"I can't do th_____ _____ _____, ___ ᵥoice a deep drawl that slipped from his lips like dark honey. "Not if you're going to leave. Not if you're going to turn away from me again."

Tori stared long and hard into those fathomless gray eyes, her own filling with tears. "I will never leave you, Guy," she whispered. "Never." And at that moment, no matter what else happened, no matter what she had to do, she knew she meant that. He had become everything to her, and she never wanted to lose him.

"Physically maybe," he said, still apprehensive, "but what about your heart?"

"It is yours, my love," Tori whispered, "for all time."

And his mouth descended on hers in a kiss that released the fury of his passion. . . .

PUT SOME FANTASY IN YOUR LIFE—
FANTASTIC ROMANCES FROM PINNACLE

TIME STORM (728, $4.99)
by Rosalyn Alsobrook

Modern-day Pennsylvanian physician JoAnn Griffin only believed what she could feel with her five senses. But when, during a freak storm, a blinding flash of lightning sent her back in time to 1889, JoAnn realized she had somehow crossed the threshold into another century and was now gazing into the smoldering eyes of a startlingly handsome stranger. JoAnn had stumbled through a rip in time . . . and into a love affair so intense, it carried her to a point of no return!

SEA TREASURE (790, $4.50)
by Johanna Hailey

When Michael, a dashing sea captain, is rescued from drowning by a beautiful sea siren—he does not know yet that she's actually a mermaid. But her breathtaking beauty stirred irresistible yearnings in Michael. And soon fate would drive them across the treacherous Caribbean, tossing them on surging tides of passion that transcended two worlds!

ONCE UPON FOREVER (883, $4.99)
by Becky Lee Weyrich

A moonstone necklace and a mysterious diary written over a century ago were Clair Summerland's only clues to her true identity. Two men loved her—one, a dashing civil war hero . . . the other, a daring jet pilot. Now Clair must risk her past and future for a passion that spans two worlds—and a love that is stronger than time itself.

SHADOWS IN TIME (892, $4.50)
by Cherlyn Jac

Driving through the sultry New Orleans night, one moment Tori's car spins out of control; the next she is in a horse-drawn carriage with the handsomest man she has ever seen—who calls her wife—-but whose eyes blaze with fury. Sent back in time one hundred years, Tori is falling in love with the man she is apparently trying to kill. Now she must race against time to change the tragic past and claim her future with the man she will love through all eternity!

CHERYLN JAC
SHADOWS IN TIME

PINNACLE BOOKS
WINDSOR PUBLISHING CORP.

PINNACLE BOOKS are published by

Windsor Publishing Corp.
475 Park Avenue South
New York, NY 10016

The P logo Reg. U.S. Pat. & TM Off. Pinnacle is a trademark of Windsor Publishing Corp.

First Printing: April, 1994

Printed in the United States of America

This book is dedicated with love to my daughter,
Chantel: thanks for all your love, encouragement and
support, as well as for Chrissy and Nadine.

One

New Orleans, Louisiana
July 14, 1993

"Damn. If one thing would go right for me today, I think I'd faint!" Tori Reichourd stared down at the massive pile of suitcases gliding past on the airport's luggage carousel. She had already retrieved her own luggage, except for the little folding carrier she'd attached to one of her bags. It was missing. She watched the same suitcases she'd already seen pass at least three times go by again.

"Oh, forget it." She bent down, slipped the straps of her tote bag and purse over her shoulder, picked up a suitcase in each hand, and began to weave her way through the crowd that was milling around the large lobby. The journal in her purse made it almost as heavy as a suitcase. And her pantsuit was starting to feel warm, as if the lightweight wool outfit hadn't exactly been the smartest choice of what to wear to New Orleans in the middle of summer. Halfway to the car-rental desk, she tripped over a teenage boy sitting on the floor and rocking back and forth to whatever was coming out of the earphones cupped to his head. "Oh, sorry," Tori mumbled, trying not to lose her grip on the luggage as she stumbled and fought to regain her balance.

The teenager glared up at her with a look that said: *Drop dead, lady.*

"Lord. What did I ever do to deserve this?" She'd been scheduled to take off from San Francisco at eleven that morning for a five-hour flight to New Orleans. She should have arrived, Louisiana time, at six P.M. Instead, because of numerous delays in takeoff, and then again in landing, it was nearing ten. She was tired, hungry, and cranky—and definitely not looking forward to driving in the dark, on a road she wasn't familiar with, to a plantation she'd never seen, to meet relatives she didn't know. Even if this trip had been all her idea, it was now very definitely starting to seem like a bad one, and she'd just gotten here.

After securing the keys to a rental car, Tori stopped at a phone booth and dialed the number of Shadow Oaks Plantation. She'd stay in a hotel for the night and drive out in the morning. That would be easier on everyone concerned.

After fumbling in her purse for her address book, and finally locating it, she dialed the number to Shadow Oaks and waited. A beeping tone droned in her ear. Great. Now what should she do? She hung up, waited a moment, and dialed again. Still busy.

She sighed, picked up her luggage, then walked toward the exit door. Forget the hotel. Might as well get going before her relatives, distant as they were, not to mention complete strangers, called the police and reported her missing. Of course, with the way her luck was running today, they might have already done so, or completely forgotten she was coming.

* * *

Half an hour later Tori steered the rented compact to the side of the road and stopped. She was lost again, she just knew it. Flipping on the overhead light, she dug in her purse for the piece of paper on which she'd scribbled the directions to Shadow Oaks. Her cousin, Grant, whom she was dying to meet, had dictated them to her over the phone before she'd left San Francisco. She held the paper up to the light. The River Road. Yes, that's what she was on. She remembered having seen the street sign, and every once in a while she'd get a glimpse of the Mississippi River that wound its way alongside the road, just as Grant had described. But he'd also said it was only a "quick twenty-five minute" drive to the plantation from town, and had made no mention of its being out in the middle of nowhere.

Tori looked at the surrounding landscape. Black. Everywhere she looked it was varying shades of black: black trees, black road, and the ragged outline of a black horizon that was just a shade darker than the black sky. She shivered and tried to ignore the little knot of fear that had settled into the base of her stomach. She hadn't seen a houselight or passed another car for over what seemed fifteen or twenty minutes.

Tori glanced at the passenger door to make sure it was locked. She should have listened to her mother and postponed the trip until they could make it together. But that wouldn't have been for another month, and she hadn't wanted to wait. Anyway, she was on summer leave now. She couldn't exactly take off after the school year started up again. Her principal didn't like to hire substitute teachers if he didn't have to. But the real reason she hadn't wanted to wait was that her curiosity had been too thor-

9

oughly aroused when she'd found and read her great-great-grandfather Martin's journal. It had been packed away for years in an old trunk in the attic of her grandmother's house. No one had remembered the trunk's existence, let alone what was in it until Tori, bored one rainy afternoon, had started poking around in the cobweb-filled room. She still couldn't believe it. Relatives she'd never known she had. And a plantation. A real, genuine Southern plantation. Many entries in the journal had described normal everyday events and occurrences, clothing, food, and such, though some descriptive words were in a French dialect she didn't understand and had to research to finally figure out what she was reading. Tori had found herself thoroughly enthralled, but the most curious and exciting, and admittedly shocking, thing she'd read about in the ancient diary were the murders. A series of murders no one but Martin and the murderer had known about, and Martin had kept them a secret from everyone except his journal.

"Now if I could just find the plantation." Sighing deeply, Tori shoved the car in gear and pulled back onto the road. She glanced at the clock on the dashboard. It was nearing midnight. "Great. My newfound relatives are going to love me for this one. Keep them up all night waiting for you, Tori. Terrific first impression."

Something shot across the road directly in the path of the car and Tori slammed on the brakes, nearly putting herself through the window. "Thank heaven for seat belts." She stared into the thick foliage that lined the side of the road and saw nothing but leaves and shadows. With a death grip on the steering wheel, her knuckles white from the pressure, she drove on, and her imagination began to run wild.

The car bumped over a rut in the road, and she suddenly

began to wonder what she'd do if she had a flat tire. Or if something happened to the car's engine and she was stranded out here for the rest of the night. Did the bayou country of Louisiana have snipers? Were there as many crazies running around out here in the swamps as on the streets of San Francisco?

"Stop it, Tori!" she ordered herself. "Stop it, stop it, stop it. You're going to work yourself into a ridiculous panic." But her imagination wouldn't turn off, and her hands couldn't stop trembling. "Oh, where is that plantation?" she moaned, peering out into the darkness.

Suddenly, sharp streaks of lightning filled the sky, jagged blinding bolts that slashed across the stygian blackness. Tori cringed, and barely managed to stifle a scream. She hated lightning. And thunder. They both scared her silly. Almost as much as being lost on a lonely road in the middle of the night, she thought, and then wished she hadn't. She began to nibble nervously on her bottom lip.

Without warning a flash of lightning struck the road directly in front of the car. She jerked the steering wheel to the left and rammed her foot down on the brake pedal. The car skidded across the blacktop and careened toward the shoulder of the road. Tori fought to turn the wheel back, but it was too late. Tall reeds loomed up in the glare of the headlights, and then the ground suddenly disappeared. She screamed and clutched the wheel, her fingernails digging into the heels of her hands.

For a brief moment, the car flew through the air, then its nose tilted downward and its wheels slammed back onto the earth. Tori lost her grip on the steering wheel. The car rode the sloping bank, crashed through reeds and bushes, bounced over large rocks and ruts in the ground, until it

11

crashed into the trunk of a huge live oak standing at the edge of the riverbank.

Tori pitched forward and her right temple smashed against the hard plastic of the steering wheel. An explosion of stars burst to life within her head, blinding her, and then immediately disappeared as she slumped back against the seat. A warm shroud of blackness wrapped itself around her mind and pulled her into its fathomless void.

July 14, 1859

"I do not have to stand here and listen to your accusations, Guy. And I won't!" Victoria Reichourd said. Her midnight blue eyes flashed with anger. She whirled away from her husband, the dark curls of her elaborate coiffure swinging wildly around her shoulders. Lifting the voluminous folds of her white silk gown, she marched across the lobby of the French Opera House and through its tall, ornate doors.

"Bring the Reichourd carriage," she ordered the doorman.

Shocked by her conduct and tone, but too well trained to voice his surprise, the man did as he was instructed. When the carriage arrived, he helped her mount the seat, but before he could step clear of the large buggy, Victoria grabbed the reins from his hand and snapped them over the glistening rumps of the two black horses. They bolted into motion, the carriage lurched forward, and mud splattered in every direction from its huge spinning wheels, soiling the fine gold and red livery of the doorman.

As the carriage sped through the Vieux Carré, a small smile of satisfaction tugged at Victoria's lips, but the gesture held no warmth. She would agree to Darin's plan now. Gladly agree. She had nothing left to lose. She thought of Guy, and sniffed with disgust. Nothing to lose except a pompous husband who was about to scandalize her in front of the entire city. Hah! In front of the world.

Due to the lateness of the hour, the narrow streets of the French Quarter were nearly deserted, and she soon left it behind. Victoria turned the carriage onto the River Road and flicked the reins again. The horses broke into a gallop, black horses and a black carriage, enveloped by the darkness, blending with the dusky gloom of the night. The pale glow of moonlight that reflected off of Victoria's shimmering white ballgown was the only thing that distinguished her, riding atop the carriage, from the all-encompassing blackness.

Suddenly, blinding, jagged streaks of lightning tore at the horizon, slicing across the ebony sky. The air cracked with the sound, and the dark landscape turned an eerie yellow-gray with each bolt.

Victoria clutched tightly to the reins, holding the leather strips taut. The horses strained to escape their bindings, panicked by the searing light that seemed to dance all around them like the taunting, burning fingers of death.

Desperate to keep them under control, Victoria tugged on the reins, but the large animals were too strong, and too scared. Fighting the restraint of their harnesses, pulling at the silver bits in their mouths, and resisting the commands of the reins, they ran blindly and threw back their heads to shriek their fear. Victoria jerked on the reins frantically, tightening her grip. "Whoa there, you stupid beasts. Calm down." Her arms strained with the effort to maintain her hold on the leather leads, her hands ached from the pressure of her grip, and her nails bit into the soft flesh of her palms.

A streak of lightning shot from the sky to hit the hard, dirt-packed road directly in the path of the frightened horses. Sparks flew in every direction. Terror-stricken, one animal lunged to the left. The other, connected by the harness, was forced to follow.

They bolted toward the side of the road. Victoria screamed, felt the reins ripped from her hands, and clutched the seat's railing to keep from being thrown out of the carriage. The horses plunged through the tall reeds and bushes that lined the top of the embankment, then lost their footing when the ground suddenly disappeared. They kicked wildly at the air, flailing legs searching for some type of footing, and then they fell downward, followed by the huge carriage . . . and Victoria. A frenzy of screams, both animal and human, filled the night air.

With a loud snap, the carriage hitch broke and the rig careened away from the horses. The left front wheel struck a boulder, the carriage bounced and nearly toppled, and Victoria was thrown from her seat. A second later, the carriage crashed against the trunk of a live oak tree, sending a shower of broken wood and splinters through the air.

Several yards away, Victoria Camerei Reichourd lay on the ground and struggled to fight off the blackness that threatened to close in on her.

July 15, 1859

With the first rays of the morning sun barely lighting the horizon, Guy Reichourd left the French Quarter and headed home. He rode at a casual trot, in no particular hurry to arrive at Shadow Oaks and face Victoria again. Their stay in the city had proved an unpleasant one, as he'd guessed it would, and their argument last night had merely made things worse. But at least now she knew exactly what he intended to do about the situation, and about their marriage.

He shifted his position in the saddle and a speck of white beyond the sloping ledge of the road caught his attention. He reined in, urged the horse toward the edge of the embankment, and peered over the side.

"Victoria!" His voice cut across the silence like a knife, his tone edged with shock. Guy jumped from his horse and, half-sliding, half-falling, scrambled down the steep bank. One outstretched foot rammed against the broken and half-buried forewheel of the carriage and allowed him to stop his rapid descent only inches from where his wife lay. He dropped to his knees, slipped an arm beneath her shoulders and lifted her from the tall reeds. Her white opera gown was stained and torn, the voluminous folds of her skirt limp with the moistness of the morning dew. Her head fell back slightly and waves of earth brown hair cascaded over her shoulders and away from her face, revealing an area of crusted blood, torn flesh, and bruised skin on her left temple. Lifting her into his arms, Guy cradled her against his chest and, digging the wedged heels of his tall black boots into the soft ground with each step to insure his footing, carried her up the hill.

Once back on the road he glanced down at where the Reichourd carriage lay in a broken heap, one side smashed beyond recognition against the trunk of a tree. Another few feet, he thought, and she would have been in the river and most likely drowned. The slightest flurry of a shadow darkened his gray eyes. For the briefest of moments he

15

wondered if he should be thankful she had been spared that fate. Their marriage was a travesty, their love for each other something that had been real only in his mind. He had denied that for the past six years, but last night, during their argument, he had finally admitted it to himself. Victoria did not love him. She had never loved him. Holding her against himself with one arm, Guy climbed back up into the saddle and, drawing her to him, positioned her across his lap, her legs beneath the flounced silk gown resting atop one of his. He looked down into her face, and a wave of guilt washed over him at the realization that he had nearly wished her dead.

Her thick brown lashes fluttered slightly, and a soft moan escaped her lips.

"Victoria?" Guy said. "Can you hear me?"

The sound of his voice, so rich and smooth, was a velvety caress that briefly pulled Tori's thoughts away from the pain that consumed every muscle in her body. She struggled to open her eyes.

At first he was all hazy, a forbidding form silhouetted against the morning light. Then her vision cleared, and Tori found herself staring up at a stranger. Thick, wavey locks of black hair swirled about his head and framed a face that was strong and square, each feature chiseled to perfection. Yet something about him made her cower and draw away. And then she realized what it was: his eyes, gray eyes that were the dark, infinite color of steel, and just as cold.

July 15, 1993

With the hazy yellow light of dawn, the ambulance pulled to a stop upon the shoulder of the old River Road, just behind the police car parked there. The driver reached overhead and flipped a switch, and the van's siren abruptly stopped its ear-piercing wail, leaving the desolate area once again in eerie silence.

"Here. Down here," someone called from beyond the road. The two paramedics grabbed a gurney from the back of the van and hurried down the sloping bank.

The first thing they saw was that the driver's side of the small car was smashed against the trunk of a tree, and almost every window on the driver's side of the vehicle, including the windshield, had shattered.

"Hurry up," came a deep voice from inside the crumpled mass of metal.

The paramedics ran to the open passenger door. "What's her condition?" one said, poking his head into the car.

"She's alive," the policeman answered. "But her pulse is erratic and her breathing's shallow. We have to get her to a hospital. Fast." He had unbuckled the woman's seat belt and was holding her head up off the seat, which was covered with broken glass.

As gently as they could, the three men began to lift the unconscious woman from the seat while they slid the gurney beneath her.

Suddenly, her thick, dark brown lashes fluttered slightly, and a soft moan escaped her lips.

"It's all right, lady. We've got you," the policeman said. "Soon as we get you out of this wreck, we'll take you to a hospital."

At the sound of the man's voice, a comforting, strong sound that briefly pulled her thoughts away from the agonizing pain wrenching every inch of her body, Victoria opened her eyes. The man was nothing more than a shadowy form silhouetted against the morning light. He moved

17

slightly and his face came into view. She blinked rapidly and looked up at him again, her vision still slightly blurred but clear enough so that she could see he was not Guy. Nor was he Darin. The man was a stranger. Victoria attempted to sit upright, and as she did, she looked at the mass of crumpled metal and broken glass that surrounded her, at the mannish-style clothes she wore . . . and screamed.

Two

New Orleans, Louisiana
Shadow Oaks Plantation, July, 1859

For a few short seconds, Tori fought to get out of his arms, to pull away from that cold, unfeeling gaze, but he held her securely captive within his hard, unyielding embrace, one arm at her back and holding the reins, the other wrapped around her waist. And then the darkness beckoned her return, swirling around in her mind like a tidal wave, consuming her consciousness and drawing her into its endless abyss. Her hands fell away from his chest, and her head slumped forward to rest against his shoulder.

Guy kept the horse moving at a slow pace for the remainder of the ride to Shadow Oaks, unwilling to risk further injury to her. His thoughts were in turmoil as a welter of conflicting emotions warred within him.

They passed the tall wooden gates of the entry drive, and the main house of Shadow Oaks came into view, perfect in every curve and plane, strong and immediately impressive like its owner. It resembled a precious white jewel set on a small knoll and surrounded by a lush carpet of carefully manicured emerald lawn. Like a mighty Grecian temple, the two-story dwelling was surrounded by twenty-eight white Corinthian pillars. Two dormer windows graced the sloping roof on each side, and wrought-iron railings, painted a dark green to match the cypress shutters that adorned each tall window, encased the first- and second-story galleries that ran the entire width of the house.

Guy looked at the house that had been his home since the day he'd been born, and then glanced down at the unconscious woman in his arms. That was why she'd wanted him to marry her so badly: to become mistress of Shadow Oaks, the largest and most prosperous plantation in Louisiana. She had come into his life like a firestorm, consuming his attentions and desires, but they had known each other such a short time he had been reluctant to commit himself to marriage. Then, at his hesitancy, she had informed him she was carrying his child, and he had known he no longer had a choice. But it hadn't mattered. He'd been in love with her, wanted her as his wife, wanted their child, and so, like a fool, he had proposed, as she'd known he would, as she'd planned. After the marriage she had immediately rejected her husband's attentions. He had tried to be understanding, assuming her desire for him would return after the birth of their child. But again he'd been wrong. After Alicia's birth, Victoria had turned her back on their daughter, as completely and with the same finality as she had turned from her husband.

Guy cursed softly, damning himself for being every kind of fool, for falling in love with Victoria's beauty and finding out too late it was nothing more than a mask, an exquisite, carefully maintained disguise that concealed the ice that flowed in her veins.

But all that was behind him now. It was over. He would

see her safely to the house. He would summon the doctor to tend to her injuries, and he would give her time to heal. Then they would resume their conversation of the night before, and she would see that he would not put up with her treachery any longer, that this time she had gone too far. And when she was well again, he would move her to one of his other plantations, preferably up north, near Baton Rouge, and proceed with the divorce.

After that he would deal with his brother Darin.

Guy stopped his horse before the sweeping entry stairs of the house. "Hannah, Moses," he called loudly.

The short, generously built black housekeeper appeared on the gallery almost immediately, large brown eyes wide with alarm in a pudgy face deeply creased by age. A second later Guy's tall, gangly manservant, Hannah's husband, Moses, appeared behind her, his thick gray-white hair like a halo around his dark thin face.

"Lord almighty," Hannah said, her words little more than a strangled gasp. She rushed down the stairs. "What done happened to Miss Victoria, Michie?"

Moses took hold of the reins and held the horse steady while Guy, swinging his right leg over the animal's neck, slid from the saddle with Tori still cradled in his arms. "There was an accident." He strode toward the house and took the entry stairs two at a time. "Hannah, get her bed ready. Boil some water and get the liniment. You'll need to clean these cuts." He paused at the door and looked back over his shoulder. "Moses, ride to town and fetch the doctor. You can use my horse."

Hannah hurried across the wide foyer toward a rear door that led to the warming kitchen. Her long muslin gown swayed around her generous form, its black and white checkered pattern almost a miniature version of the larger marble tiles of the entry's floor.

Guy began to climb the elegant cherrywood staircase that curved its way from the center of the foyer to the second floor, his steps silenced by the floral patterned carpet that covered the stairs.

"What the hell happened?" The sharp words echoed in the huge entry.

Hannah paused abruptly, a glint of worry in her dark eyes and her shoulders stiff with apprehension, but she refrained from turning. After a second of uncertainty she pushed open the door to the warming kitchen and disappeared.

Guy stopped in midstride and turned to stare down at his brother, Darin, who had just entered the foyer through the still-open front door. He stood with black gloved hands clenched into fists and propped upon his slim hips, small spots and streaks of mud evident on his highly polished black riding boots. A scowl, which had become almost a permanent expression of late, darkened the handsome face that was, at first glance, a near mirror image of Guy's.

"There was a carriage accident," Guy answered, his eyes cold and hard as he looked at his brother. He turned and continued up the stairs.

Darin bounded up after Guy and followed him down the hallway. "Is she . . . ?"

"She's alive. I've sent for the doctor."

"Well, *you* were certainly lucky, dear brother," Darin said with a sneer. He looked Guy up and down. "There doesn't appear to be a scratch on you."

Guy entered Victoria's room and set Tori on the huge, ornately carved poster bed that dominated the blue and white bedchamber. He pulled a coverlet of pale blue wool and lace over her, then turned back to face his brother who'd followed him into the room. A blaze of anger flared in his eyes, but he steeled himself and determined to control his temper. "I wasn't in the carriage, Darin, if you really must salve your curiosity. Victoria left town last night. I found her this morning on my way home."

"Last night?" In the flash of a millisecond Darin's shocked expression turned to one of suspicion, and both his voice and his attitude grew even more surly. "Why, Guy? Why would Victoria do something like leave town at night alone? She knows better than that."

"We argued."

"Humph! That's not so unusual; in fact, it's rather a daily occurrence between you two," Darin taunted. He continued before Guy could retort. "But why did she leave town, Guy? At night? And why did you allow her to travel unescorted, big brother? You know how dangerous that is, let alone improper."

Guy's jaw clenched momentarily, the only outward sign of the fury that boiled within him. "Victoria has never been one to worry about propriety, Darin, as you well know. Anyway, we were at the opera. I thought she was going back to the hotel. I didn't think she was foolish enough to try to return to Shadow Oaks in the middle of the night. When I found out she had"—he shrugged—"enough time had passed so that I assumed she'd have already got here. I had business in town this morning that couldn't be postponed, and"—he looked down at Tori—"Victoria and I had nothing further to say to one another."

"Well, if she were my—"

Guy whirled around, the taut control he held on his temper visibly slipping. "If she were your what, Darin? Your

23

wife? From what I gather, you've enjoyed all the pleasures, if not the responsibilities."

Darin blustered, and an ugly purple stain colored his cheeks. "That's a lie."

"Is it?" Guy challenged.

"Will she be all right, Doctor?" Guy asked, as the older man entered Guy's study. His tone was hollow and distant. The words echoed in his mind. Why did he care, after what she'd done? But, he knew he did. He hated himself for it, but he couldn't deny that deep down there was still a part of him that cared about Victoria. Not as much as before, and it was definitely not love, but he did care enough to not want her to have been permanently hurt. If this had happened a few months ago his feelings might have been different, there might have been more concern. He doubted it, but it was possible. A few months ago he hadn't suspected that his own brother was his wife's lover.

The old doctor shook his head, pushed a pair of spectacles onto the bridge of his nose, and took a drink of the brandy Moses had poured for him. He settled into a tall wing chair of burgundy leather and shifted his near ancient frame around in an effort to get comfortable before he answered. "She doesn't have any broken bones, Guy, but her left wrist is slightly sprained. She has quite a few nasty bruises. And scrapes. Though not as many as I would have expected considering what happened." He took another sip of his drink, set the crystal glass down on the marble-topped table situated next to his chair, and continued. "But it's that large bump on her temple I'm worried about." He drew a gold watch from his vest pocket and flipped open

24

its lid. "Eleven o'clock. She's been unconscious now for . . . how long did you figure? Almost ten hours or so?"

Guy nodded. "She left the opera house last night a little after midnight. I found her this morning, around eight."

"About ten or eleven hours then. That's not a good sign, Guy. Not good at all."

"Benjamin, tell me the truth. Is there a chance her mind might be affected by the blow on her skull? Could she end up . . . touched?" He'd almost rather see Victoria with Darin than shut up in an asylum for the insane.

The doctor sighed, rose to his feet, and picked up his bag. "It's hard to say. Unfortunately, with injuries to the head there's always that chance, Guy. We'll just have to wait and see."

The two men walked from the parlor and stood at the front door. Guy shook the doctor's gnarled hand. "Thanks, Doc."

The older man nodded. "I'll stop by again tomorrow afternoon to check on her. Keep her quiet if she wakes, Guy. Make her stay in bed, and see that she gets plenty of that laudanum I left with Suda. Victoria needs to rest. If you need me before I return, send Moses to my office. My nurse will know where to find me if I'm out."

Guy remained at the door until the doctor's carriage was out of sight, then turned back toward his study, his concentration deep within his thoughts. He had told her last night that he knew about her betrayal, and that he was going to petition Judge Beaudronneaux to grant him a divorce. She had left the opera house in a rage. But he would not feel guilty about that, or the carriage accident that had resulted. The incident changed nothing. Merely delayed it.

"Papa?"

The soft voice drew his attention, and Guy turned, look-

25

ing back into the parlor for his daughter. Alicia ran toward him, a small rag doll that Hannah had made for her clutched tightly in one arm. "Is Mamière sick, Papa? Is she going to die like Ol' Abraham and Uncle John did and go to heaven to be with them?"

Guy bent down, balancing on toes and bent legs, and gently grasped her small shoulders. Alicia's long black curls slid over his fingers, and she stared at him with eyes whose blue-gray color was a blend of both her parents.

"No, Licia, Mamière's not going to die. She just needs to rest, that's all. You go on now and play like a good girl." He looked over the child's shoulder for her playmate and servant. "Where's Ruby?"

Alicia giggled. "In the garden. We were playing hide and seek, but I couldn't find her, and I saw the doctor leave so I came to see if Mamière was going to heaven."

Guy smiled. It was a wonder Alicia cared at all whether her mother went to heaven, or anywhere else, considering the amount of time and caring Victoria gave the child. Which, since the day Alicia had been born a little over five years before, was practically none. "Don't you think you'd better go back and find Ruby? She might be getting tired of waiting for you to find her."

"All right." Alicia spun around and skipped back toward the stairs as Guy stood. She stopped at the landing and looked back. "Will you come play with me, Papa? Ruby can be it."

"Later, *chérie*. We'll play a game later. You go on now and play with Ruby."

The moment his daughter was out of sight, Guy's black mood returned and his handsome, patrician features turned dour and resolute. He took the stairs in no great hurry, his long muscular legs moving easily, his steps quiet. He pushed open the door to his wife's bedchamber and stood on the threshold looking in, his stance rigid.

Suda, Victoria's maid, rose from her chair beside the bed and hurried to Guy. "She ain't woke yet, Michie," she said barely above a whisper and using the term of address that he'd ordered all the Reichourd slaves to use. It meant the same as the more widely accepted term, *master*, but had less of a godlike ring to it. At least, Guy thought so. And if there was one thing he wasn't, it was a god.

He gave no indication that he'd heard Suda's comment. Instead, he brushed past her and moved to stand beside his wife's bed. He stared down at Victoria and again was assailed by emotions, feelings that fought within him for control and threatened to tear him apart: pity, anger, jealousy, and—finally—sorrow. His eyes narrowed slightly. Sorrow. That was the one that plagued him most; that dwelled in his mind and refused to be vanquished. It haunted his dreams and turned them to nightmares so he received little sleep or rest. Everything he'd hoped for from his marriage, everything he'd dreamt of and cherished, would never be. And his children also suffered. Damn, how they suffered. His thoughts momentarily turned to Alicia and her ten-year-old half brother, Martin, Victoria's son from her first marriage. Neither had ever really known their mother's love, and Guy finally admitted, neither had he. A little over six years ago Victoria Camerei had swept into his life like a ray of sunshine, vibrant and warm, lighting up his otherwise quiet and mundane existence. Now, her presence was like a black cloud that hung ominously, and continuously, over Shadow Oaks—and over him.

"If only I had known . . ." Guy murmured.

He pulled his thoughts from the past and gazed down at his unconscious wife. Her long hair spread across the

27

pillow like strands of silk, the dark, earth-rich color a stark contrast to both the white bed linen, and the chalky pallor of her face. Even like this, he thought, without the color she insisted on painting on her face every morning, without the elaborately coiffured hair styles and expensive jewels and gowns, she was beautiful. But only physically, Guy reminded himself. Victoria's beauty was only physical.

A movement beneath the coverlet drew his attention. Tori's head rolled to one side, and a faint moan escaped her throat. Guy took a step back, and then another, but never moved his gaze from her face. Her eyelids fluttered briefly, and then opened wide. Dazzling midnight blue eyes looked up at him for a long moment, and a frown pulled at her brow. Suddenly, she bolted upright in the bed.

The breath caught in Tori's throat and threatened to strangle her. She licked her lips quickly, then swallowed hard. Her hands trembled, her heart thudded madly, and she clutched at the coverlet and jerked it up to bunch at her neck. Pain assailed almost every inch of her body, and her head began to pound mercilessly.

"Who . . . who are you?" Her voice was nothing more than a ragged whisper as she stared, wide-eyed, at the darkly attractive man who stood across the room.

"Oh, Miss Victoria," Suda cried, and rushed forward. "You're awake." She drew back the window curtains, just enough to let in a little light, and began to fuss about the bed, plumping pillows and straightening the coverlet.

Tori pulled her gaze from the man who seemed to be glaring down at her and glanced at the short, young, black girl. Her skin was the color of creamed coffee, her hair a beautiful dark brown, and her almond-shaped brown eyes were accentuated with thin slivers of silver. Obviously she was a teenager, but a very beautiful one. Tori frowned and felt a stab of pain as her forehead tightened. Her gaze jumped back to the man who stood, foreboding and silent, several feet from the bed. Who were these people? Where was she? And what had happened? The first stirrings of fear melded with her confusion, and quickly she looked around at her surroundings.

Sunlight streamed into the room from two ceiling-high windows, filtering through the sheer lace panels that hung between heavy, hooked-back, dark blue damask draperies. The light cast the room in a golden haze and reflected brilliantly off the many pieces of highly polished furniture. A tall armoire of cherrywood with an elaborately carved crown piece stood against the far wall, and opposite the bed was a fireplace, its white marble face streaked with veins of pale blue. But what drew Tori's attention, and held it, was the large, rosewood-framed mirror above the marble-topped dressing table set against one wall.

Tori stared long and hard at the woman whose reflection peered back at her from the silver glass. Long dark hair cascaded over and around her shoulders, finely arched dark brows curved over deep blue eyes that were thickly lashed, and a full bottom lip quivered in fear. Her forehead had a bandage wrapped around it, and she wore an ivory nightgown with a plunging, embroidered neckline. Tori knew she was looking at herself, yet it was as if she were staring at a stranger. A complete and utter stranger.

Panic threatened to engulf her. Nothing was familiar. Not her own image in the mirror, not the room, and certainly not the man and woman who stood beside her bed. Her mind was a total blank.

Who am I? *Who am I?* Her brain screamed the question, and then whirled in search of an answer—any answer—and came up with nothing. She fought back the onslaught

29

of tears that suddenly blurred and stung her eyes, gulped down the scream that strove to burst from her lips, and struggled to remain calm.

She would remember in a minute. This was just temporary confusion. Maybe she'd had a bad dream, a nightmare, and her mind hadn't yet reoriented itself to reality. She closed her eyes, counted to ten, and slowly reopened them. Nothing had changed; no rush of memory swept over her. Hysteria began to build in her breast, and her hands shook uncontrollably. Her mind filled with more and more questions, while at the same time it probed frantically for answers . . . and found none.

Unconsciously dismissing the woman, who was really little more than a girl, Tori looked back up at the man. She wanted to scream at him, to demand that he tell her what had happened, why she couldn't remember anything. She wanted him to make everything all right again, to answer her questions and make her remember, but mostly she wanted him to calm the terror that threatened to consume her. But she remained silent, sensing somehow, inexplicably, that to demand answers of him would only make things worse. Instead, she studied him, as he, in turn, studied her.

He reminded her of a pirate. She didn't know where the thought had come from, but it seemed an apt description. It fit him. He was tall, the ruffle that trimmed the bed's canopy only an inch above the raven strands of his hair, and he exuded an aura of strength, like a man made of iron and steel rather than flesh and blood. His broad shoulders were muscular and full beneath a white silk shirt whose flaring sleeves enveloped arms now crossed atop a wide chest. Snug trousers held tight to his long legs, and disappeared into black leather boots that reached nearly to his knees.

His face was an interesting blend of aristocratic features and ruggedly cut contours. A strong jaw, straight nose, and high cheekbones. Tori stared, as if hypnotized. He was a Creole. She didn't know how she knew that, she was just glad to find she knew something. Other thoughts and memories would follow, she felt certain. In the patrician lines she could see the nobleness and passion of the French blood that coursed through his veins, and in his sharp, shadow-filled contours lurked the iron will and harsh persona of the Spaniards who had once ruled New Orleans, many of their families having melded with the conquered French. Tori met his gaze, and a shiver raced up her spine. Handsome would be the perfect word to describe him, except for one thing: his eyes. They were as gray in color as the fog that hung over an English moor, and they stared down at her now with the same penetrating coldness as that elusive mist.

Tori shuddered, and as her gaze remained pinioned by those depthless silver pools, she remembered where she'd seen him before. "You . . . you brought me here."

Guy's eyes narrowed. He continued to stare at her, but did not respond to her comment.

"What happened?" Tori tried to keep the fear from her tone, and failed. "Please, tell me. Where am I?" She was aware of the quaver in her voice, of the tremors that began deep within the recesses of her body, and she clutched the coverlet tighter to her throat. Her instinctive resolve not to push him, not to demand answers, deserted her. "Answer me, damn it. Who are you people? Where am I? What's happened to me?"

Without a word Guy turned and walked from the room. A few seconds later, the sound of a door being slammed echoed through the large house.

Tori stared at the empty bedroom doorway, not sure what had just happened.

"Miss Victoria, would you like some *café au lait,* or maybe some tea? It'll warm your insides and maybe help to calm you some," the black girl said. She clasped her hands together at her waist as her fingers busily twisted and twined around one another.

Victoria. Tori looked at the girl. She'd called her Victoria. Was that her name? She felt a thread of hope, yet a wave of disappointment at the same time. It sounded familiar but not quite right. She looked up at the girl, and for the first time *really* looked at her. She couldn't be more than sixteen, if that. Her body was slight, almost tiny, and her face wore an anxious, fearful, expression. But it was the girl's clothing that drew Tori's immediate attention. Her attire seemed strange somehow, out of place. The skirt of her long, plain red muslin dress reached to the floor, a bleached apron was tied around her waist, and she wore a turban on her head made of the same fabric as her gown.

"Tell me what happened. Please," Tori said.

The girl twisted her hands together nervously. "You was in a carriage accident, Miss Victoria. Last night. Mr. Guy found you on his way home this morning. Don't you remember?"

"What . . . what's your name?" Tori asked.

"Sudalena, Miss Victoria. But everyone calls me Suda. You knows who I am." The girl smiled nervously. "I'm your maid. Been your maid three years now, since I was twelve." Her eyes widened in alarm. "Don'tcha remember me, Miss Victoria?"

She stared at Suda. Three years. And she didn't remember. "Can I have a robe, please?" Tori asked, fighting the desire to give in to her panic. Something was wrong, terribly wrong, and she had to find some answers. She started to throw the coverlet back, slide her legs off the bed—and nearly screamed. Every muscle in her body suddenly filled with pain, shocking, mind-numbing excruciating pain, while at the same time the movement caused her head to throb viciously. She lifted a hand to the bandage on her head, touched her temple and felt the swollen lump at her hairline. The flesh on either side of the bandage was tender, and her probing fingers only aggravated the injury further, bringing on another onslaught of agony.

Suda held up a robe of ivory batiste, its yoke and cuffs heavily embroidered with small pink roses to match the gown Tori wore. She waited patiently as Tori slid slowly, and cautiously, from the high bed. Tori tied the wrap closed at her waist, savoring the soft feel of the rich fabric against her skin while trying to ignore the aching pain in her body. She moved to stand at the dressing table, and leaned forward until her face was only an inch from the mirror. "Who are you?" she whispered to the reflection that stared out at her from the glass. Tears filled her eyes, and she fought to stem their tide. Crying would not help her. She reached up and touched the cold reflection of herself with the tip of her index finger. "Good God in heaven, who *are* you?"

Three

"Miss Victoria, you wants I should tell Moses to fetch the doctor back?" Suda's voice faltered when she spoke, revealing the obvious fear and alarm she felt at her mistress's behavior.

Tori pulled her gaze away from the mirror and looked over her shoulder at the girl. She shook her head. "No. I just need . . ." She paused in confusion. She didn't know what she needed, except answers, and there didn't seem to be any. But she had to find a way, she had to. She remembered the man who had stood near her bed and looked down at her in obvious distaste. He would offer little help, somehow she knew that as well as she knew that she would do everything she could to find the answers herself without asking him.

She straightened slowly and looked around the room. She felt nothing, no familiarity, no warmth, nothing. It was as if she'd never been here before, and yet this was obviously her own bedroom. She had to see the rest of the house. Perhaps she had recently moved into this room from another. She looked at the girl hopefully. "Have I always occupied this room?"

"Oh, yes, Miss Victoria, ever since you come to Shadow Oaks."

The name Shadow Oaks rang a bell of familiarity in her mind. She tried to grasp onto it, to draw it out into a more detailed memory, but that eluded her. "And how long ago did I come to Shadow Oaks, Suda?"

"Huh, six years. My sister was your maid for three years, but she died, and Michie give the job to me and I been with you three years."

Tori nodded. Six years, and she didn't remember even one day. Anxious to see everything, to jog her memory somehow, Tori ignored the nausea in her stomach, the throbbing in her temple, and the pain in her trembling limbs, and walked toward the open door that led to the hallway. She paused on its threshold and clung to the doorjamb, fighting dizziness. "Damn," she whispered, more at the circumstances than the physical discomfort. She closed her eyes, then reopened them slowly and the world stopped its maddening, out-of-control spin. A step forward into the hallway brought with it a sudden sense of dread. What if she didn't remember? What if she found nothing familiar and never regained her memory?

"Where you going, Miss Victoria?" Suda asked. "You's too weak to be up. Doctor Benjamin say you should stay in bed."

"I just want to walk around the house a bit and . . ." Tori stared at the girl in panic. What was her name? Soona? Suta? Suda! She sighed in relief. Sudalena, that was it. A spark of triumph brightened her mood. "I'll be all right, Suda, really. Don't worry." She smiled and took another small step. She had to get her bearings. The need to remember was overpowering, urgent. Her name was Victoria, and she lived here—but she couldn't remember!

Maybe something she saw downstairs would look familiar, and then it would all come rushing back, everything she'd forgotten. She glanced back at the maid who was still wringing her hands and looking worried. Or was it fear rather than concern she saw in the girl's eyes? "I'll be back in a few minutes, Suda. I just want to move about a little so I don't get any stiffer than I already am."

The hall was extremely wide, thickly carpeted, and seemed endlessly long. Dark paneling covered its walls from the floor to waist height. They were painted a soft cream from there to the high ceiling. She came to a petticoat table set up against the wall, its mirrored bottom reflecting the hem of her robe. A lone candle sconce was set in the center of the table's marble top. She glanced up at the ceiling, its borders trimmed with scalloped molding, then back toward the window at the far end of the hall, opposite the direction in which she was walking.

Suddenly everything changed. The hallway became narrow, its walls and ceiling plain of molding and painted white, the doors shorter. Tori snapped her eyelids closed, shook her head, and looked again. The hallway was as it had been before; its dark paneling glistening in the soft reflection of the sunlight that filtered in through the lacey panel-covered window, the ceiling trimmed with fancy molding, the doors only a foot or so shorter than the twelve-foot ceiling.

Shaken, Tori turned and continued down the hallway. She finally reached the landing and, breathing hard, paused to compose herself. Holding tight to the gleaming mahogany railing she looked over it to the foyer below. Her gaze moved quickly from one object to another, searching and not finding what she sought . . . familiarity, a sense of belonging, a feeling of being home.

Dominating the room, its chain emerging from the center of an elaborately designed ceiling medallion, hung a huge triple-tiered crystal chandelier. Each of its three hundred candles was ensconced in its own finely etched crystal bowl, and hundreds of teardrop prisms caught and reflected the bright rays of sunlight that streamed in through the fanlight window above the entry door. Gleaming black and white marble tiles covered the floor, resembling a chess board, and murals of a country scene papered the walls.

Tori gripped the banister and began to slowly descend the stairs, the muscles of her legs protesting in pain with each step. Halfway down she stopped and stared at the large, gilt-framed portraits that lined the curving white wall of the staircase. From the small plaques attached to the bottom of the individual frames, she realized that each painting was of a member of a family named Reichourd, the portrait near the top of the stairs, closest to her, dating back over a hundred years. She moved down several steps and paused in front of a portrait she recognized. Then, staring at it, she realized slowly that she was wrong. It looked like the man who had been in her room earlier, but it wasn't him. Their similarities in appearance were remarkable, but the man in this painting—she glanced at the plaque at the bottom of the frame—John Reichourd, had gray hair at his temples. The man in her room had not. There was the hint of a smile on the man's lips, and Tori found herself wondering if the man who had been in her room ever smiled, or if he even could. "Oh, stop it," she admonished herself, "of course he can smile. Anybody can smile if they want to." But did he ever want to? she found herself wondering as her own words hung in the air around her.

She descended several stairs to the next portrait and stopped with a start, her gaze drawn and pinioned to the face she had just been remembering. The artist had captured him in near perfection, using shades of dark blue and gray as a backdrop which accentuated the aristocratic lines of the acquiline nose and black hair while intensifying the hard line of his jaw and the ruggedly sharp cuts of his cheekbones. Here was a man of definite poise and polish, as well as strength and power; and a thinly veiled savagery lay just below the surface, coiled and ready to strike whenever needed. Tori shivered slightly. This was the man who had entered her room, stared at her in open disdain, and then left without a word. Her eyes moved to the brass plaque and she read its engraving; Guy Reichourd, 1829 to . . .

Tori's mind spun, and the painting seemed to blur in front of her eyes. She put a hand out toward the wall and leaned against it. The sensation stopped and Tori frowned. Evidently the injury to her head objected to the wandering around she was doing. She looked at the plaque again. 1829. Obviously his birth date. But what year was it now? She had no idea. She looked at the portrait again. In it he looked slightly younger than he did now. And not quite so sardonic and hard. Twenty-three or -four, maybe. He appeared about thirty now. So that would make it 1859? Or maybe it was 1860?

Tori moved to the next portrait. It was of herself. Or at least she assumed it was her. It was definitely of the face that had stared back at her from the mirror a few moments before. She stared at the painting with a feeling of unease. Clearly a portrait of her, yet she had a feeling it wasn't. There was an unexplainable wrongness about it. As if something was there and yet not there. Tori studied it and

38

determined the painting to be near exact; brown hair that was just a shade too light to be black, dark blue eyes, a slightly turned-up nose, and full lips, the bottom one a bit fuller than she'd ever liked. In the portrait her hair was pulled up toward her crown in a profusion of curls that cascaded down and over one shoulder. It was obviously her, but the feeling of unease and alarm persisted.

"Oh, stop it. This is ridiculous. Of course it's me." She looked at the portrait's plaque. Victoria Camerei Reichourd. 1833 to . . . "That proves it," Tori mumbled, becoming angry with herself. "Victoria Reichourd. That's me. And these others must be my brothers." But even as she said it, she had the feeling that she was wrong. Moving down several steps she came to the next portrait, which at first glance could have been mistaken for another of Guy Reichourd, until one looked closer. The plaque beneath the painting read: Darin Reichourd, 1831 to . . .

Tori shuddered unexplainably, and though she suddenly wanted nothing more than to look away from the painting, she forced her eyes upward, to the man's face. It was obviously Guy and John's younger brother. The three men looked too much alike and the birth dates were too close for it to be any other relationship. She glanced back at Guy's portrait. He and Darin could almost be mistaken for twins, and yet. . . . She looked closer. There was a difference in Darin's features: a subtle narrowing of the chin, a lightness to the gray eyes that caused them to appear almost translucent, and a slight thinness to lips which seemed to hold just a touch of contempt. Guy's dark hair was wavey, the ends curling over the collar of his shirt and the tips of his ears, as had that of the older brother. Darin's hair was thick and full, but straight. The longer she stared up at the portraits, the more pronounced the dissimilarities between the younger Reichourd and his two older siblings seemed to become.

"Oh, of course there'd be differences. They're brothers, not identical triplets," Tori mumbled to herself.

She looked back at Guy's portrait, and again at Darin's, and then forced herself to move on. The last canvas on the wall was that of a young boy, no more than nine or ten years old. The plaque read: Martin Camerei Reichourd. 1849 to . . .

Martin. Tori stared at the name and felt a tickle of familiarity. Excitement filled her at the sensation. She quickly closed her eyes and willed herself to feel more, to remember. Murder. Her eyes shot open as the word popped into her mind. Murder? Her hands trembled, and she looked back up at the boy's innocent face but nothing further came. No memory, no flash of recognition, no explanation of the unusual thought. Why would she think of murder when she looked at this portrait? She began to move away, but as she did, glanced again at the plaque beneath the boy's portrait. Martin Camerei Reichourd. Her eyes shot back to the middle name. Camerei. She glanced back at the plaque beneath her own portrait. The middle names were the same. Her son? The thought stopped her cold and she clutched at the banister. Could the boy in the portrait be *her* son?

No, her mind screamed. No. She would remember if she'd had a child. She would know, somehow; she was sure, she would know. A mother could not forget her own child, no matter what. And yet, if this boy were her son, then . . . then these men were not her brothers. One of them must be her husband. She looked back at the portraits of John, Guy, and Darin Reichourd. But which one? she wondered. Which one?

40

A shiver of trepidation rippled through her, but she forced herself to continue down the stairs. Remaining close to the wall in case she needed additional support, Tori crossed the foyer and entered a spacious parlor. The room was decorated in a mélange of green hues and pale ivory. Heavily fringed, forest green damask drapes framed several near ceiling-high windows, and they, as well as their accompanying sheer panels, had been pulled back and looped behind gold hooks attached to the wainscoting and sculpted to resemble oak leaves. The tall windows were raised, nearly disappearing into the upper walls, and the jib doors beneath each window had been opened, creating doorways, though Tori guessed they were open more to let air circulate through the room than to use as passageways.

She moved to stand at one of the windows and looked out. The vast expanse of the plantation sprawled before her in a never-ending scene of luxuriant splendor. Verdant lawns rolled over soft knolls and sprawling meadows, lush fields spread as far as the eye could see, and thick-leafed magnolia trees, their limbs heavy with white blossoms lined the long, winding entry drive. Rising above all of this beauty, like sentries guarding a queen's treasure, giant oak trees dotted the landscape, their gnarled, wide-spreading limbs draped with heavy veils of Spanish moss that resembled curtains of gray lace.

The beauty of the scene was enough to make Tori gasp in appreciation, and then wonder why since she'd obviously looked upon this view every day and should be accustomed to it.

Off to one side of the house several horses grazed in a large pasture that was enclosed by a tall white rail fence, and just to the side of its gate two black men worked on the wheel of a gold-fringed carriage.

Tori stared at the buggy and suddenly felt a thrill of excitement. She remembered! She remembered Guy Reichourd lifting her from a wrecked carriage and into his arms. That's why her head was bandaged, she had injured it. And the bruises on her body, and the aches. All were a result of the accident. She remembered him cradling her against his chest as they rode on a horse back to the plantation. She frowned. Then there had been an argument. She had heard it, like a muffled conversation. Guy had been arguing with someone, another man.

But the unpleasant memory was not enough to keep the smile from her face or the excitement from her heart. It was coming back. Her memory was coming back. She whirled around and nearly fell flat on her face as, at the movement, the room spun crazily. Tori grabbed for the back of a nearby chair and closed her eyes until the spinning sensation stopped. She took a deep breath, reopened her eyes, and looked around at the room again, anxious to jog her memory further. There were rosewood-trimmed double settees set before a black, marble-faced fireplace, and conversation chairs were placed randomly here and there throughout the room, their damask coverings matching the draperies at the tall windows. An étagère stood in one corner, each shelf holding an array of delicate china statuettes. A grand piano occupied the opposite corner. A gilded harp another.

Tori walked around the room, trying to ignore the pain in her forearms and ribs, the throbbing of her head, and to concentrate on her surroundings. Her gaze swept over each piece of furniture, each art object and bit of bric-a-brac, studying, assessing, touching, and recognizing nothing.

"You seem to be recuperating swiftly," a deep voice said from behind her.

She spun around and the sudden gesture brought forth another moment of dizziness. She shook her head and tried to focus through the blurriness her hasty movement had caused. Guy Reichourd stood in the doorway. Or was it Darin? Or John? She wasn't sure.

Tori took a hesitant step back, suddenly uneasy, and felt the smooth curve of the piano at her back. "I . . . I felt stiff and needed to move around."

He entered the room and began to walk toward her. "I doubt the doctor would approve."

"I had to try to remember . . ." Tori's lashes fluttered, and she reached out to grip the piano in an effort to steady herself. The room whirled around her in a brilliant haze of green and ivory, and then darkness began to invade the light, consuming everything, drawing her into its abyss of infinite blackness once more.

Moving swiftly, his long strides taking him across the room in the passing of a second, Guy caught her in his arms, effortlessly lifting her against his chest. With a softly mumbled curse, he climbed the wide staircase and carried her back into her room. He settled her gently in the center of the huge bed and looked around for Suda, but the young maid was nowhere to be seen. Without conscious thought to his actions, Guy sat on the edge of the mattress and reached out toward her. He gently stroked a few wisps of rich brown hair back from Tori's temple, and let the dark satin tendrils slide slowly through his fingers.

He sighed deeply. The first time he'd met Victoria her beauty had taken his breath away. After all that had happened between them, it still gave him reason to pause. This was the first time he had actually touched her in years,

43

and he was surprised to feel desire for her warm his veins. He had thought even that was dead. He forced himself to ignore it. The love he'd felt for her, or believed he had felt for her, was gone, he knew that, yet it was still hard to admit. He had thought himself so deeply, irreversibly, and totally in love in the beginning. Until a few months ago, in spite of everything, the dream had persisted, the image of the way he had wanted their lives to be refusing to leave him. For almost five and a half years he had lived the illusion for both of them, nourished it, kept it alive, and never fully realized that Victoria had completely removed herself from it, or, what was probably more true to fact, had never shared it.

He had made excuses for her behavior, for her coolness toward him, her lack of a mothering instinct toward Alicia and Martin. He had even made excuses for the fact that she had refused to share their marriage bed since Alicia's birth. Her excuse was that she wanted no more children, but Guy knew it was more than that. She didn't want *him*.

He had heard rumors that she'd taken a lover, but she'd always denied it and he'd believed her. Then, a few months ago the rumors had started again. He hadn't wanted to listen to them, had denied them, but he had only been fooling himself. Hannah had told him of things she'd heard. Moses had told him what he'd seen with his own eyes. And still Guy had refused to believe it. But that had been before he'd seen them himself, and there had no longer been any way to deny the truth. He had been in town on business and had planned on staying the night. But the next day had been Alicia's birthday, so he'd decided to get home the night before in order to have breakfast with her. He'd arrived home late, well after midnight. On the way to his bedchamber he'd heard a soft scream from

44

Victoria's room. Thinking something was wrong he'd barged through the locked door. The sight of his wife in bed with his younger brother, their naked bodies glistening in the moonlight from the window, would stay with him forever, seared into his memory. Whatever little thread of feeling for her still burned within him had been totally and cruelly extinguished that night.

The memory brought anger with it and Guy let it seep into his veins and invade the bittersweet thoughts of what might have been. He pulled it around him, warming to its shroud, and knew he had learned his lesson well, finally. Never again would he give his heart or trust to a woman. He stared down at her. "Moses was right, Victoria," Guy whispered harshly, "I never should have married you."

Tori slept soundly through the remainder of the afternoon and early evening, waking only long enough to down a few spoonfuls of soup and a dose of laudanum. The next morning she found her limbs and ribs still extremely sore; the occasional dizziness caused by the blow to her head had subsided, though not the nagging headache. She refused the laudanum Suda offered in the morning after a light breakfast of cream-laced coffee and biscuits, wanting to remain awake. An hour later, however, after a visit from the doctor and endurance of his probing touches to her temple, Tori accepted the laudanum willingly, almost eagerly, praying that more sleep and the rest it brought would finally vanquish the throbbing ache in her head and restore her strength.

The day passed in a slumber fraught with dreams and nightmares, flashes of images she didn't understand, scenes that made no sense, and each enveloped within a shroud of danger. Several times Tori woke filled with terror, anxious to see Guy Reichourd, to warn him he was in danger, but of what kind, or from whom, she didn't know.

After a light supper, she tried to read a book of prose that she had noticed lying on a table near the bed, but the effort only made her head ache, which in turn drained what little strength she had.

Leaning over the edge of the mattress she reached to switch off the lamp that sat on the table. She turned the flat metal switch. The lamp's light suddenly exploded into brilliance and wisps of black smoke curled up from the glass chimney. Tori hurried to grab the switch again and turn it in the opposite direction, back to where it had originally been set. She stared at the lamp in surprise, and a feeling of puzzlement filled her, yet she was at a loss to explain it. She peered beneath the glass shade that covered the base of the glass chimney. Flame. She hadn't expected to see a flame. She continued to stare at the lamp, her eyes moving from the ornate, but squat, brass legs to the pale blue globe whose front was painted with a bouquet of white magnolias and twisting green leaves, to the keylike knob that protruded from just above the blue globe, a good inch below the base of the etched crystal hurricane top. So what had she expected to see? She thought hard for a moment, but no answer came to mind.

"You getting tired, Miss Victoria?"

Tori turned to see that Suda was in the process of spreading out her bedding on the floor at the other side of the poster's tall footboard. "Suda, you don't have to stay all night with me again. Go on and be comfortable in your own room. I'll call you if I really need something."

The girl looked at her, clearly perplexed. "But I can't

hears you from my cabin, Miss Victoria, if you should call for something."

Tori frowned. "You don't have a room here in the main house?"

"No, ma'am. But I always sleeps with you when you're sick. You know that, Miss Victoria." She began to fluff out the moss-filled cot she used as a bed.

"Go on home, Suda. I'm fine, really. There's no need for you to sleep on the floor. Anyway, another spoonful of that laudanum and I'll sleep the night away like a newborn baby." She smiled in an effort to emphasize her words.

With a few curious peeks in Victoria's direction, Suda rolled up her thin mattress and blanket, and quietly left the room, unable to banish the concern and bewilderment she felt at the unusual order.

Once alone, Tori sipped her second teaspoon of laudanum and lay her head back on the mound of pillows Suda had placed behind her earlier. With a sigh she let herself sink into their softness. She stared up at the sunburst pattern of the dark blue silk canopy overhead and found her thoughts drifting to Guy Reichourd, as they had done almost constantly when she was awake and not preoccupied with terror at the loss of her memory. He had not returned to her room since the morning before, when she'd first awakened after the accident and hadn't recognized him.

Earlier that afternoon she'd talked with Suda, asking the girl several pertinent questions. She'd gotten her answers, though they hadn't helped jog her memory, and in the process it had seemed that Suda would rather be informing someone they were about to die than supplying the information Tori had requested. Martin was her son, from a previous marriage, and Guy was her husband. And no they didn't share a bedroom.

47

Tori thought about this last response for a long time, then finally dismissed it. She obviously couldn't ask Guy why they didn't sleep in the same room together. And she felt that his coolness toward her, and his aura of anger, had been there for a long time, that they were not caused merely by her inability to remember him. A heaviness began to pull at Tori's eyelids and they drifted closed.

Minutes later, sleep finally settled over her thoughts and drugged her consciousness, pulling her into its mind-numbing cocoon of darkness.

Night shrouded the earth and filled the room, wafting across the wide gallery outside and drifting in through the open windows. A soft breeze ruffled the curtains, carrying with it the heady fragrance of jasmine as the tiny orange and white blossoms, whose vines wound around the massive pillars of Shadow Oaks, spread their petals wide in welcome of the night.

Tori burrowed deeper beneath the coverlet but did not wake, the laudanum she had taken holding her securely within its grip. But it could not ward off the nightmares or the flash of images that upon wakening she would remember but neither recognize or understand. She tossed fitfully, but remained deep in sleep.

With barely a whisper of sound the entry door to her bedchamber opened, and the soft click of its latch as it closed echoed in the silence of the spacious room.

A dark figure moved stealthily and hastily toward the bed. Long, slender fingers gripped the lacey edge of the coverlet, lifted it, and pulled it back from her body, revealing her lithe form to hungry eyes.

He had been hot with desire upon entering her room, the burning need to once again taste her passion, to satiate himself with her eating relentlessly at him. He stood at the

48

side of the bed and looked down at her, feeling himself becoming even further aroused by the sight of breasts pushed against the sheer fabric of her gown.

Tori moaned as a sweep of cool night air rippled over her, and she snuggled deeper against the mattress and pillow, pulling her arms and legs in tight about her suddenly chilled body.

The dark figure hovered over the bed for a long second, watching her, then hastily untied a sash at his waist and shrugged out of the black velvet robe wrapped around his otherwise naked body. He sat on the bed, swung his legs up onto the mattress and settled down beside her. The mattress shifted slightly beneath the added weight. "Victoria, my sweet," he whispered in her ear.

Tori moaned again, stretched her legs out, and attempted to roll over.

Darin smiled as she inadvertently pressed up against him in her attempt to change positions. His lips brushed against the curls of hair at her temple. He slipped an arm beneath her waist and pulled her against his body. "I know you're bruised and sore from the accident, *jet'aime,* but I couldn't resist the temptation of coming to you any longer. It's been too many days, *chérie.* Over a week." His hand caressed her derrière, and pushed her against him, against the shaft of his need, which was swollen to rigid hardness in its hunger. "I'll be gentle *jet'aime.*" His tone had grown harsh and ragged with the passion that was threatening to explode within him. "But I need you, chérie, I need you now."

A soft whimper left Tori's lips, and she snuggled against his warmth as her body responded to his tender caresses and her dreams filled with images of Guy Reichourd.

There was no anger between them now, no coolness to keep them apart. He was with her, and loving her.

A soft chuckle escaped Darin's lips. "And you obviously need me." His body was on fire, his blood boiling within his veins, and he knew he could not wait much longer. "Show me how much you missed me, *chérie*," he commanded, his voice little more than a rasp now. "Show me." His fingers slipped beneath the sheer fabric of Tori's night-gown, skipped lightly over her thigh, and up across the smooth curve of her bare back.

She shivered at the intimate touch, and a deep rumble of satisfaction at what he took as her burgeoning passion echoed within Darin's throat.

Tori pressed against him, the haze that controlled her mind and fed her dreams leaving her with thoughts only of Guy, of fulfilling the passion that he had awakened within her. "Oh, yes," she whispered, "yes."

Darin's lips caught hers in a savage kiss, a feral mating that demanded her immediate acquiescence, the urgency of his passion, the hunger of his own need, abruptly over-shadowing any display of tenderness.

Tori pressed herself to him, her hands sliding over his shoulders and wrapping around his neck. She parted her lips and his tongue instantly plunged into her mouth, fill-ing it. His fingers moved to the delicately embroidered neckline of her nightgown and slipping downward, quickly and with the expertise of a man very used to doing so, released the small pearl buttons that held it closed. He pushed the frail fabric aside and bared her breasts to his eager touch.

His hand moved to cup one subtle mound, his fingers playing roughly with the pebbled nipple they caught in their grasp.

50

Somewhere, deep in the hazy center of Tori's mind, a small voice suddenly yelled a warning, tried to rouse her from her drugged state, to alert her that her dream and reality were not one and the same. She winced in pain as Darin's fingers squeezed her breast and woke with a start at feeling the hungry suction of lips closing around the swollen mount, his teeth grazing tender flesh.

"No," she protested weakly, her mind trying desperately to struggle out of the haze the laudanum had induced. Her limbs felt lethargic and heavy. Guy . . . Guy was with her, but . . . cruel . . . not loving . . . not the way he should be. Her mind swirled in a fog of half consciousness, half delirium. He was hurting her.

His mouth crashed down atop hers again, his teeth pressing against her lips, his tongue probing hungrily, greedily within her mouth.

She struggled to lift her hands, to push out against him and met the solid resistance of his chest. This wasn't the way it was supposed to be between them. She tried to twist away, but her legs seemed imprisoned and unable to move, and she felt weak. Oh, so weak.

The hungry-hot mouth that covered hers suddenly disappeared, and Tori gasped for breath. "I have been without you for far too long, *chérie*," Darin said. His hand clutched at her breast again, and she felt a squeezing pain.

"No," Tori said, the word little more than a weak gasp. "Stop—"

"Teasing you?" Darin said, a cynical chuckle muffled within the curve of her neck as his lips moved over her bared flesh.

"Please," Tori whimpered. Reality began to return to her with agonizing slowness. "Please."

"So, you are hungry for me too, hey, *chérie?* Good,"

Darin said, and laughed, "because I am about to spill on you."

Tori strained to move away from him, only to feel the return of the sucking vortex seconds later as his mouth enveloped the taut peak of her breast. His teeth cut into her flesh as his tongue laved her nipple.

"No, no, stop," she said, her words barely a raspy whisper. Tori stiffened and tried to pull away, pushing at his shoulders with the heel of her hands, but his grip on her was too strong, his embrace secure, and her resistance too feeble. She looked down at him, but in the inky darkness that surrounded them she could make out little more than a black shadow that had wrapped itself around her. Was this Guy? An unexplainable denial coiled in the pit of her stomach.

She blinked her eyes rapidly and struggled to focus on him, to clear her mind of the mind-numbing haze the laudanum had plunged her into.

"We have to get rid of him soon, *chérie,*" the man whispered against her as his mouth moved to her other breast. "No more waiting, no more."

She felt his hand slip between her legs and urge them apart. Tears stung her eyes and poured over her lids, streaming down her cheeks. Good God, what was happening? Tori pushed against his shoulders, and arched her back to pull away from him. She wanted to scream, yet her throat felt paralyzed.

Suddenly, the door slammed open and crashed against the wall with such a resoundingly loud thud that it reverberated throughout the entire house.

Startled, Tori jerked around to stare at the open doorway, her mind still too muddled to permit her to think of drawing the coverlet over herself.

Light from the hallway streamed into the room, circumvented the figure who stood in the doorway, and turned him to little more than a black silhouette. The narrow beams fell directly onto the large canopied bed and bathed its two occupants in golden illumination.

Four

Darin rolled lazily onto his back, his nakedness and arousal clearly revealed as the sheet slipped from his hip. He stared insolently at his brother, and then a sly smile pulled his thin lips upward. "Good evening, Guy. I was just saying goodbye to Victoria before my trip to Baton Rouge." He released an exaggerated sigh. "And as usual you have"—he glanced down at the hard shaft of his erection—"extremely bad timing."

Guy stood in the doorway, his silhouette creating an ominous figure that, to Tori, loomed larger than life. His broad shoulders were held tightly squared, his arms stiff like steel rods that flowed into clenched fists of iron at his thighs. With the light streaming in from behind him and the unyielding posture of his stance, he seemed to exude pure fury.

Tori blinked hard and shook her head, trying to clear her mind of the stupor which enveloped it. As the blurriness of her vision finally cleared she looked back at Guy and, trembling uncontrollably, down at her half-naked body. The verity of the situation instantly impressed itself on her and chased away the last gripping effects of the laudanum. A gasp escaped her as she was overcome with horror at the situation. She pulled a pillow in front of her, and turned to gape at the face of the man next to her. Darin!

Her mind reeled in disbelief. The man in her bed was Darin Reichourd, not Guy.

"And I can see that you were about to receive a very *warm* farewell from my wife, little brother," Guy said. The steel-sharp tone of his voice, edged with bitter rage, cut through the dimly lit room and sent a chill skipping over Tori.

"No." The word left her lips as little more than a release of breath, though every instinct had pushed it from her lungs as a scream. She wanted to reach out to Guy, to tell him she hadn't known it was Darin in her bed, that she'd been half-drugged with laudanum and out of her mind, but before she could move, before she could formulate the words, he was gone.

Darin chuckled softly, and ran his fingers lightly across her shoulder. "Well, *chérie,* there's no question that he knows about us now. I guess we'd better do it soon then, hey? Before he does something to spoil our plans."

Tori scrambled to the far edge of the bed, away from him. She dragged the coverlet with her and stared at Darin. His long lean body stretched nearly the length of the bed, and the skin tone of his natural heritage glowed golden beneath the light still streaming in from the open entry door. She kept her gaze studiously averted from his sexual organ, though a furtive glance while he'd been talking had provided her relief at the realization that it had shrunk back down to its unaroused size. Obviously Guy's interruption had cooled Darin's ardor. "Do?" she echoed, while her mind spun in bewilderment and more than a little fear. Though she was unsure of what *it* was Darin thought they should do soon, both the insinuating words and his tone made her cringe.

Darin lay back against the pillow and smiled up at her, making no effort to cover himself. One dark brow rose slightly in cocky assuredness. "I have it all figured out, *chérie*. I leave in the morning for some business in Baton Rouge I must attend to. On my way back I'll stop in the Vieux Carré to see Mariah Chartonneau. You remember her, I'm sure. The old witch who operates that little potion shop down on Dumaine?"

Tori shook her head. What in heaven's name was he talking about?

Darin shrugged. "Oh, it's not important. Anyway, I've been told she has a potion we can use. A little in his food every day, or in a drink, and before you know it, we'll be rid of my dear brother. And the best thing, *chérie,* is that it will merely seem as if his heart failed." The malicious smile turned to laughter, a deep, throaty, evil sound that filled the room and left Tori's heart clutched within the cold, gripping fingers of fear.

"You . . . you mean to kill Guy?" she asked, gawking at Darin in disbelief and horror. "Your own brother? You want to kill your own brother?" A shiver rippled across her shoulders and she felt suddenly as if she were experiencing a sense of déjà vu, yet she couldn't be. She couldn't be, because she never would have agreed to anything like this.

The laughter abruptly stopped, his eyes narrowed, and Darin shot up in the bed so fast that Tori jumped back. He eyed her coldly. "What kind of question is that? You know what our plans are. You helped contrive them." His eyes narrowed in suspicion, and their pale gray became cold, resembling the sleet of a sunless winter's day. "Or are you thinking of betraying me, *chérie?* Has something happened to change your mind while you were in town with him all last week? Did your beloved husband bribe you with his money, perhaps? Buy you expensive gifts? Promise you the world, like when you were first married?"

"Betray you?" Her mind spun in confusion, unable to register anything he had said past those words.

"What has he promised you, Victoria?" Darin raged suddenly. He scrambled up onto his knees, towering over her, and smashed a fist against the headboard of the bed. The entire frame shook with the force of his blow. "You will not betray me, *chérie.* Do you understand? We are in this together—together!" His fist smashed against the headboard again. "We have waited too long for this, Victoria. Too long. But now the time is right. It will happen. We will have everything! Think of it, Victoria, everything. The plantations, the money"—he looked at her sharply—"and we will have each other." His hand snaked out toward her arm. "Now, no more talk. Come here."

She threw a quick glance toward the apex of his hips, to the thatch of black hair curled there and saw that, with his anger, had come renewed arousal.

"N . . . no." Tori hastened from the bed, pulling the coverlet with her, and backed toward the dressing table, aghast more at the implications his words wrought than his body. Murder. Darin intended to murder his own brother, and she had evidently helped him plan it.

"Victoria?" Darin's tone invited no rebuke.

Tori clutched the coverlet tighter about her body. "I . . . I don't remember any of this."

Darin jerked up from the bed and, with a string of curses tumbling from his lips, grabbed his robe and jerked it on. He paused in the middle of tying it closed and stared at her across the width of the bed, his passion once more effectively doused by words. "What do you mean, you don't remember? What are you talking about?"

"The accident . . . don't remember anything before the accident."

For what seemed an eternity, silence hung over the room as he regarded her thoughtfully, his dark brows drawn together as he pondered the situation. When he finally spoke it was as if a band of tension within him had snapped and he was once again calm. His voice softened as he spoke. "You mean you don't remember what we planned?"

Tori shook her head. "I mean I don't remember anything, Darin. I don't remember Guy or the children. I don't remember you, or these plans. I don't remember this place, this house. I don't even remember myself!"

Darin smiled. "Then I guess I will just have to make you remember. *Je t'aime.*" He walked around the bed and moved to pull her into his embrace again. "Surely you cannot have forgotten what we mean to each other? What we share?"

Tori eluded his outstretched arms, and knew instantly it had been the wrong thing to do. Anger flared as an instant and bright spark in Darin's gray eyes, and an ugly sneer pulled at the corners of his mouth. His arms dropped to his sides and he pinned her with his stony gaze. "You will remember in time, *chérie.* Until then, do remember this: I can always purchase enough potion for two, or even more, should the need arise."

Tori sat at the table and peered across its width from beneath slightly lowered lashes. Guy ignored her and concentrated on the food on his breakfast plate, eating silently and steadily. She didn't know what to say to him, how to breach the barriers he'd erected around himself and against her, yet she knew she must try. His life depended on her finding a way to make him listen. She only wished their son had been at the table, maybe then Guy would have been forced to at least acknowledge her presence. But Martin, she had been informed by one of the kitchen maids, had taken his morning meal early and was already out riding. Her troubled reflections wandered from Guy for a moment, and Tori thought of the boy in the portrait above the staircase. Martin Camerei Reichourd. Her son. It felt odd to think of him that way. Almost as odd as looking at Guy and telling herself he was her husband. None of it felt right. Yet, Guy was her husband, and Martin was definitely her son. Everyone said so. And she could not deny that there was a physical resemblance between her and her son. He had her coloring—and her eyes, the same set, the same blue, the same thin black line around the iris. She turned her attention back to Guy. "Could we talk? Please?"

He pierced her with his gaze, and Tori shivered at the cold contempt she saw in his eyes, the dark gray orbs turned to icy pools of silver. His fury and indignation resonated from every harsh line of his body, from rigid jaw to stiffly held shoulders, and it was directed at her, unerringly and pointedly. But there was something else she sensed rather than saw beneath the cool veneer of his controlled rage, something not quite concealed: a sense of power and virility, raw and tightly leashed but still potent and untempered.

Tori shook off her hesitancy and forced herself to continue. "Guy, please, I . . . I know you're angry but . . . there's something we need to discuss. Something important." To emphasize her words she reached across the table and laid her hand lightly on his. The touch sent a shock of warmth flashing through her fingers and spiraling up her arm.

He didn't move, but merely stared down at their hands, at her fingers atop his flesh. When he finally looked at her, his eyes still held a chill as icy as the fiercest of winter storms, and just as impenetrable. He laid his fork down, reached to lift her hand from his, and, holding her hand as if it were something he found thoroughly distasteful, placed it back down on the table.

The silent rejection cut through her. Was this how their relationship had always been? Was this why she had accepted his brother's advances and helped plot her own husband's murder? Because Guy rejected her?

"Mamière! You're up. Papa said you wouldn't go away like Ol' Abraham and Uncle John did, and you didn't."

Tori turned in her chair, startled at the child's voice.

Alicia skipped happily into the room, the tiered blue muslin ruffles on her skirt and the white petticoat underneath bouncing with each step she took, her long black hair, coiled in numerous sausage curls, rebounding merrily off of her shoulders. She paused before Tori, curtsied smartly, and then ran to Guy.

An instant smile curved his lips as he lifted the child onto his lap.

"See, Miss Pansy," Alicia said to the rag doll she propped on her own small lap, "Mamière didn't go away. I told you she wouldn't, 'cause Papa said so. Didn't you, Papa?" The child twisted around to look up at Guy.

Tori stared at Alicia. Mamière?

"Yes, *chérie,* that's what I said."

"And grownups never lie, Pansy." Alicia looked at Guy again. "Do they, Papa?"

His eyes met Tori's for a brief but intense second before they flitted away and he answered, "No, *chérie,* they don't."

"Suda said Mademoiselle Sabrina isn't coming today. Is that right, Papa?"

"Yes, *chérie.* I thought it best to postpone your dressmaking session since your mother isn't feeling well because of her accident."

"Oh." Alicia's mouth dropped into a pout.

Tori couldn't take her gaze from the child. This was her daughter? Her mind reeled with the newfound knowledge. A husband, a son, *and* a daughter—and she remembered none of them, felt no sense of familiarity, no bond. She forced a smile to her lips. "But I'm . . . I'm feeling much better than I was," Tori said quickly, "so we'll do it soon." She looked helplessly from the child to Guy.

"Alicia," he said softly, providing the name that would not come to Tori's mind.

Tori nodded. "Alicia," she repeated.

Guy ran a hand over Alicia's dark head, then lifted her against his chest and rose. The glacial tinge had disappeared from his eyes, replaced by a warmth that Tori suddenly wished was meant for her. He kissed the end of the child's nose and smiled.

Alicia giggled and held up Miss Pansy for a kiss.

Tori couldn't take her gaze away from the child. She was beautiful. The top and sides of her ebony hair were pulled to her crown and secured by a pale blue ribbon, while a halo of black ringlets draped about her tiny shoulders and cascaded down her back. Her nose was pert, her mouth curved in a continual smile, and her eyes were at once the brilliant blue of the sky and the soft gray of a winters fog. "Now that you've seen for yourself that Mamière is all right, Licia, I suggest that you and Miss Pansy say good morning and run along back upstairs," Guy said. He nuzzled his forehead against hers playfully. "You're supposed to be doing your studies with Ruby this morning, aren't you?"

"She was setting out books and stuff, and I sneaked out. I wanted to see you, Papa. . . ." She bit her bottom lip and glanced quickly at Tori. "And Mamière," she added.

Guy carried Alicia to the door that led to the foyer and bent to set her on her feet. "Well, now you've seen us, *chérie*. So, you and Miss Pansy go on back to the nursery like good girls, and I'll be up later to check on your numbers, all right?"

"Yes, Papa," Alicia said happily, and skipped toward the stairs. She paused at the door and looked back. "Will we get a new teacher soon, Papa? It's not so much fun doing my figures with just Ruby and Martin."

He nodded, and, satisfied, she raced off.

"I can teach them," Tori said suddenly, then frowned. Why had it seemed so natural that she teach the children their lessons.

Guy didn't even look at her when he answered, instead turning his attention to pouring himself another cup of coffee from a silver urn that sat on the sideboard. "No."

Tori, who had been staring at the empty doorway, looked at him. "Why?"

"Because it's not necessary. I've hired a teacher, and she'll be here in a few weeks."

"I can teach them until she arrives."

"No, I think it's better that you don't."

She felt a sudden urge to cry, to break down and allow

62

the tears that until this moment she had fought so desperately to control to overtake her. She wanted to scream her outrage at the unfairness of her situation, to demand that God rescue her from the cimmerian cavern that had swallowed every memory of her life before the carriage accident. She had a beautiful home, a strong, virile husband, a handsome son, and a darling little daughter, and she remembered none of them. And, though she felt loath to admit it, she also had a lover. Her own brother-in-law. Tori's shoulders sagged slightly and her gaze dropped to her lap, fixing momentarily on the silk daygown with its ivory grosgrain and lace trim. Was there nothing she remembered? Some shred of her life? Of her family? Her eyes rose and met Guy's. "I . . . I don't remember her."

"Maybe you don't want to."

Tori rose, shocked at his statement. "But why? Why wouldn't I want to remember my own daughter?" She was losing her grip on the terror that had been eating at her, on the self-control that she'd staunchly hung onto while hope of remembering had carried her through each minute of the past forty-eight hours. She knew her composure was quivering on the brink of collapse, but she couldn't stop herself.

She grabbed the back of the chair she had just vacated, and leaned on it for support as her legs trembled. "Why do you act as though you hate me, Guy?" As tears filled her eyes, she blinked them back. "Please tell me, what did I do? Don't you understand that I can't remember anything?" Even as she voiced the questions Tori wanted to shy away from his response, to run and hide from the brutal answers that were so obvious from the stoic set of his face, the frosty gleam of his eyes.

He moved to stand before her, every muscle exuding

indignation and mordacity. "Oh? It seemed you were remembering a few things quite well last night."

She knew he was referring to Darin being in her bed, and she wanted to cringe away from him, to hide from the loathing she saw in his eyes. But she couldn't, because she felt the same way about herself. Tori placed her hands on his chest. "I . . . I thought he was you, Guy. I thought he was you."

Guy threw back his head and laughed. "Oh, please, Victoria. I'm certain you can do better than that."

The tears she had fought to control filled her eyes once more and spilled onto her cheeks, and a burning ache sparked within her breast. An unexplainable fear gripped her heart. He wasn't going to listen to her, not to anything she said. She clenched her hands into fists and pounded his chest, the terror she felt momentarily overwhelming her better senses. "It's true, Guy, it's true. You've got to believe me. Please, you've got to."

"Victoria." His voice thundered down upon her, harsh and commanding.

"I don't know what's happening, can't you understand that?" Her fists pummeled him and tears streamed from her eyes. "I don't remember, Darin. I don't remember anything before the accident."

He grabbed her flailing arms and held her wrists against his chest in a steely grip. "Even if I believed you, Victoria, it wouldn't change anything. Inside, where it counts, you are the same woman you were before the accident. And if you are telling the truth and don't remember anything, I wouldn't worry about it too much. The doctor said your memory would most likely come back to you in time." He started to push her away, stopped, and looked back at her. "You want me to refresh your memory? Maybe hasten things up a bit?" When she didn't respond he continued, his tone hard and cold. "Fine." He looked long and deep into her eyes. "You never wanted us, Victoria. Not Martin, not Alicia, and certainly not me. You married me for my money, that's all you care about. All you've ever cared about. We don't fit into your life, Victoria. Not the life you want for yourself."

She clutched at his lapels, holding him to her when he tried to move away, remembering what she *had* to tell him. What she had to make him listen to and believe. "No, no, Guy, wait, please. You have to know. Darin plans to—"

His fingers closed around her wrists again, bands of steel that jerked him free of her, yet held her prisoner against him. "I know all about my dear brother, Victoria. Darin covets everything I own, he always has, and he'll do whatever he can to possess all that is mine."

Before she knew what was happening, his arms crushed her to him, and his lips claimed hers. His kiss was hard and demanding, as if punishing her for all the betrayals he claimed she'd committed, while at the same time tempered with a hungry passion softened by the yearning need Guy had, and would not admit to having, for love.

The fierceness of his kiss shocked Tori into physical stillness, but her emotions ran rampant, wildly out of control. She had seen strength in him, tenderness, and love, if only directed toward the children, but something within her yearned to have him spend those emotions on her as well . . . and now he was, her mind whispered. Fire erupted in her veins, turning her body into a seething flame, while her heart seemed at once to stand still and to race madly against her breast. Her breath caught in her throat, her limbs trembled, and she leaned into him.

Caught in a trap of his own making, wanting to both

push her away and hold her to him, Guy tore his lips from Tori's and stared down at her, his breath coming in ragged bursts as he fought to regain control of himself. "That's what you've rejected, Victoria," he said finally. "Everything I have, everything I am, was yours, and you turned your back on it all." His arms dropped from around her, and he turned away. "I meant what I said the night you ran out of the opera house . . . the night of the carriage wreck. But in case you've forgotten, perchance conveniently, I will refresh your memory. I want a divorce, Victoria. I want this charade we call a marriage to end." His arms dropped away from her, and he took a step toward the door; then as if remembering something more, he wheeled back to face her. Tori flinched at the hardness that had returned to his features. "I'll give you one of the plantations I own in northern Louisiana, Victoria, and enough money to keep you comfortable for several years. As soon as you are physically able, and at least part of your memory returns, I want you to leave Shadow Oaks."

Tori gasped. "No, Guy, you can't mean this. Please, I . . ."

He held up a hand to silence her. "You will leave, Victoria, but Martin and Alicia will stay here with me. Martin may only be my stepson, but he is more my son than he ever was yours. He will stay, Victoria, and you are never to return or make a move to enter their lives again. And understand this, my dear wife, if you do, if you attempt to see Martin or Alicia at all after you leave, everything I give you will be immediately taken away."

Tori paled under the assault. Everything that had happened since the carriage accident—his remarks, his attitude—told her she should welcome his rejection, that she should not care about this man, but suddenly and irrevocably she knew that she did. Why, or how deeply, she wasn't sure. But, God help her, she did care. "Guy, I . . ."

"It's over, Victoria. The charade is—" He abruptly paused and gripped the ledge of the sideboard that stood beside the door, his knuckles turning white as his fingers dug into the polished mahogany. His face creased with pain, his eyes squeezed shut, and his flesh suddenly took on a ghostly pallor.

Tori rushed to his side and wrapped an arm around his waist. "Guy, what's wrong. What is it?"

"Pain . . . in my stomach." His knees nearly buckled. "Get Hannah."

Tori helped him back to the table and he settled heavily into the chair he'd occupied earlier while dining.

Fear clutched at Tori. She lifted the voluminous folds of her skirt and hurried toward the door that led to the warming kitchen. "Hannah, Hannah," she called as she ran into the kitchen. It was empty. She looked about frantically and saw that the back door was open. She ran toward it, stepped out onto the wide gallery that wrapped around the entire width of the house and spotted Hannah in the middle of a small garden a few yards away. The old woman was just rising to her feet. "Hannah, hurry. Guy's sick."

Before Hannah took two steps, Tori whirled around and ran back into the house and through the kitchen. On the threshold to the dining room she stopped abruptly.

On the opposite side of the room Darin slouched arrogantly against the doorjamb that led to the foyer, his hands pressed together before him, outstretched fingers creating a steeple upon which he rested his chin. The smile on his face chilled Tori to the very bone.

"What have you done, Darin?" she said, her voice tinged with fear. "Tell me! What did you do to Guy?"

67

Five

"Answer me, Darin," Tori demanded, "what did you do to Guy? Did you put something in his food?" Her heart raced in fear. "Did you?"

Darin's smile turned to a smug sneer, but as he caught sight of Hannah approaching from the kitchen, his expression turned to one of complete innocence and concern. "Me? I'm not the one who practices that black magic voo-doo stuff, Victoria, and since I wasn't the one just at the table with him . . ." He didn't finish the sentence, but instead smiled serenely, shrugged, and left the insinuation hanging in the air. It served her right, after the way she'd acted the night before.

Hannah rushed past her to where Guy sat on a chair, hunched over and still holding his stomach.

Tori ran toward Guy, saw his eyes closed in pain, and whirled around to face his brother. "Darin, tell me the truth, dammit. What did you do to Guy?" She glared at him through eyes full of suspicion and her voice held a warning note.

He shrugged and turned away. "It's just another of his

spells. I'm sure he'll be fine, Victoria. He always is." With that, Darin disappeared into the foyer.

Always is? Spells? What did that mean? Tori turned back to find that Moses had entered the room and both he and Hannah were helping Guy to his feet. Though Guy seemed a little weak, and his face was ashen, he appeared to be regaining composure and strength.

"Are you all right?" Tori asked him. Could his brother have already started to poison him? She thought quickly back to what Darin had said to her earlier in her bedroom. No, he still had to go to town, to some woman's shop, and buy the potion. She glanced back at Guy who was now standing on his own and straightening his coat while Hannah fussed over him and Moses stood beside him looking deeply worried.

"Guy, what's wrong?" she questioned, the fear in her voice evident to all in the room.

"Your display of sudden"—he grimaced slightly as another stab of pain struck, though obviously not as severe as the first—"concern is overwhelming, my dear."

Tori was taken aback by the caustic words. She watched him shrug off Hannah's hand from his arm. But if not poison, Tori wondered, then what was wrong with Guy? Why had he doubled over in abrupt pain like that? "Guy, what's the matter?"

He ignored her and instead tried to reassure Hannah that he didn't need the doctor.

"But Michie Guy, you had another attack. You should call Doctor Ben. Get some medicine."

He shook his head and squared his shoulders, which seemed to underscore the fact that he towered over both Hannah and Moses. "I'm fine, Hannah, really. It's gone now."

The old housekeeper continued to flutter around him nervously, brushing imaginary lint off of his greatcoat and clucking her concern like a worried hen tending one of her chicks.

Tori stared at him quietly, trying to understand what had just happened, to make some sense of it, and instead found herself once again mesmerized by Guy's powerful presence and near devastating handsomeness.

The dark blue of his greatcoat somehow accentuated his eyes and caused the gray to appear darker, and its cut emphasized both the broad width of his shoulders and chest, and the narrow span of his waist. The white shirt he wore, the tips of its raised collar nearly brushing the sides of his jaw, contrasted starkly with the deep bronze of his skin.

Tori's gaze traveled over him as he continued to converse with the servants, and completely ignore her presence. His hands, she noticed, were square and strong, his legs, encased in trousers of the same color and fabric as his greatcoat, were long and lean, accentuated by the fact that his trousers were held taut by straps of leather that ran beneath the insole of each black boot.

"Sous pieds," Tori mumbled softly, staring at his feet.

The other three occupants of the room heard and turned to stare at her in puzzlement.

"What about them, Victoria?" Guy asked.

She frowned. *"Sous pieds,"* she repeated, louder this time.

Guy's brow creased. "I heard that. What about them?" His tone was sharp, hard, and impatient.

"Sous pieds," Tori said again, almost shouting it in her excitement. "Guy, I remember. Those straps under your boots that hold your pants taut, they're called *sous pieds.*"

70

"Pants?" He looked momentarily confused. "Oh, you mean my trousers. Yes, so?"

"I remember what they're called."

He nodded. "Wonderful," he said drily. "You remember my *sous pieds*. Let's celebrate."

Hannah and Moses quietly left the room, each casting her a look of distaste as they did, and Tori moved to stand before Guy. "But don't you see, Guy? I remembered something. It's coming back. My memory's coming back."

"Yes, you remembered my boot straps, Victoria. A milestone of recovery, I'm sure." He brushed past her, moving hastily, as if he could no longer stand to be near her. He walked toward the door leading to the foyer, paused, and looked back. "I'll be away most of the day, Victoria, and I would appreciate it if you would remain in your room while I'm gone."

"My room? Why?"

"Because I do not want you around Alicia or Martin anymore than necessary. You will be leaving soon. It would be easier on the children if you remained away from them now as much as possible." He turned on his heel and disappeared from her view.

Tori stared after him, his words coldly reminding her of his earlier edict that he wanted a divorce, that he was, in essence, banishing her from both his life and his home, as well as from her own children.

"You can't do that," she said softly to the empty doorway where he'd stood. But somehow she felt certain that Guy Reichourd, master of Shadow Oaks Plantation, could do whatever he wanted, and would. Suddenly she wondered why the thought of being separated from her children did not bring with it an agonizing ache in her heart,

71

a sense of extreme loss. Shouldn't she feel more than concern? More than mild consternation?

She should . . . *if* they were her children, she reasoned. She shook her head to rid herself of the ridiculous thought. Of course they were her children. But then, that left only one answer: she must be the type of woman Guy had indicated she was—cold, uncaring, and greedy. Or at least she had been that way before the accident, before she'd forgotten everything, including her own identity. Was it possible for a person's personality to change so drastically because of a bump on the head?

Tori felt tears sting the back of her eyes, and an ache swell within her breast. She wasn't the woman Guy had described, she wasn't. Her vision blurred and tears slipped over her eyelids and streamed down her cheeks. She wasn't like that, yet so many things indicated that she had been exactly as Guy had said.

Hadn't Darin come blithely to her bed, expecting a warm welcome? Hadn't her own son, Martin, ignored her since Guy had brought her home, making sure to stay away from her, not even coming to her bedroom to see that she was all right? And didn't the servants look at her with disdain, or in Suda's case, with fear?

Tori tried to wipe the tears from her face, only for them to be immediately replaced by more. And her daughter, Alicia. Even though the little girl had seemed pleased to see that her mother was indeed alive and well, she had physically maintained a goodly distance between them. One which at the time Tori had not noticed, but in thinking back on the scene could not help but see. Alicia had stayed well out of Tori's reach, but had skipped merrily into her father's arms.

"Miss Victoria, I assume you're finished here?"

Tori whirled to see Hannah standing beside the table. The old woman stood with her arms crossed atop her round belly, the huge muslin apron she wore draped across her girth like a tent. Her brown eyes, set deep above puffy cheeks, were hard and disapproving as she stared at Tori and waited for an answer.

For a brief moment, Tori thought Hannah was referring to her presence at Shadow Oaks. Was the woman making a reference that she should leave now?

Then she realized the housekeeper meant the dishes on the table. Relieved, she brushed hurriedly at her tears. "Yes, yes, I'm finished, Hannah. Thank you."

A spark of surprise shone in Hannah's eyes, but was gone as quickly as it had appeared. "Thank you, humph," she mumbled under her breath. "That's a new one. Didn't think she even knew the words." She began to gather the dishes together, but stopped abruptly when she realized Tori had not left the room and remained by the doorway, watching her. Hannah straightened and looked Tori in the eye. "It ain't right what you done to him, Miss Victoria. Might not be my place to say, but that ain't never stopped me before. You ain't no good for him. No good for the children either. Sooner you gits and goes about making a life for yourself somewhere else, the better for everybody."

Tori stood frozen, shocked. She didn't know what to say. She wanted to deny the woman's accusations, tell her that she was wrong, that she could be good for Guy and the children, but how could she? Everything that had confronted her since the accident, everything, served to prove exactly what the housekeeper was saying.

Yet Tori couldn't accept that. It all felt wrong. Not only what they said she was really like, but everything—the house, her husband, her so-called lover, her clothes. She sighed. These cumbersome, seemingly archaic clothes . . .

She looked down at the beautiful apricot silk gown Suda had helped her into that morning. Its skirt was a mass of ruffles, its scooped neckline trimmed with crocheted ivory lace, its sleeves puffed and then gathered just above her elbows. Beautiful, she thought, but with all the petticoats, pantaloons, and other undergarments, it seemed she had donned enough clothes to outfit two or three people. Not one.

And Guy. Tori's mind spun in confusion, seeking answers, and finding none. She was his wife, yet the very thought of her even being married seemed strange. There was no denying she was attracted to him, in spite of his brusqueness and obvious antagonism toward her. There was something between them, an unexplained magnetism or allure. She had felt it even that first time right after the accident, when she'd opened her eyes to find him standing over her.

Tori's confused gaze rose to meet Hannah's cold one, but she still did not respond to the woman's comment. Her mind continued to swim in a quandary of unanswered questions and speculation. Even her own children seemed like strangers to her, but not so much because of her memory loss as the strange feelings she was experiencing at the thought of having children, of being someone's mother. Someone's wife. It didn't feel right. In fact, her entire life seemed alien. Strange. Uncomfortable. Hers and yet not hers.

Finally, she knew what she had to do. "I am not leaving, Hannah," Tori said calmly, surprising herself more, she sensed, than the servant. "I am not leaving Shadow Oaks." At that moment, without warning, without reason, without

74

even conscious thought, she had resolved to stay at the plantation, at least until she could find a way to stop Darin from harming Guy. She knew it wouldn't be easy, since Guy refused to listen to anything she had to say, but she would find a way.

"Humph! We'll just see about that, missy," Hannah spat, and turned back to the table. "I don't think you have a whole lot to say on the matter."

Lifting the heavy folds of her skirt, Tori moved hastily from the room and rushed through the foyer toward the front door. She needed air. Fresh air. Solitude and time to think. And she needed to see more of the place that she had called home for the past few years and did not remember. Later she would approach Guy again and try to make him listen to reason, to make him believe her and understand that his brother meant to kill him.

She stood in the shade of the wide gallery for several long minutes and stared out at the scene before her. The plantation grounds spread in every direction, and in the front a winding drive, framed by azalea bushes, curved between and around tall, sprawling oaks whose limbs were heavy with moss, to an unseen road in the distance. The scene nearly took her breath away, yet as one who would look at a beautiful landscape for the first time, not as one who had seen it a hundred thousand times before.

"But then, I don't remember seeing it before," Tori mumbled to herself, in an effort to explain her feelings. "Not even once." She descended the four steps to the ground and paused as the drive's white covering crunched beneath her feet. Crouching slightly, she scooped up some of the drive's covering and held it up for closer inspection. It was some type of crushed shell. Tori let the shell bits fall from her fingers, then stood and began to follow a narrow brick path that branched off the drive. It led to a wide expanse of formal garden that sat to the left of the house. The roses were in bloom, as well as a half-dozen other varieties of plants and shrubs she recognized but couldn't name. The area was heavy with the combined fragrances of the flowers so that, when one breathed deeply of the sweetened humid air, it seemed almost an aphrodisiac, leaving one's senses tingling and one's blood warm. Reluctantly, Tori moved past the gardens and toward the stables a few yards farther on.

A boy of about ten years was in one of the corrals with a young bay colt, the horse's bridle attached to a long lead rope which the boy held in one hand. The animal cantered smartly in a circle around the lad. Tori smiled and approached the white corral fence.

She watched for long minutes, but the boy seemed oblivious to her presence, all of his concentration centered on the colt. Tori needed no one to tell her his name. He was the same boy whose portrait hung over the stairs. Martin Camerei Reichourd. Her son. Tori felt a niggling of uncertainty, of doubt, but pushed it away. He was definitely her son. She could see some of herself in his features and coloring.

"Hello, Martin," she called, inflecting her voice with a cheeriness she didn't really feel.

He glanced at her and immediately returned his attention to the yearling, not even bothering to answer her greeting.

Trepidation filled Tori, and a sense of confusion at his attitude. God, had she been that bad? Forcing herself to smile, she persisted. "Martin? Can we talk?"

"I'm busy," he answered over his shoulder. His tone was sullen, his eyes hard. He flicked a small whip over the horse's flank, though making sure to keep it high enough so that it did not touch the animal.

"I can wait," Tori offered.

The boy sighed, visibly, almost exaggeratedly, and brought the yearling to a halt. He deftly removed the bridle from the horse's head and as the animal trotted away Martin turned to Tori. "What do you want?"

Tori felt a sense of shock and disappointment at his curtness and the near snarl of his tone. This was her son. Did he hate her, too? "I . . . I just want to talk for a few minutes," she said finally, almost hesitantly now.

"About what?" He had walked toward her and now stood only a few feet away, arms crossed over his chest, legs spread. His stance was defiant and unyielding, as was the expression on his face and in his blue eyes.

"Did your father . . ." She paused, remembering that Guy was not Martin's real father, and started again. "Did Guy tell you about my accident?"

He nodded.

"Did he tell you that I've lost my memory. That I can't remember anything?"

Again he nodded.

Tori felt a rush of frustration. "Martin, talk to me, please. I'm your mother."

"You're not my mother," he said sharply, his tone impassive.

Tori started, confused. "But . . . I am."

His young face suddenly blazed with outrage, his features contorting somewhat with his wrath. "You're not my mother. I have no mother."

Tori took an unconscious step back, her hands suddenly trembling at the ferocity of his statement. "Martin . . . I'm—"

"You're nothing to me. You hear? Nothing! I have no mother!" Spinning around he stalked toward the stables and disappeared into its dim interior.

"I thought I asked you to stay away from the children."

Tori whirled around, startled at the deep voice.

Guy sat abreast a huge black stallion only a few yards away. A white blaze slashed across the animal's forehead and muzzle, and the short, silky hairs that covered his sleek, powerful body glistened like raw coal. Guy had removed his greatcoat and tied it to the back of the saddle. His snowy white shirt gleamed brightly beneath the sun, intensifying the golden bronze of his skin, and its flaring sleeves covered yet could not conceal the muscular outline of the arms that had held her in their embrace earlier. Several locks of hair had rebelliously fallen forward onto his forehead, giving him a rakish air, and the strands were so black the sunlight caught blue shadows within their waves.

All of this Tori noticed as Guy waited for her response, and it caused her heart to beat faster, her pulse to race. That confused her further. From his attitude, from all she had been told, she should feel nothing for him, yet that wasn't the case. In Guy she sensed the strength, warmth, and goodness she had always sought in a man. The thought stopped her. Always sought in a man? But he was her husband, and according to him, she had rejected him. Tori's head began to ache again, and she frowned. "I . . . I didn't hear you approach."

"Obviously."

The stallion tossed his head and his long mane whipped through the air. He raised one huge front hoof and stomped it on the ground impatiently, then lifted it again to repeat the gesture. Guy tightened his grip on the reins and reached out with his other hand to soothingly pat the animal's neck. "In a minute, Satan, we'll go in a minute," he murmured, his hard gaze never leaving Tori.

"I just wanted to . . . to talk to Martin."

"Leave him be, Victoria. Or don't you think you've done enough to him already?"

"I'm his mother," she said uncertainly, the word still feeling strange on her lips.

Guy's mouth curved in a sardonic smile. "Mothers love their children, Victoria. At least most do. I doubt you even know the meaning of the word." He pulled the reins to the left, and the horse instantly took several prancing steps, then paused, his muzzle only inches from Tori's face. The animal's hot breath wafted over her. "Leave the children alone, Victoria. I won't warn you again."

She watched him ride away, into the fields, and a myriad of emotions warred within her breast, each in conflict with the other, each struggling for conquest. But the memory of Guy's kiss only hours before, his lips ravaging hers, his touch turning her blood to flame, was stronger than the anger and frustration she felt at his attitude. An attitude formed by things she didn't even remember doing, by a person she didn't remember being.

Long minutes later, when he was finally out of sight, she turned toward the stable to which Martin had retreated earlier. She wanted to talk to him, in spite of what Guy had ordered.

Tori stepped through the huge, open double doors and into the dim cavern that smelled strongly of horses, hay, and leather, but the odors did not repulse her as she'd expected. Rather, she found them somehow soothing and likeable. A memory tugged at the back of her mind, she could feel it. She stood still for a moment, while her eyes adjusted to the dim light, and tried to pull the elusive memory forth, but it drifted away without providing her anything more than that flitting sense of familiarity.

As the interior of the stable came into focus, Tori looked around curiously. All along the left wall were horse stalls. She counted them. Fourteen. They were empty, as all the horses had been let out to pasture. To the right were six more stalls, monstrous piles of hay, and two large three-walled rooms that held riding gear: saddles, bridles, reins, bits, and blankets, as well as grooming supplies and tools.

Suddenly Tori had a longing to ride, to speed across the land and feel the wind whip at her face and hair. She approached the half-dozen saddles that straddled a rail inside one of the open rooms and looked them over.

"English," she murmured, not knowing why. Evidently it was what they were called. Another memory, but a useless one. She went on. At the end of the rail she stopped. The contraption in front of her looked like a torture device rather than a saddle. Its stirrups both hung from the same skirt and it had a rather grotesquely shaped horn sticking out and curving up from the side of the saddle several inches below the seat.

"Did you want me to hitch you a carriage, Miss Victoria?" The voice came behind her.

Tori swung around, surprised. Martin had been nowhere in sight, and she'd seen no one else upon entering. A young boy about the same height and build as Martin stood in the doorway. His skin, Tori noticed was the color of light oak, and his curly hair as black as night.

For the briefest of seconds Tori was lost in confusion. He was not a member of the family, at least not the immediate family. If she hadn't already known that, it was obvious by his clothes. Though clean and well sewn, they were not of the quality Guy, Darin, and Martin wore. He had an almost exotic look about him. His speech was good, and he stood with his shoulders straight, head held high. Tori continued to stare at him. Something about the boy that puzzled her, something she couldn't quite put her finger on.

"Miss Victoria," he repeated, "you want I should hitch you a buggy?"

"Uh, no, thank you," she stammered, finally. Tori took a few steps toward him, still experiencing a deep impression of familiarity and not understanding it. "I'm sorry, but since my accident, I don't seem to be able to remember names." A drastic minimizing of her condition. "I feel that I know you, but I don't know your name."

"Robert, Miss Victoria," he replied, though he seemed to do so reluctantly. Long black lashes swept down over eyes that were an almost indescribable color. Gray swirled close to the pupil and then faded into the darkest, deepest brown she'd ever seen. His lips were full, his nose straight, near classically aquiline, his hair a shimmering black. Only the rather weak line of his chin spoiled the aura of near perfection.

"Robert," she repeated and smiled. The boy was obviously uncomfortable in her presence. He wouldn't even look at her now that she'd moved closer to him. "Thank you for the offer of the buggy, Robert, but actually, I came in here looking for Martin. Have you seen him?"

He nodded his head, but still didn't look up at her. "He rode out toward the south fields."

"Oh." Disappointment filled her. "Thank you." She walked back along the narrow brick path toward the house, and suddenly brightened. Alicia. She'd find the little girl and renew her relationship with her. After all, Alicia was her daughter, even if Guy didn't want to consider her as such.

Tori entered the house by the front door. A servant was on hands and knees in the foyer, polishing the black and white marble floor, and Tori could hear faint sounds of conversation coming from the warming kitchen located toward the back of the house. She ignored both and moved to the staircase. Lifting a handful of gown in each hand, she began to climb the steps. Why did everything feel so awkward and unfamiliar? Even to the simple task of moving about in the huge bell-shaped skirts? If she didn't know better, she'd believe she had never had on a hoop-cage before, or shoes that buttoned past her ankles, or a corset, or pantalettes, let alone that this was her house, that Guy was her husband, that Martin and Alicia were her children, and that Darin was—she shuddered—her lover.

Tori shook herself and turned her thoughts in another direction . . . a safer direction. She thought of the long procedure of getting dressed that morning. Everything Suda handed her from the tall armoire had seemed strange. Tori had stared at each garment as if never having seen one like it before: the thick white stockings that she felt, for some reason, would have been more appropriate for an old lady; the white muslin camisole with its blue ribbons and ruffles that had impressed her as old-fashioned; and the pantalettes with their ruffled leggings and split crotch that had sent her into a gale of laughter. But her mirth had abruptly stopped when Suda had brought out a whalebone corset. Tori had adamantly refused to wear it, calling the corset a medieval torture contraption. But thinking back she had to admit that the gowns she'd seen in the tall wardrobe were exquisite as was the elegant apricot silk she had on, except that it was proving just a little snug around the waist and bosom.

Halfway up the stairs Tori tried to lift her skirt and petticoat a bit higher in order to avoid tripping on the hems. The wide bottom rim of her hoop-cage bumped against the wall. She tried to compensate for the sudden shift of balance by hurriedly placing her uplifted foot on the next step. The small pointed heel of her shoe wrenched beneath her and snapped off. She felt leather twist tightly around her ankle, felt herself begin to fall, and grabbed frantically for the banister.

On the landing above her, Darin stood silently, his eyes hard and unreadable as he watched Tori trip but made no attempt to help. He wore a tan-colored waistcoat and form hugging trousers, and both they and his knee-high black boots showed signs of the early morning ride from which he'd just returned.

Tori's fingers brushed over the staircase railing. She felt the touch of wood against her flesh as the tips of her fingers brushed the balustrade, but found no hold. The voluminous skirt twisted around her, and the petticoat and heavily ruffled pantalettes entangled about her legs. She opened her mouth to scream.

Strong arms caught her as she fell backward, encircling her waist. Her shoulder rammed into a wall of hard muscle and she heard the sound of suddenly released breath and smelled a rather masculine blend of spices, horseflesh, and leather.

"You two have a lover's quarrel?" Guy said. He looked down at Tori in his arms and then pointedly up toward Darin, who still stood on the landing above them.

Puzzled, Tori frowned and stared up at Guy, then, at his words, followed his gaze.

Darin smiled and descended toward them. "Not at all, dear brother. I would have attempted to rescue Victoria, but as usual, you were there."

Guy sighed, tired of the age-old argument between them. "Perhaps if you had married her in Europe when you two first met, I would never have had the chance and we'd all be better off now."

"Better off?" Darin sneered. "With you and John controlling everything? I don't think so."

Guy felt his temper slipping, as it always did when Darin talked of the Reichourd estate. "Father divided his properties as equally as he saw fit."

"Equally?" Darin laughed insolently. "John got almost everything, Guy, and when he died you got his share, while I'm left with father's piddling handout."

"I would gladly give back what I've inherited of John's, Darin, if I could change the fact that he died."

Darin laughed, a malevolent sound that sent chills racing up Tori's spine. She stopped her efforts to move from Guy's arms and became still.

"Oh, that's so noble of you," Darin said, the words laced with venom. "But John is dead, and you have it all." He stared down at his brother, his eyes as cold and hard as death.

"Yes," Guy said softly, "John is dead."

Tori's gaze swept to Guy. He sounded so sad, so full of hurt that it surprised her. Black lashes quickly lowered over eyes whose expression was hidden and inscrutable.

"Yes, John is dead," Darin mocked. "And you're still grieving for him, aren't you, big brother?"

Guy's glance jerked back up to meet Darin's. His eyes narrowed, his mouth tightened, and his jaw turned rigid. "Someone has to, Darin, you certainly never did."

Mesmerized by the encounter, and unexplainably terrified by its content, Tori's gaze moved from one brother to the other. Her breath lodged in her throat, her heart thumped madly, and her pulses raced; but why this conversation seemed so important to her, she didn't know, she just knew it did.

$\mathcal{S}ix$

New Orleans General Hospital
July 15, 1993

Victoria's eyes fluttered open. White. Everything was white. Fear gripped her. Was she dead? She bolted upright to a sitting position and looked around frantically, momentarily ignoring the pain in her limbs and head. She was in a bed. At least she thought it was a bed. It was terribly narrow and had metal rails on each side. The blanket, extremely thin and tucked tightly over her legs, was white, as were the walls, ceiling, and floor. A window to her right had some kind of white slatted covering hung in front of it through which sunlight streamed. Two chairs sat by the window, their arms and legs made of metal, their cushions covered by what appeared to be a cheap brown fabric that had seen better days long ago. Victoria shifted position and something pulled at her arm. Her neck ached terribly when she tried to turn, but she forced herself to pay it no mind. Not yet. She glanced down at her arm and nearly screamed. Something was stuck in her flesh, a needle; and it was attached to some kind of wire. Her gaze followed the wire to a big bubble that hung from a metal rack next to her bed. Water, or a solution that resembled water, dripped from the bag and into the wire.

Terror swept through Victoria. Guy had put her in some kind of asylum. She stared down at her arm again. They were trying to poison her. Outrage flared in her breast. "No, Guy, my darling," she whispered through her fury, "you're not going to get rid of me that easily." The fingers of her free hand grasped the cylinder that was attached to the needle in her arm and ripped it out. She pushed the white sheet and blanket from her legs and began to climb from the bed. She felt pain but ignored it. Instead, her attention was riveted on her gown. She stared down at it in horror. It was nothing but a flimsy piece of cotton. A draft swept up her back, and she reached a hand around behind her. The gown had no back! It was open, and she had on nothing underneath it. Absolutely nothing. Victoria's cheeks flamed with embarrassment and indignation. Were the people at this asylum animals? "I'll see you rot in hell for this, Guy," Victoria swore. She turned her attention to the bed's railings. Her knuckles whitening as she shook them. They wouldn't move. God, what kind of place was this? She scrambled to her knees and swung one leg over the railing.

"Miss Reichourd, what are you doing?"

Victoria looked up sharply and met the startled gaze of an older woman. She was built like a dray, big and square, her gray hair coiffed in short curls around a face that Victoria instantly compared to that of an ugly dog. Victoria's judgmental gaze swept over her. The woman was dressed in white, but her gown had no crinolines or hoop cage beneath it, and the skirt only covered her to the knees. Victoria stared at the woman's white stockinged legs in shock. Evidently she wasn't the only one half-dressed around this godforsaken place.

"Come on," the woman said in a tone of exaggerated patience, "you mustn't get out of bed just yet." She waddled forth and began to gently push on Victoria's shoulders. "Lie down now."

Victoria jerked away from her. "Where's Guy?"

Seven

"Perhaps if you remain in here, Victoria, as I instructed earlier, you will avoid further trouble or harm," Guy said. Anger resonated from him and permeated each word. With his hand on her arm, he nearly propelled her into the bedchamber.

Tori whirled to face him, angered by his heavy-handed arrogance. "Just who the hell do you think you are, Guy Reichourd? Muammar Qaddafi?"

The sharp retort he'd been about to utter fell to silence, and confusion clouded his eyes. "Who?"

Tori stared dumbfounded, her outrage suddenly forgotten. Who was Muammar Qaddafi?

Guy looked at her as if she'd just muttered an incantation in tongues. It was obvious he didn't know whether to be concerned about her or to walk away and go on about his business. He damned himself for not immediately turning his back on her and instead took a step toward her. "Victoria?"

Tori shook her head and moved to sit on the edge of the bed. "I'm all right, Guy. I . . . I'm just tired, I guess. Perhaps you're right, I should stay in my room . . . and . . .

and get some rest." While I'm trying to figure out what in the devil is wrong with me besides memory loss, Tori thought. She hadn't forgotten her little experience in trying to turn off the lamp, or the lone word that had popped from her mouth while staring at the saddles in the barn. And now this. What was a Muammar Qaddafi? Or maybe it was a who?

She peeked at Guy from beneath lowered lashes. At the moment, she wanted nothing more than for him to leave the room so she could think. Something strange had just happened to her, and she needed time to mull it over, to try to reason her way into some kind of rational action. She put a hand to her forehead and closed her eyes, repeating the unusual words over and over in her mind in an attempt to make some kind of explanation come with them.

Guy turned, but paused at the door and looked back at her, his brows nettled together in a deep frown. "Heed my words this time, Victoria."

She nodded absently and heard the door click closed. Then her eyes shot open and she sprang from the bed. Nervous energy propelled her around the room at a frantic pace. Back and forth, back and forth, from one side of the spacious bedchamber to the other.

"Muammar Qaddafi," she muttered beneath her breath. "Muammar Qaddafi, Muammar Qaddafi, Muammar Qaddafi." What did that mean? Was it a person's name? A place? A food? What? She searched for an answer . . . any answer, and none came.

Maybe it was a city she'd heard spoken of lately. It did kind of have an Egyptian sound to it. Muammar Qaddafi. Or perhaps it was the name of an actor in the opera Guy had said they'd attended the night of her accident. Tori brightened. That must be it. Stage people always had strange names.

Relieved at the thought, she stopped pacing and moved to the window. It had been raised and someone, most likely Suda, had opened the jib door beneath it to create a tall breezeway and a door onto the gallery. Tori stepped past the heavy blue damask draperies that framed the window and moved across the gallery to the green wrought-iron railing that spanned the open width between each massive white Corinthian pillar.

Her gaze roamed the landscape, searching, assessing, waiting for recognition to come. It didn't, and she finally gave up and just let herself enjoy the view. Shadow Oaks was indeed beautiful. The most beautiful sight she had ever seen. A small smile tugged at the corners of her mouth. Of course, she couldn't remember what other beautiful sights she'd seen. Paris? London? She didn't know, regardless, this had to be one of the very best.

Suddenly, she froze. Her hands gripped the railing, her knuckles pushing hard against her skin from the pressure of her grasp. "No," Tori whispered. She felt a rending deep in her chest, as if her heart were cracking into a million pieces. She closed her eyes in an effort to banish the sight, to make it a figment of her imagination, but when she reopened them, nothing had changed.

A hundred yards or so from the house an ancient oak tree spread its gnarled, twisted branches wide, each limb heavily surrounded by clusters of dark green leaves and draped with long, curtainlike blankets of gray Spanish moss. But it was not the tree that held Tori's attention; it was the couple who stood within its shadow.

Though they were too far away for her to see their features clearly, Tori thought she recognized Guy from his clothes: they appeared to be the same dark blue jacket and trousers he'd had on earlier. Before him stood Suda, or rather, Tori thought derisively, clutched in his arms stood Suda. She remembered the feel of Guy's fingers around her own arms, like bands of steel, unyielding and hard. Now they were wrapped around Suda. Suddenly, the young maid tried to turn away. Guy jerked her back to face him and roughly pulled her to him. Her petite body was crushed against his tall frame. She was forced to stand on tiptoe, nearly lifted from the ground by his grasp on her as his lips covered hers.

Tori gasped and turned away again, sickened by the sight that had unfolded before her. Why? Why was Guy forcing himself on Suda? The girl couldn't be more than— what had she said?—fifteen or sixteen years old? Tori looked back. Was this what she'd driven her husband to? Seducing the servants?

Suddenly, Suda tore herself out of Guy's embrace, but he reached out and grabbed her arm, viciously yanking her back against him.

Tori stared, both mesmerized and terrified.

Suda's free hand shot forth and slapped Guy's cheek.

Tori jumped reflexively, the sound of Suda's hand connecting soundly with Guy's flesh echoing on the still air. "Oh, my God," Tori muttered softly, suddenly deathly afraid.

Guy caught Suda's wrist and twisted it back cruelly, forcing the young girl to arch backward awkwardly. His face lowered until it was barely an inch from hers. Tori could see that he was saying something to the girl, but she was too far away to hear the words. Then he abruptly flung Suda away from him, spun on his heel, and strode toward the stables.

Suda's arms flailed the air, and she scrambled to maintain her balance.

Tori watched Guy's retreating back until he was out of sight. She saw Suda run, stumbling and obviously crying, toward the back of the house and disappear. What had just happened? Puzzled, and deeply distraught, Tori settled onto one of the wrought-iron chairs that graced the gallery and stared out at the landscape, though this time she didn't really see it. She was too deep in thought, too preoccupied by the scene she had just witnessed between her husband and her maid.

It was obvious Suda didn't welcome Guy's advances, but it was also obvious that particular point did not matter to Guy. Unconsciously, Tori bit down on her bottom lip. She had to do something. But what?

She sighed in instant defeat. How could she do anything? She couldn't even remember why she had turned away from her own husband, why she had taken her brother-in-law as a lover, or why she had obviously paid little attention to, or had little feeling for, her own children. How could she hope to right all of those wrongs and change her family's opinion of her until she knew why she had done those things? And she did want to change their opinions of her. She wanted that more than anything in the world.

Finally she got up. She needed to move around the house, to look at familiar things and touch them or hold them in her hands. She needed to talk to the other servants, to question them, watch their reactions to her. Lord, she needed to find something that would jog her memory.

The sound of hooves moving over the crushed oyster shells that covered the entry drive drew her attention, and Tori paused. Someone was approaching the house on horseback. She turned back from the doorway to her room and returned to the wrought-iron railing, looking down at the drive.

"Hi, beautiful," Darin said from his seat upon a sleek bay stallion. He was dressed in a brilliantly white shirt, its sleeves full and flowing, a pale blue silk cravat at its collar, and snug-fitting midnight blue trousers. Black riding boots, highly polished, wrapped around his legs to the knee. His jacket was folded and tied to the back of his saddle. He seemed in remarkably better spirits than he had the evening before when he'd left her room. "We haven't been riding together in a while. I thought maybe you'd like to go this morning. Especially since I'll be leaving tomorrow."

"Leaving?" Tori repeated. The idea of Darin leaving brought a sudden brightness to her mood.

"For Baton Rouge."

"Baton Rouge?" Tori echoed.

The smile left Darin's face, and his expression turned to one of surly frustration. "Victoria, will you stop repeating everything I say. Now"—the sly smile returned—"do you want to go for a ride with me or not? We could stop for a while in the meadow?"

She nearly said *The meadow?*, but caught herself. "Why are you going to Baton Rouge, Darin?" she asked instead.

Darin sighed, not bothering to mask his annoyance with her. "To look at a string of stallions Émile Latrotte is selling. I also want to attend a meeting of the Knights. Now, are you satisfied with that? Can we get back to planning our ride together?"

"What are the Knights?"

"Victoria, this is becoming tiring. I feel like I'm talking to a child."

94

Tori bristled. "I'm sorry, Darin, but I told you, I don't remember anything."

"That's becoming painfully obvious, and more than a little annoying. What I'd like to know though, is when is your memory going to come back so we can get on with things?"

"Things?" The moment she muttered the word, she regretted it, even before she saw the scowl darken his face. He was referring to their plan to kill Guy. She should have realized that immediately.

Darin yanked viciously on the reins and the stallion's head jerked up and to the left. The horse's front hooves rose from the ground, its body swung around, and it lunged forward, carrying Darin away from the house . . . and Tori.

Tori moved slowly around the bedchamber. She ran her hand over one of the thick posts of her bed, tracing the ornately carved rosewood grape leaves and vines with the tips of her fingers. She touched the silk coverlet draped over the bed, fingered the lace at its edges, ran her hand over the base of the lamp on the table, then around the blue crystal globe, and finally the clear, etched-crystal hurricane glass that surrounded the wick. No memories came forth, no sensations, and no feelings of familiarity. She moved to a tall étagère that sat in one corner, its shelves filled with various pieces of porcelain, china, and crystal bric-a-brac. Again, the memories she wanted so badly to flit into her mind eluded her.

She swung around and stared at the room. This was *her* room. This was where she lived, where she dressed and slept. This was her private retreat. Why couldn't she remember it? Tori felt suddenly like screaming. Why didn't her own bedroom evoke some feeling within her? Some comfort?

She left the room and moved along the wide hallway toward the landing. At the top of the stairs she looked down at the portraits that lined the curving wall. Her family. The Reichourds. A family she didn't know. A family who, it seemed, wanted nothing more than for her to be gone.

Except for Darin, she thought with a shudder of revulsion. How in heaven's name could she ever have taken that man for a lover? He impressed her as nothing more than a pale shadow of his brother, Guy. No, she quickly corrected that thought. Darin's physical appearance resembled Guy's, but that was all, and there were even differences there, weaknesses maybe not discernible at once, but definitely there for anyone to see upon really looking.

Lifting the heavy skirts and hoop-cage with one hand, she clung to the banister with the other and began to slowly descend the wide staircase. A little more than halfway down she paused and looked at the portraits of Guy and Darin, but it was the painting next to Guy's that piqued her curiosity. Engraved on the brass plaque attached to the bottom of the frame was the man's name, but she didn't need to read it again to know what it said: John Reichourd IV. Guy and Darin's older brother. The man whose name had entered their heated conversation on the stairs earlier. She remembered Darin's sneering reference to John's death, and Guy's remark that Darin had never really grieved the loss of their brother.

She studied the portrait. John had looked much like Guy, though his eyes held an illusion of blue within their gray depths and his chin possessed the barest hint of a cleft.

"What happened to you, John?" Tori mumbled softly, reaching out to touch the canvas with the tip of her finger.

"He was murdered, that's what happened. As if you didn't know, missy," Hannah spat.

Tori started, shocked at the woman's insinuation. She stepped hastily away from the portrait and looked down at Hannah.

The hefty old housekeeper glared up at Tori from the bottom of the staircase. Rage burned in her eyes, and her generously fleshed full lips were now nothing more than a thin, hard line.

"What"—Tori was forced to clear her throat—"what do you mean, murdered?"

"You may have fooled Michie Guy, missy, but you ain't fooled me." Hannah shook her head. "No, ma'am. I know all about you and what you've done. You just remember that when you get them notions in your head about staying here and pulling any more of your deviltry." With that, Hannah turned and marched toward the door leading to the warming kitchen. The skirt of the red and white checkered gown she wore on her more than ample frame swayed about her short legs, making it appear she floated rather than walked.

Tori's mouth hung agape. What did Hannah mean? That *she* was responsible for John Reichourd's death? A chill swept up her back. She turned to look back at the portrait and suddenly, as she stared into those gray eyes that so resembled Guy's, the room dimmed and blurred. Her knees began to grow weak and tremble, then, as if the bone and muscle within her legs had turned to little more than mush, they buckled beneath her weight. Blackness swirled around her like a ravenous whirlpool, closing in on her, engulfing her in its darkness and shutting out the world, the light. Tori opened her mouth to scream, and nothing came out. Then, as quickly as it had descended and enveloped her, the vortex cleared and she was no longer standing on the staircase over the foyer, but in the murky, dimly lit recesses of a swamp. Dozens of tall cypress trees surrounded her, the base of their narrow trunks a bulbous swell that disappeared beneath the black surface of the still bayou waters. Overhead thick foliage clung to the trees' thin, tangled limbs, allowing little sun to penetrate the area, and what little did, filtered down in pale, luminous streams. Covering the dank ground was a profusion of lush ferns and wild grasses, all pressing together, their fronds and reeds entwining as they struggled for space and what little sun was afforded them. Tori stood on the muddy bank, her feet slowly sinking into the soft, wet quagmire, and shivered at the deadly silence. Nothing stirred. It was as if life, all life, had ceased to exist.

A shape protruding above the surface of the stagnant black water caught her attention, and she turned to stare down at the mire-covered marsh. Horror wrapped a boney hand around her heart and began to squeeze the life from her, but she could not pull her gaze from the sight that drifted before her.

A scream ripped from Tori's throat as she watched a man's limp body slowly float nearer to where she stood. His arms were stretched wide, and his hair spread around his face in dark, curling black tendrils, each coated with muck and drifting aimlessly on the current. Tori stared, both fascinated and scared beyond comprehension, her body convulsing in an onslaught of terror-instilled tremors as the body floated, ever so slowly, toward her. Realization of the corpse's identity sent a shock of hysteria through her.

As the man's head became illuminated by a faint stream of sunlight that broke through the trees, Tori screamed again, the sound ripping from her throat as a cry of pain, a blood-chilling wail echoed within the endless curves and corridors of the swamp. But try as she might, she could not tear her gaze away from his sightless eyes, nor keep his name from repeating over and over in her mind and in her heart: *Guy, Guy, Guy.*

"Lord 'a' mercy, what's that woman up to now?" Hannah said, rushing from the warming kitchen and into the foyer at hearing Tori's scream.

"Sounds like something done scared her good," Moses replied, following on Hannah's heels.

"Humph, only the Devil hisself could scare that one, and I ain't too sure about him."

At the bottom of the staircase Hannah came to an abrupt halt, and Moses nearly collided with her back.

"Oh, Lordy," Hannah said softly. Hastily lifting her skirts and apron in both pudgy hands she rushed up the steps to where Tori lay unconscious.

"What's the matter with her?" Moses asked, remaining at the base of the staircase.

The old woman bent down beside Tori and placed a hand on her forehead. "Best fetch Michie."

Moses didn't move.

Hannah looked up sharply. "You hear me, old man? Go fetch Michie Guy—and hurry. I ain't sure what's wrong with her."

"Maybe she's dead," Moses said quietly.

"Lord ain't blessed us with that yet, I can tell you that much. She's still breathing. Now go on—get yourself moving before she does up and die and it be your fault."

Moses released his hold on the banister and turned to go. The entry door opened just as he approached it.

The imposing silhouette of a man blocked the sun so

99

that its rays streamed in around him. "What the hell happened now?" Guy asked. He looked past Moses to the two women on the stairs.

Moses glanced back at Hannah. The old woman shrugged. "Moses and me was in the kitchen. We heard her scream and we come running. Found her like this."

Moving quickly up the stairs, Guy knelt beside Tori, a frown of confusion and concern knitting his brow and shadowing his eyes. He laid a hand over her heart, felt its strong beat beneath his fingers, and sighed in relief. She was alive.

Tori moaned and stirred slightly.

"She fainted," Guy said softly, tossing the words over his shoulder. He slipped an arm carefully around her shoulders, the other beneath the immense folds of her skirt and then rose to his feet, lifting her in his arms as he straightened. Tori's head came to rest against the curve of his shoulder. "Hannah, get me a cool cloth for her forehead and some smelling salts, just in case." He mounted one step, paused, and looked back. "Moses, send someone to town for the doctor."

Hannah clucked her tongue and watched in disgust as Guy carried Tori up the stairs, but she did as she was ordered, though mumbling disparagingly to herself all the way back to the kitchen. Moses nodded at Guy's request, remained silent, as was usual for him, and hurried out the door.

Guy reached the landing, turned, and walked down the hallway to the door of Tori's bedchamber. The door was unlatched, and slightly ajar. He pushed it open with his foot, entered, then kicked it closed with the heel of his boot. He walked directly to the poster bed that dominated the room and set Tori on it, then straightened to his full height and looked down at her for several long minutes.

He was filled with an upheaval of emotions, but which emotion was in control, if any, he wasn't sure. Anger at her disobeying his order that she remain in her room blazed within him, while relief that she was alive tore at him and fueled the rage he felt at himself for even caring. But more than that, and this emotion upset him the most; passion gnawed within him, dark, hidden, and intense. It simmered just below the surface, ate at him mercilessly, and craved—demanded—satiation.

Ever since he'd made the mistake of kissing her, of holding her in his arms again, Guy had been consumed with the need for her, and the fact riled him near to rage. It had been months since he'd wanted her, since he'd even thought of her that way. He had convinced himself that all desire for her was dead, killed for all time when he'd discovered she had taken his brother as her lover. But he had been wrong. He still wanted her, now it seemed more than ever.

In spite of the turmoil roiling inside of him, Guy reached out and gently touched her cheek, a featherlight touch that seemed to burn his fingertips and deepen his need. He stared down at Tori for a moment that seemed more an eternity, as if trying to see beyond flesh and bone. There was something about her that was different than before. He felt it, sensed it, and at times thought he could even see it. Ever since the accident, there was a strangeness about her. She wasn't the same person she had been, and yet he knew, beyond any doubt, that the woman before him was his wife, Victoria. At the same time he couldn't shake the feeling that she wasn't. And it wasn't only the amnesia, the loss of memory that made her seem different to him, he reasoned, it was something else, some elusive quality he couldn't quite grasp.

The door behind him opened and Hannah entered the room. "I got the cold cloth you asked for, Michie, and the smelling salts, too."

Guy jerked his hand away from Tori's face and moved to stand at the window. "Good. Take care of her then," he said gruffly. "I think she merely swooned, though since my dear brother, Darin, wasn't around I don't know why." He crossed the room and stepped into the hallway. Whatever there was about Victoria that had ignited his long-dead desire was better left ignored. As soon as her memory returned she would be the same Victoria he'd decided to divorce, the same greedy, self-centered woman who had scorned both him and the children. Until then, he would keep a tight rein on his passions, and stay as far away from her as possible.

"Guy?"

He spun around at the sound of her voice.

"She's shaking something terrible, Michie." Hannah stepped from the room and shook her head. "She won't let me put the cloth on her, and won't stay lying down. Says she's got to talk to you."

Guy nodded and moved back into the bedchamber, taking hold of Tori's arm and leading her back to the bed. "Victoria, I don't have time for this," he said brusquely, hating himself for his seeming insensitivity, yet knowing it was necessary. It was the only way he could maintain his barriers against her, the only way he could keep her out of his life.

"Guy, you have to lis—"

He forced her to lie down, then turned to leave.

Hannah had closed the window and jib door. The room

was dim, only a faint stream of sunlight penetrating the slight space between the drawn drapes.

"Guy, please . . ." Her voice sounded uncertain and scared.

It gave him reason for pause. Never in the five years they'd been married had he ever known Victoria to be either uncertain or scared of anything.

"Please . . . listen to me?"

Guy paused, hating himself for giving in to her, yet unable to refrain. "All right, Victoria, I'll listen." He stood beside her bed. "But it will change nothing."

Tori reached up and took his hand in hers. The touch sent a shock of heat through his fingers and he instantly jerked his hand away.

She sat up. "Please, Guy, I need you to listen to me, to help me," Tori said softly, and reached out to him again. "I'm frightened."

He tried to steel himself against her, against her touch, but it did no good. He allowed her fingers to wrap around his, felt his blood turn to flame and the gnawing hunger in his groin deepen. "Of what, Victoria?" he finally forced himself to say, fighting to keep his tone hard. "Just what is it you are frightened of?"

Tears filled her eyes and fell from her thick lashes, coursing over her cheeks in thin, silvery streams. "Everything. I'm frightened of everything. And nothing." She shook her head and clung to his hand, wrapping it tightly in both of hers. "I feel so lost, Guy, as if I don't belong here."

"I don't think you do, Victoria."

"No, I don't mean it that way, not about us, about you wanting me to leave. I mean . . ." She looked up at him then, and he was drawn into the fathomless depths of her

103

blue eyes, like a drowning man caught in a whirlpool and pulled down into the unknown deeps of the sea. He tightened the rein he held over his self-control.

"I mean I feel really lost, Guy. Nothing here seems familiar to me. Nothing feels right, like it's mine, like I've seen it or felt it before."

"The doctor said it would take time for your memory to come back."

"If it comes back." She looked up at him through her tears. "Isn't that what he said, Guy? *If?"*

Reluctantly he nodded.

"So I might never remember who I am?"

God, how he wanted to pull his hand away. But then again, that wasn't true. He didn't want to pull away from her. What he truly wanted was to wrap her in his arms, to smother her with kisses, to feel her body crushed against his, the warmth of her flesh melded to his own. He wanted to cup her breasts within the curves of his hands, slide his fingers through the silken curls between her thighs. . . . He threw a roadblock in front of his runaway thoughts. What the hell was the matter with him? Why, just because she'd lost her memory, were his feelings changing toward her?

"Guy?"

He forced the traitorous thoughts from his mind. "You are Victoria Marie Camerei Reichourd."

"But that's just a name to me, don't you see? It doesn't mean anything. In fact, it even feels strange . . . like it's mine, but not really mine. Do you understand?"

The pitch of her voice was rising with each sentence, her fear of the situation building toward hysteria. Guy wished the doctor would arrive. He didn't really know

104

what to say to calm her, to make her feel better about things.

"It's my name, but it doesn't feel like my name, Guy. I mean, it does, but—"

"Victoria, you're only scaring yourself with this rambling. Believe me, you are Victoria Marie Camerei Reichourd. That's one thing I wouldn't lie about. Now," he forced her to release his hand, "the doctor will be here shortly. Lie back down and rest until he comes."

"Will you stay with me?" Her eyes implored him as much as her words. "Please?"

"Where's Suda?"

She merely stared at him, not knowing how to answer his question.

Guy exhaled a deep breath of resignation. "All right." He took a chair near the fireplace, a goodly distance from her, and ordered his body to calm down, to rid itself of the hungry ache of desire that had filled him as he'd stood beside her bed, as she'd touched him. What in blazes was the matter with him that he should want *her* again? Had he learned nothing from their five years of hell? A hell he had endured only because of Alicia and Martin—and his own foolish dreams.

A few minutes later, her voice broke the silence that had descended on them with his moving to the chair. "Guy, was I really so terrible before?"

He stared at her, a hard, cutting stare that held almost total disbelief and cynicism. He found it almost impossible to consider that Victoria's basic personality could ever change. At least this much. What was easier to believe was that this was all a ruse, just another of her schemes. Perhaps in collusion with his brother, Darin. Yes, he nodded to himself, that he could believe. Easily.

"Guy, Darin hates you," Tori said abruptly, the words hastening from her lips and breaking the silence that hung between them.

"I know."

She stared at him in disbelief.

The door from the hallway opened then and Hannah stepped into the room. "Doctor Benjamin's here," she said, and moved aside to allow the man's entry.

Guy rose, shook the old doctor's hand, and walked toward the door. "I'll be in my office if you need me, Doc," he said, and closed the door without a word to Tori or a glance in her direction.

Guy didn't bother to draw back the heavy cinnamon-colored damask curtains, nor did he light a lamp. Instead, he sat in the tall, winged-back leather chair behind his desk and stared into the gloomy dimness. After a few minutes he lifted the silver lid of a crystal jar that sat on one corner of his highly polished oak desk, removed a cheroot, and replaced the silver lid. He snipped off one end of the thin cigar and slipped it into his mouth, holding it in place with his teeth, then struck a lucifer against the heel of his boot. The tiny match burst into flame, throwing an eerie yellow glow over the immediate area surrounding Guy but not reaching the book-lined shelves that graced each wall. He cupped the flame, held it to the end of the cheroot and inhaled deeply of the whiskey-soaked tobacco.

White smoke drifted in thin spiraling streams toward the ceiling and instantly filled the room with the cheroot's fragrance. Guy sat back in his chair, settling into the well-worn cushions, and letting his mind wander.

Something about Victoria nagged at the back of his

mind, but he couldn't quite put his finger on it. There was a definite difference about her, a strangeness, but for some reason, he felt certain it had nothing to do with her memory loss. It was something deeper, more basic, yet exactly what it was eluded and bothered him.

She had tried to work her wiles on him before when she wanted something, acting sweet, seductive, innocent, or caring; and every time he had been able to see through her performance. Why not this time? Why now did her words and attitude seem so sincere? So genuine?

Frustration swept over him. Guy stood, crushed the burning tip of the barely smoked cheroot in a silver plate that sat on his desk, and strode toward the door. She had to leave, that was all there was to it. Before something happened. Before this damned ache he had to once again possess her overwhelmed him and he lost control. Then it would be too late.

He slammed the door of his office and marched away from the small building that had been built as an almost miniature version of the house. She had to leave now. Right now.

Eight

Guy mounted the stairs to the second floor two at a time, in a hurry to get to Victoria's room. The doctor was just stepping into the hallway when Guy ascended the landing and turned in his direction.

"I gave her some laudanum, Guy. She was upset but wouldn't say why," the doctor said. "She'll sleep for a while now."

Guy felt a swell of disappointment, almost overriden by a sense of relief. The latter emotion nearly unnerved him. He had to get her out of here, away from Shadow Oaks, away from him. But there was no way she could leave now. In the morning, though, she could go. He would pack up her things and move her to one of the other Reichourd plantations.

He turned and accompanied the doctor downstairs. In the front parlor Guy poured the older man a glass of bourbon, which was accepted gratefully, and then poured one for himself.

"Tell me something, Ben," Guy said, "this loss of memory, is there any way Victoria can be faking it?"

The old doctor shook his head. "I don't think so, Guy.

I mean, there have been some people who've tried, naturally, for various reasons." He chuckled. "And some have gotten away with it too, but only for a while. Anyway, I believe Victoria's case is too severe. And take into consideration, Guy, that she's scared. Damn scared." The doctor took a long, appreciative swallow of his bourbon. "Fear is something a person usually can't fake with much success. Either you're really scared or you aren't, and it's not too hard for most people to tell the difference."

Guy stared into the drink he held in his hand. The amber liquid picked up the light of the sun that streamed through the tall windows of the room and sparkled brilliantly. He had been determined to make Victoria leave Shadow Oaks right away, but he'd also managed to convince himself she was pretending her memory loss. If she wasn't, how in the name of human decency could he force her to leave her own home? He looked up at the doctor, his eyes troubled. "Will she get it back, Doc? Her memory? Will it all come back?"

"Probably, though I can't really say for sure. These cases are all different. Some people make a complete recovery and remember everything, others remember only some things, and there are those who never remember a thing. Unfortunately, we don't know a whole lot about what goes on in there." He tapped a finger to his head.

"Is there any way to help her remember?"

"Familiar things usually help, but in Victoria's case, she's already home, surrounded by things she should recognize and people she loves."

Guy almost laughed at the doctor's words, but refrained.

"From what she tells me, though," the doctor continued, "she doesn't recognize anything or anyone."

"So she claims."

The doctor shook his head. "No, Guy, it's the truth. That woman is scared. Terrified would be more like it, actually. To her it's like she's been born all over again, new and fresh, but everyone's telling her what kind of person she's supposed to be, what she likes and dislikes, and she's having a hard time accepting it all."

Guy took a deep breath and released it in a long sigh. "She's changed, Doc, a lot. It's almost as if she's another person, a stranger. The woman upstairs in that bedchamber is not the woman I married."

"Well, physically she's the same woman, but emotionally"—the doctor shook his head again—"emotionally you're right, she's not the same, at least not right now."

Guy had been staring into his drink, but at the doctor's words his gaze jerked up to meet the older man's. "Physically she's different too."

Ben frowned in obvious puzzlement.

"Ever since the accident I've noticed things about her that are strange, Doc. Like her skin. Victoria always took great pains to avoid the sun. Her skin was like alabaster."

"As most women's," the doctor agreed.

"Yes, but no more. It seems, and suddenly so, that Victoria had developed quite a nice golden tone to her flesh, and it doesn't seem to bother her. I've even seen her out walking the grounds several times without a parasol."

"Yes, but—"

"And her voice. Have you noticed the rather clipped way she speaks now? Not at all in the slow, lilting drawl she had before the accident."

"Umm, that is a bit strange." The doctor smiled. "But nothing to worry about."

"Maybe not, but"—Guy shook his head—"she's so different now."

"And she might stay that way, Guy. She may never be the same person she was before the accident."

Victoria woke to find herself surrounded by darkness, an impenetrable blackness without end. She bolted upright in the bed and clutched the coverlet to her breast. Her heart pounded in her chest, a fast, thundering beat that nearly exploded in her ears. She felt her way off of the bed, swinging her legs to the floor, and then stood up. Her legs were only slightly sore now, as were her ribs, and the bruises she'd received in the accident were nearly gone, having faded to faint yellow splotches that blemished her skin here and there. But the bump on her head was still tender to the touch, the headache having subsided to a nagging, steady, ache; and the gash was now covered by an ugly mottling of dried and bloodied skin.

She reached out with her hand, searching the blackness, and her fingers touched the crystal lamp that sat on the table beside the tall poster bed. Tori breathed a sigh of relief. She was in her room. But why was it so dark? She tried to remember coming to bed, and couldn't. She thought back. She'd been on the stairs and . . . she clamped a hand over her mouth to stifle the scream that gurgled within her throat.

She'd been in a swamp, not on the stairs. And there had been a body floating in the murky water. Her hands began to tremble at the memory. The body . . . Guy's . . . no, John Reichourd's body, had drifted near where she stood on the bank and . . . Tori frowned, trying to remember. She'd fainted.

Feeling her way, Tori moved to the window and drew open the heavy drapes. A brilliant sunset greeted her, its

fast-dying rays bathing the landscape in an almost iridescent glow and turning the plantation into a surrealistic fan-
tasyland. The white oyster shells that covered the entry
drive and several pathways around the grounds glowed
pink, the leaves of the giant live oaks shimmered silver,
and the ivory petals of the closing magnolia blooms held
a rosey blush, while their huge dark green leaves glistened
almost black. The scene was too inviting, too tranquil to
resist.

Slipping into the batiste robe that lay across the foot of
her bed and the silk slippers near the table, Tori stepped
from her room into the hallway. She tied the robe's sash
around her waist and stood still, listening for a moment,
but she heard nothing. There seemed not a sound of life
in the house. She moved quietly toward the back staircase.
It was narrow, the steep steps curving in a sharp spiral.
She felt her way down. At the back door she let herself
out and walked across the gallery, breathing deeply of the
cool night air.

The shadow-entombed earth came abruptly alive around
her. The chirruping of a bird danced merrily on the still
air, an owl hooted from a perch somewhere within the
thick boughs of the trees, and in one of the far pastures,
a horse whinnied. Tori smiled. The night was peaceful and
serene, unlike the day, which brought so many turbulent
thoughts and feelings with it, so many confrontations and
suspicions.

She stepped from the gallery and moved along the path
that led to the formal gardens. Rosebushes formed a cres-
cent in the center of the garden; like walls, boxwood
hedges lined the path in certain areas, impenetrable and
tall, creating an almost mazelike effect. Azaleas bordered
marble benches set here and there in small alcoves cut

from the hedges, and jasmine vines grew thickly over a trellis that spanned the width of the path in one spot.

Tori breathed deeply, inhaling the blend of sweet fragrances. She walked slowly, enjoying the night and its solitude. All worrisome thought was temporarily banished from her mind, and she felt, for the moment, at peace with herself, with the world, with everything. But no sooner did the feeling envelop her, than she lost it. Suddenly the hair on the back of her neck rose, and a chill swept up her spine. The sense that she wasn't alone in the garden assailed her, and along with it came fear, unexplainable, but distinct nevertheless She paused and looked around, squinting into the darkness in an effort to define the shadows that surrounded her, to discern if one concealed human flesh rather than leaf and bark.

Nothing moved, and the thought that the garden was as still as a cemetery, as silent as death, filled her mind and turned her blood chill. "This is a perfect set-up scene for a horror movie," she muttered. "Like *Friday the 13th, Part X.*"

Tori stopped abruptly, almost tripping over her own feet, the fear of being watched, of not being alone in the dark garden was momentarily forgotten as she realized what she'd just said, but did not understand. Horror movie? What was a movie? And *Friday the 13th, Part X?* What did that mean? It sounded like a date and an act from the theater. Part X. But somehow she sensed it was not.

A rustling sounded behind her in the bushes, and Tori started. She shouldn't have come out here alone, not in the dark, not to the garden with its inky shadows, wall-like hedges, and meandering, directionless paths. Panic invaded her breast, filled her mind, and sent her fleeing down the narrow, foliage-bordered path in search of a direction that would take her back to the house.

The hem of her robe caught on the low, protruding branch of a rose bush. Tori nearly fell forward as the fabric pulled taut.

Someone had grabbed her! She twisted around and a gurgled shriek escaped her lips. Tori raised her hands, ready to fight off her attacker, and nearly fainted in relief at seeing it was only a rose bush which held her imprisoned. But hysteria pressed her to flee the garden and the night, pushed her in haste toward the house, did not leave her or lessen its intensity. She jerked on the batiste fabric and it pulled free, a shred of the delicate fabric left behind on the protruding thorn. Tori turned, took a hasty step, and fell forward as the thinly padded sole of her slipper was pierced by a sharp rock. Pain shot through her foot. She threw her hands out in front of her in an effort to break her fall, and winced as the tiny pebbles that covered the path sliced into the heels of her hands and knees upon impact with the ground.

Tears swelled in Tori's eyes. A nearby bush rustled and a small animal darted across her path. The scream that had been about to erupt from her throat died a quick death, but the frantic beat of her heart did not slow. She clamped her jaws together, struggled to her feet and began to hastily move along the path again. She rounded a corner of the hedge and, glancing back over her shoulder at what she thought was the sound of a footstep behind her, ran straight into a draping curtain of Spanish moss that hung from the branch of a tall oak set just to the side of the garden. Its dark gray prickly needles, almost invisible against the night, caught in her hair and snagged the delicate threads of her robe.

"No, get away." She flailed her hands in an effort to ward off the offending attacker, and felt the thorny moss scrape at her flesh. Within seconds she was running blindly down the path, unheedful of anything in her way, intent only on getting back to the sanctity of the house, of her room.

Gasping for air, Tori moved around the corner of a massive boxwood hedge and collided with the tall figure of a man, the impact nearly knocking him and her off balance and to the ground. Tori screamed and spun around to run in the direction she'd just come, but he grabbed her arms and prevented her escape.

"Victoria, what the hell are you doing out here?" The voice was deep, the tone concerned and surprised.

At hearing him speak, she stopped struggling against him and her head jerked up. "Guy?" Relief swept over her. "Oh, Guy, thank God. I thought . . . I thought . . ." Tori threw her arms around his neck and clung to him, her breasts crushed to the wall of his chest as her head nestled against the lower curve of his shoulder.

"Victoria, what happened? What's wrong?" He reached up and gripped her wrists in his hands, then forced her arms from around his neck and her body from his, but maintained his grasp on her hands. A plethora of pithy oaths raced through his mind as he looked down at her and felt the hot betrayal of his body that her mere touch had invoked. Moonlight pierced the thin fabric of her gown and robe, transforming the fragile ivory threads to a shimmering veil that caressed her body, but hid nothing from his sight.

She looked up at him. Tears glistened in her eyes and turned their depths to endless pools of shimmering blue, the tiny specks of gold blazing into points of fire. Her bottom lip, full and enticing, quivered with fear.

"I . . . I was taking a walk, and . . . and I thought . . . someone was . . ." A sob choked off the words.

With the swiftness of a winter's squall, Guy's self-control deserted him, fleeing into the unknown and leaving him vulnerable to her. And their circumstances and their surroundings—the velvety blackness of night, the peace and tranquillity that came with the darkness, the heady fragrances of dozens of blooms, and the soft glow of the moon that filtered down around them to turn the garden into a place of golden magic, only served to weaken his resistance and deepen his desires. Tiny diamonds of light sparked from beneath the ebony waves of Tori's hair and danced from deep within the infinite depths of her eyes.

"There's no one else out here," he finally said.

Tori nodded, but did not speak or try to move away from him.

Guy knew he should flee from her, knew that he was courting danger, *deadly* danger by staying in her company for even one more moment, and yet he could not turn away, could not force himself to release her. Her eyes held his gaze, and the tremulous quiver of her bottom lip instilled within him an insane desire to kiss her again.

Tori, too, seemed spellbound, mesmerized by the man who stood before her and gripped her wrists within the iron circle of his hands. Her gaze roamed, fascinated, across his features—the lock of black hair that had fallen forward to dangle rakishly over his forehead, the square jaw that seemed more an angle of granite than flesh and blood, the full mouth suddenly softer than usual, and the gray eyes deepset and haunting. Moonlight turned the hollows of his cheeks to inky valleys, created shadows beneath his jaw to intensify its already sharp lines, and left arches of darkness over his eyes as it played across his face. "Thank you, Guy," Tori whispered, and a small smile curved the corners of her lips.

The smile broke the last threads of his resistance. He could no longer deny the desire she aroused within him, or control the hunger that her closeness induced. Nor did he want to. Lord help him, all he wanted was to possess her, to make her body burn with the same fire that her nearness caused to flame wildly within his, to feel her want him as he—damn the saints—wanted her.

Guy released her wrists and his arms encircled her waist to drag her roughly up against him. His head lowered toward hers, but rather than the resistance he expected, the rejection he had become so used to, Tori's face lifted toward his, inviting his kiss. His mouth crushed hers and he moved his hands brusquely up to press them against her back, holding her tightly, as if in an effort to meld the lithe length of her to his hard frame. He could feel the rapid thump of her heart against his chest, and his own matched it beat for beat, a wild crescendo that raced out of control. He felt her tremble in his arms, and he tightened his embrace, unwilling to let her go, to return, even for a moment, to the barren wasteland his life had been for the past several years.

Her arms slid up to encircle his neck, and her fingers slipped within the ragged curls of black hair that brushed the collar at the nape of his neck. A deliciously warm sweep of desire, like a slowly devouring cascade of hot lava, spread languorously through her body, invading every cell and leaving her weak with want in his arms. She bent her head back as his lips moved to press against

117

the long column of her throat, his touch turning the flesh to flame.

A moan of defeat and self-loathing escaped his throat. He was lost to her now, he knew it with the certainty of a man facing death. Yet he, himself, had brought on this defeat, and if truth be told, he'd wanted it ever since she had awakened after the accident. Desperately, hungrily, undeniably, he'd wanted it.

He swore inaudibly, hating himself for what he knew he was about to do, and unable, unwilling, to stop. Nothing mattered to him anymore, nothing but that he taste once again the passion of the woman he held in his arms, the woman who had damned his soul and nearly destroyed his heart.

His lips claimed hers again, his kiss a savage demand that strove to brand her with the mark of his possession, and attested silently to the depth of his need. Fire burned in his groin, hot and molten. It engulfed him, swiftly, mercilessly, and raced through his length so that every cell, every muscle, every fiber of his being was conscious of nothing but the tantalizing body he held in his arms.

Her lips parted, but whether in protest or invitation, Guy was not sure, nor did he care. He acted on instinct now, without thought or reason, without conscience, guilt, or fear. He took instant advantage. His tongue darted forth to entwine with hers and fuel the conflagration of need that had already begun to hungrily consume his body.

His hands roamed her back, caressed, held, and crushed her tighter against him. He was burning with a need he had thought long dead, extinguished years ago by her neglect and indifference, the need to make her his once again, to show her that she belonged to him and no one else had the right to claim her. No one.

Oblivious of the time and place, Guy was conscious only of the soft lips beneath his, of the lithe body in his arms, the small, hard breasts pushed against his chest. He did not see the figure which lurked in the shadows only a few yards away . . . watching with barely controlled rage.

Hot, hungry emotions that both shocked and startled her in their intensity clawed through Tori at Guy's ravaging kiss. She felt his mouth on hers, hard and hot, consuming her in his hunger. Some basic instinct deep within her recognized the loneliness in his kiss, the need for her response, and she gave it willingly, happily. Somehow, deep inside where her passions slept, Tori knew that no one, not even Guy, had ever kissed her like that before, and the blaze of pleasure that seared through her left her almost weak with want and joy.

She tightened her arms around his neck and pressed closer to him, locking her body against the hard, ropey bulwark of his. Reality vanished, all the harsh words and cold feelings that had passed between them in the last few hours were forgotten, at least for the moment. This was her husband, a man she'd thought despised her, wanted nothing to do with her; and yet he was kissing her with a desire like none she'd dreamt could exist.

His hand moved to cup her breast, and through the fabric of her gown she felt his thumb brush rhythmically across her nipple, teasing it, caressing the hardness until she ached with need.

It was Guy who eventually, though reluctantly, pulled his lips from hers. His breathing was heavy and ragged with desire, and his heart seemed to pound in his ears. He looked down at her for a long moment, a moment in which Tori stood suddenly terrified in his arms, not knowing whether he would kiss her again, as she so desperately wanted, or cruelly reject her, as he'd done before.

She stared up at him, trying to read his expression, but his handsomely chiseled features were lost to her in the darkness of the night. "Guy?" she finally said, her voice hesitant and breathless.

"I want you, Victoria." His deep drawl was husky with desire. "God help me, I want you."

Both the words and the sensual tone of his voice wrapped around her like a velvet shroud, warming her flesh, heating her blood, and sending tingles of pleasure skipping through her. She stood on tiptoe, and pressed her lips softly against his in answer, and then added in a whisper, "I want you, too."

At her words Guy swept one arm around her knees and lifted her from the ground. He cradled her against his chest and began walking down the path, his strides long and purposeful.

Tori slipped her arms around his neck. She had thought they were going to the house but was pleasantly surprised when, only seconds later, Guy veered from the path. He stepped between two draped curtains of Spanish moss and climbed several steps into the trellis-walled confines of a white gazebo. With the soft creak of the plank flooring beneath his steps, Guy moved to the wall opposite the arched entry, bent, and gently lay Tori on a cushioned seat that curved around the entire length of the gazebo.

Swiftly removing his cutaway coat, he bent over her and his mouth found hers again as he slid onto the cushion beside her. His tongue pushed between her lips, urgently seeking the inner softness that awaited it as his hands moved to explore the tantalizing curves sheathed only by the thin gown.

A trembling weakness swept through Tori at the ravishing claim of his lips, followed by a searing heat that turned her blood to boiling rivers beneath his touch. But this kiss was different from the one of moments before. It began as a strangely gentle kiss, tender in its seeking, cautious in its demand, and yet became, within seconds, powerful in its fervor, feral in its capture of her senses.

His hands caressed her, moving slowly, teasingly, over the cloth of her gown. She could feel the heat of his fingers through the fabric, scalding her flesh and inciting the passion within her that now threatened to overwhelm and engulf her. Tori felt his hand slide between her breasts. A few seconds later, the thin silk ribbon which held the front of her gown closed released its hold. He pushed the frail barrier of material from her, baring her flesh to his touch. His hand encircled one naked breast, and his fingers tenderly caressed the rosey, taut nipple until it throbbed.

Tori's breath caught as she lay spellbound by the sweet torture the stroke of his fingers brought to her. His lips left hers and she felt suddenly deserted. She reached for him, aching for his return, for the taste of his lips on hers again, until she felt his mouth graze her bare breast. His warm tongue curled intimately around that swollen mound in a laving caress, and then flicked over the aching tip of her nipple. A soft groan escaped her, and she instinctively arched her body up toward his mouth, silently, unconsciously, begging him to continue his rapturous assault.

He complied readily, needing no encouragement, no pleas. His mouth moved from one nipple to the other, teasing, the intoxicating caress of his tongue seducing her senses and causing the painful ache of pleasure that was coiling in her loins to deepen.

Soon she was no longer capable of reason. All thought

121

centered on the man who was causing waves of unbelievable pleasure to course through her, this darkly virile man whose words scalded and wounded her, but whose passions carried her to ecstasy.

"Victoria," he mumbled against her flesh, his tone filled with the ache of need and loneliness he had lived with for so long. He said her name again and again as his mouth moved from her breast and his lips traced a burning trail of kisses to the taut, smooth plane of her stomach.

His fingers slid through the triangle of dark hair at the apex of her thighs.

Her body jumped with shocked pleasure as his fingers slid to the moist, throbbing center of her need and turned her senses to flame. She was totally unprepared for the raw desire that coursed through her, an infinite abyss of hunger that seized her in its grip and demanded, cried, for fulfillment. She trembled with the force of the sensual emotions his touch had so violently unleashed, and cried out his name, the soft sound echoing on the still night and wafting over the dark gardens of Shadow Oaks.

His finger slipped within her, plunging into the dark depths of her need, while his thumb caressed the tiny nub of sensuality that ached with hunger.

Tori gasped and writhed beneath him, his touch, his body, now all that existed in the world for her, all that she wanted or cared about.

His mouth moved to recapture hers, once again kissing her with the demanding, ravaging passion that had blazed within him for so long and had been pent up, ignored, and denied.

For Guy too, nothing mattered at the moment but that she respond to his touch, that this mysterious, magical moment that had erupted between them, bringing them together, last forever.

His body was on fire, every nerve ending alive with anticipation. It had been so long—so damned long since he'd been with her, since he'd wanted to be with her. He had thought his love for her dead, his passion for her nothing more than a withered, nearly forgotten memory. But he had been wrong. God, how wrong. He wanted her more than ever, and most likely, he always would.

Suddenly Tori twisted away from him. She didn't know why she'd done it, since every instinct within her wanted nothing more than to be in his arms, to be loved by him, but something told her it was wrong. He aroused her emotions to heights she felt she'd never experienced before, and she shouldn't feel that way, memory or no. It was as if she had never been in Guy's arms, never felt the press of his lips, or the caress of his tongue.

Through the agonizing ache of his desire, through the drugging haze of his passion, Guy felt her rejection. It cut through him like a knife, an old, familiar knife, destroying all the newly awakened feelings for her that had overtaken him. For several long seconds he stared down at her as he fought to control his runaway emotions, forcing his ragged breathing to return to normal, ordering the accelerated beat of his heart and the headlong speeding of his pulses to slow. Realization of what had happened between them came slowly, but when it finally came, his mind reeled with the confrontation and his arms instantly dropped from around her waist as if touched by fire. A wave of utter disgust engulfed him. He had taken her into his arms, kissed her, let the basic savagery of his emotions, his lust for her, overwhelm his better senses. He closed his eyes as another surge of revulsion swept over him and he silently damned himself for his weakness, for betraying not only himself but his children. Guy pushed himself hastily away from her and rose to his feet.

"I'm sorry." Tori sat up. "I just . . ." She couldn't finish. She didn't really know what to say. He had made her feel things that, though wonderful, felt strange and new. She knew they shouldn't, and that scared her.

Guy looked down at her, the passion he'd felt only seconds before now gone, replaced by a burning anger and a self-loathing so intense he trembled from it. "Even without your memory of our past you seem still to be able to maneuver around my defenses, Victoria," he said, his voice as cold as his rage was hot. "But it won't do you any good. You may work your wiles on me and arouse my basic needs, but you cannot change my mind about anything. It's too late for that."

Tori shuddered. He stared down at her through eyes as cold as steel, shuttered and unreadable. His face was an implacable landscape of rigid flesh, his full, sensuous mouth slanted in a tight grimace. She wanted to say something, to reach out to him and crack the icy barrier he had so quickly erected between them, but the words stuck in her throat, and her hands refused to obey her commands and rise toward him, remaining instead stiff at her sides.

Guy saw the hurt in her eyes and steeled himself against it. He had never been a cruel man, but circumstances in the last few years had made him a hard man, a man distrustful of his own wife and brother, and a man who, out of necessity, had cached his heart away and vowed never to let it feel anything again. As he stared down at Tori the suspicion came to him that, in spite of the doctor's words, this was more than likely another of her ploys, probably a scheme thought up by her and Darin. A cleverly planned maneuver to wheedle her way back into his trust. She had used her beauty, her body, to seduce him before, and he'd been fool enough to fall for it. His fists clenched hard at his sides. But not again. He would not fall into that evil web of enchantment again.

Yet his rage, the hot fury that roiled within him was more at himself than at her, at the realization that he had almost fallen into her trap again. With gray eyes now cold and icy, and having taken on a hardness that was impenetrable, he looked down at Tori. "If I take you to my bed, Victoria, it will be to satisfy my lust, which I will admit you can easily arouse." His tone was hard and menacingly even. "But it will change nothing between us. Be assured of that. No matter what, it will change nothing."

Nine

Dawn crept slowly into Tori's room, filtering in through the tiny crevice of space between the drawn drapes to settle in a hazy spotlight of gold at the center of the room and leave its outer reaches in darkness. But she didn't need the light to know that the night had passed. She hadn't slept a wink since her encounter with Guy. Instead she had tossed, turned, flounced, and paced. She had wracked her brain in search of answers, cried at her lack of them, and cursed God for his cruelty. But she had received no miracle, no answers, and no memory. Nor had Tori managed to sort out her feelings toward Guy.

According to everything she'd been told, she was supposed to care nothing for him. And yet that was the farthest thing from what she was feeling. She was still confused by her passionate reaction to his kiss, hurt by his announcement that it had been nothing more to him than pure lust, the need to satisfy the hungers of his body. But most of all she was angry that she couldn't remember a thing past the moment she'd awakened after the carriage accident. Maybe if she could remember she'd understand Guy, as well as her own feelings and reactions.

"Except for the lamp," she muttered, looking at it as she spoke. How in the name of heaven could she forget how to turn off a lamp? And that thing about Muammar Qaddafi, and the other about *Friday the 13th, Part X*. There was no explaining those things. Or why she had the nagging sensation that she was a stranger in her own house, and not because of her memory loss. It was as if she were really a stranger, someone who had never been to Shadow Oaks before, had never known the Reichourds, including Guy.

"And if I say any of this they'll all think I'm crazy and most likely lock me away somewhere."

Her thoughts only served to torment her, for there were no answers to her questions, at least none that she could find. Even now, several hours after Guy had walked away and left her standing alone, dumbfounded, in the gazebo, she could feel the warm taste of his lips on hers, tremble to the sensations it had caused within her, and she was aching to know the touch of his hands and mouth again. If she were to believe everything that had been said to her of the way she was, the kind of person she had been before the accident, if she were to believe it because of the attitudes of her husband and children, of the servants, and of her "lover," Darin, then what was left?

She walked to the large armoire that dominated one wall of the bedroom and swung open its tall doors. A rainbow of colors spread before her in gowns of satin, silk, chintz, poplin, muslin, and taffeta. Tori frowned. She didn't want a gown. She wanted a pair of pants. Boots. And a shirt. She hadn't gone riding the other day when she'd wanted to, but she was definitely going now. She needed the fresh air, the solitude, the mindless dash across the landscape. She needed time just to be, without thinking or worrying.

Turning back to the bed, she pulled the tapestry bell cord that hung beside it and then returned to rummage through the drawers of the wide closet.

Several minutes later a soft knock sounded on the entry door.

"Come in," Tori called over her shoulder. She pulled a corset from the drawer and held it up in front of her. "Why in heaven's name would anyone wear one of these things?" she muttered.

"Because it's proper, Miss Victoria," Suda said.

She had entered the room so quietly that Tori hadn't been aware anyone had come in. She turned. "Proper or not, it can't be comfortable."

"No ma'am," Suda said, keeping her eyes downcast.

Tori suddenly remembered the scene she'd witnessed earlier, of Guy and Suda in the garden. She sat on the edge of the big bed. "Suda," she said, a bit hesitantly, not quite sure how to approach the subject.

"Yes, Miss Victoria?" The girl's eyes remained downcast, and she twisted her fingers together in front of her.

"What was Guy saying to you, when you were in the garden with him?"

Suda looked up in surprise. "He didn't say nothing, Miss Victoria. I wasn't in the garden with Michie Guy."

"I saw you Suda."

The girl shook her head vehemently. "No, Miss Victoria. No, not with Michie Guy."

"Was it Darin?"

Suda's head shook so much Tori thought it was going to fall off.

Tori frowned. Obviously Suda was lying. But why? The answer came almost immediately. Because she was afraid. But of whom? Tori determined to persist. "Suda, I saw you. Guy forced you to kiss him and then nearly threw you to the ground."

"No, Miss Victoria, no. It wasn't Michie Guy."

"Then it was Darin."

Tears slipped from Suda's eyes to stream over her dark cheeks.

"It was Darin, wasn't it?" Tori said, feeling anger begin to burn within her.

Suda nodded. "I'm sorry, Miss Victoria."

"You're sorry?" Tori couldn't believe her ears. "What do you have to be sorry for?"

"I know you likes Michie Darin, and I wouldn't do nothing like that, to hurt you, but he says I have to or he'll sell Robert."

"Sell Robert?" Tori's mind was spinning. "What has Robert got to do with this?"

"He's Michie Darin's son, and my half brother."

"What?" Tori felt as if the earth had just tilted. "Robert is Darin's son?" No wonder the boy had such a look of familiarity about him. He was a Reichourd. "And"—she looked incredulously at Suda—"and Darin is threatening to sell the lad if you don't sleep with him?"

Suda nodded, a look of abject misery in her eyes. "Michie Darin used to sleep with my mama, but she's old now and he don't want her no more. He says he wants me but—"

"But you don't want him?" Tori provided.

Suda shook her head.

"Suda, the next time Darin tries to force himself on you I want you to tell him I know what he's doing."

The girl looked at her in astonishment.

"Do you understand? Tell him you told me and I said if he didn't stop I'd tell Guy about his plans. Understand?"

Suda nodded.

"Good. And don't worry, no one's going to sell Robert. Or anyone else for that matter. The idea is reprehensible." She shook her head. "Selling people. Lord, how could anyone do that." She looked back at Suda and forced a smile to her face. "Well, now that we've got that settled I'd like to go riding, but I don't see any pants in my closet."

The girl's face screwed into an expression of complete incomprehension. "Pants, Miss Victoria? What's that?"

"Pants, Suda. You know, like Guy wears."

Suda's eyes widened in shock. "You mean trousers, Miss Victoria? You want to wear trousers?"

"Yes. Don't I have any for riding?"

Suda shook her head. "No, ma'am." She walked to the armoire and pulled out a light brown gown with a matching jacket. Both were trimmed in dark brown velvet cord. "This here's your favorite riding habit, Miss Victoria."

Tori sighed. "Suda, will you please stop calling me *Miss Victoria?*"

Suda started. "Then what am I supposed to call you, Miss Vic—?"

"Tori. Just call me Tori." The comment surprised Tori almost as much as it did Suda. She didn't know how she knew that was what she was used to being called, she just suddenly knew it. She also realized, at that same moment, that this was why the name Victoria had felt so alien to her. No one called her Victoria.

"Tori, Miss Vi—?"

"Yes, Tori." She looked at the riding habit in distaste. How in the world could anyone ride a horse in that thing?

"But I've always called you Miss Victoria. Everybody does, Miss—"

"No, everyone calls me Tori." She smiled to soften her words. "Don't I have any pants, Suda?"

"It ain't proper for a lady to wear trousers, Miss Victor—Miss Tori. You knows that."

Tori sighed. "Fetch me a pair of Guy's, please, Suda. And a needle and thread."

Suda backed her way out of the room, almost as if she were afraid to turn her back on Tori.

Tori moved to stand before the tall window. A movement caught her eye, and she looked beyond the pasture that bordered one side of the drive. On a path that led around it she saw Guy astride a huge black horse. He seemed to be heading for the cotton fields.

For some unexplainable reason her eyes filled with tears as she watched him. She was supposed to care nothing for him. Everyone said so, including him. But instead, every time she saw him, every time he was near, she seemed to want nothing more than to be cradled in the security of his arms. It was unreasonable, it was insane. She knew it, yet she couldn't help it or deny it. Nor did she want to. "But what happened between us?" she murmured to herself. "What happened to make us strangers? To make you hate me so much?"

A tear dropped from her eye, sliding down her cheek in a silvery path, shimmering beneath the soft rays of the sun that streamed in through the window and warmed her flesh. She remembered the hurt she had seen in his eyes after she'd pulled away from his kiss. It had only been there for the briefest of moments, but she had seen and recognized it. And she wanted nothing more now than to make it go away, to never see that in his eyes again.

Suda returned to the room just then, carrying a pair of Guy's trousers and one of his shirts. "You want I should fit these to you, Miss Victoria?" She paused a few steps from Tori and looked slightly abashed. "Huh, I mean, Miss Tori."

Tori brushed away her tears. "No. Help me get into that riding habit, Suda. We'll do that later." Tori pulled the brown outfit from its hook in the armoire. "Hurry, Suda."

The girl did as she was ordered, hastily retrieving a pair of pantalettes and a camisole from the armoire's drawers and holding them out to her mistress.

Tori stared at the pantalettes. "I have to wear those when I ride?"

Suda frowned and looked at Tori in obvious discomfort. She wasn't used to seeing her mistress confused . . . about anything. And she certainly wasn't used to her being nice.

Tori stepped into the pantalettes and tied the ribboned waist. She laughed. "I feel like a clown in these things."

Suda remained silent, not knowing what to say. She wasn't exactly sure what a clown was.

"Please don't tell me I have to wear one of those hoop-cage things," Tori pleaded, eyeing the collapsed whalebone hoop that hung on one inside wall of the armoire.

Suda smiled weakly. "No, ma'am, just this petticoat." She held out a ruffled white petticoat made of soft cotton.

"Thank heaven," Tori said, and hurriedly slipped into it. She quickly buttoned the white silk blouse Suda handed her and then stared down at her breasts in surprise. "Have I gained weight, Suda?"

The girl looked up from where she knelt with Tori's shoes in her hands, and her eyes followed Tori's. The center buttons were slightly strained in their bindings, just enough to pull the material a bit too taut.

Tori slipped her feet into the shoes and winced slightly as Suda hooked them up. They were tight, binding her ankles like some medieval torture device, too narrow, and ugly. But they were her shoes. She was off the settee and to the door almost before Suda knew she'd risen.

"What about your hair, Miss Vic—Tori? I haven't put it up yet."

Tori paused at the door and looked back at the young girl, who was just rising to her feet. "I always wear it down, Suda." She paused at seeing the little frown tug at Suda's brow. "Don't I?"

Suda forced a smile to her lips and averted her gaze from Tori's. "Yes, ma'am. Down. You always wear it down."

Tori practically ran down to the stable, or at least she tried to. She held the skirt of the brown habit off the ground and rushed down the path, remembering her last episode in shoes like these and taking care where and how she placed her feet.

"Robert? Robert, are you in here?" Tori called as she entered the dimly lit stables. She wondered suddenly if the boy knew Darin was his father. "Robert?" She stopped in the center of the stable and looked around. There didn't seem to be anyone else about. "Drat." She turned to the railing that had the saddles mounted on it. Tori had the oddest feeling that the one that looked like some kind of disfigured cow's head and had both stirrups hanging from the same side was most likely the one she was supposed to use. She went directly to one of the others. "Suicidal I am not," she mumbled, throwing a glance at the strange saddle as she passed it with another in her arms.

"Can I help you, Miss Victoria?"

She whirled around at the voice. Robert stood in a doorway that led to one of the outside corrals. His face was completely in shadow as sun streamed into the stable from behind him, but she had recognized it.

"Yes, Robert, please. I saw Guy ride out a little while ago, and I thought I'd like to join him. Could you fetch me a horse?"

"You want Rogue, Miss Victoria?"

"Rogue?" she echoed.

Robert nodded. "I've got him all groomed up for you. Brushed him myself." He turned and disappeared from the doorway. A minute later he reappeared at the wide opening through which Tori had entered, leading one of the most beautiful stallions she'd ever seen. The horse's coat was a glistening silver, yet beneath that pale coat could be seen spots of black, giving the animal a mottled, rich look. His mane and tail were white, pure white, as were the short stockings just above each black hoof.

"He's beautiful," Tori said softly, her gaze moving admiringly over the horse. He was leanly built, yet exuded an aura of power and strength. His muscles were sleek, as were his body and legs. All in all a graceful and exquisitely beautiful testimonial to his Arabian lines and breeding.

"You want *that* saddle?" Robert asked.

Tori nodded.

The boy quickly took it from Tori's arms and settled it atop Rogue's back. The horse shuddered momentarily, kicking a rear hoof into the dirt floor, as if in protest. "Come on, Rogue," Robert said soothingly, as he buckled the girth around the stallion's belly. "Calm down and be good. Miss Victoria wants to ride you today."

The horse snorted and pranced in place. Robert slipped a silver bit between the animal's lips, then shrugged a leather halter over his ears. Rogue shook his head, as if in an effort to rid himself of the leather straps. "Rogue," Robert said, "stop it or Miss Victoria will think you don't want to give her a ride."

Tori watched the big horse. That's exactly what she was beginning to think; that Rogue didn't want her to ride him. She felt as if the horse was watching her and had decided he, like everyone else at Shadow Oaks, didn't like her. But that was ridiculous. He was a horse. She frowned and continued to watch Rogue sidestep away from Robert and flick his ears at the halter. "Or is it?" she mumbled softly.

Robert turned and smiled proudly. "Okay, Miss Victoria, he's ready."

Tori felt a moment's hesitation. She looked down at the young boy. "This is my horse, Robert? The one I always ride?"

"Yes, ma'am. You raised him from a colt. Three years now. And no one else rides him. Only you Miss Victoria. I make sure of that, just like you ordered."

"No one else rides him," Tori mumbled, inching her way cautiously to the obviously nervous horse. "Then why isn't he putting out much of a welcome mat?"

"Pard'n Miss Victoria?" Robert said. He looked at her quizzically.

Tori shook her head. "Nothing, Robert."

"I'll get the stairs."

"Stairs?" Tori didn't know what he was talking about, and didn't feel like waiting to find out. Guy was already probably halfway to China by now. If she was going to catch up to him she was going to have to hurry. She lifted her skirt and slipped her left foot into the stirrup, grabbed hold of the small hump of leather over the horse's shoulder and hoisted herself upward.

Rogue shied away from her, taking a step sideways just as she bounced upward into the air. Tori's foot slipped through the stirrup as Rogue moved, her fingers lost their grip on the molded leather and she fell forward. As her nose rammed against the saddle's skirt, pain shot up into her forehead. She struggled to free her foot and glared up at the huge stallion. "You did that on purpose," she said under her breath.

The horse sniggered and flicked his ears back.

"Now stand still," Tori ordered, "and let me mount."

She settled her left foot into the stirrup again, took a death grip on the leather cantle and leapt from the ground.

Rogue tossed his head upward and tried to back away from her, but this time Tori was ready for him. She swung her right leg quickly over the animal's back and slid onto the saddle, thrusting her right foot quickly into its own stirrup and holding tightly to the reins. The horse whinnied in protest at her success, and a huge forehoof pounded on the ground.

"Miss Victoria," Robert said, rushing up to her and staring in obvious shock. "You didn't wait for the stairs."

Tori looked down at the wooden structure the boy held in his hands. It was a miniature staircase, evidently made to help a person mount. Weird, she thought, then smiled. "I'll be back in a while, Robert, and I promise, just for you, I'll use the stairs next time."

Robert walked to the doorway and watched her ride away, a look of puzzlement glistening from his gray-brown eyes. As she disappeared into the distance, he shook his head and looked down at the scraggly black and white mutt of a dog that had come to sit at his feet. "She ain't like Miss Victoria anymore, dog. She's nicer, and I likes her better, but she ain't like Miss Victoria anymore."

Ten

Tori rode for over half an hour, but saw no sign of Guy. She finally gave up looking for him and just began to explore the vast plantation, letting herself enjoy its many varied landscapes. Rogue had settled down to only an occasional outburst of rebellion against her commands, but Tori found that she was a good enough horsewoman to be able to keep him under control, though she couldn't figure out what was bothering him. Robert had said he was her horse, that no one else rode him, but the sleek stallion's behavior said otherwise.

He tossed his head up just then, flinging his long flaxen mane into her face, the coarse tendrils stinging Tori's cheeks as they slapped her flesh. "Boy, for being my horse you've got a real weird way of showing your affection." Rogue tossed his head again and whinnied. Tori kept a tight grip on the reins and urged the stallion onto a narrow path that led away from the fallow ground and open pastures. But again, as she had in the house, she had the feeling that she was a stranger, both to the land that surrounded her and to the people that inhabited it. "And now to my horse," she mumbled disparagingly. She came around a

137

thick copse of dogwood, the clustered white blossoms that littered its thin, gnarly branches preventing view of the cotton field until she'd cleared the trees. She pulled up on Rogue's reins, ignored his snicker of distaste, and stared at the infinite stretch of white that spread before her over the wide expanse of planted acreage.

Tall brown stalks, looking dried and brittle, grew in long, endless rows, and on the short branches of each plant were the burst pods of blooms, each revealing a large puff of cotton. Working within the vast white landscape were several dozen slaves: black men, women, and some children. Most of the men wore floppy old hats and tattered shirts, though some remained bareheaded and shirtless. Their ebony hair and skin, glistening from both the sweat of their labors and the already mercilessly hot rays of the late morning sun, provided a stark contrast to the pristine color of the crop they toiled over. Bandanas, like turbans, were wound around the heads of most of the women, providing the black and white landscape with spots of yellow, red, blue, and green.

Tori rode aimlessly along the path that bordered one side of the cotton field, watching the workers move down the rows, their fingers deftly and quickly picking the cotton from the thorny pods. She felt nearly mesmerized by the sight before her, but it was a hypnotic trance that filled her with disgust and revulsion, not for nature's gifts, but for the people toiling here.

Tori shuddered with a frustration borne of helplessness, yet didn't understand her own feelings. This was the way of the South. She had been born into these traditions and customs, raised within them. Why should these things bother her so intensely now? They obviously had not bothered her before the accident. At least that was what she had to believe, *if* she believed that she had been the way everyone was intimating.

She sighed. Why did everything they told her seem so alien and strange? That question had been haunting her since the accident. Why did her whole life seem so unreal? Nothing felt familiar. And as each day, each hour, passed and no memories returned, she began to worry that they never would.

The field slaves threw furtive glances her way, their dark eyelids raising slightly, then lowering quickly, like shutters over dark windows. A tattily dressed overseer with a stub of a cigar protruding from the corner of his fleshy lips sat astride a big gelding beneath the shade of an oak tree's sprawling branches and watched the workers toil. He tipped his hat to Tori as she passed, and his whiskered cheeks puffed in a wide, rather lewd smile. The overseer's assistant, a scraggly young man who continually paced the length of the field, grinned toothlessly up at her. But none spoke, and Tori, feeling disheartened once again, recognized no one.

Deep in thought, and paying no attention to the direction Rogue took, Tori continued to ride, though her mind was no longer on the scenery around her. Nor was it on the rising temperature as the sun moved higher into the sky and its rays grew hotter, penetrating the silk blouse to heat her shoulders and the light wool of her habit's skirt to make her legs seem to be encased in a cocoon of fabric. Tori's eyes became shadowed with the darkness of her thoughts. Somehow she had to make the first twenty-seven years of her life come back to her. She had to remember. How else could she go forward?

Rogue moved along a narrow path that led between the two tracts in which Guy had decided to plant tobacco this season. Tall, purplish green stalks grew close together, their leaves like pointed spears that shaded the earth and reached skyward for the sun.

Beyond the tobacco fields was a fallow tract, the earth unplowed and covered with a tangle of tall wild grasses and flowers. Rogue paused to lower his head and pull a clump of thin green reeds into his mouth. At a nudge of Tori's heels to his ribs he continued his shuffling pace, though she sensed it was begrudgingly.

She caught a movement, or shadow, out of the corner of her eye. Turning, she gasped softly, startled. She yanked back on the reins, hard, and Rogue stopped, pulling his head downward and straining against the sudden tightening of the reins. "Be still," she commanded harshly, her voice low. On the crest of a small rise of land several hundred yards to her right, with the sun behind him, sat a man astride a horse. Relief swept over her instantly. Guy. She waved, but instead of returning the greeting, the rider swung his horse around and disappeared down the opposite side of the hill.

Tori frowned, then dismissed the incident. It had probably been Guy, and he obviously preferred his own company to hers. She urged Rogue back into a slow walk. They crossed an open tract, the big horse nipping at the tall grass every now and then, the comfortable warmth of the morning sun intensifying. Tori spotted a wide copse of trees at the end of the tract and turned Rogue toward it. Both her back and shoulders were beginning to feel the effects of the blistering heat, to say nothing of her legs swathed beneath the light wool skirt, cotton pantalettes, and stockings. The thought of a little respite in the shade was just too tempting to pass up. Anyway, her rear end was a bit sore. Her body had still not gotten over the accident, as the few bruises that remained attested.

She dismounted and looped Rogue's reins around the low-hanging limb of a bush, then turned toward the grove. The sun seemed to stop at its edge, the ground just beyond the first few trees dark with shadow. The soft song of a bird filtered out from the inky depths. Rather than sit at the base of the tree, and within its shade, as she'd planned, Tori stepped past it and into the grove. The brown of her skirt instantly blended with the dimness, but the stark white of her silk blouse was like a ray of daylight penetrating the thick foliage. She walked slowly among the trees, admiring the almost primitive beauty. Pine, oak and cypress grew in close proximity of one another, so close that their branches twisted and entwined together, prevented little more than a few weak rays of light to penetrate the area, and supported dripping sheets of gray Spanish moss that in some places hung to the ground. After wandering only a few yards into the grove Tori was surprised to find the earth turn soft beneath her feet and in spots give way to canals of murky, slowly swirling, or stagnant water.

A thin stream of sunlight shone down onto the center of one of the pondlike canals, directly onto a leaf, flat and round, that floated on the water's surface. A large flower, its pinkish petals open wide toward the sun, rested on one end of the leaf. Tori watched it move with almost imperceptible slowness toward a gnarled log that had lodged itself at the opposite side of the narrow pond. The leaf and flower bumped up against the log, and Tori started to turn away, intent on exploring the rest of the primal, untouched area. Another movement in the pond, caught out of the corner of her eye, drew her attention back to the turbid water.

"Oh, my God," Tori breathed, her heart instantly accelerating to a hammering beat. She stared at the two yellow eyes that had appeared toward the top of the "log" as it had risen higher in the water and begun to move toward her. Alligator! Crocodile! Alligator! her mind screamed, uncertain which she was actually looking at. The silent scream of terror was accompanied by an order for her to run. But the ability for swift movement had deserted her. Instead, her limbs seemingly frozen, she could barely take a stiff, awkward step back from the bank, her gaze riveted on the ugly, prehistoric reptile that was now in the center of the pond.

A cracking sound, like that of a small, brittle branch being broken from a tree, or being stepped on, sounded behind her, but Tori couldn't turn, couldn't look. She didn't dare take her eyes off the thing floating toward her, didn't dare breathe or make a sound. Suddenly something small and dark soared over her shoulder, so close to her head she felt the drift of wind it caused as it passed. Tori jerked to the side and heard, rather than saw, it hit the water with a plop. A thunderous splash followed, and she jerked around just in time to see the alligator's massive tail slap at the water and his jaws clamp down viciously around the small dark object. A squeal filled the air as whatever had hurtled into the pond met its death between the reptile's huge jaws.

Tori shivered in both revulsion and fear, and abruptly finding the power to move, she scrambled back several steps from the water's edge. Her fingers clenched into tight fists, but it still did not thwart the shaking that had gripped her at the horrible sight. Her gaze remained pinioned on

142

the alligator as satisfied, albeit temporarily, it closed its yellow eyes and sank slowly beneath the water's muddy, black surface.

Still shaking violently, Tori took another step back and realized, too late, that it had been a mistake. Her foot floundered helplessly in space in search of solid ground, and found none. Tori tried to throw herself forward and her arms frantically flailed the air in an effort to change the direction in which she was falling. The back of her shoulder slammed against a tree trunk and the breath shot from her lungs. At the same moment her foot splashed into the water and she felt the heel of her riding shoe sink into the quagmire that was the swamp's floor. Mind-rending fear seized her as her imagination reeled out of control. She sucked in great gulps of air and scrambled with lightning speed to perch precariously on a dead cypress stump that protruded from the water.

A sigh of relief left her lips. At least she was out of that ugly black water.

A soft chuckle, deep and throaty, suddenly echoed through the eerie stillness of the shadow-filled swamp.

Tori's head jerked up, her heart slammed against her breast, and her eyes tried to pierce the surrounding darkness. Someone was in the swamp with her. She didn't want to look, but she couldn't stop her eyes from straying to the tall trees and dank shadows that surrounded her. Who was watching her? It had been insanity to come in here. Especially alone. She had to get out. There was one tree between where she stood and the thin strip of land she'd fallen from. She lunged for it, praying she wouldn't end up in the water again. Her fingers clawed desperately at the bulbous trunk as her feet scurried to find a hold on the moss-covered root that disappeared beneath the murky surface. Panic lodged in her throat, preventing the scream that wanted to tear from her lungs. Her fingernails dug into the damp bark, and she managed to push herself upright, her hips feeling the drag of the water-soaked woolen skirt as it lifted from the water, its hem lost in a clumped layer of clinging muck.

Suddenly, without warning, the vision of John Reichourd's body floating lifelessly in the stagnant waters of just such a place as this assailed her. Tori froze and her eyes darted around wildly. This was the same place! The place where the body floated!

The laugh sounded again, this time instilled with such malice, such unmistakeable evil that Tori, frightened now beyond all reason, did scream. The sound ripped from her throat and shattered the peaceful silence of the swamp. She threw herself back onto the muddy bank and scratched, clawed, and tugged her way up its slope, panting with each effort, gasping at each milestone of ground achieved.

Blind terror gave her strength. A thick root from one of the trees protruded through the earth. She grabbed it, her fingers curled tightly around the sodden wood, and Tori hauled herself upward.

Gasping and heaving, she made it back to the top of the narrow bank and looked around frantically for the alligator. It was nowhere in sight, but relief was not forthcoming, and wouldn't be until she was out of the swamp. She was suddenly aware of a pulling sensation on her forearm, like a tightening of her flesh. Someone had hold of her! Oh, Lord. She twisted and flung her arm outward. There was no one there, but the feeling continued. Tori looked down. The button that had held the cuff of her sleeve secured was gone, and the sleeve itself, now wet and covered with mud, hung loose and half pushed up toward her elbow. Something black and shiny clung to her forearm.

She screamed and violently shook her arm, trying to break its hold on her, but the parasite remained secured to her flesh. "Off. Get off," Tori screamed, tears of fear streaming down her cheeks now. Her pulse was racing, blood rushed through her veins at breakneck speed. "Get off," she shrieked through her tears, and slapped at the thing with her free hand.

It maintained its grip on her.

Hysteria filled Tori. She pulled up the heavy folds of her skirt and, stumbling and half-blinded by tears of panic, ran along the narrow path of land that snaked between the canals of water. She broke from the grove into the sunlight and slammed against something hard and solid. Strong hands clasped her upper arms in an iron-tight grip before she had a chance to avoid them.

"No, let me go, let me go." Tori twisted frantically.

"Victoria, stop it," Guy ordered, his deep voice hard and controlled. His grasp on her remained firm.

Tori stopped trying to pull away from him, her eyes shooting to meet his. "Guy?"

He opened his mouth to respond, but her hysteria would not be so easily contained.

"Guy, get it off me, please. Get it off." Her gaze fell to the ugly black creature that still clung to her forearm.

Guy's eyes followed the direction of hers. He released her immediately. "Good God, a bloodsucker." He grabbed her upper arm again and began to push her toward the ground.

"What are you doing? You've got to get it off." Her voice was ragged with fear, her body trembling almost out of control now.

145

"Sit down, Victoria," Guy said, his words harsh, his tone meant to instill compliance.

Tori dropped to the ground, her knees shaking so badly that she wasn't sure it had even been voluntary. "Please get it off," she cried weakly, tears streaming down her cheeks.

Guy ran to where Satan stood grazing and tore his jacket from the pommel where he'd rolled and tied it. He turned and hurried back to where Tori sat, digging a lucifer out of the breast pocket of his jacket as he approached. "How long has it been on you?" he asked brusquely.

"I . . . I don't know." She looked at him in fear. Did it matter? "A few minutes, maybe."

He crouched before her and flicked the sulfur tip of the lucifer against the heel of his boot. One end of the wooden match burst into flame. He cupped it with his other hand and moved the match toward Tori.

She cringed away from him, her eyes wide with alarm.

"Stay still," he growled.

"What are you going to do?"

"Get that thing off you. Or would you rather it continue to suck your blood?"

"Suck my blood?" she gasped.

His brow arched condescendingly at her words.

She closed her eyes and held her breath, waiting for the match to touch her flesh, waiting to feel the searing sting of burning skin.

"There, it's off."

Tori's eyes shot open in surprise and she looked down at her arm. Relief filled her. The slimey black thing was gone. "What was it?"

Guy looked at her with blatant suspicion.

"Guy?"

"Victoria, you know damn well it was a bloodsucker. A leech." His eyes blazed with fury. "How long are you going to continue this charade, Victoria? This act about not knowing anything. Or is this just the beginning of another of your schemes?"

The hard words were the last attack her fragile senses could take. The frail barriers of self-preservation that had held through her flight from the swamp, that had remained erect around her ever since the carriage accident, though unsteady, now crumbled, and with them so did Tori. She had desperately wanted to be comforted by him, to be pulled into the refuge of his embrace, where, God help her, she felt safe, in spite of his antagonistic attitude toward her. But that avenue of solace was closed to her. She sank to the ground, buried her face in her arms, and let the tears flow unhampered. "I'm not pretending, Guy. Much as I wish I were, I'm not," she said between sobs.

He remained on his haunches, his arms settled on his thighs, hands dangling down between his knees. His gray eyes studied her, his ears heard her words, his mind registered their meaning, but in the end his heart rejected them as false. He had to, in spite of the burning hunger that lay coiled deep within him, in spite of the gnawing ache of desire that swept over him every time he neared her. If he even thought to allow himself to believe her he might begin to feel compassion for her, and then he might begin to feel something else, something he didn't want to feel. He could never again allow that. Guy sighed and rose to his feet. "I have a lot of work to do, Victoria," he said, his words hard and cold. "I suggest you return to the house." He started to turn away.

Tori lifted her head and looked after him. "Guy, someone was . . ." The words died on her lips as what she had been about to say registered in her mind. *Someone was in the swamp . . . watching me . . . laughing.*

Guy turned at her words. "Someone was what?"

She stared up into his eyes, at the gray pools that had turned as hard and dark as obsidian. It could have been Guy in the swamp watching her struggle, hoping she would . . . she remembered those evil-looking yellow eyes looking up at her from the dark water and shuddered. She didn't want to believe it had been Guy in there, taunting her with his laughter, amused at her fear, but . . . her mind raced for a reason to refute the suspicion and found none.

Eleven

Tori watched him ride away, unable to decide whether she was relieved or disappointed. She rose shakily to her feet. If it had been Guy in the swamp, could he have circled around and beaten her to the open field? She didn't know. Would he have pretended he didn't know what had happened? But why would he have taunted her? What would he have hoped to accomplish, other than to frighten her?

She glanced back over her shoulder at the dark edge of trees. It would be much easier to believe it had been Darin. She wanted it to be Darin. Though what would be his reason for watching her like that? For trying to scare her half to death? Tori shivered with fear. Could he still be in there? Watching her even now? Grabbing up the wet and muddied folds of her skirt, she hurried to where Rogue stood grazing. The horse skittered away from her as she shakily unwound the reins from the bush, but Tori held tight to them and the saddle. This was no time for games. "Whoa, there, Rogue. Take it easy," she crooned, "take it easy." But the fear in her voice belied the soothing words. Rogue's ears flicked, his eyes darted constantly in every direction, and one huge hoof pounded the ground relentlessly, nervously.

Tori rammed her foot into the thin silver stirrup and, bending her right knee, pushed against the ground and thrust herself upward. She settled instantly into the saddle, then, once astride the tall stallion, chanced another glance back at the swamp, squinting hard in an effort to pierce the darkness beyond the first line of trees.

The soft, short hairs on the back of her neck rose as she felt someone returning her intense gaze. From somewhere within that darkness someone was still watching her.

"But Darin's gone," she murmured, suddenly remembering that he had told her he was leaving for Baton Rouge that morning. He was, most likely, already more than a few dozen miles from Shadow Oaks. "And Guy rode in the opposite direction." She turned to stare in the direction Guy had ridden, and found no sight of him.

A swell of fear clogged her throat. Tori yanked on Rogue's reins to turn the horse back toward the house, jamming her heels into his ribs. The silver stallion lunged forward, breaking into an immediate lope, his long, powerful legs stretching across the earth and carrying them forward with what seemed almost effortless speed. The wind caused by their flight whipped at Tori's hair and pulled it from the thin silk ribbon she had used to tie it at her nape, leaving the dark tresses to stream out behind her.

She rode through the open tracts, past the tobacco fields, the cotton fields, and the formal gardens, urging Rogue to keep up his frightening pace the entire way, allowing the big horse no slack, no thought of deviance from their direction. Tori wanted nothing more than to get back to the house, back to the sanctity of her bedroom. If it had been possible to jump to the ground before the horse completely stopped in front of the stable doors, Tori would have, but she was encumbered by the voluminous folds and weight of her muddied skirt and pantalettes. She jerked back on the reins, forcing Rogue to a sliding stop as Robert ran from the stable and grabbed the horse's bridle. Then she swung her leg over the saddle and slid to the ground.

"What's the matter, Miss Victoria?" Robert said, his eyes wide with alarm at seeing her mud-spattered skirt. "Did Rogue throw you? Is you hurt?"

"I'm fine, Robert," Tori said, gathering up her gown. Sight of the boy momentarily vanquished the harrowing episode of less than an hour before and brought back the memory of what Suda had told her, that Robert was, unfortunately for him, Darin's son. "Robert."

"Yes, Miss Victoria?"

"I want you to come to the house tomorrow when Martin and Alicia do their lessons."

"You want me to bring my shoe-polish box, Miss Victoria?"

She ignored a shiver and smiled. "No. I want you to take lessons with them."

The boy stared at her in shocked astonishment, but Tori didn't notice. She had already turned away and was hurrying toward the house, her hands trembling beneath the stiffening wool of her habit. A shudder shook her. She was chilled to the bone, in spite of the blistering heat of the afternoon sun. Her fingers felt nearly numb, her flesh was covered with goose bumps, and her teeth were rattling. Tori ran up the path that led to the house, took the shallow fan-shaped steps to the gallery two at a time and burst through the front door.

Hannah, busy polishing a cherry and lemonwood petticoat table that was set against one wall of the foyer, turned at Tori's brusque entry. A frown of disapproval drew her

151

black brows together and narrowed her eyes. "Now what she gone and done?"

Tori heard the softly muttered words, but ignored them. She moved toward the wide staircase, holding her gown up with one hand, the other sliding along the polished banister as she ran up the steps, the sound of her footfalls silenced by the thick Aubusson runner that covered each step. Halfway up the stairs she stopped and whirled to stare at the family portraits that hung on the curved wall. Her gaze rested first on the painting of Guy, wanting to see only good in the handsome face, searching for some semblance, some spark of warmth, compassion, or love. Her eyes then moved to the portrait of Darin. Tori was immediately assailed with a feeling of evil, but was unsure if it was real or merely brought out by the fact that she didn't like him. Lastly her gaze came to rest on the face of John, the eldest Reichourd brother. The dead Reichourd brother. Once again memory of the nightmare filled her mind, as well as the image she'd had the last time she'd looked at his portrait. The feeling intensified the trembling that shook her. Had they actually been visions of John's death? Was she seeing what had happened to him? Or had she . . . ? No, she didn't want to think that. But she had to. Or had she been there? Had she witnessed his death? Was she merely starting to remember it? Then another thought struck her, and she almost reeled in rejection of it. Could it have been, rather than a dream, a premonition? An image of death yet to come for one of the two remaining brothers?

"Oh, God," Tori mewed. She ran down the hallway, flung the door to her bedchamber open, and slammed it shut behind her. Leaning her back against it and closing her eyes, she sighed as relief, swift and sure, swept over

152

her. She was safe now, but she continued to tremble. Tori walked on shakey legs toward the bed and pulled a coverlet from it. She wrapped that around her, then moved to the royal blue settee that sat at an angle before the cold fireplace and let herself collapse onto its brocade cushions. The silken fabric was a soothing caress to her cold flesh, as the silence and safety of her room was to her jangled nerves. She held her legs tightly pressed together, wrapped her arms around her torso, and bent forward, rocking slightly back and forth.

Someone had been watching her, first while she'd been riding, and later in the bayou. Someone had wanted her to meet disaster in that swamp, maybe even death, but they'd wanted it to happen naturally, to look like an accident.

"But who?" The words were spoken in barely a whisper, but seemed to scream out and reverberate against the silence that hung over the room. She didn't want to think about the obvious conclusions. Her lover? Or her husband? All logic said it had to be one or the other.

She rose and, letting the coverlet slip from her shoulders, walked to the dressing table across the room, settled onto its tapestried cushion, and stared at the image that looked back out at her. "Remember," Tori commanded the reflection that looked at her from the silver glass. "Remember your life and maybe things will start to make sense again." She closed her eyes and waited, willing it to come, but her memory remained elusive, dwelling within the dark regions of her mind just out of reach, taunting her. Tori sighed and opened her eyes. The image in the mirror did the same, and Tori sat quietly, resigned, and stared at the woman in the looking glass, a woman who was supposed to be Victoria Camarei Reichourd yet who couldn't remember being anybody. Her brown hair was a tangled dark

153

mane that cascaded down her back and about her shoulders and nearly covered her breasts. She had smudges of dirt or mud on one cheek and temple, and her face had lost all of its color. Her pallor was nearly as white as the blouse she still wore, though its natural color was only sparsely visible through the splatters of mud, grit, and ugly brown water stains that covered it.

A knock sounded at her door. Soft as it was, Tori jumped and whirled around, startled and afraid. "Who . . . ?" The word came out as little more than a strangled gasp. She coughed to clear her throat. "Who is it?"

"It's Suda, Miss . . . Tori."

Tori sagged in relief. "Come in, Suda."

The door opened and the maid entered. Her eyes were wide with alarm. "Hannah said something was wrong. Can I get you anything, Miss . . . Tori?"

Tori noticed that Suda still hesitated each time she had to use her name, or rather the name Tori had instructed her to use. But why was it so difficult? Wasn't that what she'd always been called? Tori. Not Victoria. She turned to stare at her own reflection in the mirror again. The name felt right. She sighed. It was the only thing that did feel right, yet if Suda's reaction to it was to be considered, it wasn't.

She shook her head and turned back to the mirror. "No, I'm fine, Suda."

The girl started to go.

"No, wait," Tori said, turning in her seat again. "Maybe a bath. I think I'd like a bath. A very hot bath. And maybe some coffee."

Suda nodded. "I'll fetch both right away." She disappeared instantly, the door closing quietly behind her.

Tori began to release the laces of her mud-caked riding

154

shoes. Once the ankle-binding shoes had been discarded she wiggled her toes and rotated one foot from side to side, reveling in the sudden freedom. "They certainly aren't Nikes," she muttered, then froze. Her head jerked up and spun around so that once again she was facing her own reflection. "What are Nikes?"

Whatever they were, her mind was refusing to tell her any more. Tears of frustration stung the backs of her eyes. "I hate this," she snapped. "Why do I only remember these stupid little things that don't make any sense? Why can't I remember my life, damn it? Why?" Anger born of frustration burned within her. Tori jumped to her feet and tore at the hooks at her waist. The mud-stained skirt slid over her hips and dropped to the floor. She stepped from the heap of material, then bent to pick it up and tossed it across the chair before her dressing table. A movement in the opposite corner of the room caught her attention and Tori whirled, surprised and suddenly afraid again. Relief swept over her at discovering that it was only her reflection in the tall cheval mirror.

Except for the darkness of her hair she looked almost completely white, discounting the mud stains on the bottom ruffles of her pantalettes and the pale blue ribbon that zigzagged its way back and forth across her camisole to secure it around her midriff and breasts. Its shoulder straps were trimmed with tiny lace ruffles, as was its yoke and hem at her waist. The pantalettes were ruffled from her hips to her ankles.

"I look like a poor imitation of an undressed Scarlett O'Hara doll," Tori muttered. She turned away from the mirror, then stopped and looked back. "What in blazes is a Scarlett O'Hara doll?" she asked the image that stared back at her. But nothing more was forthcoming. She

155

sagged onto the edge of the bed and made no effort to stem the tears that filled her eyes. "Why can't I remember something worth remembering?" she cursed, slamming a fist down on the firm mattress. "Why, why, why?"

A soft knock on the door instantly brought her out of her self-pity.

The tall door opened and Suda entered, carrying two large buckets of steaming hot water. Another maid, one Tori didn't recognize, followed in her footsteps, and also carried two buckets of water. They disappeared through a doorway to the left of the tall armoire. It led to the dressing room.

The unknown maid immediately reappeared and hastened toward the door to the hall. Tori walked to the dressing room and peered in. Suda was busy pouring scents into the water and splashing it up into foamy white suds. She had already laid out several towels and a batiste wrapper. Tori entered the room and stood quietly waiting for her maid to finish.

The young girl straightened and turned toward Tori. "Your bath is ready Miss . . . Tori, and I'll have that coffee waiting in your bedchamber when you come out."

Tori nodded, but made no move to finish undressing.

Suda stared at her, as if waiting for something. Finally, Tori couldn't stand it any longer. She wanted to get into her bath and relax, and she wanted Suda to leave. "Is there something else, Suda? Did you want to say something?"

The girl looked shocked. "Oh, no, Miss Victoria. I was just waiting to help you undress."

"Undress?" Tori looked at her as if she'd just said she wanted to help her jump out a window. "I can undress myself."

"But I always help you undress. And then I wash your back and hair for you."

"Wash my . . . I don't usually wash my own hair?"

Suda shook her head. "No, ma'am. I always help you."

"Well, not this time," Tori said decisively. "I'm perfectly capable of washing my own hair, and I'm sure you have better things to do."

Suda remained rooted to the spot, her eyes full of puzzlement.

"Go on," Tori said, trying to make her tone light. "Take a break." Actually, she wanted to be alone. Her nerves were shot, her heart had beaten such a drumroll in the last few hours it was a miracle it could still beat at all, and her pulse still hadn't slowed to a normal rate.

"Take a break, Miss Tori?" Suda echoed.

"Yes. Go do whatever you want to do. Eat, take a nap, whatever." She ushered Suda toward the door. "You can come back and help me dress for dinner if you want."

Suda left quietly, though confusion at Tori's words was clearly etched on her face as she shuffled from the room.

Tori closed the dressing-room door, but waited until she heard the one leading from her bedroom into the hall close before turning back toward the green tin tub that sat on a raised dais in the center of the room. She quickly untied the camisole, shrugged it over her shoulders and tossed it on a nearby chair. The pantalettes fell to the floor as their waist hook was released, and she left them there. Her stockings immediately followed. Stepping onto the dais Tori lifted one leg over the tub's tall side and slipped her foot into the midst of the foamy white bubbles that covered the water's surface. Her toes met stinging hot water. Shifting her weight to that foot, she brought the other into the tub, a small hiss escaping her lips. The water was ex-

157

tremely hot, as the steam rising from within the bubbles attested to, but oh, it felt so good against her still aching muscles and icy flesh.

Tori slowly lowered the rest of her body into the water and then leaned against the tub's sloping back, slipping down so that her head lay on the scalloped design that trimmed the rim. She closed her eyes and let the water caress and soothe her, let its heat work relaxing miracles on the tension that had held her body in such a tight grip. A soft sigh of contentment whispered from her lips, and as she inhaled deeply, the scent of jasmine enveloped her.

Sleep came over her quietly, easily, consuming her consciousness like a slowly drifting fog rolling over an unsuspecting landscape. It cajoled her into its womb, offering peace, comfort, and warmth; and Tori succumbed without hesitation.

The body rode the gently swirling waters until it floated mere inches from the bank where she stood. His outstretched arm reached toward her, and his fingers beneath the murky water strained to touch the toe of her shoe. Bits of swamp grass, leaves, and bark chips clung to his clothes and moved about the surface of the black water. An eerie silence surrounded her, as if every creature of the bayou was holding its breath, standing motionless, watching, and waiting for her to do something. Trembling in fear, Tori forced herself to look down at his lifeless face. The once golden pallor of life was now, in death, a pasty, almost translucent gray. His hair was littered and tangled with debris, and his mouth hung agape, as if in a silent scream or a denial of whatever had happened to rob him of life. The body moved slowly, the water causing it to turn horizontally to where Tori stood, transfixed. Her eyes met his, saw the vacuum of emptiness within their dark gray pools, the absence of spirit. Unable to help herself, Tori screamed, over and over. Heart-rending screams tore from the depths of her soul, ripped her senses to shreds, and left her teetering on the brink of sanity.

Suda and Guy reached the door to Tori's room at the same time. Suda had covered her dress with a muslin apron, and it, as well as her hands and face, were half-covered with flour from helping her mother in the kitchen. She stared at Guy in embarrassment, not for her own attire but for his. Having returned early from the fields and deciding to bathe before dinner, he was clothed only in a black and burgundy brocade robe that reached to his mid thighs. Beads of water still clung to the dark hairs that covered his bare legs and chest, and his bare feet had left wet marks on the hall carpet behind him.

He threw open the door and rushed into Tori's room. Suda hung back in the hall, unsure of whether to follow. Guy looked around in puzzlement at the empty bedchamber. He turned back to Suda. "Where the hell is she?" he thundered.

Suda pointed toward the dressing-room door.

Guy stalked toward it, more concerned and alarmed than he wanted to be, and furious to have to acknowledge it. The door was slightly ajar. He pushed it open and strode into the dressing room, but stopped before taking more than two steps inside.

Twelve

A soft whimper escaped her lips and shook the golden shoulders that rested against the tub's sloping back. Guy stood rooted a few steps away, the open door at his back, his breath trapped in his throat. A hard, burning knot began to coil deep within his stomach. He stared at the lovely creature before him and felt his restraint and self-control quickly deserting him. Never had he been able to deny that his wife was one of the most beautiful women he had ever seen on the face of the earth, yet since the accident, something about her had changed. It wasn't so much a physical change really, and yet it was. She seemed softer somehow, almost fragile and delicate, and yet strong at the same time; but it was a gentle strength, and she had traits he would never before have attributed to Victoria.

The dying rays of the afternoon sun shone through the lone window of the dressing room, filtered and softened by the heavy lace panels that hung before the glass panes. Her golden brown hair hung down her back and spread like silken threads in wild disarray across her shoulders, the sunlight turning it to strands of sable, her shoulders to planes of shimmering amber. As he watched, her arms rose from the mist of white foam that hid the rest of her body from his view. She covered her face, shuddered, and began to weep into the cradle of her hands.

"I don't want to see any more," she murmured softly between sobs. "Please God, no more, no more. Don't make me see any more of this."

Guy took a step to his left, bringing himself farther into the room and into view of her profile. The saffron glow of the setting sun had begun to fill the room and played across the scene before him. It sprinkled her dark hair with glistening points of light, like tiny diamonds amid the wild curls, and turned the soft ivory mounds of breasts peeking out from the foamy white covering to golden swells of flesh.

Unaware of his presence, and still drowsy with sleep, Tori let her hands fall away from her face and slip once again into the now lukewarm water as her head lay against the tub's back. "No more," she murmured again. "No more." A stream of tears ran from both eyes, appearing from beneath the long, dark ruche of her lashes to course over her cheeks, thin trails of moisture turned silver by the sun's rays.

His first reaction to the scene had been scorn, followed by puzzlement and curiosity. Each had vanished quickly, to be replaced by the one emotion he wanted desperately to deny and could not: passion. It consumed him, choked him, and held him its prisoner, its slave. All the hunger of his past dreams, of his long-forgotten fantasies and vanquished hopes rose up to assault him, to conquer his good intentions and override his vacillations. He felt it in the pit of his stomach, in the depth of his chest, felt it invade every muscle, every fiber of his being, and knew he was lost to it, knew that to fight it would only prolong his

161

surrender but not prevent it. Like a man suddenly lost in a daze, or overcome by an unexplainable trance, Guy walked slowly toward the green tub, shedding the heavy robe as he moved and letting it fall quietly to the floor. He knelt behind her and slipped his arms over her shoulders, his hands disappearing into the foam of white bubbles, his fingers cupping the taut swell of her breasts.

The soothing touch of his hands on her flesh, of his thumbs rhythmically circling the rosey flesh of her taut nipples, chased away the last of Tori's nightmare and replaced it with a spark of desire. Her eyes fluttered open and she started to sit up in the tub, but the pressure of Guy's arms against her shoulders, his hands on her breasts, prevented this movement. Instead, she twisted around to face him.

"Oh, Guy," she cried softly, a new onslaught of tears filling her eyes. An ache, so devastating she felt as if it were tearing her apart, heated her insides. She slid her arms around his neck and pulled him toward her as a sob left her lips. The nightmare had been all too real, all too ghastly, but now she was awake and knew it was nothing more than a bad dream because he was with her, loving her, and she didn't have to be scared anymore, at least for a little while.

It was the last straw for Guy. If he had had any intention of pulling away from her, of escaping her web of seduction, it was gone. His hands plunged deeper into the warm, sudsy water, his arms wrapped around her and he rose to his feet, lifting her with him. He held her tightly, her slender, wet body pressed to his hot damp one. Soap bubbles clung to her skin and slid slowly downward as she rose, curving, snaking bubbles of whiteness dripping from her arms onto his back and shoulders, dropping from her

162

breasts to slide within the dark, satiny mat of curls that covered his chest, and sliding from her hips and legs to travel the muscular contours of his limbs until finally reaching the floor and settling into tiny puddles.

His lips sought hers in a savage capture of her mouth, in a kiss that was at once a languorous caress and a plundering conquest. Her lips parted willingly, inviting his ravishment. He took instant advantage, his tongue plunging into her mouth, a twisting, caressing sliver of fire that explored every cavern, every secret hollow, tasting her honeyed sweetness, taking what she had to offer, and demanding more.

And more she gave, pressing her body ever closer to his, tightening the arms that wrapped around his neck, until there was not a hint of space or a shred of light between them. Her lips returned his kiss, her tongue matched his hungry exploration with one of her own, fire touching fire, passion inciting passion.

His hands had begun a featherlight exploration of her body, circling one taut breast, his thumb teasing the pebbled nipple with a few rhythmic strokes, then moving to slide tormentingly down the curve of her ribs, to dip within the curve of her waist and then over the subtle arch of her hip.

Her body melted farther into his with each new touch, wanting nothing more than to be possessed by him, to know and savor the ritual that would make them one.

A strangled sound of unbearable desire filled her throat, and she pressed against him, her own hands sliding up and down the length of his body, her mouth tasting his flesh.

The evidence of his hunger for her pressed against her stomach, a hard, pulsing rod of flesh that ached to know

163

her touch, to know the sweet torment of being inside her again.

Suddenly, with an abruptness that startled her, Guy tore his mouth from hers, and his hands disappeared from her body. He stepped away from her, and Tori nearly cried out in despair. He couldn't leave her now. He couldn't!

She looked up at him as he towered over her. Sunlight filtered through the window behind him, through the delicately woven lace panels to create a patchwork of golden pink light on his body and glisten within the thick, dark strands of his ebony hair. Unconsciously she let her eyes drop to the wide shoulders that seemed a rippling landscape of muscles which continued down into the long, well-honed arms that hung at his sides. His chest was a broad wall of strength, its muscular plane covered with a thick sprinkling of black hairs that came together in a vee at the inward curve. It dropped in a thin line past a taut stomach to culminate in the tangled patch of dark hair that surrounded the protruding, hard shaft of his arousal.

Tori reached a hand toward him, and the tip of her fingers brushed softly, gently, over the sensitive head of that straining rod of flesh.

Another barrier within him crumbled at her touch as the fire of passion swept through him. With sudden swiftness Guy bent down and swooped her up into his arms, cradling her against his chest. "If you're going to reject me, Victoria, do it now," he said, his eyes riveted to hers. "Because in a few minutes I can't promise I'll heed your words."

She tightened her arms around his neck and leaned forward to press her lips to the curve of his bare shoulder. "Make love to me, Guy," she said softly. "Those are my words."

She felt the ferocity of his need as it crescendoed with

this response and his arms tightened around her. Turning, he carried her across the room and, pausing for one brief second beside the bed as if giving her a last chance to deny him in spite of his earlier words, lowered her onto the coverlet.

She lifted her arms toward him, and with the fluid grace of a great cat, he lay down beside her.

Tori's arms slipped around his neck, welcoming him. His lips captured hers, his probing tongue filled her mouth, and his hands roamed her bared flesh.

He kissed her slowly, taking his time, allowing himself to enjoy, for the first time in longer than he could remember, the assuaging relief her touch brought his body and mind. She writhed beside him, her legs entwined with his, and his satisfaction that her desire had become as strong as his fueled the gnawing hunger that had uncoiled within him.

She snuggled tighter against him, and her stomach pressed against the rigid maleness that jutted proudly from between his legs.

His lips moved from hers as his head rose. Eyes dark with passion stared down at her, assessing, questioning, and for one brief moment, one flash of time that was so quickly gone she wasn't sure it had even been there, Tori thought she saw a glimmer of mockery in his gaze. Then his lips curved in a smile that tugged at her heart, and no other thought filled her mind or heart but that she wanted to be possessed by him, to truly be his wife, and know his love.

She had no memory of the other times he had taken her, the other nights they had shared their bodies and feelings, but she would remember this night always, for to her it would always be the first time. Her body arched against his, begging for more, each caress a further intoxication of her senses.

Guy lowered his head and pressed his lips to the smooth valley of flesh between her breasts. His tongue slid teasingly over sensitized skin to which the heady fragrance of her violet-scented bath clung, and the honeyed taste of her flesh stoked his already burning desires.

Tori trembled with pleasure, and then responded convulsively, hungrily, as his lips found one breast and closed over its hardened nipple. His tongue turned to a blaze of flame that flicked, teased, and burned as he moved from one breast to the other.

With each touch, each stroke, a whole new plethora of sensations assailed Tori and left her hungering for more.

At a soft whimper from her, his mouth reclaimed hers, and his hands slipped from her breasts to brush lightly down the curve of her waist and across the taut landscape of her stomach. When his fingers slipped between her inner thighs and touched the delicate fold of flesh that hid the core of her need, Tori gasped, a bolt of raw desire, like lightning, flashing through her. She twisted against him, and his hand gently nudged her legs apart, silently urging her to open herself to him.

With a soft moan of pleasure trembling within her throat, Tori did as he indicated, her mind, her senses, her entire being now nearly lost to the tight ache of anticipation that held her in its grip.

She felt his fingers move between the silken pleats of flesh, the juice of her desire spreading over him, coating his fingers as they probed and explored. His thumb circled the small nub of her sensitivity, brushed over it and repeatedly caressed it, while his finger delved inside of her, each thrust causing a shudder of ecstasy to wrack Tori's body.

Never had he felt so out of control yet in control at the same time. His body was trembling with the force of his need for her, every emotion, every yearning and desire that he had kept under tight rein, under strict control or denial for the past several years was now suddenly unleashed. He might never again know the taste of her passion, he might never again want to, but this time, at this moment, he wanted to make her desire him as much, if not more, than he desired her, to make her realize that she belonged to him, and that no other man, no matter who, could love her as he could.

Dragging his lips from hers, Guy growled softly, "I need you now, Victoria."

Tori looked up into those brilliant gray eyes through the joyous blur of tears that filled her own. "Please," she whispered, the softly muted plea barely more than a breath of air from her lips. It felt so right being in his arms she couldn't imagine ever wanting to be anywhere else, or why she ever had been anywhere else.

Please, yes . . . or please, no. He didn't know how she had meant the word. He closed his eyes and tried to gain control of the raging torrent of desire that had gripped his body. Regardless of what she had done to him in the past, regardless of his earlier threat that he wouldn't stop, he wouldn't make love to a woman who didn't want him. He wouldn't rape her.

Her mouth brushed against his, and he felt her tongue slide, hot, moist, and hesitant, across his bottom lip.

He needed no further invitation, and with a deep groan of both defeat and conquest rumbling in his chest, Guy rose to cover her body with his. Her arms slid around his neck and her mouth pressed hotly against his as her tongue pushed into his mouth and fueled him with her hunger.

He plunged into her then, and she felt herself fill with him, the warmth of her inviting, aching flesh surrounding the invading shaft of his hard flesh. Her hips rose up to meet him, and he thrust deep within her, pulled back, and entered again, and again, and again. She writhed joyfully beneath him, matching his rhythm, rising toward him when he drove into her, melding with him, fusing her body to his, until finally, they moved as one.

Tori was overwhelmingly conscious of everything about him: the fragrance of musky spice that permeated his hair, the faint hint of horses, leather, and tobacco that clung to his skin, the glistening, slick sheen of perspiration that covered the bronzed range of corded muscles across his shoulders and back; his long legs, sinewy and puissant framed hers, and his hands, embodied with might caressed her with infinite gentleness. But most of all, she was aware of his strength and virility, of the power contained within him, and the tight rein with which he controlled it.

Suddenly, for the first time since the accident, she felt safe, loved, wanted, but above all, at home. This was where she belonged, where she had always belonged; in this man's arms, in his bed, and in his life. Perhaps before the carriage accident she hadn't realized it, but she did now and nothing or no one was ever going to take this away from her. With that thought in her mind, Tori gave herself up completely to the erotic abandonment that his lovemaking had infused within her. Her legs entwined around his buttocks, her hands roamed his back, and her mouth returned his ravaging kiss with fiery urgency.

Suddenly, like the onslaught of a tidal wave, or the rolling assault of a summer storm, a rush of sensations indescribably delicious, intense, and rapturous swept her into a whirlpool of soul-routing pleasure.

Feeling her release, Guy gave one final, deep thrust and spilled his seed within her, his body wracked by trembling as he, too, delved within the maelstrom of ecstasy that had consumed Tori.

Guy rolled onto his side, leaned the weight of his upper torso on his bent arm, and stared down at her. She looked so peaceful as she slept, so beautiful and . . . he smiled ruefully, so innocent. As he thought of nothing more than the physical enjoyment being inside of her had brought him, his eyes moved appreciatively over her body.

She lay on her back, long tendrils of her dark hair spread across the white pillow, one arm raised so that her hand, with fingers curled slightly, lay near her face. Her breasts were perfect swells, her waist tiny, her hips slender yet curved just enough, and her legs seemed to go on forever. Guy's gaze roamed freely, enjoying the wanton exploration, but as it traveled back up the long trail of her thigh, it suddenly stopped.

He frowned. Why was her flesh tinged slightly golden? Though he had noticed it before, his mind suddenly registered the oddness of it with abrupt clarity, even as his body surged with the fire of renewed passion. Victoria had always maintained a porcelain quality to her skin, abhorring even the slightest evidence that she had remained outdoors unprotected from the sun for too long. He ignored the throbbing hardness of his need swelling beneath the sheet that draped his hip and instead forced his eyes to move over her again, more quickly this time confirming what he had already known. Just above the small triangle of darkness at the apex of her thighs, his roving gaze paused again. The flesh there was white, as was a thin white line of flesh that ran from there over each hip. His eyes moved to her breasts. Both creamy white, like a magnolia, but in stark contrast to the rest of her body.

He wanted desperately to touch them, to hold her breasts in his hands, to cover each rosey nipple with his mouth, caress the pebbled flesh with his lips and flick the taut peaks with his tongue. He tried to shake the impulse away and pushed himself up from the mattress to stare down at her. What had she done? What did this coloring of her flesh mean? And suddenly, with that question, with that revelation, came others, some he had noticed and ignored, others he had only that moment become aware of. Her speech. He had mentioned it to the doctor, but Benjamin had provided him with no acceptable explanation. Why had her speech changed so much? She no longer talked with the lilting, almost exaggerated drawl he had almost come to hate hearing. Instead her words were slightly clipped, spoken quickly, and her tone didn't seem to echo the antagonism he had gotten so used to ignoring.

He felt an urge to reach out to her, to reaffirm that this person he had made love to only a few hours before was really lying next to him. She was his wife, Victoria, and yet she wasn't. A shadow flitted across Guy's face. It was as if, since the accident, Victoria had become another person. That thought stopped him, only to be followed by one he had never thought would come to him; she had become the woman he had always wanted her to be, the woman he had thought, all those years ago, that he had married.

He stared into the darkness. Was it possible she had really changed that much? That she was actually a different person now?

Tori stirred then, drawing Guy's attention, and he quickly discarded the ridiculous notions that had been going through his head. He was being maudlin, trying to fantasize her into something she wasn't. Obviously this was just another of her schemes, another ploy to get into his confidence. And he'd fallen for it. As had happened so many times during the past few months when he'd least expected it, an image of Victoria and Darin, their naked bodies entwined, flitted into his mind. Guy slid off the bed and stood looking down at her. She'd gotten him into her bed, and he had to admit, there had been something about their lovemaking, a delicious, soul-stirring quality, that had never been there before. He took a step away from the bed, almost as if in fear. But it wouldn't work. He was not going to fall into one of her traps again.

Moving almost stealthily in the darkness of the room so as not to make any noise, Guy found his robe on the floor and slipped into it. Taking care to close the door behind him quietly, he stepped into the hallway. It was a long, silent cavern filled with moonlight that streamed in from the tall window at each end, yet it was also a maze of shadows and dark crevices.

From one of those dark crevices, an inky, shadowed alcove set in the exact center of one wall that ran the length of the long hallway, dark eyes stared out and watched Guy step from Tori's room toward his own.

Thirteen

Tori woke slowly, forcing her eyelids to flutter open and her body to rouse from the contented comfort of deep sleep. She yawned contentedly. This had been the first good night of rest she'd had since the accident. It was not yet morning, she knew, as the heavy drapes were still drawn across the tall windows and only the palest stream of moonlight seeped into the room through the thin slit of space left where the thick damask folds met. Desire rekindled instantly within the recesses of her body as memories of her lovemaking with Guy warmed her and resparked the passion that had been satisfied only hours before.

She rolled onto her side, wanting to snuggle against him, needing to feel the ironlike circle of his arms around her again, the steely length of his body pressed tightly to hers. Her leg moved across the mattress, unhampered, her hand slid freely over the cool sheet, and Tori sat up, stunned. She stared down at the empty portion of bed beside her. A lone strand of ebony hair lay within a slight indentation on the white pillow next to her own, the only indication that she had not dreamed his presence, that Guy had really been there and had held her in his arms.

She stared down at the pillow, at the single black curl. He *had* been there, if her mind had any doubt of that, her body did not. She could still feel the caressing explorations of his hands on her flesh, the glorious melding of his body with hers, the pleasure that had been such sweet torment as to be almost unbearable. Tori slid a hand from beneath the covers and ran her fingers lightly across her mouth. Their tenderness was further, though unneeded, evidence of the kisses that had branded both her lips and soul with Guy Reichourd's mark.

She lay back against the pillow and looked up through the shadows at the canopy's *ciel de lit*. It was a sunburst pattern, its center a large, flat, silk-covered button, and its rays folds of the same blue silk damask fabric that adorned each window. But even though her gaze remained riveted on the gathered material, her thoughts were elsewhere. Their lovemaking had been wonderful, and yet, as she thought of what everyone had said she was supposed to be like, of what the relationship had been between husband and wife, she couldn't shake the feeling that it shouldn't have been, and that it shouldn't have happened at all . . . not if what they said of her past, of their past, was true.

Guy had told her that on the night of her accident he'd announced he was going to seek a divorce. It had been only natural to assume, then, that he no longer loved her. He had even stated as much. And everyone had told her she didn't love Guy, she'd only married him for his money and for the prestige of being mistress of Shadow Oaks. Tori felt a swell of frustration fill her breast. So why didn't she believe what they'd said? And if it were all true, why now did she want nothing more than the love of her husband? That thought brought with it the memory of Darin lying naked, arrogant, and uninvited in her bed. A sense

173

of foreboding swept over her and dragged her farther from the warm happiness with which she'd awakened, leaving her trembling.

Somehow she had to find out the truth; about herself, about Darin, and about Guy. She closed her eyes and tried to will her body to relax, but her limbs remained stiff with tension. Suddenly, images from her dream swept into her mind. Tori resisted the urge to open her eyes and terminate them. Instead, she tried to concentrate on them, to make them clearer. Whose lifeless body was it she saw floating atop the murky water, its sightless eyes staring up at the sky? Was it Guy and Darin's brother, John? Had she witnessed his death? Was she reliving a scene that she had been a part of? She shuddered.

Or was the corpse Guy's? Was it his fate she was seeing? His murder by Darin? The image suddenly faded and disappeared. Defeated, Tori opened her eyes and sat up. A cold shiver snaked its way up her spine and Tori wrapped her arms around her torso in an effort to thwart it. In spite of how she felt about him now, was she still a danger to Guy because of her previous involvement with Darin? Or was she the entire danger? Somehow she had to thwart Darin's plan. But how?

Tears filled her eyes. He had come to her when she'd cried out during her nightmare. He had stayed to comfort her and had ended up making love to her. The intensity of his need, of his wanting of her was evident. But did he love her? Was there any hope, after everything she had done to him, that he could still find love in his heart for her? Somehow she had to make him love her again, because she knew now, with a certainty beyond any she'd ever felt, that she couldn't live without Guy in her life.

Tori rose from the bed and walked to the window. With

a sweep of her hand she pushed back the drapery and slipped its heavy folds behind the gold, leaf-shaped hook attached to the wainscotting. Her gaze moved over the sweeping landscape of Shadow Oaks. He'd said that she didn't love him, that she had married him for only two reasons, one of which was to become mistress of this grand plantation, one of the largest in Louisiana. So why now did it mean so little to her when compared with his love?

A movement in the gardens below her window caught her attention. She leaned toward the glass and squinted slightly in an effort to see through the darkness.

Guy stood at the tall window in his study and stared out at the dimly lit landscape of Shadow Oaks. The morning sun would be at least another hour in rising, its pale rays now visible as only the feeblest of light on the distant horizon. He didn't know how long he had been standing there. An hour, perhaps more. The room had been dark when he'd entered, and he had not bothered to light a lamp or even a candle. His fingers loosely cupped the glass of brandy he'd poured himself but had not yet bothered to taste. A silent curse filled his mind. He had given in to the desires that had burned within him for the past several days, that had gnawed at his body like hungry animals, and he had expected that to be the end of it, had thought his body would be satiated of its lustful cravings. Instead, the need for her had deepened within him, and his mind was in turmoil. What was it about her that had suddenly aroused all of his old feeling for her? That had made him take leave of his senses and throw restraint to the winds?

He downed half of the brandy, set the tumbler on his desk, and took a cheroot from the crystal decanter that sat

175

toward one corner of the wide expanse of cherrywood. A flick of his wrist caused the tip of a lucifer to scrape across the heel of his boot, and the tiny match burst into flame, throwing a momentary cast of yellow-orange light over his face yet leaving the curves and hollows of that finely chiseled vista in shadow. Guy settled into the leather chair that sat behind his desk and turned toward the tall windows again. He let his eyes rest on the scene before him while his mind continued to contemplate the events of the night.

He couldn't fault her, exactly, for what had happened. She hadn't enticed him into her room with unspoken promises, nor had she lured him into her bed. He'd gone there willingly. Hell, if the truth be known, he'd gone there eagerly, hungrily. Guy inhaled deeply of the whiskey-soaked cheroot and watched for long, silent seconds as the tip of the simmering tobacco flared bright against the night. But hadn't it been her screams that had brought him to her? Cynical suspicion, long a companion in the years after his marriage to Victoria, loomed large and ugly. She had lied to him from the beginning. She had married him in order to become mistress of Shadow Oaks. Money, luxury, and social standing. Those were the things that mattered to Victoria. The only things. Love had no place in her heart. It never had, and he'd been foolish to think it ever did or would. The Reichourd fortune, that was all she'd ever wanted.

Memory of Victoria lying with Darin came back into his mind like a descending sword, swift and brutal, shattering what little calm and contentment he still clung to. Guy tossed down the last swallow of brandy left in the tumbler and stabbed out the end of the cheroot in a small silver tray that sat beside the decanter. His gray eyes had turned the color of a midnight storm. John had warned him against Victoria, against marrying her, but he'd refused to listen. Darin had coveted her since the moment Guy had brought her back to Shadow Oaks, but Guy had refused to believe anything could come of it. Even when he'd discovered she and Darin had known each other in Europe a year before she'd arrived in New Orleans, he had refused to believe, in spite of the rumors and Darin's leering remarks, that they had been anything more to each other than acquaintances. He poured himself another glass of brandy and returned to stand before the window. She had played each brother like a marionette and he'd been too blind to see because he hadn't wanted to. He'd told himself it was for the sake of the children that he'd endured her antics and schemes for so long, but deep down Guy knew it had been as much for himself. He had not wanted to admit how much of a fool he'd actually been.

So why had he succumbed to her again? Why, only a few hours ago and after all these years, had he lost all reason and sanity? All self-control and restraint? She had drawn him into one of her schemes again, and he had no idea what it was, though that it had something to do with his brother Darin, he had no doubt.

He closed his eyes and let the events of the past few days move through his mind, examining each, cataloging it, and trying to make sense of the entire picture. In some ways the Victoria he had found in the broken carriage was an entirely different woman from the one he had been living with for the past five years. Yet he knew that was impossible. She was the same person. He exhaled slowly. And yet she wasn't. For over five years she had treated him with contempt and indifference and had forbade him her bed. Now she was warm, compassionate, almost fragile, and more than willing to share both her bed and her body with him. But why? What was she up to?

Frustrated beyond all reason, Guy whirled and threw the brandy glass at the fireplace that graced the adjoining wall. The crystal tumbler struck the black marble surface and shattered. Glass flew about the room, raining down on tapestried settees, burgundy velvet chairs, tables, and the flowered Aubusson carpet that covered the floor.

She had somehow planned what had happened tonight. For days now her sweetness and smiles had tempted him, and if he hadn't gone to her tonight, it would have been tomorrow night, or the next. Seducing him was a calculated move in her game to entrap him. But into what? And did it involve Darin? Was the affair between his wife and brother merely that—an affair—or had they joined forces against him? Darin had killed John, of that Guy had no doubt. He had no proof, but as far as he was concerned, he didn't need any. John's body had never been found, it had simply been as if he had vanished off the face of the earth. But John had had no reason to voluntarily leave Shadow Oaks. Many, including Darin, had pointed an accusing finger at Guy, since he had inherited John's portion of the Reichourd holdings.

A stabbing pain in his stomach caused Guy's ruggedly aristocratic features to twist in a momentary grimace. Ben's medicine wasn't working, but he wasn't concerned with that problem at the moment. His thoughts returned to Victoria and his brother Darin. He didn't know what to believe anymore. Before the accident it had been simple, but now—he shook his head—now she was so different. Memories of her in his arms, her naked body writhing beneath his, matching him movement for movement, hunger for hunger, filled his mind and turned his body hard

178

and hot with renewed need. "Damn it!" he growled. Regardless of everything he knew about her, and everything he suspected, he wanted her again. She was a seductress, an enchantress who had weaved a spell over him, inciting his passions, and he was at a loss to explain how or why. It wasn't just her beauty. He had lived with that for five years and had maintained control over his physical needs . . . until now. The hand at his side clenched into a fist. In spite of all his misgivings, his suspicions and doubts, he wanted her, and the knowledge filled him with the bitter taste of defeat.

Pushing the window up, Guy unlatched the paneled jib door beneath it and stalked out onto the wide gallery that surrounded the house. Fury filled him. Why had he succumbed to her? And why did he still want her? "Why, damn it?" he snarled into the night. He moved down the shallow steps and walked along the narrow path that led to the formal gardens. He needed fresh air and time to think, time to be alone to try to figure out what her scheme was this time, and why he was so willing to fall into her trap again.

He paced the weaving pathways of the sprawling garden for over an hour, his brow nettled tightly, his mind moving from one event of the past few days to another, trying to find something to latch onto, some shred of reason for his feelings.

Dawn slipped silently over the horizon without Guy noticing. Its soft yellow light spread across the earth, vanquishing the night's shadows, warming everything in its path, and waking both the blossoms and the small animals who inhabited the garden.

Guy walked aimlessly, taking note of none of the changes wrought around him by the coming of the new day's light, or the fact that he was not the only one in the thickly foliaged gardens.

He cursed softly beneath his breath, as seemed lately to be a habit. There were no answers to the many questions that streamed through his mind, he realized. At least, no easy or ready ones. He could accept that fate, or some other miraculous force, had intervened and somehow caused the carriage accident to truly change his wife's personality. Or, he could believe that he had once again fallen victim to one of her machinations, been ensnared by a scheme so devious that no one, not even the doctor, could see through it this time. If he accepted the former possibility, might there be a chance for their marriage? Could they find the happiness, the love, he had always dreamed of and that they had never found before? Yet what if the latter was true? If he chose to dream, to hope, to chance, and was proven wrong . . . it could mean his life. And even though he might gamble on that, if he lost, what would become of the children?

With a long sigh, and having made no decision, Guy turned back toward the house. Nothing in life had proven easy since he'd brought Victoria to Shadow Oaks, but this was a tangle he would wish on no one.

For the entire time Guy had paced the gardens, more than an hour, Darin had slouched lazily against the massive trunk of one of the sprawling oak trees that bordered the manicured formal tract and watched. Long drapings of Spanish moss hung from the tree's gnarled and reaching limbs, creating a veiled curtain of gray whose tips swept the ground and whose folds offered inky shadows within

180

which a person could stand undetected. Darin's pale gray eyes had followed his older brother's movements, the hint of venom in their near translucent depths accentuated by the sneering upturn of his lips.

He watched Guy return to the house, and the sneer turned into a smile of sincere satisfaction. An almost joyful anticipation suddenly energized him as he reviewed, in his mind, the details of the plan he had devised to rid himself of the obstacles that stood between himself and fulfilling his ambition to become sole master of the Reichourd estates.

Long minutes after Guy had returned to the house, Darin remained standing beneath the tree, surveying what he'd always felt should have been his. The sun had risen high enough by now for the gardens to be brilliantly colored. The leaves of the oaks, myrtles, chestnuts, and willows glistened in varying shades of green, while the brilliant yellow black-eyed Susans, the red, pink, and white roses and azaleas, the purple iris, the white and orange jasmine, all spread their petals wide to capture every available ray of warmth and light. And beyond the gardens and the mesmerizing blanket of emerald lawn sat the house, situated like a crown on its slight rise of land, gleaming pristine white, its tall window shutters rivaling in color the green of the leathery leaves of the nearby magnolia trees. Only beneath the ancient oaks, within their concealing sheers of moss, did shadows linger, as if in defiance of the sun.

Darin's gaze moved to the row of windows set on the second story of the house and came to rest on one set in particular: Victoria's windows. The heavy drapes had finally been drawn, so that now only sheer white panels of lace hung before the glass panes. It was enough to obscure his view, but then, he didn't need to see in. He knew she was there, and he also knew she had not spent the night alone.

Fourteen

In spite of the anxiety that filled her, Tori forced herself to go slowly with her toilette. Suda patiently pulled three gowns from the armoire before she made a decision on which to wear. She finally chose a light muslin of pale yellow, its scooped neckline and pagoda sleeves, as well as the gathered flounces of fabric that draped over both hips, trimmed with a short ruche of white Valenciennes lace. She was beginning to get used to the long, ruffled pantalettes, the massive petticoats, and even the cumbersome hoop-cage that made her feel like a walking bell, but the corset Suda kept pulling from the armoire and trying to get her to wear was another matter altogether. She'd tried it once since the accident, the first day she'd gotten up, found it an almost impossible task to breathe with the contraption binding her ribs, and refused to even consider wearing it again, much to Suda's chagrin. How women stood those whalebones sticking into their flesh, and their ribs being crushed together, she'd never understand. The design of the corset was masochistic, and the wearing of it seemed archaic, yet she knew the undergarment was in

183

fashion to the point of it being considered improper for a woman to be attired without one. But she didn't care.

It had taken three tries to finally feel satisfied with her hair. She had had Suda brush it and tie it at her nape with a ribbon, and then had decided against that style. The second coif had been a mass of curls piled on her crown. She hadn't liked that either. Finally, brushing it loose again, Suda had swept up the sides and tied them with a ribbon high on her crown, leaving the back cascading loosely and the top and front fluffed softly. A touch of rose petal to her lips and cheeks had given her just the right amount of color.

Guy was just crossing the foyer as Tori moved down the wide staircase. He glanced up at her, with no intention to linger, and found himself instantly mesmerized and suddenly in no hurry to get to his study. She looked more breathtaking than he had ever seen her. Lustrous strands of rich, earth-tone waves cascaded over her shoulders, at once complementing and highlighting the soft golden pallor of her skin. Guy was still puzzled over the sun-kissed flesh, and how it had occurred so suddenly, but at the moment the puzzle was one that his mind refused to dwell on. A tremulous smile curved her lips, and uncertainty flashed from the blue depths of her eyes, furthering the impression of fragility and innocence. The voluminous folds of the yellow gown swayed gently, the movement seeming somewhat seductive, as she descended the stairs toward where Guy stood.

She neared him, and their gazes locked. Silence hung thick in the spacious entryway, and though he remained stoically in place and silent, Guy was painfully conscious of the need to possess her that again simmered within him.

Tori faltered slightly on the last step, the intensity of

Guy's gaze unnerving her. She had expected, hoped for, a warm greeting from him, especially after what they had shared only hours before. Instead she was being met by a stone wall. An icy stone wall, yet one that still had the power to unnerve her severely. Even as he stared up at her, the light at his back leaving his patrician features partially shadowed and emphasizing the wide breadth of his shoulders, Tori felt the arousing effect of his presence, and her pulses quickened. Earlier, in her room, she'd worked it all out and had known exactly how she was going to approach him, exactly what she was going to say to him; but now all of the carefully planned words and entreaties disappeared from her mind. Regardless of what they had shared the previous night, now, staring down into those steel gray eyes, Tori knew with a sinking feeling that he would not believe anything she had to say. Swearing that she remembered nothing of their life before the accident, that she did love him, that Darin meant nothing to her and planned to murder Guy—he would accept all of it as lies, because as everyone kept insisting, one of the things she did best was lie. Yet somehow she had to find a way to make him listen, to make him believe—before it was too late.

But if Tori hoped Guy would break the strained silence that had developed between them, her hoping was in vain; Guy was too busy trying to decipher the myriad emotions that had erupted within him to worry about mere words. Fear and apprehension urged him to demand that she leave Shadow Oaks instantly, that very morning, that very instant if possible, while other emotions, ones he wished he could ignore, urged him to sweep her into his arms, to capture her lips with his and kiss her until she could think of nothing else, until she could want nothing else. Yet he stood frozen, rooted to the spot, staring at her as if suddenly helpless.

Tori took a deep breath and stepped from the last stair, bringing herself within three feet of where Guy stood. A sense of disappointment crept over her at his coolness. The man who had swept her from the warm cocoon of her bath, who had comforted her through the aftereffects of her nightmare, then used his body to carry her to a realm of ecstasy like none she could remember visiting before, was nowhere in evidence. She stared into his eyes and searched his shuttered face, but the persona Guy had assumed held no hint of the dark lover she had lain with only hours before.

What had happened? What had turned him so aloof? He had left her bed sometime during the night, after their lovemaking . . . but where had he gone? Was there another woman? Tori remembered her first impression of the boy in the stables, Robert. If Darin had slept with the women in the slave quarters, wasn't it also possible that Guy did? Especially if it were true she had kept him from her bed for the past several years, as he'd claimed? Suddenly questions she had never given thought to loomed in her mind. Could that be what had happened between them? Had she turned away from him, rejected him, because he had slept—was perhaps still sleeping—with one of the slaves?

Unable to stand the silence between them any longer, Guy finally found his voice. "I was just on my way to the study, to do the books."

His words pulled Tori from her gloomy speculations. She forced a smile to her lips. They had to talk, she was convinced of that, and now was as good a time as any. Hopefully she wouldn't lose what little courage she was

186

struggling to maintain. "I'd hoped we could breakfast together."

"I've already eaten." His words were curt and hard, and not at all what he wanted to say to her, but he'd thought it over carefully for the past few hours, and it was the way it had to be. The only way. He just couldn't allow himself to believe her, to become ensnared within her web again, no matter how enticing it seemed.

"Would you at least join me for coffee?" Tori persisted. She could feel the frantic beat of her heart as both anticipation and fear lodged there.

His first instinct was to decline, to get away from her as quickly as possible. And he would have, if Martin hadn't appeared on the stairs behind her at just that moment. The boy's young face, resembling hers, hardened as he looked down at his mother, and Guy noticed the boy's hands clench into fists before he began to descend the staircase.

Tori saw Guy's gaze stray from hers and heard the slight fall of footsteps on the stairs behind her. She stiffened, and then instantly remembered that Darin was gone. Smiling again, she turned. "Martin, what perfect timing. I was just going to breakfast. We can talk."

"I'm not hungry." His face had a surly cast, and his gaze gleamed with distaste. He began to brush past her.

"Martin."

The boy stopped at Guy's voice, and the hardness immediately left his eyes. "Yes, sir?"

"You need to eat breakfast, son. If you prefer, you can have Hannah serve you in the kitchen with Moses."

"I'd like that," Martin said. He threw a scathing glance at Tori and then quickly descended the stairs past her. "Is Uncle Darin home today?" he said as he approached Guy.

187

"I believe he's gone to Baton Rouge for a few weeks," Guy answered.

Martin nodded and a look closely resembling relief came over his features. He crossed the foyer quickly and disappeared through the door that led into the warming kitchen.

A flicker of pain struck Tori's heart, yet something about it bothered her. It didn't feel like the pain of a mother who had lost her son's love, but more the pain of rejection. Could loss of her memory obscure or camouflage her true feelings toward her own children? Tori slowly turned toward the dining room. Martin hated her, that was obvious. But why? Because before the accident she had rejected Guy? Were her son and husband so close that her son would choose Guy over his own mother? Guy held a chair away from the table for her, and pressing a hand to the huge folds of her gown, Tori sat down.

Guy settled into a chair at the head of the table, just around the table's corner from her own. From a small silver pitcher he poured a generous dollop of cream into her coffee cup and then, lifting a larger server, filled both cups with hot coffee.

Tori stared at him in confusion. "Why did you put cream in my coffee?"

Guy looked at her as if she'd just asked him why he'd gotten dressed that morning. "You always take your morning coffee *au lait.*"

She shook her head. "I prefer it black, like yours."

He stared at her for several seconds, so long that Tori thought he was going to ignore her comment altogether. Then, just as she was about to do it herself, Guy retrieved a clean cup from beside the silver server, poured coffee into it, and set it before her.

"Thank you." She picked up the cup and sipped the hot coffee. Her nose instantly crinkled in distaste. "It's bitter."

Guy frowned and picked up his own cup. The coffee had been fine earlier. He sipped slowly, replaced his cup on its saucer and looked back at Tori. "It tastes fine to me."

"But it's so . . . so"—she searched for the right description—"so sharp tasting?"

"Victoria, are you trying to tell me that you don't even find the taste of coffee familiar?" Guy said, his voice hard, his tone unbelieving.

She heard the disbelief in his tone and bristled. She was getting just the tiniest bit tired of his overbearing attitude. Why couldn't he always be gentle and warm as he'd been last night? But then, maybe last night was nothing more to him than what he had earlier claimed it would be if he came to her bed: the satisfying of his physical needs. She returned his derisive glare. "No, Guy, I don't find the taste familiar. In fact, I rather dislike it. Especially black."

"I told you, *au lait* is your usual style."

She allowed him to push the creamed coffee back in front of her and, picking up the cream pitcher, poured another generous dollop into her coffee. A quick sip confirmed her suspicion. "I don't much care for it that way either. It's still bitter."

He took a long swallow of his own coffee before answering. "Since we are talking about familiarities, Victoria, let me ask you a question. When did you go out in the sun?"

"The sun?" Her brow pulled together as she failed to understand his words. What did going out in the sun have to do with familiarities? She shook her head. "I don't understand. I've been walking in the garden, if that's what

189

you mean. And I did go out on horseback the other day. So what?"

"The night of the opera your flesh was as white as alabaster, Victoria, which is the way you always insisted it should be. If you had been sun-touched that day I assume you could have partially accomplished the whiteness with rice powder, but"—he shrugged, then continued—"but now your skin is golden, very golden. You have obviously been out in the sun for more than just a few minutes, or even hours, yet it was that way right after the accident. So, I'll ask you again; when did you go out in the sun? And how did it happen so quickly?"

Tori looked down at her arms and then at the swell of breast revealed above the scooped neckline of her gown as if to confirm his words on the tone of her flesh. "I . . . I don't know." She looked back at him. "Is it important?"

"Only so far as it is unusual, as is the sudden clip to your speech. Is this a new style, Victoria? Or just another part of one of your schemes?" A sly smile curved his lips and one dark brow cocked smartly.

From everything she'd learned she knew Guy had reason to be suspicious of her, to dislike her; nevertheless, his attitude was getting tiresome, and her restraint was a bit weak. "I know you won't believe me, but there is no scheme."

"No scheme," he echoed, reminding himself again of what she had been like before, of what she most likely was still like, and of her involvement with his brother. It was the only way he could keep the hard edge to his voice, keep his passions cooled. "You're right, Victoria, I don't believe you. And I'm getting tired of this charade. Whatever you're up to, whatever you've got planned, it won't work. I warned you of that more than once, but consider this warning again."

Tori counted to ten. "I'm not up to anything, Guy." She sighed, her anger abruptly defused by a sweeping sense of defeat. Nothing she could say would get through to him, she knew that now. And she also knew, in that instant, that if Guy were to survive Darin's plans, it was going to be up to her to protect him, though how she was going to protect someone who wanted nothing to do with her except in bed was a problem she had no solution for, at least at the moment. "I'm sorry if you find my unfamiliarity with things inconvenient, Guy. I, personally find it a lot more than inconvenient, I find it downright frustrating and un-explainable. Everything about my life seems strange, in-cluding having you as a husband. No, that's wrong," she quickly amended. "Having a husband at all seems strange. I feel as if this isn't really my life, as if I'm not the person everyone says I am, yet I know that's ridiculous. I'm Vic-toria Reichourd, that's obvious from looking at that portrait in the foyer and then in the mirror, but I don't feel like Victoria Reichourd. In fact, I don't feel like anyone."

"You ordered Suda to call you Tori."

"I requested she call me Tori."

"You've never gone by any name other than Victoria."

Tori inhaled deeply and let the air slowly slip out through her lips. "I can't explain that. All I know is that the name Victoria doesn't seem exactly right. I mean, it's right but it's not. Victoria is not comfortable. Tori is. It's about the only thing that is. I don't feel that room upstairs has anything of me in it. My clothes seem alien, and some are too snug, like my shoes. I walk around in this house, on the grounds, and feel like a stranger, as if I've never been here before."

"But you have."

"Yes, obviously I have, but I don't remember."

"Convenient, you must admit."

The taut rein with which she had struggled to hold her temper in check suddenly snapped. Enough was enough. Tori bolted out of her chair. The whalebone hoop-cage beneath the voluminous folds of her skirt abruptly popped back into shape and pushed against the chair. It teetered momentarily on its slender, curved legs, then toppled backward, crashing loudly atop the hardwood floor.

Both Tori and Guy ignored the chair and glared at one another.

"No, it's not convenient, Guy. It's damned annoying, and as a matter of fact, so are you."

"So you've said a few dozen times before."

Tori trembled with rage. How in the world was she supposed to get through to a man who saw only what he wanted to see? She wanted to slap the self-righteously smug smile off of his face. At the same time she wanted to kiss him, and lose herself within the powerful circle of his arms. Neither was a viable choice. She lay her hands palm down on the table and leaned over until her face was only inches from his. "All right, Guy, I give up. I'm tired of trying to convince you I'm telling the truth, but if you believe nothing else I say, at least believe this; Darin is going to try to kill you." There, she'd said it.

If she hadn't been certain she was looking down at Guy Reichourd, the murderous gleam that came into his eyes at her words would have caused her to think it was Darin at the table.

He had known there was a scheme, he just hadn't known what it was. Now he at least had an idea, sketchy as it was. He had tried his damnedest to believe the best of his brother. It had been difficult most of the time, but he'd tried. That is, up until the moment he'd caught Darin with

192

Victoria. Memory of that scene had been burned into his mind, and on his heart, but even if it hadn't, even if somehow he had chosen to block it out as if it had never happened, Darin wasn't about to let him forget. He had taunted him, offering insinuating remarks almost daily, especially if anyone else was around. And there were other things. Darin took no interest in the daily operations of Shadow Oaks, claiming that since it had passed from John to Guy, why should he bother? But he found no hesitation in spending the Reichourd money. That he was quite adept at. One of his favorite pastimes was visiting the Quarter's casinos, and sometimes the less respectable houses on Magazine. Even after John's disappearance Guy had told himself repeatedly that he was being ridiculous in his suspicions. Sleeping with a brother's wife, refusing to share the responsibilities of work, even spending lavishly, and foolishly were undesirable traits, but murder?

Much as he'd tried to deny his suspicions, he hadn't been able to discount them. His long, black lashes closed slowly over his eyes, momentarily blocking Tori's sight of the gray pools that had turned black with suppressed rage.

She shuddered as she watched him, regretful now that she'd said anything at all. She had hoped to jar him from his complacency, to shake the walls he had obviously, and hastily, erected around his emotions since they had been together, and it hadn't worked. Instead all she'd done was deepen his suspicion and dislike of her.

Guy fixed her with his gaze, a riveting glare that pinioned her in place and seemed to bore through her flesh, straight into her soul.

"And what is your role in this grand scheme, Victoria?" He sneered. "Are your instructions to lure me to a certain spot where Darin is waiting? Entice me to your bed again

193

when Darin is home, wait until I'm asleep and then allow him into the room to slip a knife into my heart? Or perhaps something a bit more simple, such as poison mixed in my food?"

Tori was seized by such unadulterated outrage at his accusations that she was, for a few seconds, utterly speechless. "Why you . . . you . . . you insufferable, ornery, stubborn, bull-headed . . ."

"Stupid?" he volunteered.

"Idiot," she snapped. "Your life is in danger. Darin told me he planned to kill you. Are you going to just let him attempt it?"

"No."

She breathed a sigh of relief. "Well, thank God for that." She sank back into the chair. "What are you going to do?"

He smiled, a sly smile that brought no warmth to the cool gray eyes. "Now, it wouldn't be too wise of me to tell you that, would it, Victoria?"

Tori fought down the humiliation and anger his adequately veiled accusation provoked. She was tired of this battle of wills, of this cat-and-mouse conversation where more times than not she felt like the mouse. She stood again, and when she spoke her words were tight and controlled, though threaded through with rage. "I should have known you wouldn't believe me, Guy, but I had to try. Now, if you will excuse me, I have better things to do than waste the rest of the morning on a man who is so stubborn and bullheaded that he would rather risk death than believe in his wife."

Guy's eyes remained fixed on Tori's departing figure, a swirl of yellow moving swiftly toward the doorway to the foyer, sable waves cascading down her back and across her shoulders. "Not stubbornness," he murmured beneath his breath, "merely a sense of self-preservation."

Tori heard the softly spoken words, and for one brief moment was tempted to turn back to him. But she knew it was no use.

Fifteen

New Orleans General Hospital
July, 1993

Victoria snapped her hand away from the venetian blind and turned from the window to cast a scornful glare toward the two people who stood near her bed. "You are not my parents. How many times must I say that?" Her tone was hard and abrasive, yet within it was a hint of mounting hysteria. "My parents were killed in a carriage accident while on a visit to London in eighteen forty-seven."

"Now, honey," George Reichourd said. He brushed a hand through the shock of thick white hair that covered his head and tried to smile. "You've had a nasty bump on the head, and you're confused, that's all."

"You're not my parents," Victoria snapped. She stalked toward the bed, pushed a chair out of her way and ignored the crash of its arm against the metal nightstand. "And this book, this diary," she said, holding up Martin Reichourd's journal, "it's wrong. It's all wrong. Someone's obviously tampered with it. Changed it. To make me think

I'm crazy. But I'm not." Her voice rose. "You hear me? I know the truth, and you can't change that."

Carrie Reichourd slapped a hand over her trembling lips and blinked rapidly in an effort to stem the tears that came to her blue eyes. "Tori, please, you're delirious," she said, her voice quaking badly. "Get back in bed, honey, and let Dad call the nurse for a sedative."

Victoria whirled on the petite woman who insisted she was her mother. "I am not delirious, old woman, nor do I want a sedative."

Carrie gasped, unused to being talked to in such a manner by her daughter.

"Don't speak to your mother like that, Tori."

Victoria's hateful gaze pounced on the man who had introduced himself moments earlier as her father. "Don't tell me what to do. And don't call me Tori. My name is Victoria. Victoria Marie Camerei Reichourd."

Carrie shook her head in denial of Victoria's words. "Your middle name is Elizabeth," she said softly.

"Why am I being kept in this place?" Victoria demanded. "And who wrote this ridiculous journal? It's not Martin's. It's a fake." She laughed then, and waved the journal at them. "All these accusations! And this little fairy-tale ending. That will never happen for Guy, no matter how much he wishes for it. Especially with me!"

Carrie and George both frowned. George reached out and took Carrie's trembling hand in his. "That's the journal you found in the attic a few weeks ago, Tori. The one written by your great-great-grandfather, Martin."

"My great-great-grandfather's name was Pierre."

"Martin," George repeated softly, as if trying to correct a child.

"My son's name is Martin, you foolish old man."

George shook his head sadly. "You don't have a son, Tori."

Victoria's eyes widened with rage. "My husband put you two up to this, didn't he? This is some kind of asylum, and he's trying to prove me insane. He couldn't get the divorce so he decided to lock me away. That's it, isn't it?" She threw the journal across the room. It crashed against the wall and dropped to the floor with a loud thud.

"Tori," George said, "you don't—"

"Stop calling me Tori, old man. That's not my name."

He nodded. "All right, all right. Victoria. But listen, sweetheart"—he glanced nervously at his wife—"you don't have a husband either."

Sixteen

Guy stood at the window, his eyes looking out onto the moon-touched landscape without actually seeing it. His mind was in too much of a turmoil to register something as mundane and common as scenery.

It had been a rather quiet day, considering the circumstances. He had remained in his office, even taking the noonday meal there, and worked on the plantation books. He'd spotted Victoria walking the grounds several times, but had resisted the urge to join her. Guy sighed quietly. He had never been a hard man. Strong, yes, but never truly hard. And never cold, though in the last few years, while married to Victoria, there were some who would argue that last point. But it was the daily disillusionment he'd felt from the failure of his marriage, the pain of his wife's rejection, that had caused him to erect the icy barriers around his heart. And now she was pulling them down, and there seemed to be nothing he could do to stop her. Nothing short of removing her from his house and from his life. Maybe then he could forget her and get on with living. "How do we tell, Doc?" Guy said, breaking the momentary silence that had fallen between the two men. "How do we tell if her memory loss is real?"

Ben absently rotated the tumbler of brandy he held cupped in one hand, watching the amber-colored liquor swirl and catch the light, sparkling like liquid gold; and then he moved to stand beside Guy. His white hair seemed to glow softly as it picked up the moon's light. "There really isn't any definite procedure, Guy, though I must reiterate what I said on my last visit here; I don't believe she's faking. I spoke with her for quite a while this evening, and I just don't see any hint of deception. She is genuinely confused about quite a number of things, not the least of which is being your wife. That seems a point she wants to accept, but finds extremely difficult to do."

"Because she never did accept it."

The old doctor shook his head, his eyes dark with puzzlement. "I'm not sure about that, Guy. She said that it just doesn't feel right somehow, being your wife, that just the thought of even being married seems strange to her."

"Maybe that's because our marriage was little more than a charade. A well-conceived farce concocted to fool the world, and me. But then, obviously I'm not that hard to fool."

"Umm, you might be right, but I don't know. There are other things."

"What other things?" Guy asked. He didn't want to know, and yet he did. He wanted her gone—and he wanted her to stay. In the past few hours his emotions had been pummeled in first one direction and then the other by the battle that engulfed him. No decision was right; yet he had to make one before it was too late. He had walked through the day like a zombie, his mind asking question after question, and coming up with no answers. How could she have changed so drastically? Was it permanent? Did he dare hope that she would remain this way, gentle, warm, and caring? And even if she did, would she eventually turn away from him again? Was she really suffering a memory loss, or was this another scheme? Another deception? Perhaps this time, in collusion with Darin's greed.

"She says words keep popping into her head, words that don't make any sense." The doctor turned to look at Guy. "Do you know what Nikes are?"

"No."

"How about *Friday the 13th, Part X?*"

"Sounds like something out of the Bible."

Benjamin shook his head. "Muammar Qaddafi? Scarlett O'Hara?"

Guy remained silent.

The doctor frowned. "Those last two are obviously people's names, at least I think so, but who are they? And why would their names come to her mind when little else does? Of what importance are they?" A thoughtful expression crossed his features as another idea struck him. "Guy, what words did you two exchange just before her accident—did you two have an argument or disagreement about something?"

Guy laughed ruefully. "I told her I was going to Judge Beaudronneaux to request a divorce. You might say we disagreed on that."

Ben nodded. "I see."

"It's something I should have done a long time ago, Doc. I just kept hoping things would get better." Guy laughed again. "I was a fool."

The doctor looked at his friend. "No, you were a man who wanted to keep his family together, who wanted his wife's love. There's nothing wrong with that, Guy."

201

"Unless the woman in question is Victoria." He exhaled deeply, as if in resignation. "You know the truth, Doc. What I haven't told you, I'm sure you've heard, so there's no need to be polite to spare my feelings. Victoria and I have been married five years, and in that time she's had a variety of lovers."

"You can't always believe rumors, Guy."

"I never did, or at least I told myself I didn't, though it was damned difficult at times. Victoria never was one for subtlety. According to local talk she's taken our mayor, one of my neighbors, and a fencing master to her bed. I've tried to tell myself this was just gossip against a beautiful woman. But when she turned to Darin"—he shook his head—"and I saw it with my own eyes, I could deny the truth no longer."

The doctor remained silent. There wasn't much to say. Victoria Reichourd was definitely not the most popular woman in New Orleans. Unless, that is, one asked the men she reportedly dallied with. Only a few months back he'd heard that she'd had an assignation with Jermonde St. Croix. Benjamin shuddered at the very thought, but not for Victoria. His concern with the affair was for his friend, Guy. Jermonde St. Croix was not one to have his feelings dallied with, by man or woman. He was a ruthless businessman who had no mercy for those who fell under his power—or his wrath. And he conducted his personal affairs in the same manner.

Ben glanced at Guy, but his thoughts remained on Jermonde St. Croix. The man's reputation with the rapier was renowned. He was a *maître d'armes,* one of the best fencing masters in the city, and would challenge an opponent to a *duello* at the slightest provocation. What was worse, Jermonde fought to kill. Drawing first blood, he had been heard to say on many occasions while standing over the lifeless body of his victim, was not worth the effort of the *duello.*

"I want to move her to my Baton Rouge plantation, Doc. I want Victoria out of this house and away from the children, as soon as possible."

"Are you sure it's not you, Guy, who needs her out of the house and not the children?"

Guy sighed deeply. "Is it that obvious?"

"I'm afraid so."

"I thought I hated her, Doc." He wasn't talking to Benjamin Lecoix, the doctor now, but to Ben, his good friend. "I thought, after everything she's done, after finding her with . . ." he faltered at the memory, then stiffened and forced himself to continue, though his voice dropped noticeably. "After I came across her and Darin, I thought any feelings I had left for her were dead, and—"

"And you were wrong," Ben interjected.

"I don't know. She's changed, Ben, drastically. She's an entirely different person since the accident. Someone I never knew, yet want to." He looked at the doctor sharply. "Can this amnesia thing do that to a person, Ben? Can it cause someone's personality to truly change?"

Ben shrugged. "We don't know that much about amnesia, Guy. There have been cases where those afflicted have changed, sometimes only in minor ways, other times quite radically, but in most cases the changes were only temporary."

"So sooner or later she'll revert back to the way she was." It wasn't a question but more a statement of what he felt was true while wishing desperately it wasn't.

"Most likely. But that's not a certainty. Anything's possible."

Guy nodded. "But, as you said, not likely. I just wish this was over. I'm not so coldhearted that I would force her to leave Shadow Oaks when she can't remember anything, but—"

"She may never get her memory back, Guy. And her personality could remain just as it is, indefinitely. Maybe forever. Then what?"

Guy shrugged. "I don't know. How could I live with that, Doc? Knowing that any day, hell, any minute, she could suddenly change again."

"Do you love her?"

The question hung in the air like a black cloud waiting to unleash a torrent of rain.

Love her? Guy balked physically and mentally at the thought. His body stiffened, his muscles held taut by the unconscious tightening of ligaments at the mere thought of loving her. His mind instantly and coldly rejected even the remotest possibility that he loved her, yet something within him, something deep down where he seldom looked—was afraid to look even now—left him uncertain of his conviction.

The doctor, taking a step past the open jib doors and onto the gallery, broke the spell of the conflicting emotions that held Guy in their grip. No, he did not love her. He would not love her. He could not allow himself that emotion—no matter what.

"It's your decision, Guy," Ben said. He took a long swallow of brandy from the tumbler he held in one hand, and then let his gaze scan the vast acreage of Shadow Oaks as he waited for his friend to respond. Several long minutes passed in silence. He glanced over his shoulder. Guy was still standing inside. "You can send her to Baton Rouge," Ben said, deciding to go on since Guy wasn't answering,

204

"even if she doesn't remember anything of her life before the accident. And perhaps that would be better. She can start anew up there, and you can start anew here." He turned around to face Guy. "Anyway, what's to be accomplished by waiting? It might be harder to make her go if you wait until she recovers."

"I don't know, Doc. I guess I just feel like I'm throwing a helpless animal to the wolves, you know? How can she function without knowing who she is?"

"She knows who she is, Guy. We all do. She's Victoria Reichourd." He walked over to Guy. "I think what you have to decide, old friend"—he patted Guy's shoulder—"is whether you truly want her to leave."

Guy downed the last of his brandy and walked back into the study. Two feet from the corner of his desk he stopped abruptly and gasped. The glass toppled from his fingers to the floor, landing on the carpet with a soft thud and rolling under the desk. Guy's face turned white and he grabbed at his stomach, his knees nearly buckling beneath him.

Ben rushed into the room, instantly assuming the persona of the doctor again. "Another attack?"

"Yes," Guy hissed through tight lips. He sunk into the chair behind his desk and let his head drop back onto the leather cushion. His eyes closed, his skin tightened by the grimace that twisted his face. "They've been getting worse."

"Did you take the medicine I gave you?"

"It doesn't do any good." The pain slowly subsided and color gradually began to return to Guy's face. He opened his eyes and loosened the grip he'd clamped on the chair's arm. "Tell me the truth, Ben." His unrelenting gaze pierced the doctor's. "Am I dying?"

"Dying? Well, I certainly hope not," Ben said. "Who the hell would I play chess with if I let you die?"

Guy smiled, but his stomach still felt too tender to chance a laugh.

"Seriously though, have you noticed what you've been doing just before each attack? Anything similar? Like eating a certain thing? Having a drink? Pursuing an activity? Anything?"

"No, nothing."

"Damn it, man, you've got to help me with this thing." Ben pulled open one of the desk's drawers and retrieved a piece of paper and a writing quill. He slid both in front of Guy, as well as the cut-crystal inkwell that sat toward the front edge of the desk's top. "From now on you keep a journal, Guy. Everything you eat, everything you drink, everything you do, and everywhere you go. When you have an attack, note it."

"And if we come up with nothing?"

"Then I'll split you open like a damned catfish and take a look inside."

"Very funny."

Ben Lecoix chuckled and took a sip of his brandy. "Just wanted to see if you'd lost your sense of humor, old friend, that's all."

Tori stood just beyond the doorway, well enough into the dark foyer so that she was swallowed up within its shadows and her presence was undetected by the two men. She had come downstairs to try to speak with Guy, to try once more to convince him she was being truthful, but had stopped before entering the room when she'd heard another man's voice and then seen Guy suddenly stagger and clutch at his stomach. She'd clamped both hands over her mouth to keep from screaming when he'd nearly doubled over in

206

pain. Though she'd wanted desperately to run to him, her body had become paralyzed with fear, her limbs refusing to heed the commands of her brain, her feet rooted to the spot, while her heart beat so frantically she had thought it about to burst from her breast.

Darin was doing this. She remembered the diabolic look that had come over his face when he'd talked of his plan to murder Guy. Whatever was wrong with Guy, she knew Darin was behind it. Somehow. Regardless of what the doctor said, of the medicines he was giving Guy, of his suspicions as to what the problem was, she knew Darin was the cause of Guy's attack, knew it with a certainty that chilled her to the bone.

Her hands began to tremble, and a shudder coursed through her. But what could she do? And how was Darin doing this when he was more than a hundred miles away in Baton Rouge? Had he poisoned the food? Her brow furrowed deeply. But then why wasn't anyone else feeling the effects? She glanced at the tumbler that had rolled under Guy's desk. The brandy? Her assessing, still frightened gaze moved to the doctor. He seemed fine, and she had to assume he had been drinking the same brandy as Guy. Tori remembered Darin saying something about a shop in the Quarter . . . and buying a potion there. But he was to do that on his way back to Shadow Oaks.

She saw Guy rise from his chair, take a deep breath, and allow the air to leave his lungs in a slow exhalation. He shook his head, as if to clear it, and looked at the doctor.

"The pain's gone now," he said. His color was back to normal and he was once again the picture of strength and power, but his tone was ragged.

Ben nodded. "Remember what I said about that journal." He set his empty brandy glass on a marble-topped table beside the tapestried settee that faced the fireplace and then picked up his medical bag. "Write everything down. I'll stop by again in a couple of days."

"I have to go into town for a few days," Guy said. "Let me notify you when I return. I'm not sure how long I'll be, and I'd like to be here when you talk to her again."

Ben nodded. "I'll wait to hear from you."

The two men started to walk toward the door, and Tori quickly moved away from it, not wanting to be caught eavesdropping. She hurriedly ran into the room to the right of Guy's study, then stopped. The door swung silently on its hinges behind her. As her eyes scanned the room, she felt uneasy. It was a sort of kitchen, but like none she'd ever seen before. It was primitive; yet she wasn't really sure why she thought that. Counters ran along two walls, their wooden surfaces scarred by knife cuts, in some places scorched. Doorless cabinets lined another wall, their shelves piled high with pots, pans, and metal cooking trays. The fourth wall was a massive brick fireplace, its grate huge. A large brass pot hung from the hook attached to the metal arm over the hearth, and set within the bricks to one side of the opening was a black metal box, like an oven, its metal door hanging open. Tori stepped closer and saw that it was empty.

The door to the back gallery opened, and Hannah entered the room. She spotted Tori, sniffed disdainfully and waddled toward a large tublike metal sink set into one of the counters. "What you want in here, missy?" Hannah said, making no effort to conceal her animosity. She turned her back on Tori and dumped a large bundle of fresh vegetables, just picked from the garden, into the sink.

"I . . ." Tori looked around quickly. "I thought I'd . . .

208

I'd"—she said the first thing that popped into her mind—
"fix myself a quick cup of coffee."

Hannah sniffed. "You gonna fix your own coffee? Hah!"

Tori hurried toward an open doorway through which she could see shelves of canned and dried foods. It was little more than a small closet. She looked about. "Hannah." She turned back to the old housekeeper who had lifted a porcelain pitcher and was in the process of pouring water over the vegetables in the metal sink. "Where's the instant coffee?"

"Instant coffee?" Hannah's eyes shone with scorn. "What you mean, instant?"

Tori started to answer and then stopped, her mouth agape. She didn't know what she meant by instant coffee. The words had just popped into her mind and out of her mouth before she'd even had a chance to think about them.

Hannah glared. "I don't know why you're looking in there, but if'n by instant you mean you want your coffee right now"—she sniffed and turned back to the sink— "you're just gonna haf to wait, missy. I gotta clean these vegetables and get them out to the kitchen so Sally can put them in her stew."

"Out to the kitchen? You mean," Tori stepped farther back into the room and looked around in confusion, "this isn't the kitchen?"

"Warming kitchen, as you well know. Cooking kitchen's out there." She nodded her head toward the window.

Tori looked out and saw a small cottage set several hundred feet from the rear of the house. From its smokestack puffed a continual stream of white smoke. To one side of the entry door several women stood around huge black pots that were set over log fires. As steam wafted up from each pot, the woman stirred its contents with long wooden paddles. Another woman was hunched over in the center of a small garden, hoeing weeds from around the base of the plants.

Tori looked back at Hannah. "Then what's this room for?"

"I done told you," Hannah said, not bothering to look up. "It's the warming kitchen. Food's cooked out there, kept warm in here." She flopped the mound of vegetables into a huge bowl she'd placed on the counter then, clenched fists on her wide and well-padded hips, turned to glower at Tori. "Now, if you ain't got no more silly questions 'bout things you already know, I got work to do."

"No, I . . . I'll just go for a walk."

"This late?"

Tori shrugged. "What else is there to do? There's no TV."

Hannah had just hefted the huge bowl of vegetables into her arms, but at Tori's words she looked up sharply, her brow pulled tightly into a frown. "What's a TV?"

"A . . ." Tori's eyes moved back and forth as her mind raced for an answer to Hannah's question. She couldn't find one.

"Another of your secret things again, huh?" Hannah spat. "You shoulda heeded my warning, missy. You don't play around with old Doctor Yah Yah. He don't like nobody doing that. 'Specially white folks. You mess with him and his, you be the sorry one."

Tori followed Hannah to the door. "Doctor Yah Yah? Who's that? And what things?"

"You know better'n me, missy. I don't fool with none of that voodoo stuff."

210

Seventeen

Tori woke the next morning to find the sun already high in the sky. She had gotten little sleep during the night, tossing and turning restlessly. Every time she had finally managed to fall into slumber, the nightmare returned, each time with more clarity, more reality, and more horror. The body drifted closer to where she stood on the bank, its hand reaching out to her, its eyes seeking hers, its mouth open in a soundless scream that nevertheless she could hear.

But whose lifeless body was it floating atop the murky swamp and beckoning to her? John Reichourd's? Had she witnessed his death? Been a part of his murder? A cold chill rattled through her. Or was it Guy's body drifting toward her? Could she somehow be seeing the fate yet to befall her own husband? Or was it Darin's corpse?

She didn't know.

Finally, toward the wee hours of the morning, her body and mind exhausted, Tori fell into a deep, dreamless sleep.

Sunlight streamed into the room through windows whose drapes had been drawn hours before. The windows had been opened, as had the jib doors beneath, but the lace panels hung still over the openings, no breeze wafting the air to rifle the sheer fabric. A gown of the white muslin, its ruffled and flounced skirt embroidered with tiny yellow flowers, its scooped yoke decorated with a twisting vine of green leaves, lay across the settee before the tall armoire. Beside it had been set a freshly laundered camisole, pantalettes, and stockings.

Tori threw the bedcovers from her legs and swung them over the side of the tall bed. She ignored the little stepstair and slid to the floor. The bruises on her body were still visible, though faded, and the pain they'd caused had subsided considerably. Her toes had just touched the rug when she heard someone softly singing. It was a beautiful, lilting tune, one filled with sadness, and seemed to be coming from her dressing room. Slipping into a batiste wrapper that lay across the foot of the bed, Tori padded across the room. "Suda?"

The girl stopped singing and turned quickly, obviously embarrassed. "I'm sorry, Miss Victoria. I didn't mean to wake you. I was just preparing your bath and I guess I—"

"It was beautiful, Suda," Tori said. "You should sing more often."

"Michie Darin don't like it."

"So?"

Suda's eyes turned as big as saucers, and Tori laughed. "I mean, if Darin doesn't like it, he doesn't have to listen, now does he?"

"No, ma'am," Suda said. But her physical demeanor was in direct contrast to her verbal agreement as her gaze dropped to the floor, her head drooped, and her shoulders sagged.

Tori sighed. "Suda, Darin's not going to hurt you anymore. And he's not going to do anything to Robert, so stop worrying. In fact, Darin's not even here. He went to Baton Rouge."

"Yes, Miss Tori," Suda said, though her tone relayed her hesitancy to believe what Tori told her.

"Robert's going to be joining the children in their studies, Suda, and when Darin returns I'll speak to him about leaving you alone."

"Yes, Miss Tori," Suda repeated. She kept her eyes downcast.

Tori sighed. Well, actions spoke louder than words. Maybe when Suda saw that Tori meant what she said, things would improve. She smiled. "Suda, I'd like to just relax in the tub for a while. Could you bring up some coffee and rolls?"

The girl nodded and exited immediately, as if glad to escape.

Tori shrugged the wrapper from her shoulders, tossed it across the petit-point cushion of a nearby chair, and then pulled off her nightgown and lay it atop the wrapper. She submerged one foot and calf into the hot, bubble-topped water and stopped, her thoughts flying back to another time . . . and another bath. Could it really be that only a day had passed since he'd lifted her from the warm waters of that bath? She looked toward the doorway, half-expecting to see Guy standing there. It was empty, but the hot stirrings that suddenly erupted deep within Tori, invading her limbs and turning them dangerously languid, were not a result of the heated water.

She closed her eyes for just a moment, remembering his strong arms around her, his warm, exploring hands on her body, the press of his lips over hers, and all of the delicious sensations he had awakened within her . . . and shuddered.

213

"I brought your coffee and rolls, Miss Victoria, I mean, Miss Tori," Suda called out from the bedroom.

Tori's eyes flew open. "Oh." She stepped quickly into the tub, submerged her body beneath the bubbles, and began to run the violet-scented soap over her arms and legs.

Guy had left the house early that morning, well before dawn. His sleep had been fitful and restless, the doctor's words repeating themselves over and over in his mind. He rode the fields aimlessly, his eyes seeing, but his mind failing to register the stages of harvest, the number of hands in the fields, the state of the tobacco crop. When he'd finally noticed that the sun was directly overhead, signaling the noon hour, he turned his horse back toward the house. Maybe with a decent meal in his stomach—he'd skipped the morning repast—and a splash of water on his face, he could get his mind onto business. And unless he wanted to lose everything, that was exactly what he had to do.

Hannah had his noonday meal waiting when he entered the house. He looked at the mountainous plate of food on the table. Fried catfish, potatoes with peppers and onions, string beans, grits, butter biscuits, sliced tomatoes, fried plantains, and beef stew. "Am I sharing this with someone?" he asked, and chuckled.

"You went skedaddling out of here this morning with no breakfast," Hannah scolded, her chubby arms folded across her more than ample breasts. "A body can't do right with no food in it." She waddled back to the kitchen, and Guy, settling into his chair at the head of the long dining table, picked up his fork and sunk its tines into the mound of potatoes Hannah had scooped onto his plate.

Twenty minutes later, with his stomach full and his hunger satisfied, Guy ascended the stairs to his bedchamber. He changed into a clean shirt in preparation for a meeting he had scheduled that afternoon with the overseer of Shadow Oaks, then left his room. At the landing of the staircase, however, he paused as laughter drifted to him from an open door midway down the opposite wing of the house. Guy immediately identified the door as that of the nursery. He smiled and felt an instant desire to see Alicia before he left, just for a few minutes. Martin, he knew, was out in the corrals with his young foal. They had spoken earlier that morning and agreed to meet after dinner in Guy's study for a game of chess. His stepson was proving to be an apt pupil, so apt in fact that he had begun to beat Guy every now and then. Guy felt a surge of pride.

He walked quietly down the hall, his footsteps hushed by the thick carpet that ran the hall's length, and stepped into the nursery. He stood silently by the door for several long moments. He hadn't expected to find Victoria in the room. In fact, as far as he knew, she had never before stepped foot in the nursery. His first reaction was anger, hot and swift. He had warned her to stay away from the children, *ordered* her to stay away from them, and she had defied him, again.

Alicia was reciting her lessons aloud. He didn't want to upset his daughter, or her playmate, Ruby, so he remained silent, and his anger turned to astonishment and then, surprisingly, to pleasure.

Alicia would read a line, stumbling over a word here and there, and then look to both her mother and Ruby for approval or help. Guy was shocked to see Ruby remain silent while his wife helped their daughter.

"That's a hard one," Tori said, smiling, as Alicia suddenly stopped reading and looked up. "Let's sound it out."

215

She took the book from Alicia's hands and pointed to each letter, while making its sound. "Leaves."

"Leaves," Alicia repeated dutifully.

Both laughed, and Guy became choked with emotion. Why hadn't she always been this way? Why couldn't she stay this way? His fists clenched tightly at his sides. He backed silently out of the room, turned, and hurried down the hallway toward the staircase, his eyes dark as he reminded himself that this new Victoria was only temporary. She would change back to her normal self, he felt certain, and when she did he didn't want her to be here at Shadow Oaks, didn't want the children to have to experience again the coldness, the rejection, the lack of love that was all they'd ever known from their mother. Hell, if truth be known, he didn't want to go through it again himself.

Tori thought she'd caught a movement behind her, felt certain she'd seen something toward the back of the room out of the corner of her eye as she'd turned, but no one was there. The door stood open, but the entryway was empty. She dismissed her curiosity and smiled down at Alicia. "Okay, honey, shall we read another?"

The child's eyes lit with happiness. "Oh, yes, Mamière, let's," she said, and clapped her hands together.

Tori looked at the slave who'd said she had been appointed Alicia's guardian-playmate since the child's birth. Ruby was barely fourteen, just a few years younger than Suda, but much smaller in stature, resembling more a girl of nine or ten. Her skin was darker than Suda's, her features not nearly as delicate, and her eyes were almost black in color. Tori knew there had been a teacher hired for both Alicia and Martin, but the man had recently married and returned to Boston. Michie Guy, Ruby explained, was looking for another teacher. "Can't you give Alicia her lessons in the meantime, Ruby?" Tori had asked her.

The girl looked stricken. "Oh, no, Miss Victoria. I can't read nor write, honest. I never stayed when Mr. Morse gived his lessons." She shook her head vehemently. "No, ma'am. I waited downstairs, in the warming kitchen, just like you said to."

"Like I said?" Tori felt suddenly sick.

"Yes, ma'am. I always do just what you say."

"And I said you couldn't take part in the lessons?"

"Yes, ma'am. It against the law for slaves to have schoolin', and I sure don't wanna break no laws."

Tori nodded, but the feeling still didn't sit well. Just the thought of the word "slave" seemed to stick in her craw and poke at her temper. But what was so bad about slaves learning to read and write? It was a question she knew would remain with her until answered, though now was not the time nor place. "Ruby, why don't you run downstairs and get some milk and cookies for all of us?"

"Yes, Miss Victoria," the young girl said. She curtsied and hurried from the room.

"Tori."

Ruby stopped in midstride and looked down at Tori, confused. "Pardon, ma'am?"

Tori smiled. "Call me Tori, not Miss Victoria. Please."

"Yes, ma'am."

"Mamière, let's read," Alicia said, bouncing impatiently on the settee and tugging on Tori's sleeve.

Tori looked down at Alicia and the smile immediately left the child's face, to be replaced by an expression of fear. "I'm sorry, Mamière, I'm sorry," she said quickly. Tears filled her gray-blue eyes.

"Alicia," Tori said softly, alarmed at the sudden change

217

in the child. She wrapped an arm around her and pulled her close in a tight hug. "What's wrong, honey? Why are you sorry?"

"I pulled on your dress, Mamière, and I didn't mean to, honest. I'm sorry."

Tori chuckled. "But isn't that what sleeves are for, sweetheart? To pull on?"

"But you said—"

"Never mind what I said before." She bent down and pressed her lips lightly to the top of Alicia's head, feeling silken black curls against her mouth. "You can tug on my sleeves anytime you want to, okay?"

The child brightened instantly. "Yes, Mamière." She opened the book on her lap to the next story. "Oh, can we read this one, Mamière? It's my favorite."

They sat that way for another hour, Alicia content to read her stories, Tori content to listen and help Alicia whenever she stumbled on a word, both munching on cookies and sipping their milk. Then Alicia began to yawn and her eyelids drooped. Finally, right in the middle of a word, she slumped against Tori and the small book fell to her lap.

"Ruby," Tori whispered over Alicia's head, "I think Alicia has decided it's nap time."

The young nanny nodded and lifted the child into her arms. "I'll put her to bed, Miss Vic—Miss Tori."

Tori left the nursery. She had found the time spent with Alicia satisfying and fun, in direct contrast to what she'd expected after being told how little time she'd spent with the children before and how uninterested in them she'd been. In fact, the time spent with Alicia had felt comfortable and natural, as if it was something she was used to doing. A thoughtful frown creased her brow as she moved toward the landing. Again, here was something to ponder. Had she changed that much? Once downstairs she found the house desolately quiet. There did not seem to be a soul about. Walking into the warming kitchen she looked out through the window and discovered the reason. The cooking kitchen was a bustle of activity, both inside and out. The chimney was once again spurting a steady stream of gray-white smoke into the sky, and just to the right of the entry door were several wooden tables upon which dozens of glass jars had been set. Several women were busily filling the jars, scooping something out of huge bowls or pots they carried, while more women hunched over the garden, picking vegetables and tossing them into baskets attached to their backs. To one side of the kitchen house several more women were harvesting fruit from the trees.

Tori sighed and turned away from the window. All she'd accomplish by going out there would be to gather a dozen glares and interrupt the work. She peeked into Guy's study. It was empty, as were the remaining rooms downstairs.

Dare she look into his bedchamber?

An intense curiosity and a sudden need to know more about the man who was her husband urged her up the stairs and toward the door to his room. It opened immediately when she turned the knob. Her eyes hurriedly took in the damask drapes of burgundy and white, the matching cushions on a tête-à-tête near the fireplace, and the ornately carved post of the huge bed set against one wall. Its canopy and coverlet were of burgundy-colored silk trimmed with gold fringe, and the armoire that sat in one corner was massive, square, and unadorned. Tori stepped into the room and looked around, then nearly jumped out of her skin when she spotted someone standing in the corner staring back at her. Her heart hammered furiously, then began

219

to subside into normalcy as she realized she was looking at her own reflection in a free-standing cheval mirror. "Great, now you're afraid of your own reflection," Tori admonished herself.

She took another look around the room, her husband's room, and her gaze came to an abrupt halt at the portrait hanging over the fireplace. It was an oil painting of three young boys. Tori stepped closer. The Reichourd brothers when they'd been children. She looked first at the tallest, and obviously eldest, boy. She assumed this was John. He'd been about ten when the portrait was done. Tori looked quickly at the base of the frame. There was no plaque to confirm her guess. Her eyes traveled back up to the portrait, to the young male faces that seemed to be returning her gaze. John's face was open and friendly, very much like Guy's, who stood in the middle. But there was a distinct difference between the two older brothers and the youngest. Darin's eyes, even though paler in color, held a darkness to them that was indescribable. His expression was serious, yet one corner of his lips was turned upward. Tori shivered and took a step back. It was more a sneer than a smile, and seemed, even on that boyish face, to translate into a threat.

"What you doing in here, missy?"

Startled, Tori jumped and whirled around.

Hannah filled the doorway with her generous girth, her plump hands rammed onto her hips, her dark brown eyes glaring at Tori. "Michie Guy don't let no one in here, and you know it. And he especially don't want you in here."

"I . . . I just opened the wrong door," Tori said, knowing the excuse sounded totally ridiculous.

"Humph. Musta been in a daze, too. Your door's on the other side of the hall, missy, as if you didn't know it."

Hannah backed up several steps to give Tori room to exit, but kept her gaze riveted on her.

Tori swept past Hannah and made for the stairs. Guy was obviously not in the house, but her need to see him, to talk to him and be with him was stronger now than ever. She had to ask him about the nightmare. Somehow she had to get him to talk to her about John . . . and his death. *If* it was John's body she was seeing. Tori shivered again. It had to be. It just had to be . . . otherwise . . . she fled down the stairs. The alternative was unthinkable.

She first checked the small building that was set just beyond the formal gardens. It was an exact replica in miniature of the main house, and Suda had said it served as Guy's office, aside from his study. She knocked lightly on the door, but there was no answer. A peek through one of the windows confirmed that there was no one inside. Tori walked rapidly toward the stables, but halfway there she realized she was not dressed for riding. She paused and looked back at the house. Returning to change into her habit would take too long, and she'd given up on the idea of pants, since everyone had seemed scandalized by that idea. Anyway, she didn't want to face Hannah again. At least not right now.

Robert was in the process of sweeping out the stables when she entered. He didn't hear her footsteps over the *swish-swish* of the broom, and she stood watching him for a long moment, assailed again by the impression of how much he resembled the Reichourds. "Hello, Robert. How have you been?"

"Fine, Miss Victoria. You wants me to saddle Rogue?"

"Yes, that's fine, Robert, thank you."

The boy disappeared outside for several minutes and returned leading the tall silver stallion. Tori stood to one side of the stable's open area, resting one bent arm atop a stall rail. The horse spotted her instantly and snorted loudly, as if in protest, then tossed his head, his black mane whipping wildly through the air. His tail switched continuously, and one huge fore hoof pounded the ground, sending a cloud of dust rising about his leg.

Obviously the stallion was no more pleased to see her than he had been last time. But why? she wondered. This was supposed to be her horse. What in heavens had she done to make him so apprehensive of her?

"You want your sidesaddle today, Miss Victoria?"

"No, Robert," Tori answered.

The boy looked at her in puzzlement.

"Just put a regular saddle on him. My skirts are full enough for me to ride astride."

Robert frowned but did as he was told. "Sure has changed," he mumbled under his breath as he lifted one of the saddles from a nearby rack. He glanced about quickly to make sure his words hadn't been heard, but Tori had wandered to another stall in which a mare and her foal stood. "Riding astride." He shook his head in disbelief. "If that don't beat all." Robert settled the saddle on Rogue, buckled the cinch around the horse's belly, and then turned to Tori. "You want me to get the stairs?"

Tori remembered the little wooden steps he'd brought out for her the last time. She looked down at the voluminous folds of her gown. "Yes, please," she said. "I don't think I could even find my foot beneath these skirts, let alone hike them up and find the stirrup."

Robert pushed the little stairs into place beside the horse.

Tori mounted the steps, swung her right leg over Rogue's back, and settled onto the saddle. She easily found the stirrups, but her skirts and petticoat were hiked so that her legs were revealed from the mid calf down. Not exactly proper, she knew.

Robert frowned as he stared at the bottom ruffles of her pantalettes.

Tori caught his worried look and laughed softly. "Robert, you didn't come up to the house for lessons this morning."

He stared at the ground.

"Don't you want to learn to read and write?" Tori asked.

"Yes, ma'am."

"Then why didn't you come?"

He kept his gaze averted from hers. "I was afraid Michie Darin mighta come back."

"It wouldn't have mattered, Robert. I want you to come to the house in the mornings for your lessons, whether Darin's here or not, understand?"

"Yes, ma'am," he said softly.

Tori smiled. Perhaps she'd just come down to the stables tomorrow morning and escort him to the house. "Robert, do you know where Guy went?"

He shook his head. "Saw him ride out toward the tobacco fields, but that was awhile ago."

"Umm, he could be anywhere by now. Well, I'll be back in an hour or so." She pressed her heels to the stallion's ribs and the horse bolted forward, lifting his long legs in a high-stepping prance and throwing his head about, as if to let her know he would do as she commanded but not willingly.

Tori rode past the cotton fields, several acres of fruit trees, the tobacco tracts; she even skirted the fallow tracts that had not been planted this season. She purposely kept clear of the swamp. That was one place she had no desire to revisit. She might not have a choice when she was asleep, but while awake she certainly did.

Finally, after having ridden for more than two hours, and failing to spot Guy anywhere, she decided to return to the house. She had been enjoying the peacefulness of her ride so much that she'd failed to notice the lateness of the hour. The day was nearly over, the sun sinking quickly toward the horizon. In the distance, glowing above the ragged black treeline, the sky was a brilliant pinkish orange, and the land was quickly turning to a landscape of shadows. Physically she had made a near total recuperation from the accident, though admittedly she was beginning to feel a bit stiff, and her derrière was getting sore. She turned Rogue back toward Shadow Oaks, and then suddenly reined in. On a small knoll, almost directly to her right, and silhouetted by the fiery light of the sinking sun, a figure sat on horseback, watching her.

Eighteen

Tori's fingers tightened around the reins. She stared at the shadowed horseman, trying to determine his identity, as he in turn watched her while remaining still as death atop the raised mound of earth. A cold chill stole up her spine. How long had he been there? How long had she been unknowingly under his scrutiny? Who was he? And why was he watching her?

The questions raced through her mind and held her momentarily immobile. Suddenly horse and rider turned toward her and began to descend the knoll. She wanted to flee, to kick Rogue's ribs as she suspected he'd never been kicked before and send him racing toward the stables. But she didn't.

The wide brim of a hat kept the man's features in shadow, and a long cape flared from his shoulders and draped down over the animal's rump. He rode with a grace and fluidity that made it appear man and beast were one.

As he neared Tori realized that it wasn't only the sun at his back that had caused him to appear in silhouette. He was completely dressed in black: his hat, cape, trousers, and cutaway coat, as well as the silk shirt beneath the jacket

225

and the kid gloves that covered his hands. Her gaze moved to the animal he rode, its glistening body as rich as silks and as dark as a moonless night.

Lucifer, Tori thought suddenly. Lucifer and his mount come up from the fires of Hell.

"M'amie, I was worried," the man said. His voice was as dark and rich as his appearance. He reined in beside Tori, facing her.

Tori stared into the deepest, most infinite eyes she had ever encountered. Surrounded by a thick ruche of sable lashes, his eyes were neither brown nor black, but a gleaming, swirling combination of both, yet sparked by tiny slivers of amber that gave them an unearthly quality. Waves of hair, the same brown/black color as his eyes, swept back over his ears and curled over the black collar of his shirt. He stared at her from beneath finely arched brows and from above gently jutting cheekbones that gave his eyes a rather slanted appearance. His nose was straight, almost aquiline, his lips full, his jaw square and hard, his flesh swarthy in tone. Everything about him served to emphasize Tori's first impression of a magnificiently handsome Satan rising from the fires of Hades astride his devil-horse. And even though she knew this to be untrue, a ridiculously silly notion, she couldn't shake the feeling.

"What is this, Victoria?" the man purred deeply. He reached out a hand and ran the back of one finger along the line of her jaw, a featherlight touch that sent a chill racing through her. "Why have you not answered my note?"

"Note?" Tori echoed. Somehow she knew, sensed, that to admit she had no idea of who he was would infuriate him beyond reason.

"Yesterday, I sent a note to you."

"I didn't get a note," she said, truthfully.

"The flowers, they were delivered, my man told me, and he wouldn't lie. He knows better."

Tori shook her head. "I didn't get a note. There is a vase of flowers in my room, but they didn't have a note with them."

He looked at her through narrowed eyes, suspicion etched on his handsome features. "You are sure that you did not merely decide against meeting me?"

"No, I . . . I wouldn't do that." How could she? She didn't even know who he was.

"Then someone intercepted my note. But who? Who knows our relationship continues?"

"No one," Tori said quickly, sensing immediately this was the answer he wanted. Good Lord, who was he? And what did he mean *relationship?* Fear lodged like a knife in her chest.

"Darin?"

"He's in Baton Rouge," she said quickly. "He left the other day."

"Your husband? He suspects?"

She shook her head, feeling panic rise. What was this all about? "No, I don't think so."

"Good, I would hate to have our plans interrupted."

Plans? Tori's mind repeated. She'd made plans with this man, as well as with Darin?

His brow nettled again. "But if it wasn't Darin who intercepted my note to you, and not your husband, then who?"

She shrugged, trying to appear nonchalant. "Perhaps it was just an oversight. Maybe one of the servants received the flowers and didn't see the note, or put it aside to give me later and forgot."

"Then I would say that is a slave we should consider selling. Wouldn't you agree, Victoria?"

We? her mind repeated. What did he mean *we*? "Perhaps," she said instead, sensing her acquiescence would appease him. "I really must get back to the house now though. It's late."

"In a moment." He suddenly pulled her from her seat and onto his lap. "Now, that is better, *chérie*. Much better. I have missed you."

Tori fought down her panic.

His arms wrapped around her waist, held her tightly, while his lips trailed a line of kisses along her cheek and his hot breath wafted over her flesh. "A St. Croix is not to be put off, *chérie*, not when he wants something as badly as I want you. And I *do* want you."

"But not here," Tori said, struggling to sound calm. Instead she sounded breathless, and could only hope he thought it because of desire, not fear. "And not now."

"Yes, here," he breathed against her cheek. "And now." His lips descended on hers, swift and unavoidable. His hands flattened against her back, pressing her tightly against him until the subtle mounds of her breasts were crushed to the hard iron wall of his chest. His tongue forced her lips apart and plunged inside her mouth in a raping kiss. He stole her breath, held her prisoner, and released his hunger upon her.

Tori twisted in an effort to escape, but it was no use. She was no match for his strength or the passion that drove him. Her hands and arms were pinioned between their bodies. As his mouth ravaged hers, she struggled to push one upward until finally her curled fingers touched his neck. Positioning her bent knuckles, Tori pushed.

A choking, garbled sound emitted from his throat and

he jerked away from her, his eyes wide with shock as he gasped for air and coughed.

Tori threw herself back onto her own horse, scrambling to retrieve her seat and praying Rogue would not choose this moment to step away.

She grabbed up the reins and was about to jam her heels into Rogue's ribs when fingers curled around her wrist. Her head jerked about and she stared at the stranger in black.

His eyes sparkled with rage. "What is this, Victoria? What has happened to you?"

"Nothing." She tried to pull free, but his fingers, like steel bands, refused to release her.

"Ah, but something has happened," he said evenly, the calmness of his voice holding more menace than anything he said. "You are different somehow."

"I . . . I don't remember anything," Tori stammered. "Not since the carriage accident."

He released her arm and straightened, but his eyes were black with suspicion and swirling with thought and something else that she could not identify. "I had heard you'd lost your memory, but I thought, knowing you, my sweet, that it was merely a ploy to further our plans."

"It's not a ploy," Tori said softly. "I don't remember anything, including you."

His eyes narrowed to little more than mere slits. "You do not remember Jermonde St. Croix? How much we have meant to one another? The plans we've made?"

"Plans?" Tori repeated, almost afraid of what he would tell her.

"To be rid of your husband and marry."

"We'll . . . we'll talk later." She jammed her heels into Rogue's ribs and the horse lunged forward. Tori tried to

229

appear calm as she rode away from Jermonde, but in actuality she was shocked, scared, confused, and outraged. Jermonde had almost echoed Darin's words. She looked back only once. There was no evidence of his remaining on the horizon; yet she couldn't shake the persistent feeling that she was being watched. She clutched the reins with trembling hands. Guy should be warned, she knew, but she also knew he wouldn't believe her or put any stock in what she said. Hadn't she tried to tell him about Darin? Suddenly she realized that the eerie feeling of familiarity that had come to her when Darin had mentioned killing Guy, as if she had heard of the plan, or about it, before, had not come to her when Jermonde mentioned they'd made plans. Was that because she had been in on the ploy with Darin, as he'd said, and not in on Jermonde's plot? If so, why would he mention it now?

Tori knew a frustration beyond description. She would be no more successful in warning Guy about Jermonde than she had been in warning him against Darin. But she had to try. Somehow she had to find a way to stop this insanity, to save Guy, even if he didn't believe he needed to be saved.

Robert was brushing down one of the horses when Tori rode into the barn. Forgetting that she was clothed in the cumbersome skirts and petticoats, she leaned her weight onto the left stirrup and swung her right leg hurriedly over Rogue's rump in preparation for sliding to the ground. She managed instead to get the heel of her shoe tangled in the lacey ruffles of her petticoat. Tori grappled frantically for the pommel as her weight shifted and she began to fall backward.

Rogue whinnied and shuffled to the side in an effort to

get away from her weight, which was now dangling to one side of the saddle.

"Whoa, Rogue, stand still," Robert yelled over the horse's protests.

Tori's fingers found a grip on the pommel. She tried to yank her left foot from the stirrup while her right remained tightly secured within her own underskirt and cocked over Rogue's rump, her derriére protruding in the air.

"Perhaps this is why ladies always ride sidesaddle," Guy said, his voice full of amusement. His strong hands clasped her waist, and he half caught, half lifted her away from Rogue, who had begun prancing nervously and swishing his tail in Tori's direction.

Robert released a loud sigh of relief at Guy's appearance, then hurriedly led the snorting animal to one of the outside corrals.

Tori turned in Guy's arms at the same moment that her feet touched the ground. She placed her hands on his chest, feeling the heat of his flesh through the thin silk of his white shirt. She looked up at him and laughed. "Perhaps this is why ladies should wear pants while riding, not skirts."

The glint of amusement that had been in his eyes instantly vanished. That was the second time she had said pants, rather than trousers. Not a big thing, but big enough in light of the other things about her that he had begun to notice and which seemed strange. And all since the accident.

Tori stared up into his gray eyes. "What is it, Guy? What's wrong?"

He pulled away from her. "Nothing." He glanced at Robert as the boy reentered the stable carrying the saddle

231

from Rogue's back. "How long have you had this desire to ride astride like a man, Victoria?"

"Like a man?" Tori echoed. "Women don't ride astride?" She knew instantly it had been a stupid question.

He looked down at her long and hard, each second feeling to Tori like an eternity. "I just don't know what to believe about you anymore," Guy said, his words little more than a whisper.

"Believe me when I say that you're in danger, and that I don't want to see you hurt," Tori said.

One finely arched dark brow soared upward at her words, and an expression of mocking disbelief swept over his features. "You don't want to see me hurt," he repeated.

"No, I . . ." She could sense his withdrawal and the coldness that came back over him as the barriers he had erected against her once again settled into place.

"Is that why you have never been a wife to me, Victoria? Because you didn't want me to be hurt? Is that why you have had so many affairs that I've lost count?"

"Guy, please, you must listen," Tori pleaded.

"Oh, and by the way, my dear wife, contrary to your claim that there was never anything between you and Jermonde St. Croix, you received a bouquet of flowers from him the other day. I assumed you wouldn't want the card and had Hannah throw it away."

Her heart nearly jumped into her throat. Guy started to turn away, and she lunged at him, grabbing his arm.

He paused and looked back at her over his shoulder, but there was no longer even a hint of the warmth and amusement he had shown only moments before. Now his gray eyes were as frigid as the waters of a northern sea, as hard as the polished steel their color so closely resembled.

"Guy, please, you have to listen to me."

232

"I think I've spent too much of my life listening to you, Victoria."

"They're going to try and kill you, Guy, and I can't stop them alone."

He laughed then. "Them? So now it's not just Darin but Jermonde, too? Guy shook his head as if in wonder. "Why would you want to stop them, Victoria? Isn't that what you want? To be rid of me and still have Shadow Oaks?"

Tori's temper snapped. The man was being an absolute ass. "Guy Reichourd, if you won't listen to reason for yourself or for me, will you please do it for the children?"

He instantly sobered, fury blazing in his eyes and emanating from every pore and cell of his body. She waited for the explosion, but none came. Instead he held himself in control. "Perhaps we should finish this discussion at the dinner table," Guy said, his voice more a rush of rage than a trail of calm words. "Hannah will be waiting to serve."

Tori walked beside him to the house, but neither spoke. In the foyer she excused herself and rushed upstairs, needing to wash and change her gown before dinner. The ride, for the most part, had been thoroughly enjoyable, but she smelled like a horse. Suda was nowhere to be seen, consequently it took Tori several long minutes to unfasten the row of tiny buttons at the back of her dress. Finally she let it fall to the floor. A pitcher of tepid water sat on her dressing table. She poured it into the matching bowl and, dipping a cloth into it, washed quickly. "I'd give a hundred dollars right now for a shower," she muttered, then stopped. Lord, she was doing it again; saying things that made no sense. She hastily donned a hoop-cage, then fresh crinolines, and slipped into a shimmering gown of pale blue silk. Its plunging neckline, trimmed with a thick ruche of

233

ivory-colored Parisian lace which came together in a deep vee between her breasts and then dripped to her waist, was a bit more risqué than she would wish, but she had no doubt Guy would appreciate it. Lace also hung from the gathered edges of the pagoda sleeves and the flounced silk that was draped at each side of her skirt. Ruffles of midnight blue silk peeked out from between the flounces and then flared to make up the hemline of her underskirt. A velvet cord, of the same dark color, trimmed the lace of the gown's neckline and wound around her arms to be tied in the small bows that hung down over the lace cuffs.

Tori ran a brush through her long hair, letting it flow freely over her shoulders. With a last look at the mirror to assess her appearance, she left her room. As quickly as she could, considering her lack of success at maneuvering down the stairs in full, bell-shaped gowns, she hurried to the dining room. Eager to continue her talk with Guy, she could only pray that he hadn't changed his mind about listening. Of course, Guy's snarled *"Perhaps we should finish this discussion at the table"* was not exactly an affirmation that he was going to listen to her. Still, she was optimistic.

She entered the dining room and was surprised to see Alicia and Martin seated at the table with Guy, both to his left. Not that she wasn't pleased to see them there, but so far, at least since the accident, which was still as far back as she could remember, they had taken their meals separately from their parents. She smiled and approached the table. "Good evening, everyone."

"Good evening, Mamière," Alicia said happily. She beamed up at Tori, gracing her with a wide smile. "Papa said we could dine with you tonight."

"That's wonderful, sweetheart," Tori said, winking at Alicia.

Guy rose and pulled her chair out for her, but rather than take it, she remained standing and looked pointedly down at her son. "Good evening, Martin," she said, in an attempt to force him to acknowledge her.

The boy looked up, begrudgingly. His eyes held the same contempt she'd seen in them when she had approached him in the corrals, but at least his words and his tone were cordial this time. "Good evening, Mamière."

Tori took her seat and Guy settled back into his. "Alicia was just telling me that you two read stories together this afternoon." His eyes pinned Tori as if trying to look past the physical facade of the woman and into whatever made up her spirit.

She smiled. "Yes, we had a very good time." Tori looked at Alicia. "Didn't we, honey?"

"Yes, Mamière, a very good time." Alicia bounced in her seat, and her ragdoll, Miss Pansy, bounced along with her. "Can we do it again tomorrow?"

Tori laughed softly. "Of course we can. In fact we can do it every day if you like."

"Oh, yes, Mamière, I'd like that." She turned to Guy. "Did you hear Mamière, Papa? We're going to read together every day. And we had cookies and milk too."

Guy nodded to Alicia and then turned his attention to Martin, who was still sitting quietly, his expression sullen. "And what about your studies, Martin? I haven't procured another teacher yet, though I have made several more inquiries. Do you need help with your lessons?"

The boy shook his head. "No, sir. I'm fine."

"I'd be happy to help you, Martin," Tori said.

"I'm fine," he repeated, without looking at her.

"Mamière said Ruby can do lessons too, Papa," Alicia offered.

"And I've instructed Robert to join us," Tori said.

Guy stared at her for a long moment, then slowly nodded. "That's a good idea, I suppose, under the circumstances." He glanced at the children, then back at Tori. "Shall I ring Hannah to serve?"

"Please," Tori said, suddenly feeling more hopeful about things than she had for days. Unable to help herself, she laughed. "I'm so hungry I could eat a horse."

Alicia giggled, Martin looked at her as if horrified, and Guy's brows rose slightly in surprise as he lifted the small silver bell that sat before him and shook it gently. A soft tinkling filled the room.

"We don't eat the horses, Mamière," Alicia said, "we ride them."

"And maybe tomorrow we could do just that," Tori suggested. She looked at Guy. "Could we all take a ride together in the morning?"

"I have to do my lessons in the morning," Martin said.

"Oh, please, Papa, can we? Please?" Alicia begged.

Guy chucked her chin with a bent finger. "We'll see in the morning, shortcake."

"Oh, please, Papa," Alicia persisted.

He looked back at Tori as Hannah set the food on the table and began ladling servings onto their plates. "Hannah," he said, though his gaze remained on Tori, "please have Suda get a pair of my trousers and fit them to Victoria."

The old woman's head swung around so quickly at his words that the vertebra in her neck cracked loudly. She gawked at Guy. "Fit a pair of your trousers to Miss Victoria?"

236

"Yes. And while Suda's at it, have her sew up a pair of Martin's for Alicia, too."

"For Miss Alicia?" Hannah squeaked, in near total shock now.

"Yes. We're going riding in the morning, and I want the ladies to be comfortable."

"Oh, goodie," Alicia said, bouncing on her seat and clapping her hands. She glanced at Martin and then poked him with her finger. "Come on, Marty, don't be an old fogey."

The boy jerked his arm away and glared at her. "I'm not an old fogey, Licia. I have lessons to do." But he refused to look at either Tori or Guy.

When their meal was finished, Guy ordered Hannah to have Ruby see Alicia to her room for the night. The youngster appeared from the kitchen almost instantly. She took the hand of a yawning Alicia and, chattering about nothing in particular, led her from the dining room. Martin followed sullenly and, Tori noticed, without saying good night.

Guy poured them both a cup of coffee and then sat back in his chair. "All right, Victoria," he drawled lazily, "you were saying that I should listen to reason."

Nineteen

He could see them quite clearly through the tall dining-room windows that looked out onto the gallery. The brass chandelier that hung overhead lit the room and even reflected out onto the gallery, but the surrounding gardens, where he stood, remained in inky darkness. The children were gone from the room now, only Victoria and Guy remained, talking, but he couldn't hear what they were saying. It was impossible to get any closer, not unless he wanted to chance being seen, and he didn't. His gaze was pinned on Guy as a wicked gleam sparked in his eyes, and his lips curled upward in a smile that held no warmth. "One down, one to go," he whispered softly, closing his mouth quickly before the laughter bubbling up from his chest could escape his lips and alert the pair to his presence. He turned his attention to Victoria. She was wearing the same gown she had worn the last time they had met in town. That had been an especially delicious assignation. It had been one of their most passionate. His tongue slid slowly over his bottom lip as he remembered.

A spark of anger lit his eyes. She shouldn't have worn it for him. He looked at the plunging neckline, and desire, hot, fierce, and instant, roiled within his loins and blended with the fury also building within him. The inseam of his pants tightened, and he cursed softly beneath his breath. "Witch," he said. She'd always had the ability to stir his passions, even when he didn't want them aroused. His eyes took in the swollen mounds of golden flesh peeking above the froth of ivory lace. It had been too long since he'd tasted her passion. He tugged at his pants, and a sly smile curved his lips. He had learned that Guy was planning a trip to town the next day. If Victoria accompanied him, she would go shopping, and he could arrange a meeting. If she stayed at Shadow Oaks, all the better, he would go to her there. A soft chuckle escaped his lips, and he hurriedly backed farther into the shadows, then turned and walked to where he'd left his horse.

Tori lay on her bed and stared up at the *ciel de lit,* its canopy. The room was dark, its drapes drawn, but a thin stream of moonlight pierced the slit of space between the drapes and allowed her to discern the pattern of the silk. Her eyes followed it aimlessly, while her thoughts dwelled on the conversation she'd had earlier with Guy. He had listened, patiently and quietly while she'd explained that Darin had said he wanted to kill him. And he'd continued to listen when she went on to reveal that Jermonde St. Croix had also spoken of murdering him. But she had been ill prepared for his reaction. Rather than understanding, which she'd hoped for but had been certain would not occur, or showing acceptance of her accusations or even anger because of them, Guy had simply waited until she had finished, then had stood, excused himself, and silently walked from the room without another word or a backward glance.

She breathed in deeply and released a long sigh. How could she possibly prevent him from getting killed if he wouldn't even listen to her? If he wouldn't help?

The sudden feeling that she was trying to change history assailed her. She sat up quickly, momentarily shaken. "Oh, don't be ridiculous," Tori muttered to herself, and sagged back against her pillow. "Change history. Humph. You can't change history until it is history. Guy hasn't been killed, so it's not history." She slipped from the bed and began to pace the room. But the feeling persisted. She pulled back one of the drapes and looked out at the moonlit landscape. *Darin shot Guy by the swamp, but his body was never found.* The words popped into Tori's head and she stiffened. "Where the hell did that come from?" she muttered to herself, and then remembered her dream. Were those words in conjunction with the dream?

By the time she finally managed to go to sleep it was past midnight, but at eight o'clock the next morning when Suda entered the room and gently shook her awake, it felt as if she'd just closed her eyes moments ago. She stared up at the girl, but didn't rise. "What is it, Suda?"

"Michie Guy says if you're going to go riding with Miss Alicia this morning, it's got to be soon 'cause he's gotta do things to prepare for his trip to town tomorrow."

Tori threw back the covers. "Have you prepared me a bath yet, Suda?"

"Yes, ma'am, it's all done and waiting for you."

"Good, I'll just pop into it and be back out in a jiffy."

Suda looked at Tori's retreating back and shook her head. "Woman talkin' stranger and stranger all the time. Pop into it and be back in a jiffy. What's that supposed to mean?" She continued to softly mumble to herself as she made the bed, laid out the trousers Guy had requested she alter to fit Tori, then retrieved a blouse from the tall armoire. She stared down at the trousers. "Now how she gonna get her pantalettes under them things?"

"I'm not," Tori said, emerging from the dressing room with a towel wrapped around her still damp body.

"But it ain't proper not to wear your underthings, Miss Tori."

"Get me a pair of scissors," Tori said.

Suda scurried from the room without another word and returned momentarily, a pair of scissors in her hand. She handed them to Tori who immediately picked up the pantalettes Suda had laid on the bed, and cut off their legs.

"Oh," Suda gasped. "Miss Tori, what you doing?"

"Making myself some comfortable underpants." She laughed. "Here." She threw the cut-off leggings to Suda. "You can give these to Hannah to use as dusters or something."

Suda stuffed the leggings into the deep pockets of her apron. "I'll get your coffee and biscuits, Miss Tori, and then help you with your hair, if you want me to."

"I think I'll just leave my hair loose, Suda, but I'd love some coffee and a biscuit." She shrugged on the blouse, stepped into the altered trousers, and then moved to stand before the mirror. The white blouse fit snugly across her bodice, the material so delicate that the blue ribbons of her camisole were clearly visible through the sheer fabric. She buckled the belt that had previously been slipped through the trousers of the pants, obviously Martin's, not Guy's, and turned her attention back to her reflection. The trousers fit perfectly, hugging the subtle curves of her hips and the long leanness of her legs.

241

"Oh, Miss Tori," Suda exclaimed as she walked back into the room. "You ain't going out like that?" She set a silver tray laden with a plate of biscuits and a cup of coffee on the table near Tori.

"Of course I am, Suda." Tori laughed and picked up the cup of coffee. "It will be much easier to ride in these than in one of those silly riding habits."

Suda shook her head. "Sure hope nobody sees you, Miss Tori. Don't know what they'd say."

Tori swallowed a chunk of biscuit. "I don't really care what they say, Suda. I just don't want to fall off Rogue again."

"You fell?"

"Well, not really, but I almost did." She drained the last of her coffee. "Anyway, I'd better get downstairs before Guy and Alicia leave without me."

Tori hurried toward the stairs and at the landing saw that Guy and Alicia were waiting below in the foyer.

"Oh, Mamière, look what Ruby made for me," Alicia squealed as Tori descended toward them. The child pirouetted. "Aren't they wonderful?"

"Wonderful," Tori agreed, laughing. Alicia had on almost the exact outfit as Tori, only in miniature.

"Heaven knows what people will say," Guy said, but his words were soft and there was a smile on his face, especially when he looked down at Alicia.

"Martin's not coming?" Tori asked, looking around the empty foyer.

"He insists that he has lessons to do," Guy said.

"He's just being an old fogey," Alicia added.

Tori laughed, knelt before Alicia and tweaked her nose gently. "Well, if Martin wants to be an old fogey and study

242

rather than go riding, we'll just go without him, won't we, honey? Are you ready?"

Alicia nodded eagerly.

"Good, then let's go," Guy said.

Alicia was out the door and skipping toward the stables before Tori had even half risen to her feet.

"Suda said something about you going into town tomorrow," she said as she and Guy walked side by side toward the stables.

He shot her a quick glance. "Yes, I have some business to attend to."

"Would you mind if I joined you?"

He sighed deeply. "If I am merely transporting you into town so that you can have an assignation with one of your lovers, Victoria, then yes, I do mind."

Her mouth almost dropped open in shock, and her temper flared, but she caught both reactions before he noticed. "I merely thought it would be pleasant to go into town, Guy, maybe spend a little time together, do some shopping, and have dinner out."

"With me?" he said, his tone one of sneering disbelief.

"Yes, dammit, with you."

His brows rose at her curse. "Why, Victoria?"

"Why what?" she parroted.

"Why this sudden change in you? I have a very hard time accepting that this is all due to a memory loss." He looked at her long and hard. "In fact, sometimes I find myself wondering if you're even my wife."

For several seconds she couldn't answer. It was as if he had spoken the same thoughts that had haunted her ever since the accident. Everyone said she was his wife, Guy had insisted she was, and somehow she knew that she was; yet somewhere, deep down, where she almost feared to

243

look, remained a feeling that something was wrong, that all she was being told, all she was accepting as fact, was not true. "But, you . . . everyone says I'm your wife."

Guy shook his head and continued on toward the stables. "Of course you are, I was just being momentarily foolish."

They rode aimlessly for almost an hour, through one field after another, admiring the scenery and saying little except to Alicia, who rode in the lead on her brown and white pony.

Tori shot a sideways glance at Guy. He sat astride the same black stallion he'd ridden before, the animal's coat a satiny landscape of ebony stretched over rippling, powerful muscles that flexed with each step or prance. Its legs were long and sleek, its flanks well curved, its neck a graceful column adorned with a flowing mane of black strands that looked more like threads of silk than hair. The stallion's thick tail nearly touched the ground, its ears remained pricked, listening for the slightest unusual sound, and its eyes, as black as its coat, remained alert and watchful. She had heard Robert call the huge horse Satan, and wondered if Guy had named him for appearance or temperament.

Satan switched his tail, the long, coarse strands slapping against Rogue's rump. Her horse skittered forward several frantic steps and whinnied his displeasure, throwing his head and yanking against the reins. Tori held them tightly.

Guy touched a heel to Satan's ribs and applied the reins to the side of the animal's neck. Satan instantly sidestepped several feet away from Rogue and Tori.

"I don't think they like one another," Tori said.

Guy looked first at Rogue, and then at Tori. "They never have."

244

The words were simple and straightforward enough, yet Tori had the distinct feeling that he was referring as much to the relationship between husband and wife as to that which existed between the two horses.

They rode past the cotton fields, where Tori noticed that over half of the prickly plants had been relieved of their puffs of cotton, pristine as snow. At least a hundred slaves were busy in the far off rows of the tract harvesting the remainder of the crop.

"Papa, can we go into the bayou?" Alicia called back to them as she reached the edge of the cypress swamp.

"I'd really rather not," Tori said to Guy. Memory of the last time she'd been in there, and of what had happened, instantly assailed her, followed by the eerie specter of her dream, the man floating atop stagnant, leaf-covered black waters, his fingers reaching toward her, his eyes looking at her. A cold chill swept up her spine, and she shivered, then shook her head to rid herself of the morbid thoughts. The man had not been reaching toward her or looking at her. How could he? He was dead.

But the feeling remained, weighing on her, persisting.

"Not this time, shortcake," Guy called out to his daughter.

Tori turned to him. "Guy, I don't want to leave."

He looked at her quickly, his features devoid of emotion, hard and cold.

"I want to stay here, Guy," Tori continued, swallowing her fear. "With you and the children."

Suddenly, a shot rang out, the deadly crack piercing the quiet morning air.

Twenty

"Guy!" Tori's scream echoed through the dense growth of cypress and pine that made up the bayou, blended with the still reverberating crack of the gunshot, and instilled further panic into the hearts of several white egrets who had taken flight from the tall branches of the trees at the outburst.

Alicia sat astride her pony, horror stricken, her wide eyes fastened on the limp body of her father. He lay on the ground, half-concealed by the tall reeds that surrounded the swamp and the wild grass that quickly took over any unplowed land.

"Alicia, get down," Tori screamed, afraid another shot might break the silence of the tract and find her daughter as its target.

The child scrambled from her pony's back and ran toward Tori. "Mamière, Mamière, what's happening?" she cried.

Tori, unhampered by petticoats and long skirts, jumped to the ground and ran past Satan, who was still snorting and nervously pounding the ground with one hoof. She grabbed Alicia as the child threw herself forward, and pulled her to the ground beside Guy. "Stay down, Alicia."

But there was no need for the words. Alicia, crying softly, huddled against Tori's back as she looked around hurriedly and then turned her attention to Guy. If the shooter was still out there, maybe intent on killing all of them, there really wasn't much she'd be able to do to prevent it since they weren't armed. Their only cover would be in the swamp, and she wasn't sure the shot hadn't come from in there. Anyway, Guy was in no shape to go anywhere.

A thick, ugly rivulet of blood streamed across his right temple and curved its way down over one high cheekbone. Tori, her hand shaking violently, reached out and hesitantly placed her fingers on his head, just above the hairline. It was moist with blood. She probed gently, trying to determine the extent of his wound.

"Please, God," she prayed softly, "don't let him die. Please."

Alicia hiccuped. "Is Papa dead, Mamière?"

Guy flinched as her fingers pressed against his skull, and Tori felt a sudden burst of joy. "No, sweetheart, he's not," she said quickly, "but stay down. We don't know who's out there."

Guy's eyes opened and he moved to sit up, then grimaced and sucked in a short hiss of breath. "What the hell happened?" He reached a hand toward his wound, but Tori grabbed it.

"Someone shot you." She saw the dark suspicion that came instantly to his eyes, recognized the apprehension and mistrust that distorted his features as he looked up at her.

He struggled to sit up. "I've got to get Alicia out of here."

"No, you can't, not yet." Tori placed a hand on his shoulder to hold him down, though she knew if he truly meant to rise there would be little she could do to stop him. Fear clutched at her heart. Someone had tried to kill Guy, and had nearly succeeded. Then another thought struck her, one that turned the blood in her veins as cold as ice; or had the shot really been meant for her? They had been riding side by side, an extremely close shot for anyone but an expert marksman, difficult even at that. But why would someone want to kill her? She looked over her shoulder toward the swamp and then back at Guy. It couldn't be Darin. He had gone to Baton Rouge, and anyway, she couldn't see him using a gun. He'd mentioned poison; she felt certain that was more his style. The memory of Jermonde St. Croix and his ominous words filtered back into her mind.

She rose to her feet. If it was Jermonde out there, she was in no danger, but Guy and Alicia were. "Do you have a pistol?" Tori turned from the swamp to look back down at Guy.

He forced himself to sit up, and Alicia immediately flung herself onto his lap. "What do you mean . . . ?" His jaws clamped shut as his face contorted in pain. One hand clenched into a tight fist at his side, the knuckles turning white from the pressure of his clasp, the other held Alicia to his chest.

Knowing there was no time to spare if she was going to find out who was out there, Tori hurried around a still-twitching Satan and remounted Rogue. "I'm going to find out what in the hell is going on."

"Victoria . . . damn it!" Guy said, but before he could

248

protest further she had jammed her heels into Rogue's ribs and the huge silver stallion had lunged forward in a smooth lope. Guy watched her ride away from them, and a feeling of dread assailed him. He struggled to get to his feet, but felt Alicia's weight against him, her tiny hands tightly clutching his shirt in which her face was buried. He sank back down. He could not leave his daughter, and he couldn't risk taking her with him to go after Victoria. And much as he didn't want to think it, he couldn't help but wonder if this was just another of Victoria's ploys. Why would she brave riding toward a gunman unless she knew she was safe?

Guy sat silent, confident he could easily, and swiftly, reach the gun he always carried if he had to. Someone had shot at him. An inch more to the right and he would be dead, a bullet securely lodged within his brain. Had it been one of Victoria's lovers who'd fired the shot? Perhaps even his own brother? And had she ridden into the swamps hoping that Guy would follow her—to receive a second bullet more deadly than the first?

His temple throbbed. He couldn't follow her, but he couldn't just sit here either, because if this wasn't another of Victoria's schemes, then a killer was around, possibly approaching, and his daughter was in danger. He grasped Alicia's arms and forcibly set her away from him. "Sit there, shortcake," he said. "And don't move."

"Papa?" Alicia squeaked, her eyes filled with fear.

"Shh." He forced himself to his knees. "I'm just going to get something from my jacket, on Satan's back." He pulled his feet beneath him, but remained crouched. "Be quiet, honey. I'll be right back."

Tori urged Rogue along the narrow bank of land that wove its way through the dank bayou. The moment they had passed the first line of trees, the day had turned from one of brilliant sunshine and warmth to a vista of dark shadows and eerie stillness. It was difficult to breathe in the swamp, the air stagnant waves of humidity that seemed to pull the breath from your lungs and offer nothing in return except stifling heat.

Rogue's front hoof slid off of the narrow, moss-covered strip of land. The horse snorted loudly and sidestepped, grappling to regain his stance. Tori clung to the pommel, her gaze darting in every direction. A movement to her right, across a narrow strip of murky water caught her eye. She turned just in time to see a gator move from his bed amid a lush growth of maidenhair fern on the bank and slip quietly beneath the water, creating little more than a ripple on the black surface. Rogue snorted, as if in protest of their direction. Tori ignored it and urged him on. They moved farther into the swamp, and as the last time she'd ventured into the bayou, Tori began to feel she had wandered into a land where time had stood still, where man's progress and movement throughout the years in other parts of the world had gone unnoticed or ignored by the inhabitants of this primitive, almost prehistoric, island of life.

The sound of a branch snapping, as if stepped on, suddenly yanked Tori from her reverie. She pulled back on Rogue's reins, though there was really no need; the horse had come to an abrupt halt. Both Tori and Rogue remained still, listening, but there was no further noise.

"Jermonde?" Tori called out softly. She leaned forward in the saddle and looked around again. "Jermonde?" She waited what seemed endless seconds, but there was no answering voice. That Jermonde had fired the shot was the only logical conclusion, but why wasn't he answering her? She sighed. Because obviously he was already gone.

"Come on, Rogue," she said, and pulled on the reins, "let's get out of here."

As the horse turned and made his way back along the narrow strip of land toward the boundary of the bayou, Tori felt a chill race up her spine. What if it hadn't been Jermonde? What if it had been someone else? Another lover that she didn't remember, just as she hadn't remembered Jermonde? Or—she rammed her heels into Rogue's ribs, feeling the need to speed up their retreat—what if she had called out to Jermonde, and it had been Darin after all?

Moving stealthily through the tall grass, and remaining hunched over, Guy approached the tall black stallion. "Be still, boy," he crooned softly, and reached out a hand toward the horse. His fingers swept lightly over Satan's flanks. "That's a good boy." Guy reached up and tugged at the leather bindings that held his greatcoat secured to the cantle of his saddle. The coat fell into his hands. He flipped back one lapel and hurriedly shoved a hand deep into an inside pocket. His fingers curled instantly around the warm mahogany handle of a Colt revolver. With the advent of John's mysterious disappearance, Guy never rode the fields unarmed. He didn't like it, but he liked the idea of sharing John's fate even less.

Guy pulled the gun from the pocket and ran back to where Alicia sat huddled in the tall grass. He pulled her close with one arm, while the thumb of his other hand cocked the trigger on the gun.

"Where's Mamière, Papa?" Alicia asked softly.

"She'll be back soon, shortcake. You just sit still," Guy said. He watched the swamp, his eyes trying desperately to pierce the dark shadows into which Victoria had disappeared. Nothing stirred. There was not the slightest movement, no sign of life within the dank bayou or the surrounding tract. It was as if everything waited. The birds remained silent, the leaves on the trees and the reeds were unmoving, even the air seemed still. Finally, he could stand it no longer. If this was a ploy to get him once more into the open, then it had worked. But if it wasn't, she could be lying hurt in there. Guy stood, his gun ready, his senses alert for the slightest sound, the most minute movement. "Victoria," he called at the top of his lungs.

Horse and rider broke from the inky shadows that had swallowed them only moments before and moved rapidly into the blazing sunlight. Rogue's large hooves pounded the ground as he loped toward Guy, a thunderous sound that resonated across the earth and shattered the quiet.

A wash of relief swept over Guy as he saw them. "Why in hell did you go in there?" he demanded. Concern swelled within his chest; yet anger at the fact that he was concerned over her nearly strangled him. "You could have gotten yourself killed."

"I wanted to find out who fired at you."

"Did you ever stop to think they might fire at you, too?" Guy snarled. "Or were you sure they wouldn't?" He couldn't help the suspicion that stormed up within him. Too many times he had given her his trust, his faith, only to have it thrown back at him in tatters. He might be fool enough to desire her, might even be fool enough to still care deeply for her, but trust her? No. That he would never do again.

Tori looked at Alicia, who was clinging tightly to her father's leg and crying silently. "You're scaring Alicia," she said softly.

"I'm scaring Alicia?" As if the mocking words had suddenly penetrated his thoughts, Guy looked down at his daughter, lifted her into his arms and moved to mount Satan. "We'll discuss this later, Victoria. Please get Alicia's pony." Before she could utter any response, Guy jerked Satan's reins to the side and the big stallion whirled around and plunged into a gallop.

Twenty-one

By the time Tori led Alicia's pony back to the stable, handed both horses over to Robert, and got up to the house, Guy was already in Alicia's room, tucking her into bed for a nap and telling her a story. Tori caught him as he came out into the hall. He closed the door quietly behind him, but shook his head as she opened her mouth to talk and motioned her toward the stairs. She followed him to the landing.

"Guy, we have to—"

"I don't have time to talk right now, Victoria," he interrupted curtly. "Moses gave me a message from the overseer when I returned. There's trouble out at the mill."

A sudden image of several dozen angry, half-crazed black slaves riled up against Guy flashed into her mind. "With the slaves?" she asked anxiously. She didn't know what the vision meant, or where it had come from, she only knew it frightened her beyond belief.

But he shook his head. "No. Something's happened to the cotton gin. Hopefully it's a broken part we can easily fix. If not, we may lose half our harvest. I have to go and see."

She nodded, suddenly overcome with relief.

"I'll be late." He glanced back at Alicia's closed door. "She might wake with a nightmare after what happened out there."

"I'll listen for her," Tori said. She watched him run down the wide, curving staircase, his long legs taking several steps at a time. "Be careful," she called after him, but he was out of the door before the words had left her lips.

The remainder of the afternoon seemed to drag. Alicia slept soundly. When she finally woke she contentedly played dolls with Ruby. Tori paced, first one room, then another and another. She checked the tall grandfather clock in the foyer several dozen times, glanced out of every window on the first floor, and, stepping out onto the gallery, stared hard in the direction of the mill, once Hannah begrudgingly told her where it was.

She ate a solitary dinner in the vast emptiness of the long dining room, her eyes continually darting toward the entry from the foyer, her ears straining to hear the sounds of his return. Could he have been hurt worse than they'd thought? Perhaps he'd ridden toward the mill, become dizzy, and fallen from his horse. He might be lying somewhere, unconscious and hurt. Perhaps even dying. Panic seized Tori. Maybe the person who'd shot him that morning hadn't left. Guy could have been his target again, this time when he was alone, with no help. Tori pushed the half-full plate of food away and stood. She walked to the window and looked out again. The sun was quickly sinking behind the tall trees on the horizon, the landscape rapidly turning into a panorama of translucent colors and whispering shadows.

"Where is he?" she murmured softly.

She wanted desperately to ride out and find him, and

knew that would be foolish. If he'd been hurt some of the workers would most likely have come across him on their way in from the fields. Even if they hadn't, she would never find him in the dark. And if he was merely working out at the mill as he'd said he would be, he was bound to be angry with her for riding out there. Angry or suspicious.

Tori retreated to her room, shooing Suda out and telling her she just wanted to be alone and was perfectly capable of getting herself out of the trousers and blouse she still wore from that morning. She was capable of doing it, but she didn't. Instead, she paced, she fretted, she stared out the window, and she exhausted herself. Finally, her body and mind weary, Tori lay down on the bed. She had left her door partially open so that she would know when Guy returned. Her door was directly across from his. She would hear him when he came up the stairs, when he walked down the hall and entered his own room. Until then, she would lie quietly and rest.

The house was silent when he entered, most of the servants having retired to their own quarters for the night. Hannah and Moses were in the kitchen, having a last cup of coffee, but he didn't worry about them. The old man was half-deaf, and nature had been too generous to Hannah's girth to give her any speed. He mounted the stairs quickly, his boots making no sound on the thick carpet, then hurried down the hallway toward her door. It was partially open. A spurt of rage erupted within him. She wasn't waiting for him, so his suspicions must be correct. His fury burned out of control, hastening his steps and turning his handsome features into a grotesque mask that diminished but did not totally conceal the anger he felt at her betrayal. For he was certain now that she had betrayed him. Why would her door be open unless she was waiting for Guy? He slipped into the dark room. The door clicked softly behind him as he pushed it closed. She stirred on the bed, but did not wake.

The heavy blue drapes had not been drawn over the windows. Instead they remained pulled back and secured to the wainscotting by gold hooks. The windows were open, as were the jib doors beneath, and a soft breeze, floating in from the river at the western edge of the plantation, wafted in and ruffled the sheer lace panels, billowing them out into the room. Golden moonlight streamed in, filtered by the delicate lace curtains. It fell softly on the huge bed upon which Tori slept, illuminating the blue coverlet beneath her and shimmering softly off each silk thread.

She moved slightly, and the shadows that had rested in the cleavage between her breasts deepened. He gazed at the long column of her neck, remembering with a sense of satisfaction how many times he had pressed his lips to it, and then at the rounded curve of her breasts. He smiled, the memory of his tongue on those rosey pebbled peaks igniting a fire deep inside of him. His eyes moved down her slender rib cage, past the tiny waist, over slender, well-curved hips, and across the taut, flat plane of her stomach until finally reaching the part of her he'd always loved best. He hardened with need, swelling within his trousers until he thought their seams would burst if he didn't release himself. He licked his lips and took a step forward.

She rolled toward him.

He smiled and moved closer.

"Guy?" she moaned softly, snuggling deeper into the pillow.

The smile turned to an evil curve of his lips. It would serve her right, the treacherous bitch. "Yes, my love," he whispered softly, and caught her lips beneath his before she could awaken further. He slipped a hand to the apex of her thighs and felt her hips rise toward him. Need filled him like a conflagration soaring out of control, sweeping through him with fierce intensity and threatening to destroy his well-laid plans. But it was too late to stop, too late to deny himself what he had come for. His tongue plunged into her mouth, hungrily seeking, demanding everything she had to offer as his fingers moved to release the belt at her waist. He would have her one more time, and then she could share the same fate that would soon befall her beloved husband.

"Oh, Guy," Tori breathed.

A door slammed downstairs.

He stiffened, then pulled away from her. The moonlight was behind him, leaving his features in shadow. He almost laughed. So much the better. "Stay here, *chérie*," he whispered hoarsely. He rose to his feet, hurried toward the door to the hallway, and slipped out into the blackness.

Twenty-two

New Orleans General Hospital
July, 1993

Victoria slipped into the fuzzy lavender wrapper that she'd discovered hanging in the closet and tied it securely around her waist. She looked down at her legs and frowned. The wrapper hung only to her knees, quite improper, but evidently this asylum gave no thought to whether things were proper or not. That had been obvious the moment she'd realized her nightgown was not only short, ugly, and made of some cheap fabric she would never have willingly worn, but was completely open in the back. She sniffed. "He put me in some rat hole that he didn't have to spend a lot of money on, more than likely." Victoria shoved her feet into the slippers the woman who insisted she was her mother had brought. They were horrid little things covered with lavender fur. She'd never seen anything like them, but then, everything about this asylum, about these people, was strange. "And that's exactly what Guy wanted," Victoria mumbled to herself. "So that I would appear insane."

She walked quietly to the door, pulled it open, and poked her head out of the opening. The wide hallway was empty except for a man at the other end running a mop over the floor. She stared at the flat light overhead. How did they do that? Get the flame to burn within the ceiling like that without torching the whole building? She pushed the unimportant thought to the back of her mind and slipped out into the hallway.

A woman in white, the skirt of her gown no longer than the wrapper Victoria wore, suddenly appeared from one of the other rooms. She stood in a doorway halfway down the hall, her back to Victoria. "Now you get some rest, Mrs. Brassea, and I'll be back to see you before your daughter and husband pick you up in the morning."

Victoria pressed her back to the wall and held her breath.

The nurse let the door close and walked down the hall, her thick-soled shoes making no noise on the fake marble floor. She disappeared around a corner and Victoria let out a faint sigh of relief. Suddenly she remembered that she hadn't put a pillow under her blanket as she'd intended. If they checked on her now, they'd find her missing, and that wouldn't give her enough time to get to Shadow Oaks and confront Guy. She glanced at the door at the end of the hall, where the lighted sign proclaimed EXIT. Again wonder struck her at how they could get a flame to burn inside of a glass box with no apparent opening. She looked at the door to her room. It would be taking too much of a chance to go back in there now. She hurried toward the exit door.

Twenty-three

Tori struggled into wakefulness and sat up. She rubbed her eyes and looked around the room. Moonlight streamed in through the lace panels and a soft breeze lifted them slightly, billowing the sheer fabric into the room. She reached a hand to her mouth and ran a finger over her lips. Had she dreamed him here? She swung her legs over the side of the bed. But it had seemed so real. She had fallen asleep on the bed while waiting for him to return from the mill, and only moments before, at least she thought it was moments before, he had come into her room and kissed her. Tori looked down at the ends of her belt hanging loose. No, she hadn't imagined it. He had been in her room. She closed her eyes and tried to remember. A door had slammed shut somewhere in the house, and he had left her.

She rose and walked to the door that led out into the hallway. It stood partially open. Had she left it like that? She couldn't remember.

Someone was coming up the stairs. She heard the soft sound of footfalls on the thick carpet as they approached. The hall suddenly filled with the yellow glow of lamplight as whoever it was reached the landing and turned in her direction.

"Victoria, what are you doing still up?" Guy said.

Ignoring the lamp in his hand, Tori moved to stand before him and placed her hands on his chest. "Hoping you wouldn't be long." Emboldened by his visit to her room, Tori reached up and wrapped her arms around his neck. Whatever she had done in the past, whomever she had loved, that was no longer important. This was her husband, this dark, handsome man who had made her experience a fiery passion she knew she had never felt before, and he was all that mattered. If only she could convince him of that, of her sincerity. She pressed her body to his. "I worried all afternoon about you," she whispered, rising on her tiptoes and pressing her lips to the side of his neck. She lowered back to her heels and looked up at him, then reached a hand toward his face. The tips of her fingers touched the dried blood that still clung to the hair at his temples where the bullet had grazed his head that morning.

For several seconds neither spoke or moved. Tori remained pressed to him, one arm around his neck, the other bent between them, her hand resting on the lapel of his jacket.

Guy looked down at her, and for one long, seemingly timeless moment, allowed himself to enjoy the incredible beauty that was his wife, appreciating her more somehow in her dishevelment than in her usual state of painted perfection. His gaze roamed over her hungrily as his thoughts had that afternoon. Her long, earth-rich hair tumbled in wild disarray about her shoulders, her wide, midnight-blue eyes tilted up slightly at the outer corners, her pert nose

262

was at once sassy and aristocratic, and the faintly rosey tint of her full lips was sensuous.

He could have stood that way forever, unmoving, unaware of the world around them, Victoria pressed tightly to his length. But the opening of her mouth, her tongue sliding innocently across her bottom lip as she waited for him to respond to her words, stoked the simmering fires within him to heights he could not ignore.

Deep within him the coiled heat tightened and burned, turning into a gnawing ache that left him little thought of anything else. An oath, incoherent and smothered, slipped from his lips as he slammed the lamp onto a nearby table and pulled her into his arms.

Martin wasn't really sure what woke him. He sat up in bed and listened. He heard nothing, but a light in the hallway, showing beneath his door, drew his attention. Lit lamps were never left unattended this late. There was too much risk of fire. Curious, he slipped from his tall bed, padded to the door, and opened it quietly. His mother stood before the glow of the lamp and within the circle of Guy's arms. Martin watched dumbfounded, his mouth agape, as the two kissed. Then, to Martin's further amazement, Guy pushed open the door at his back, the door to his own bedchamber and, without taking his lips from hers or releasing her from his embrace, backed into the room, pulling Victoria with him.

The door slammed shut, and Martin jumped, his heart racing. He closed his door and scrambled back into bed. It *had* been Guy, he told himself. It *had* been Guy, not Darin. But for some reason, and it was one he really didn't want to think about, that didn't make him feel any better. In fact, it frightened him even more.

Guy kicked the door shut behind him and leaned back against the polished mahogany panels. His lips still held claim to hers, and his tongue explored the inner sweetness of her mouth; but his arms slackened their tight hold on her waist. She did not move away from him; instead her mouth teased his, her tongue darting forth to duel with his, to caress, tantalize, and invite. It was a strange kiss, fervent in its passion, hungry in its need, yet touched with a hint of hesitancy and, he thought, something like innocence.

Both wanted everything the other had to offer, yet both were afraid; afraid of giving too much, afraid of being rejected once again, afraid of knowing the joy of love and the pain of loss. But it was Guy who broke away first. Too many things had gone between them in the past, too many things had made him distrustful for him to walk blindly down that same path once more.

"I can't do this again, Victoria," he said, his voice a deep drawl that slipped from his lips like dark honey. "Not if you're going to leave. Not if you're going to turn away from me again."

Tori stared long and hard into those fathomless gray eyes, her own filling with tears. "I will never leave you, Guy," she whispered. "Never." And at that moment, no matter what else happened, no matter what she had to do, she knew she meant that. He had become everything to her; she never wanted to lose him.

"Physically, maybe," he said, still apprehensive, "but what about your heart?"

"It is yours, my love," Tori whispered, "for all time."

His mouth descended on hers in a kiss that released the fury of his passion. Since she had awakened from the accident he had known she was a different person, his wife, yes, but different. Something inside her had changed. She'd been a stranger to him; yet he had known her as he had never known another human being. She had become everything he had once hoped she truly was, everything he had ever wanted in a woman, everything he had ever dreamed and longed for. Physically she was still Victoria Marie Camerei Reichourd, the woman he had married five years ago, the woman who had given birth to his daughter, Alicia. But inside, where it counted, she had changed and become the woman he had always yearned to hold in his arms, and even if it were only for this one time, he could not deny himself what he had waited so long to possess.

"Miss Tori, Miss Tori, you gotta wake up now," Suda whispered. She shook Tori's shoulder again.

Tori moaned and snuggled her face deeper into the pillow, her hip deeper into the softness of the mattress. She didn't want to wake up; she wanted to lie here forever, in the warmth of Guy's embrace.

"Michie Guy ready to leave, Miss Tori. He said for me to tell you if you want to go to town, you have to get up right now or he gonna leave without you."

Tori's eyes flew open. *Ready to leave?* She looked at the wide space of empty bed beside her. Her hand snaked out from beneath the warm cocoon of covers to slide over the cool sheet and confirm what her eyes had already told her. He wasn't there. Disappointment filled her like a hungry ache.

"Miss Tori, you want I should tell Michie to go on and go into town without you?"

Tori rolled over and sat up. "Go where?"

Suda tried to frown, struggled not to giggle, and failed at both.

Tori looked around and felt a blush warm her cheeks. She was in Guy's room, in his bed, and she didn't have a stitch of clothing on. She yanked the sheet up to her neck. "Suda, get me a wrapper, please, and tell Guy I'll be down shortly."

The young girl hurried toward the door.

"And tell him he'd better not dare leave without me," Tori called out.

Suda returned within minutes with a wrapper.

"Have you run me a bath, Suda?"

"Run?" The girl shook her head in confusion. "I done drawn you a bath, Miss Tori, like always."

"Good, and thank you." Tori quickly slipped into the wrapper. "Lay out something pretty for me, and I'll just pop into the tub and be right out."

Suda looked after Tori as she hurried across the hall and into her own bedchamber. "Pop into the tub," she repeated, and shook her head. "Don't know how she gonna do that." She walked to the door of the dressing room. "Michie Guy says you're staying in town at least two days, Miss Tori. You wants I should pack your opera gown?"

Tori frowned. Opera gown? That seemed rather strange. She didn't even like opera; yet she had a special gown for it? "Umm, yes, that's fine, Suda. And something for shopping, too, please."

Suda pulled a billowing white gown of shimmering satin and Caldeonia silk from a hook. Obviously her mistress would need to have another opera gown made, since her favorite had been ruined in the accident. She retrieved another day gown from the tall closet, along with its accessories, and then closed the armoire's doors and began to roll the clothing and stuff it into a beaded satchel that she had pulled out from behind the cheval mirror.

Thirty minutes later, practically setting a record since Tori still couldn't seem to get used to the idea of wearing so many clothes, she was ready. Suda had chosen a lightweight muslin traveling gown of baby blue poplin. Its bodice was a snug fit, with a white collar trimmed in scalloped lace, and a yoke of embroidered white flowers that dipped in a vee between her breasts, flowed onto her skirt, and then spread out again just below the knee to cover her hem. The sleeves were small puffs of fabric that reached to just above her elbow and were then trimmed with white cord ribbons. She wore her hair loose, brushed back away from her face and secured by two white combs, one just behind and above each ear.

"Victoria."

Guy's booming voice echoed up the staircase and down the wide hall.

Suda giggled. "Michie getting tired of waiting," she said.

"I guess so." She joined in Suda's laughter. "Does he always bellow like that?"

"Only when he's in a good mood," Suda said.

"Well then, I don't want to hear how he calls me when he's not in a good mood."

Suda giggled again and handed Tori a white pelisse cape, its waist-length hem trimmed with baby blue embroidered flowers and blue cord swirls, followed by a white beaded reticule.

Tori accepted the cape readily, but stared, puzzled, at

the little beaded sack. "What's this?" She held it up by its twisted silk cord.

"Why, that's your reticule, Miss Tori."

"My reticule?"

Suda nodded. "I done put all your things in there, just like always. That little gun you like to carry, your money purse, some rice powder, and a small packet of rose petals for your lips."

Tori stared at Suda as if she'd just sprouted horns. "Gun?"

"Uh-huh."

Tori held the bag at arm's length. "Take it out."

Suda frowned in confusion. "Take it out?" she repeated, not sure what Tori wanted her to do.

"Take the gun out. I don't want it. I can't carry a gun. I never could."

"But you always do."

Tori hesitated. She always carried a gun? Even the thought made her shudder. Why did she carry a gun? She shoved the bag farther toward Suda. It didn't matter why. She didn't want it now. "Please, Suda, take it out. Get rid of it. Throw it away, give it to Guy, whatever, but please, take it away."

Suda shrugged, took the reticule from Tori, and retrieved the tiny gun. It was smaller than her hand, its barrel a highly polished silver, its small handle a curve of ivory. "I'll give it to Moses for safekeeping, Miss Tori. That way, if you want it back, it ain't gone far."

Tori hurried to the landing, but just as she turned the corner and grasped the railing to descend, she stopped. A wide smile drew her lips upward and a spark of fire lit her eyes as a fluttery warmth spread through her. Guy stood in the foyer below, peering out through one of the windows that flanked the front door. His back was to her, and as he had not heard her approach, he did not turn. Her gaze raked over him slowly. He was dressed in black from head to foot, and once again, for just the briefest flash of a second, Tori thought of Lucifer, fallen angel and lord of all that was dark. And then she remembered Guy's lips on hers, the gentle stroke of his hands across her body, the tenderness of his lovemaking, and the dark thoughts were gone.

Leather *sous pieds* beneath the instep of each highly polished boot held his snug-fitting trousers taut to the outline of well-honed long legs. A cutaway coat of black broadcloth spread smoothly across the wide breadth of his shoulders, the short cut ending at his waist and accentuating the slimness of his hips, the length and leanness of his legs, and the broad width and muscular tone of his upper torso. His deep black hair, its thick waves curling wildly over his head and edging the white collar at his neck, glistened in the morning sunlight that streamed in through the window. Tiny sparks, like diamonds, danced within the thick strands, reminding Tori of the way it had felt to run her fingers through that rich satiny veil.

He stood with his hands clasped at his back, deep in thought, and then suddenly, as if feeling her gaze upon him, as if instinctively knowing she was behind him, he turned and looked up at her.

The wariness in his eyes had not been there when he'd lain with her, nor had the questioning hesitation that she didn't know how to answer. Tori felt her heart do a funny little leap, and her hands trembled uncertainly. She stared down at him, trying to see past the gray eyes, past the unsmiling lips. He couldn't have gone back to being the cold stranger who wanted her to leave Shadow Oaks. Could he?

Twenty-four

Tori wanted nothing more than to fly down the stairs into Guy's arms, but fear held her back. What if he didn't want her? What if, in spite of his tenderness, in spite of what she'd thought she had felt from him when they'd been together, he'd had only physical needs. She looked into his eyes, waiting, praying . . . and then he smiled. The wariness and hesitation she thought she'd seen in those gray depths disappeared, and all that was left was warmth.

"Well, are we going, or shall we just stand here and stare at one another for the remainder of the day?" He laughed softly, and the last of the fear that had gripped her flitted away, instantly forgotten.

Tori swept down the stairs toward him. "Don't tempt me," she teased, "or I might choose the latter."

He pulled her into his arms and brushed his lips lightly across hers. "Don't tempt *me,* or I might let you, though I doubt the business associates I must see in town would understand."

"Well, then"—she wriggled out of his embrace and slipped an arm around his—"we'd better go. I wouldn't want to be blamed for keeping you away from all those important appointments."

He looked at her quizzically as they walked across the gallery toward the steps. As he often had since her accident, Guy felt he was gazing down on a stranger, a woman who looked like Victoria but who wasn't his wife. A sudden chill swept over him.

Guy helped her into the carriage, then settled himself on the seat next to her. He held the reins loosely in his hands, but rather than urging the horses forward, he stared at Tori. "Aren't you going to tuck in your skirt?"

Tori stared down at the voluminous folds hanging over the side of the carriage, only an inch from one of the huge metal-rimmed wheels. "Oh, of course." She hurriedly pulled the folds in around her legs.

For the first ten minutes of their journey, neither spoke. Tori was too fascinated by the ever-changing scenery. They passed bayous that seemed to go on forever. In spite of the bright sun overhead, their dank interiors remained foreboding masses of shadow in direct contrast to the open meadows that bordered the bayous, meadows whose grasses were laced with the blooms of wild jasmine, honeysuckle, and black-eyed susans. In some areas cotton fields spread as far as the eye could see, some harvested so that only the weathering brown stalks remained, while others still held puffy white blossoms waiting to be picked. Tobacco stalks rose in the air here and there, and some planters had even begun to experiment with sugar, the canes a peculiar sight among the cotton and tobacco.

"We should reach town in half an hour," Guy said finally, breaking the silence that had fallen between them.

"Oh, I could ride like this for hours," Tori said, her eyes hungrily devouring each new sight. "It's so beautiful."

271

"You always hated this ride," Guy said, his words little more than a whisper on the breeze.

But Tori caught the softly muttered sentence. She looked at him in surprise. "I did?" She glanced back at the horizon. "But why? It's so beautiful out here. So peaceful and serene."

"You always said it took too long to get to town. Many planters have a house in the Vieux Carré. I don't, and you always hated me for that."

A sudden image flashed into her mind; of herself, sitting behind a wheel and speeding at what seemed to her, breakneck speed, down a wide road. She closed her eyes, trying to pull the blurred image to her, to define it, but it flitted away, as if having only appeared in order to tease her. Tori looked back at Guy. "What's the Vieux Carré?"

"The French Quarter."

"Oh. Well, I never liked living in the city," Tori said.

A frown pulled at Guy's brow. "That's what you've always said about living on the plantation."

Tori fell silent. Could she have changed that much? It seemed that everything she liked now, she'd hated before. And everything she found unpleasant or distasteful, she had liked before the accident. Was this really possible? Or was everyone lying to her for some reason?

Over the next thirty minutes, the farther the carriage traveled, the more distinct the differences in the scenery became. The huge planted fields, swampy marshes, elegantly simple planters' cottages, and columned plantation houses gave way to smaller fields of crops and meandering creeks. The road turned north, curved, climbed a small knoll, and the city of New Orleans came into view.

Tori gasped. "I never thought it would be so big." Her gaze darted over the sprawling buildings that spread out over the flat horizon. She looked at the river that bordered one side of the city. Its wharves were crammed tight with anchored schooners, packets, keelboats, and frigates— ships of every size, shape, and color. They sat two, and in some places, three rows deep. Still more were anchored outriver, while others were in the process of arrival or departure. She watched in fascination as the *Gypsy Queen,* a white packet, plowed its way downriver, pushed along by the huge red paddlewheel at its stern, gray smoke billowing from its twin black smokestacks. The *Gypsy Queen* passed a packet moving upriver, and Tori's gaze jumped to the other boat. It seemed to be a huge moving block of cotton bales, each burlap-wrapped square piled atop another until the only parts of the boat visible to the viewer were the twin smokestacks, the huge paddlewheel at the stern, and the flat-roofed pilot house which crowned the top deck.

"It's a wonder they don't sink," Tori murmured. She stared in awe at the packet as it chugged toward the Barracks Street docks.

Guy glanced at the packet. "Some do."

Tori's attention was caught by a tall white spire. "What's that?" She pointed.

"The steeple of St. Louis Cathedral." His voice dropped, and a shadow passed briefly over his face. "It's where we were married."

Tori heard the softly spoken words and sensed the tension that filled him when he spoke them. He was still afraid of trusting her, still leery of her. She decided not to comment. Words would not convince Guy that she had changed, that she loved him. Only her actions would prove to him that she was not the same person she evidently had been before the carriage accident.

273

They entered the French Quarter by way of Levee Street, circumventing the more crowded narrow streets of the downtown section of the Quarter for the wider thoroughfares of the dock area. Even so, the streets were a bustle of activity and a maze to maneuver through. Huge drays laden with bales of cotton, kegs, crates, or luggage lumbered along the avenue, some taking their cargo to the ships waiting at the docks, others departing the wharves and heading toward nearby warehouses or businesses. Passengers of both the schooners and packets crowded the banquettes, some looking about in confusion for a carriage, others hurrying toward the vessels' gangplanks as whistles blew in announcement of imminent departure. Street vendors moved alongside the open refuse canals that separated the banquettes from the streets, some pushing two-wheeled carts, others balancing huge baskets or jugs of goods on their heads, and all called out loudly, hawking their wares to those who passed.

Tori's eyes darted from one sight to another, finding each fascinating. She felt she'd never seen anything like this; yet at the same time she knew that thought was a ridiculous one. Still, she couldn't quell her excitement.

The carriage moved alongside a long row of street merchants who were huddled beneath a long, low canvas roof, each merchant having a designated space or booth in which to display and sell his goods.

"The French Market," Guy offered, noticing her awe-struck stare.

He pulled the carriage to the side of the road and stopped. Looping the leather reins over the thin iron bar that trimmed the footboard, he climbed to the ground. "I'll be right back."

Before Tori could even ask where he was going, he was

gone. She turned her attention back to the assembly of merchants. In one of the cubicles nearest her she saw that a row of geese hung upside down from one of the rafters that supported the canvas roof. The birds' once silken feathers were now dull with the absence of life, as were the silver scales of the fish that lay on a bed of ice in the adjoining cubicle. In contrast, a huge table piled high with bright yellow plantains, rosey red apples, and green-skinned okra proved a vivid display.

She looked for Guy in the crowd that meandered through the aisles of the market, failed to see him, and once again turned her attention to the displays. Rows of brown eggs lay atop carefully spread beds of gray Spanish moss; an old man sat hunched over a table whittling at a piece of ivory; an Indian sat cross-legged on the ground amid a mountain of baskets, her adept fingers weaving yet another one; and a giant tortoise lay asleep on the ground beside a table piled high with chips of ice and mounds of shrimp and crawfish.

Tori couldn't get over the scene around her. Everything she was looking at, everything she was experiencing seemed strange, different, and totally alien. She tried to reason out her feelings, and became even more confused. This was her city. She'd been born here, raised here, married here, twice; yet there was no feeling of familiarity as she'd hoped, no sense that she had been here before, known these sights, these sounds, these smells.

God, the smells. Whereas the air at the plantation, and on the road, had been fresh and filled with the country smells of pine needles, grass, and wild flowers, the air in the city was pungent and sharp, a blend of odors that at once stung the eyes and burned the lungs. There was the piquant scent of the river; a lingering, musky tang of old wood, leather, and canvas; and the sweet, tantalizing fragrances of sugar, baked goods, and chicory coffee emanating from what appeared to be a small café or coffee house down the block. At the same time the French Market filled the air with the aromas of its vendors' wares: cheeses, fowl, fish, vegetables, fruits, and baskets.

Yet over it all, dominating these sharp but still pleasant scents, was one that made the nose crinkle in disgust. Tori looked around, searching for the origin of the offensive smell, and found it almost instantly. On each side of the street, in between the banquettes where pedestrians strolled and the roads where carriages and travelers on horseback ventured were open trenches of murky water laced with every type of garbage imaginable, including human waste.

Nausea rose up in Tori at the sight, and her stomach churned.

At that moment Guy reappeared beside the carriage.

"Guy," Tori said, her gaze remaining on the open trench, "what in heaven's name is that?" She pointed a finger at the dark, floating debris.

Guy glanced over his shoulder in the direction she indicated. "The sewer," he said simply, as if that was explanation enough for anyone.

"But why isn't it underground, where it belongs?"

"Underground?" Both his tone and eyes mocked her. "Nothing goes underground in New Orleans, Victoria, you know that."

"I might have before, but I don't now," Tori answered. "So why not?"

"Because it just rises again, that's why not."

"Rises again?"

"We're below sea level here in the city. It's sort of like

living on a marsh. Whatever goes too deeply into the ground finds its way back on top of it in no time."

"Oh." She glanced back at the trench. Where did she get these ridiculous ideas? If she kept blabbering on like this, she wouldn't have to worry whether Guy sent her to live on another plantation or not, he'd just put her in a nut house and be done with it.

Guy climbed back up into the carriage and handed her a wadded piece of wrapping.

"What's this?" Tori began to fold back the paper.

"A praline. My craving for one was becoming unbearable. I thought we might share it."

She held up the pancake-shaped object that was filled with nuts. "A praline," she repeated.

"Candy, and don't tease me with it, give me a piece."

She laughed and broke off a piece of the candy, then slipped it between his open lips. He rolled his eyes in appreciation and Tori placed a piece in her own mouth. It began to melt instantly, the sweet taste of brown sugar and molasses almost too rich to be bearable. "This is delicious," she murmured, breaking off another piece.

"I know. Now give me some more." Guy snapped the reins over the rumps of the two carriage horses, and the buggy moved forward and began to turn the corner. Across the street a huge open park came into view. In its center was a bronzed statue of a man sitting astride a rearing horse, and beyond that, bordering the opposite end of the park were two magnificent buildings. The steeple on one allowed Tori to recognize it as the St. Louis Cathedral she and Guy had discussed earlier, but she didn't know what the one next to it was, with its flatter, more squat appearance. She was just about to ask Guy about the little park when her attention was drawn to a man exiting a shop in one of the twin brick buildings that bordered the north and south boundaries of the park. She whirled around in her seat to stare at him and found that he had paused on the banquette. He stood with his back to her now as he conversed with a young lady who had just approached him.

Tori's heartbeat accelerated and a tremor shook her hands. It couldn't be. She squinted against the bright afternoon sun, trying to see better even as the carriage took her farther away from him. Finally, sighing in frustration, she turned back around. She had to have been mistaken. It couldn't have been Darin. He was in Baton Rouge and not due back in New Orleans until next week.

Twenty-five

"What is it, Victoria?" Guy said. He glanced back over his shoulder. "Did you recognize something?"

Someone, she thought, but kept it to herself. She settled back on her seat and clasped her hands together in an effort to stop them from shaking. "No, I . . . I was just looking back at the market." What was Darin doing here? And it had been Darin. In spite of the fact that she'd just tried to convince herself it wasn't, only someone who looked like him at a glance, she knew it had been him. She was certain of it.

Tori wanted to jump from the carriage and run back down the street, find Darin, and demand to know what he was up to. Instead she remained stoically silent beside Guy, frozen to her seat, her mind a morass of questions and terror.

It wasn't Darin, she told herself. It wasn't. He's in Baton Rouge. He couldn't have made it back this quickly. Could he? No. He said he wouldn't return until next week, and there was no reason for him to lie. Was there? Of course not, she admonished herself. Darin thought everything between them was fine. She'd made him think that. He was in Baton Rouge. She glanced over her shoulder again, and a small sigh escaped her lips. There was no sense trying to fool herself. Darin was back in New Orleans. Then again, maybe he had never left.

Guy pulled the carriage up before a large, ornate building. It was four stories in height, causing it to dwarf the other structures nearby, and both its second- and third-floor windows were graced with lacey wrought-iron adornments. A sign, gold-leaf letters on black lacquer, hung over the arched entryway and proclaimed the building the St. Louis Hotel.

Tori momentarily forgot about Darin. A tall black in livery of brilliant red wool adorned with gold cord stepped forward from the banquette to assist Tori in descending from the carriage, while another, identically dressed, hurried around the rear of the carriage and took the reins from Guy.

She placed her hand on his proffered arm and walked beside Guy into the hotel, but after taking no more than a half-dozen steps into the cavernous interior, she paused, totally speechless. The lobby was spacious and round, its ceiling, high above, a huge dome of various stained-glass designs that created a kaleidoscope effect with the rays of sunshine piercing them and shining down into the room. The walls were graced with elegant panels of wood into which alcoves had been cut and within which beautiful pieces of art had been placed. Grooved pilasters separated each panel and alcove. Above the lobby level a balcony with intricately carved balustrades and railings circled the entire second story and another the third upon which several dozen shopfronts faced. Several men had congregated in one section of the balcony to watch the proceedings on the lobby level.

Guy led her through the maze of people wandering about and crowding the vestibule. While he registered them at the long front desk that was tucked to one side of the room, Tori turned her attentions to the proceedings in the center of the lobby.

The entire center area was taken up by auctioneers, their podiums placed in a circle. In front of each podium, behind which an auctioneer was yelling, a crowd of people had gathered. One hawker was selling furniture. Another was attempting to auction jewelry, furs, and silks, while yet another was holding up various pieces of artwork. But it was the display directly in front of her that filled Tori with disgust and anger. Two young black boys stood on a raised stage tightly clutching one another. Neither child was more than eight years of age, and their eyes registered the stark fear each felt as he stood before the crowd of well-dressed men. The auctioneer behind the boys banged his gavel on the podium and yelled out an acceptance of a bid of fifty dollars, then began a gibberish request for a higher bid. Someone raised it to seventy-five. Another lifted hand took the bid to one hundred dollars.

Tori's insides churned in outrage.

Within seconds the auctioneer pronounced the children sold for two hundred dollars, and they were ushered off the stage. Tori was turning back to Guy, who had become embroiled in a conversation with several men near the desk, when a tall black man was ushered onto the raised auction block. Tori watched him. He seemed different from the others milling about the dais and waiting their turn to be sold. His skin, like that of the other slaves, was as black as ebony; his features were coarse and wide. He wore only a pair of ragged trousers, its legs torn off just below the knees, his feet bare. His chest was a wall of power, a developed study of muscle that flowed easily into the well-honed mountains of black sinew that made up his shoulders and arms. And, as he glared arrogantly at the men bidding on him, that black skin glistened beneath the sunlight pouring down from the skylight and those same muscles rippled, almost threateningly, when he flexed his shackled arms.

Tori watched two men roughly push him toward another block of wood on the dais and indicate he was to step up onto it. They tried to help him, but he shrugged their arms away, and as he did so his back came into view of the audience.

Tori let out a gasp of surprise, but no one else seemed moved by the sight of the dozen or so old slash marks that marred its surface. Each had left a deep, gouging scar.

The chains that bound his legs and arms rattled loudly as he struggled to hoist himself onto the block without losing his balance. It was then Tori noticed another scar on one of his hands, the skin puckered in the shape of an X, like a brand. Once on the pedestal, the slave looked down on the crowd with quiet disdain, as if he were judging them. He held his head high with pride, and defiance burned brightly in his dark eyes.

The auctioneer loudly mumbled a string of gibberish that Tori couldn't understand but which she assumed were requests for the audience to bid, then began searching the gathered crowd with his eyes, waiting for a response. No one bid. The auctioneer frowned and the black man smiled, his lips parting widely in a satisfied grin, his teeth creating a slash of brilliant white across his dark face. Tori suddenly realized it was the slave's attitude that had caused him to stand out from the others. But why was no one bidding?

She looked around, confused. The auctioneer called out again, and this time Tori was able to make out the words.

"Five hundred, wanna bid five hundred, wanna, wanna, bid, bid, gemme five hundred, five hundred, gemme."

The crowd remained silent.

The auctioneer glanced up at the tall slave who stood on the pedestal next to him, but even without the raised block the black would have towered over the majority of the men crowded around the dais.

"Two hundred, *monsieur.*"

Tori started at the softly feminine voice, and turned to see who had spoken.

A murmur broke out from the crowd as all eyes turned to the speaker. The sea of males milling around the auction area slowly parted as a woman began to make her way through their midst. She had the same defiant spark in her eyes as the man whose life she had just bid on, the same pride in the tilt of her head and lift of her mouth. But where his flesh was the tint of pitch, hers was the rich color of day old cream, where his black hair clung to his head in a thick mat, hers cascaded over her shoulders and bare back in a glistening array of sausage curls the hue of raw coal, and where his dark eyes were near black, hers were brown and the slivers of amber that danced in them turned to fire. She wore a gown of silk the same color as the fire in her eyes, its deeply plunging neckline adorned with several dripping ruches of black lace, its sleeves puffed at the shoulder, then hugging her arms, and trimmed with more lace at her wrists. A sash of velvet, only a shade darker than her gown, encircled her tiny waist before trailing down her back. Two amber-dyed ostrich feathers were nestled behind one of her ears, secured by a brilliant gold medallion from which hung several looped strands of ivory black pearls.

Every man in the crowd stared at her, hunger evident in his eyes.

"Two hundred dollars is impossible, *mademoiselle,*" the auctioneer said, his tone one of obvious indignation. "This nigra is worth five times that."

"Be that as it may, *monsieur,*" the woman said, and slowly looked around, "two hundred dollars is what I bid, and I hear no other offers."

"But you can't bid," the auctioneer blustered, his pudgy, unshaven face puffing in anger. "You're . . . you're . . ."

"I am of the *gens de couleur libres,* as you well know, Monsieur Grantham, a free woman of color, and I believe my money is as good as anyone else's in this room." She smiled slyly and pinned him with a riveting gaze. "Especially yours, *monsieur.*"

The auctioneer looked around helplessly, but no one else spoke up.

The woman smiled. "He is a problem, *monsieur, no?*" she said, managing to look both innocent and sly at the same time. "Then sell him to me, Monsieur Grantham, and rid yourself of this troublesome slave."

In obvious frustration at getting no higher offers, his outrage at the situation evident in the tightness of his features, the auctioneer slammed his gavel down. "Sold, for two hundred dollars."

"Take his chains off," the woman ordered.

The auctioneer threw her a key. "Take them off yourself, negress," he growled.

Startled by the man's rudeness to the woman, Tori took a step back and was further shocked to find a strong hand at her waist, and a whispered deep voice in her ear.

"This is no place for you, *chérie*." His hot breath stirred the wisps of hair that curled before her ears.

Guy. She turned, and the smile that had curved her lips at the thought of him behind her instantly disappeared. "Jermonde," she gasped, the word more the fluttering sound of a summer breeze than even the barest whisper.

"Oui, chérie," he said. "I did not expect you to meet me so soon, especially not here at the St. Louis."

"I . . . I am with Guy, Jermonde." She wrestled free of his hands and moved away from the auction crowd. "Please, Jermonde, this is not proper, and I am not here to meet with you." Tori frantically looked past him in the direction where Guy had been standing. He was not there. Her heart began to race in fear. Where had he gone? If he saw her with Jermonde he would assume she had planned to meet him, he would assume everything she had said to him was a lie. Tori felt like pushing the sardonic Creole out of her way, but some instinct warned her against such brusqueness. "I'll call you later." She began to brush past him, but his hand snaked out and his fingers caught her arm in a tight grip.

"Call me?" he repeated.

"Yes, later."

His dark eyes narrowed in suspicion. "What am I to do, Victoria, stand on the banquette and wait until you call through your window?"

Tori looked for Guy again. "Oh, Jermonde, really," she snapped. "I'll phone you. Now go away."

"Phone? What are you talking about, Victoria? What's this phone business?"

She immediately stopped searching for Guy and stared at Jermonde. The words had just slipped from her lips, easily, without thought, and now that he wanted an explanation of what she'd meant, she found she couldn't give one.

"Victoria?" he said again, grinding her name out through clenched teeth.

"I . . ." she shook her head. "I will send you a note, Jermonde. Tomorrow."

From across the spacious hotel lobby, within the throng of people who milled about beneath the cavernous dome, gray eyes watched Tori from the shadows of one of the overhanging circular galleries. He had suspected all along that she couldn't be trusted, that she would betray him again, and he had been right. His eyes narrowed. But it didn't really matter anymore. Soon he would be rid of them all.

Twenty-six

New Orleans General Hospital
July, 1993

Victoria pushed open the wide door beneath the queer exit sign and stepped quickly past it and into the stairwell, letting the door swing silently shut behind her before moving again. She listened for footsteps, for someone coming after her, but was met with silence. She turned her attention back to the stairs, took a step toward them, and paused, gawking dumbly. "What kind of place is this?" she asked for the hundredth time since waking from the accident. She looked at the metal stairs, at the stark iron railing painted an ugly shade of gray, and the walls that appeared to be raw blocks of concrete. A frown pulled at her brow. She was used to Aubusson step coverings, polished wooden railings, elegantly carved balustrades, and walls of paneling, murals, or exquisite French wallpaper.

"I wouldn't be surprised to discover he's buried me in some madhouse for the indigent in New York," Victoria grumbled. "But it isn't going to work. Just like that bogus journal didn't work." She shuffled forth in her lavender fur slippers and quickly began to descend the stairs. "But I have to warn Darin." Her slippers made soft padding sounds on the steps. "He has to know that Guy knows about John, and what we've planned." After descending two flights she paused before two doors. The one directly in front of her had a huge number one painted on it. The one to her left had a small sign affixed to it: EXIT. She opened the latter and hurriedly stepped outside.

Victoria squinted against the harsh brightness of the afternoon sun. It might have been better to wait until nightfall, but she hadn't wanted to stay cooped up in that awful room for one more moment. Anyway, the streets would be more dangerous at night. They always were.

The piercing sound of a horn blasted the quiet. Victoria shrieked and jumped back, flattening herself against the building's outer wall. She looked up in horror, expecting to see a packet steaming toward her. Did this asylum edge the docks?

But it wasn't a riverboat. Instead, she gaped as a conglomeration of shiny black and silver metal moved slowly toward her. She stared at the huge metal and glass box. A person sat inside it, behind a curved sheet of clear glass and beneath a roof of more black metal. Victoria's eyes bulged as the contraption moved closer to where she stood, her teeth began to chatter, and a violent series of shivers rattled her body. My God, what was this thing? It suddenly roared at her. Victoria's hands flew to each side of her face and she screamed. Then, as abruptly as the growling sound had emanated from within the shiny black box, it quieted.

Victoria clung to the wall, not daring to look away from the thing, unwilling to move lest it attack her.

Suddenly, a wing flew outward from its side. Victoria screeched again and tried to press herself into the wall.

She didn't want to look, she didn't want to see what was going to happen to her, but she couldn't shut her eyes.

A woman emerged from the bowels of the metal and glass monstrosity. Her hair was long and golden, and she wore the most outrageous gown Victoria had ever seen, worse even than the asylum attendants garb. It was a print of huge purple and pink flowers, green leaves, and yellow stems. The dress had no sleeves, and its skirt barely reached to below the woman's derrière.

"Evie."

Victoria's eyes shot to the man who'd called out to the woman. He emerged from another metal "thing," a red one that Victoria had not noticed sitting nearby. The couple moved into one another's arms and their lips met.

"Scandalous," Victoria muttered, meaning the woman's dress, not their public embrace. She inched her way behind a tall bush a few feet away. Now that she had assured herself that they were indeed people, perhaps not the likes of which she had ever encountered before but at least not disciples of Hell come to fetch her back, she had regained some semblance of courage to go on.

She moved stealthily around a corner of the building and came face to face with a sea of huge metal and glass "things" just like the ones the woman, Evie, and her lover had emerged from. Victoria felt herself begin to tremble again. What were these? She took several steps down a bricked pathway that ran parallel with them. Suddenly one roared to life. Victoria shrieked and ran toward a tree, clutching its trunk as if it were a life line. One of the huge metal boxes, a glistening red one, moved backward, away from her, swung around to the right, and began to move away.

Victoria stared after it, mesmerized. It had wheels, but

they were like none she had ever seen. Black, solid, and with large, glistening silver hubs. There were no spokes.

The thing dipped as it rolled over a slope in the banquette and out onto the street. There were no horses. Victoria's gaze followed it until it was out of sight. Good God in heaven, what were these things? She shuddered. What kind of place had Guy sent her to?

She took a deep breath and scurried from the protection of the tree's shadow. Everything looked strange. The streets were all paved, and had lines painted on them; the banquettes were also paved, and raised. Suddenly a loud wailing sound pierced the air. Victoria slapped her hands over her ears and cringed against the side of a building. Her eyes widened in terror as another of those moving "things" sped toward her. A red light flashed from its roof. It roared past and through its window she saw a woman lying on some sort of bed.

Victoria ran blindly on. She had to get away from this place. If she could just get to the hotel, to the St. Louis, everything would be all right. Guy wasn't aware of it, but she had always kept a room there. She could get her clothes and hire a carriage to take her back to Shadow Oaks.

"Hey sweetheart, didn't anybody tell ya Mardi Gras is over?"

Victoria stopped and looked at the man who'd spoken. Cold terror raced through her veins and nearly stopped her heart. He was straddling a huge hodgepodge of shining metal, which in turn was held above the ground by two of those same black wheels she'd seen on those other "things." The man stared at her, waiting for her to say something, but her voice was frozen in her throat. His hair hung in long, brown strings down his back and over his shoulders, and a band of red material was tied around

290

his head. Black glasses hid his eyes but she could feel their scathing examination of her. He wore no shirt, his brawny arms and chest bare, his upper torso covered only by a vest of black leather. His trousers were denim, though old, frayed, and torn at the knees. Black gloves covered his hands, and on one upper arm a picture of a skull resting on a bloody knife had been printed on his flesh.

"Come on over here, gorgeous, and I'll give ya a ride." The man laughed, and the sound broke the spell Victoria had felt herself under.

"My husband's seconds will call on you promptly, *monsieur*," Victoria said angrily. She held out her hand. "Your card please."

The man laughed again and shook his head. "My card?"

"For the *duello*," Victoria snapped.

"A duel? Man, you crazies down here really do take all this old time Southern crap for real, don't ya?" His hand moved on the metal bar it rested upon and the huge assembly of metal roared loudly. A second later it shot forward, with him astride it.

"They're actors," Victoria mumbled to herself. "Guy hired actors to scare me with their tricks and some kind of machinery. That's all, actors."

Suddenly a shadow swept over Victoria and blocked out the sun. She looked up and a fresh wave of terror instantly filled her. A scream gurgled in her throat as she stared at the huge silver bird soaring overhead.

"Ma'am, are you all right?"

She turned eyes filled with panic toward the voice of the young man who had addressed her. He was about her own age, with a boyish face and wide-set blue eyes, and he was climbing from one of those moving "things." It was painted black and white, and had one of those red lights on its roof, like the one she'd seen on the "thing" that had emitted the ear-piercing wail. The man was dressed in some kind of uniform.

"Ma'am, I'm Officer Pellichout. Can I help you in some way? Is anything wrong?"

"Shadow Oaks," Victoria managed to mutter. She cleared her throat and tried desperately to stop the tremors that shook her body. "I have to get to Shadow Oaks. My husband, he . . . he . . . but my carriage, it's gone, and my gown."

"Shadow Oaks," the officer repeated. "Yes, I know it. You say you need to get there?"

"I had a carriage, but there was an accident." Victoria glanced at the "things." They seemed to be everywhere now, but there wasn't a carriage or horse in sight. "Guy must have taken my carriage. And my clothes. He left me in that asylum, but I'm not crazy." She looked about wildly. "I know he just wants me out of the way, most likely so he can whore with the slaves down in the Quarter." She laughed then. "No, that's not his style either. It's Darin's, but that will all change once we're married."

"Yes, ma'am," Officer Pellichout said. He glanced back at his partner, who was standing at the driver's door. His partner raised a hand to his head, pointed an index finger toward his own temple, and moved it in a circle.

Pellichout nodded and turned back to Victoria, who was still talking.

"Everything's wrong. He's trying to make it look like I'm crazy, but I'm not. I left the opera house because I was angry, I mean, divorce would be such a scandal. The horses spooked at the lightning, that's all, the stupid beasts panicked and dashed over the embankment. Lucky for me

292

that carriage turned sideways, or I might have gotten killed."

"Pardon me, ma'am, but, ah, do you know what year this is?" Pellichout asked.

Victoria fixed him with a riveting glare and straightened her shoulders. He wasn't a soldier, he was an actor, just like the others. Guy had hired them all. An elaborate scheme to drive her out of her mind. But it wasn't going to work. "Of course I do. What a stupid question. It's eighteen-fifty-nine." She waved a dismissing hand at him. "Now, enough of this foolishness. Whatever Guy is paying you to playact this scheme, I'll pay you more to stop it."

"Yes, ma'am," Officer Pellichout said.

"Now"—Victoria's air had become haughty and arrogant—"take me to Shadow Oaks."

"Alert the mental ward that we've got one of their patients out here," Pellichout's partner whispered into his mike.

Twenty-seven

Tori spotted Guy only a few feet from where he'd been standing moments ago. She had missed him while looking earlier because several more gentlemen had joined in the conversation. A sigh of relief left her lips. At least he hadn't seen her with Jermonde St. Croix. She would have to do as she had promised and contact Jermonde later, but how she was going to convince the handsome Creole that she had no interest in a relationship with him, in spite of their past, she didn't know. She just knew she had to.

Guy broke away from the cluster of men and walked hurriedly toward her. "I'm sorry to have left you alone like that, Victoria. One of our neighbors has just returned from Washington, and it seems the slave issue is once again the main topic of conversation up there. I don't like politics, as you know, but I may have no choice but to get involved in this issue."

Tori was about to tell him that if he did get involved and his stance was proslavery, he'd lose, but she caught herself. How did she know that?

Just then the woman from the auction passed, her head held high, a satisfied smile on her lips. She nodded a greeting to Guy, ignored Tori, and continued on without pausing. The slave followed closely behind, though rather than in a subservient manner, impudently and challengingly, as he dared any man watching to reproach him.

"Guy," Tori said softly, "do you know that woman?"

He followed her gaze. "Celestine Dubois." He placed a hand on Tori's back and urged her toward a wide sweeping staircase near the hotel desk. "Do you remember her?"

Tori shook her head. "No. Should I?"

He shrugged as they slowly ascended the shallow steps. "I just thought you might, after seeing her."

"Were we friends?"

Guy laughed. "Hardly. You hated her."

Tori stopped abruptly and gawked at him. "Hated her? Why should I hate her?"

"You shouldn't, but you did. She buys slaves, educates them, and then frees them."

"But that's wonderful," Tori said. "No one has the right to own another human being."

Now it was Guy's turn to gape in disbelief. He studied her face for long moments, unmindful of the stares of the hotel guests forced to circle them on the stairs. His eyes searched, questioned, and assessed. Victoria stood before him, he knew it was her as well as he knew his own image in the mirror, and yet everything she did and said made him question what he saw, what he knew to be true. How could a simple carriage accident change a person so drastically?

"She was also John's *placée*," Guy said finally, and tensed, his shoulders stiff, waiting for the storm that he felt was sure to come.

Tori's face screwed into an expression of complete puzzlement. *"Placée?* What's that?"

A woman just passing on the steps stopped short and glared at Victoria. "Well, I never," she huffed.

"Never what?" Tori asked innocently.

The woman sniffed, lifted her chin into the air, and continued on her way down the stairs.

Guy's deep laughter wrapped around Tori and sent a shiver of delicious tingles racing up her spine. She loved it when he laughed. "I'm glad you find my lack of knowledge amusing," she quipped lightly. "But before you begin to roll on the floor, would you please tell me what a *placée* is?"

He sobered quickly as more people began to stare, took her by the arm, and urged her to continue their ascent of the stairs. "She was John's mistress," he said softly under his breath, then in a more sober tone he added, "There are some who think she killed him in a fit of jealousy."

Tori stopped again, remembering the horrid nightmare that had been plaguing her of late. "Do you?"

"No. If Celestine is guilty of anything, it's having loved John too much. Anyway, she didn't have anything to be jealous of."

They reached the landing and Guy's hand on her back urged Tori to turn left. She walked beside him down the wide hallway.

"John was betrothed to marry Janeene Labout, but he had broken the engagement. He loved Celestine and wanted to move her to Shadow Oaks."

"He was engaged to be married *and* had a mistress?" Tori said incredulously.

Guy threw her a cursory glance. Could she really have forgotten everything? Even the Creoles most basic customs? He pushed the question aside. There would be time enough to dwell on that later.

"What do you think happened?" Tori asked.

Guy shrugged and inserted a key in the door they had passed before. "I don't know. John left the house one evening. He said he was going to Celestine's and wouldn't be back until morning. When he didn't return by afternoon I went looking for him. When I got to Celestine's she was worried. She said he had not come to her the previous night. She had sent her servants throughout the Quarter in search of him, but no one else had seen him."

"How long has he been gone?" She followed Guy into the room.

A long sigh left his lips as he thought back to that night John had left Shadow Oaks. "Almost a year. That's why we're in town. I've been putting off signing the papers that would finalize the transfer of Shadow Oaks and all of John's other property to me, but it can't be delayed any longer. If it is," he moved to stand before a window that overlooked Royal Street, "well, let's just say there could be legal problems if I wait."

"With Darin?"

His head swung around sharply at her question and a look of suspicion returned to his narrowed eyes.

She recognized the expression and her heart sank. It had been the wrong thing to ask, but it was too late now. His brother's name hung in the still air between them like a black thundercloud. Tori had hoped never to see that look in Guy's eyes again, but after everything that had happened, she couldn't blame him for suspecting her at times. "It was just a natural assumption, Guy. I mean"—her eyes implored him to believe her—"as you've said, Darin covets everything you possess. I imagine he had that same feeling toward John."

Guy nodded. "Even as a child, no matter how much my

parents gave Darin, it was never enough. He always wanted whatever John and I had, though he'd been given exactly the same thing."

"Was John going to marry Celestine?" Tori asked, changing the subject in the hope of banishing the spark of suspicion that had come to Guy's eyes at the mention of Darin.

"Marry Celestine?" Guy looked at Tori as if she were crazy, then shook his head. "I'm sorry, I keep forgetting you don't remember much of anything." And hopefully never will, a little voice in the back of his mind said. He wanted her to stay this way, to remain the person she had become, the woman he had fallen. . . . He clamped a barrier down on his thoughts before they strayed too far in a direction he did not want them to go.

"Try just plain anything," Tori quipped.

His head jerked up, and he smiled. "Your sense of humor has definitely improved though."

"Thank you." She laughed. "Now, answer me. Was John going to marry Celestine?"

"No. He couldn't."

"Why not?"

"Because she's a quadroon and it's against the law."

"A quadroon? What's that?"

"Black."

"Black?" Tori echoed. "But . . . but . . . she's as white as I am."

Guy settled down on the bed, folded his long arms behind his head and crossed his feet at the ankles. "No, she's not, Victoria. She only looks it. Her father is Étienne Dubois, of Cherry Hill Plantation, but her mother was his mulatto housekeeper, Marie."

"But her skin—"

"Is white," he finished for her. "Up North or in Europe she could pass for white, but not here. Regardless of how much or how little black blood flows in her veins, Victoria, in Louisiana she is considered black. So you see, John could not marry her. Dubois freed her years ago, gave her money, even educated her in France. As a promise to Marie I've heard. Celestine could live anywhere she chooses, but she refuses to leave New Orleans."

"Why?"

He shrugged. "Who knows. I used to think it was because of John, but he's gone now, and she has no intention of leaving. I don't know."

"She must have been devastated when John disappeared," Tori said softly.

Guy pushed himself up from the bed and moved toward her. This new side of Victoria aroused his emotions, especially his passion, more quickly than he'd ever thought possible. His arms went around her waist and pulled her close. "Much as I would rather remain here and help you out of that lovely dress, I'm afraid I have a meeting at the bank in"—he slipped a hand into the pocket of his coat, pulled out a gold pocketwatch and flipped it open—"umm, five minutes ago." He brushed his lips across hers in a featherlight kiss that was a tease to her senses. "I'll meet you back here in two hours."

The moment he released her and left the room she felt cold and deserted. The beautiful suite that only a moment before had seemed bright, warm, and full of life, suddenly felt drab and empty. Even the excitement of being in town was now overshadowed by the fear she felt at having run into Jermonde St. Croix only moments after their arrival.

And Darin? her mind nagged.

He was supposed to be in Baton Rouge. Perhaps she

had been mistaken. Most likely it hadn't been Darin at all, just someone who resembled him. The same hair color and such. The thought made her feel better momentarily. She sat down on the bed. But where had Darin been the night of John's disappearance?

I saw him plunge the knife into John's back, then he rolled John's body into the water.

Tori shuddered as icy fingers tripped up her spine. She felt that someone had just walked over her grave. Now where in the name of God had that thought come from? She stood quickly, grabbed her reticule, and moved toward the door. Her thoughts were getting too morbid, and much too frightening. She needed fresh air, space, and some exercise. She should walk about, see the Quarter, look at other faces besides those presently haunting her.

Tori descended into the crowded lobby of the hotel. The slave auction was over, but several other auctions were still taking place. Hawkers were yelling for bids on everything from furniture, oil paintings, and household goods to jewelry and exotic fabrics. She watched, spellbound, as a tall, ornately carved armoire sold for three hundred dollars.

"Lord," Tori murmured. "In my time that would cost several thousand dollars at least." She was just approaching the bottom of the stairs, but stopped cold at her own words. The fingers, holding the skirt of her gown, stiffened and lost their grip on the delicate fabric. Her other hand tightened around the stair railing until her knuckles were white from the pressure. What did she mean, in her time? Her heart raced frantically. Why did her mind keep throwing out these ridiculous thoughts? What was wrong with her? Tori took a deep breath to try and calm herself. Her time? She clenched her trembling hands together, walked

300

past the crowd milling around the auctioneers' blocks, and hurried out the entry door.

A carriage was just pulling away from the banquette in front of the hotel entry, and another moved forward to take its place. The doorman looked expectantly at Tori, but she shook her head at his gesture toward the buggy. With still-shaking hands, she settled the white and blue pelisse cape around her shoulders and turned to the left. Air, she needed air; then her thoughts would clear and she'd make sense again.

She walked aimlessly, recognizing nothing, not sure of where she was going and, after having walked several blocks, no longer certain of the direction from which she had come. Turning a corner she was pleased to see the gardenlike open land they had passed earlier in the carriage. She remembered that Guy had called it the Place d'Armes and had then corrected himself, explaining to her that only a few years before the city officials had renamed the park Jackson Square, in honor of the man who had saved the city from the British, and whose statue was the park's centerpiece.

She walked across the wide roadway that separated the square from the elegant gray St. Louis Cathedral with its arched doorways and three sky-reaching steeples. At the small path that gave entry to the square, Tori paused and looked around, searching for anything that would spark a glimmer of memory. Her gaze rested first on the park itself. It wasn't really very large, just a small tract of garden in the midst of the city. Several tall trees offered spots of shade to those who chose to loiter within the park's grounds, while various arrays of rose bushes gave the square a brilliance of color. Small benches had been placed here and there along the winding paths for visitors to rest upon. Tori studied everything for several long seconds, but found nothing familiar.

She turned next to the two-storied buildings that flanked each side of the park. They were identical. Red brick, sloping roofs, their second stories adorned with wrought-iron balconies of lacey design and painted black. These upper floors appeared to be used as residences—apartments—while the ground level was composed of storefronts. Again she remembered nothing.

Tears of frustration filled her eyes, but Tori fought them back. They would not help. She turned her glance toward the river across the street. To the left was the French Market she and Guy had visited that morning. Almost directly opposite the park was a small building. A sign over its entry proclaimed it the DuMonde Café. Beyond it were the wharves, the river, and the boats. Tori sighed. "This is useless," she muttered to herself, a spurt of anger shooting through her at her lack of success.

Walking slowly along a path that cut through the center of the park, Tori paused before the tall statue of Andrew Jackson. She looked at the smooth surface of the huge granite base upon which the statue stood. Suddenly words appeared, engraved within the stone: The Union Must and Shall Be Preserved. Tori blinked and looked again. The words were gone.

She reached out and ran her fingers over the cold surface. It was smooth and uncut. "What's happening to me?" Tori muttered, the fear that had shaken her back in the hotel room returning. She turned away from the statue. Instantly her body seemed consumed with heat, her breathing ragged and difficult. A woman sat on a nearby bench conversing with a young man. In her hand she held a fan, which she fluttered back and forth before her face. The breeze caused by the fan lifted the curls at her temples. Tori opened her reticule and looked inside. No fan. She looked about the park. There was no vacant bench either. But there was a giant oak. She walked toward it. The gnarled limbs supported a thick growth of dark green leaves that acted like a parasol against the sun and were also rods for the sheer curtains of Spanish moss that, in some places, dripped to the ground. Tori moved gratefully into the tree's shadow. Just escaping the brilliant glare of the sun, even for a few moments, seemed to refresh her. She stood beside the tree's massive trunk, beneath the protection of its gnarled limbs, and looked out at the river across Levee Street.

"I knew you would come, *chérie.*"

The touch of a hand on her neck, of fingers moving lightly, caressingly, over her skin, and the words softly spoken by the deep voice startled Tori. She whirled around, and as the huge hoop-cage beneath her skirts swung, was forced to reach out toward the tree trunk to stop herself from losing her balance. Dark eyes, as infinite as the night sky, yet laughing and full of humor, met hers. "Jermonde," Tori said, his name little more than a whispered gasp that escaped her lips.

He smiled and Tori was instantly reminded of a cat that had succeeded in cornering his prey and was about to enjoy the game of live or die. "I . . . I didn't expect you."

Black fire flared within his eyes and the smile instantly lost all pretense of warmth or cordiality. "Oh? And whom did you expect, *chérie?* Another love perhaps?"

She heard the grate of anger in his voice, saw the tightening of muscles in both his jaw and neck, and knew, instinctively, this was not a man to cross. His hand rose toward her face.

Instinctively Tori began to cringe, then caught herself, sensing that would anger him further.

He touched her cheek with the back of his hand, his knuckles gliding lightly over the curve of her cheek, along the line of her jaw, and then dropping to follow the column of her neck. As his hand approached her breast, Tori stepped back. She looked around quickly. "Jermonde, please, someone will see."

"And if they do? So?" He laughed softly, a sardonically wicked sound that sent a wave of goose flesh rippling over her body. "What fool would challenge me, Jermonde St. Croix, to a duel? I am the best, as my pupils at the St. Croix *académie* will swear, and as you very well know, *chérie.*" He laughed again.

She stiffened as his hand turned abruptly and his fingers slid over the curve of her breast, his thumb intimately flicking the spot of cloth that covered her nipple. His dark eyes held hers, refusing to relinquish their power over her.

"Please, Jermonde, Guy might see. He's out here somewhere and—"

"And he would be forced to challenge me, no?" He laughed again. "Such a *mari complaisant,* your husband. Perhaps a little kiss now, *en plein jour,* will bring out a bit of jealousy in him, you think?"

Tori stared up at Jermonde in confusion. His words had meant nothing to her, but his sneering tone had relayed their message. "Jermonde, I don't want—"

Before she knew what he intended, his head lowered and his lips covered hers. Tori tried to move away from him, but one arm had slipped around her waist to hold her in an iron grip that offered little hope of escape. He drew her toward him and crushed her against his lean length.

The sharp denial she tried to utter proved to his advantage as his tongue slipped quickly between her parted lips and filled her mouth with its twisting, curling exploration.

Shocked, Tori tried to push against him, but he was too strong, his arms like bands of steel, his chest a wall of unmoveable granite, his shoulders lean curves of hidden strength. She felt the rhythmic cadence of his heart beneath her hand on his chest, its beat fast and hard, tasted the apricot brandy that still lingered on his lips, and smelled the exotic scent of island spices that surrounded him and exuded from him. And all the while that he kissed her, Tori's terrified thoughts were on Guy and on what he would think if he saw them.

It was Jermonde who broke the embrace. "So, my kisses do not please you anymore, *chérie?*"

The chastising remark she'd been about to direct at him died on her lips. She looked into his eyes and, for one brief moment, saw Jermonde's callous disregard for human life. Suddenly she knew she had to choose her words, to act toward this man with caution. "I just do not want to cause more scandal. There's been so much already. You understand that, don't you?"

He smiled then, but, as the first time she had encountered Jermonde St. Croix, she could find no warmth in the curve of his full lips, in the fathomless blackness of his eyes, or anywhere else on the handsome features.

"Au contraire, mon cœur, it is, perhaps, only scandal that will get us to where we want to be, no?"

He laughed softly then, and Tori's blood turned chill. How could she have ever felt anything toward this man but dislike? "Jermonde—"

"Non. Let us dispense with this pretense of *bien séance,* Victoria, this concern with propriety you have suddenly developed. You belong to me, *chérie,* and I want the world

to know it." His fingers slipped around to the back of her neck, and suddenly, without warning, his hand clasped her nape and his arm yanked forward, roughly forcing her close to him. "And if that means I must kill this cuckold of a husband you have"—he shrugged nonchalantly and Tori shuddered at the cold spark in his dark eyes—"then that is what I will do." His mouth slashed down over hers again. "Gladly," he whispered against her lips.

When he finally released her, Tori had to gulp deeply to regain her breath. She stepped back and brushed a stray lock of hair from her temple as his arms dropped lazily from around her.

"Now, did you not find that too enjoyable to be worried about propriety, *mon cœur?*" He laughed deeply, the musical baritone tones filling the afternoon shadows and echoing out into the bright sunshine of the surrounding park.

Tori looked around nervously. There were at least a half a dozen people looking in their direction, all of whom she did not recognize, but who most likely knew her and would, she sensed, be all to happy to tell Guy what they had witnessed.

Rage flared within his chest, its fiery flames building with each second that passed, its heat spreading throughout his body, consuming him, until it took every ounce of will power he had to remain still. It was no longer passion she instilled within him, but fury. He stood within the confines of a tailor's shop, one of the many stores located on the ground floors of the twin, red brick, Pontalba buildings, and whose storefront window faced the square. The sun was low in the sky, the afternoon waning. Its brilliant rays reflected on the face of the glass he looked through, enabling him to see the couple who stood beneath the tree, embracing wantonly, but preventing them from being able to see him. Hatred glistened from his gray eyes. He had left Celestine's later than he'd intended, had then finished with his *homme d'affaires* in a financially satisfactory manner, and on his way to Madame Chartonneau's had entered the tailor's shop on impulse.

While a cheroot burned, forgotten, between the fingers of his left hand, the white smoke drifting up before him in spiraling, translucent wisps, his other hand, hanging beside his lean thigh, repeatedly clenched and unclenched into a fist. He had known she would betray him again, that it had been only a matter of time, yet even though he had known it would eventually happen, it did not lessen the rage he now felt.

Twenty-eight

Tori turned the key and pushed open the door to their hotel suite. She stepped across the threshold, but as she reached to close the door, paused. Guy sat in a tall, winged-back chair beside the window, the chair's gold damask fabric the same as that of the elegant drapes that hung from the tall window. Rather than return immediately to the hotel after extricating herself from Jermonde, she had wandered the streets of the Vieux Carré, looking through windows and generally just trying to recapture some semblance of composure. But the problem of Jermonde would not leave her mind, nor would the realization that no matter where in the Quarter she wandered, no matter what she looked at or touched, nothing had sparked even the faintest memory.

Evening was quickly approaching, and the radiant pink rays of the setting sun streamed through the window's lace panels to settle on Guy's shoulders and within the dark curls of his hair. "Did you have a pleasant stroll, Victoria?"

Her hand tightened around the doorknob as she searched his face for signs of suspicion and tried to determine if she had heard any sarcasm in his tone.

"Victoria, are you all right?" He pushed himself gracefully to his feet and walked toward her.

Tori smiled and closed the door. Everything was all right, otherwise he would not appear so calm. "Of course, you just startled me, Guy, that's all. I really didn't think you'd be back yet."

"My *homme d'affaires* was on another call and we were unable to meet. Actually, I wandered about the Quarter for a while, looking for you. I had thought we might dine early and perhaps partake of the opera."

Her hands instantly began to tremble. He had been looking for her. He had been in the Quarter. Perhaps at the square. "You looked for me?" she finally managed, distressed further to find her voice little more than a raspy squeak. Was he truly as calm as he appeared?

"For a while." He frowned and his eyes searched hers.

Tori felt charged with nervous energy, yet at the same time weak with fear. He stood before her now, so close she could feel his warm breath waft across her temple as she looked up at him. She could almost hear his heart beat beneath the crisp white shirt, could sense the warmth of his flesh, though they weren't touching. Please God, she prayed silently, don't let him have been near the square. "I . . . I didn't see you."

"I know. I've been back here for a while." He slipped his arms around her waist and pulled her toward him. "And I found I didn't much care for being here alone."

Tori laughed in relief and wrapped her arms around his neck, snuggling close to him. "I was out walking, but if I had known you were here, I would never have kept you waiting," she said, her voice low and sultry.

"Are you hungry, Victoria?"

"For you," she teased, and snuggled deeper into his

309

arms. "But only if you stop calling me Victoria, and call me Tori."

"Ummm." He brushed his lips over hers. "Then never let it be said, *Tori,* that I refused you sustenance." Guy's lips descended on hers, swift as the swoop of a hawk, demanding as a hunter.

The fires of passion seized him in a grip that offered no recourse but satiation. His fingers moved quickly and deftly from one button of her gown to the next, releasing each from its bindings.

He brushed the gown from her shoulders, and the soft rustle of fabric broke the silence between them as it fell to the floor, followed almost instantly by her crinolines, camisole, and pantalettes. When finally her gown and underthings lay in a heap on the floor around her feet, Guy bent to kneel on one knee, and his fingers slid lightly over her legs as he rolled her stockings down and removed her shoes.

At the seductively feather-light touch of his fingers on her thighs Tori nearly moaned in pleasure. Remaining still before him, she closed her eyes and let her head tilt back ever so slightly.

Guy made to rise, but as his gaze lifted his eyes encountered that lustrous triangle of dark curls and hesitated. Then, giving in to the basic urges that had taken over both his mind and body, he leaned forward and pressed his lips to the sensitive flesh hidden behind those curls.

He heard a sharp intake of breath and felt Tori's body quiver as his tongue darted forth and touched the delicate folds that hid the small nub of her need from view. When she trembled again, and a soft groan escaped her lips, he rose to his full height and drew her into his arms, once again claiming her mouth with his. His tongue moved caressingly about the interior of her mouth, stoking her passion as well as his own, and when he sensed—knew—that her desire was such that it would not allow her to reject him, he pulled away from her and took a step back.

Standing nude before him, bathed in the rosey glow of the sun's dying rays, Tori found herself suddenly embarrassed. She lifted her arms to cover herself from his view.

"No, don't hide yourself from me," Guy said. He reached out and gently pushed her hands back down to her sides. "It has been a long time since I have enjoyed the sight of your body, Victoria."

Tori's cheeks warmed, but she kept her hands at her sides as he had asked.

His gaze swept over her swiftly, then again more slowly, assessing each curve. She is beautiful, he thought coldly, but then he never had been able to deny that. Still, her beauty was like that of the porcelain statuettes that graced the palaces of France—cold, hard, and superficial . . . for there was none inside.

"Now it is your turn," Guy said finally.

She frowned in confusion at his words, but the sly little smile that pulled at his lips was explanation enough. Stepping from the mound of her discarded clothes she moved toward him. She quickly released the buttons of his shirt and pulled its tails from the waistband of his trousers. Her fingers slipped beneath the silk fabric and, as her hands slid slowly, seductively, over the ropey contours of his shoulders, feeling hard muscle and satiny flesh beneath them, she pushed his shirt from him and let it fall to the floor. He remained still as she unclasped the waistband of his trousers and tugged both them and his underdrawers downward. But it was her hair, the soft curling strands of brown that brushed against his pulsating, hungry manhood

311

as she knelt to remove his boots that tore the groan from his throat.

To Tori's ears it was a moan of desire and instilled her with the confidence she needed, but to Guy it was the sound of his own self-loathing, of momentary defeat and surrender to the overpowering allure she held for him.

He had wanted to punish her, to take out his anger and indignation on her, to prove to her once and for all that he could take her and feel nothing . . . and once again he had failed. But it was too late to stop, and too early for regrets. He pulled her back to her feet, swept her into his arms, and crushed her nude form to the hot, naked length of his body. His lips sought hers again; his tongue plunged into her mouth and instantly sought to rape her senses and drive her as mad with want as she had driven him.

He felt the small start of shock that went through her at his brusqueness, heard the soft whimper that echoed from her throat, and tried to ignore them. But he couldn't. Something within him, something he didn't want to acknowledge but seemed unable to deny, refused to allow him to hurt her. He loosened his hold on her, and his kiss turned to one of gentle yearning and exploration.

Each sweep of his hands inflamed Tori's senses further; each stroke of his tongue intoxicated her already piqued sensuality. Her arms wrapped around his neck, hungrily holding him to her, and her body, hot with yearning for him, arched against his in welcome. She shivered with want for him as his hands traveled over her silken skin, his fingers skipping lightly over every slender curve, every subtle mound and sweeping line.

Lifting her into his arms, Guy carried Tori to the bed and, his mouth never leaving hers, set her down and unfolded his long form next to hers. He drew her fiercely into his arms then, but rather than reclaim her lips, his mouth moved to cover the nipple of one breast, his tongue tasting the pebbled flesh, teasing it, until the tiny peak was hard and throbbing. The fingers of one hand slid through the triangle of dark curls at her thighs and disappeared within the sensitive folds of flesh on which his tongue had been only moments before.

Waves of fire suddenly swept through her at his touch, bringing his name to her lips over and over. She writhed beneath his caresses, her body pressing to his, the soft lines of her curves fitting into the hard muscles of his sinewy length.

Thoughts of revenge, retribution, and punishment had been in his mind for several agonizing hours before she had returned to the hotel. They had been in his mind when he had dragged her into his arms and kissed her, when he had stripped her of her clothes, and when he had demanded that she remove his. But they were there no longer. Now his desire for her was so intense, so mind-consuming, that it wiped out all other thought, all other emotion.

"Love me, Guy," Tori whispered. "Please, love me."

Her words caused a searing fire within him that nearly proved his undoing. Guy's mouth reclaimed hers in an urgency of need, and rising above her, he nudged her legs apart, settled himself between her thighs, and thrust inside of her. Her body rose to meet his entry, and her arms tightened around his neck. His thrusts were urgent, hungry, and deep, his need for release near desperate. He had let himself be fooled again, and his anger, his frustration at the situation, drove his passion to new heights yet left him with a coldness inside. He knew he was not being gentle with her, that he was exerting no real tenderness, no care for her feelings, but he was no

313

longer concerned with that. He was taking what belonged to him, what was rightfully his.

Guy remained awake long after Tori had drifted into sleep. He lay with one arm raised and tucked his head, his eyes staring up at the gathered gold silk *ciel de lit,* his thoughts a jumble of questions to which he desperately needed answers.

Tori stirred slightly, snuggling her head into the crook of his shoulder, and a thick lock of her long hair slipped slowly along his chest. The dark tendrils also spread across the white pillow like rich trails of earthen-colored silk. As Guy let his gaze travel her length, desire burned anew within him, the flames that seemed always to simmer when she was near threatening to erupt into an inferno of hungry need, but with them now came another emotion, one he was well familiar with—anger.

Reaching out, Guy slipped his fingers beneath a curl of her hair and lifted it slightly. He stared, mesmerized, as the wavey strands slipped slowly through his fingers, caressing his flesh like threads of satin and intensifying the need building within him to know her passion one more time.

A soft curse left his lips, and he dropped his hand to the flat of his own stomach, his thoughts returning to that afternoon. When he hadn't come across Victoria in any of her favorite dress shops, he had gone to the Cabildo. Politics was not a favorite pastime or subject with him, but it never hurt to know what was going on, especially if there was any chance it might affect his business affairs. And the talk he had heard earlier in the hotel lobby on the slave issue could definitely hurt his business. He had spoken with several friends who'd been at the Cabildo and then, on his way out of the old government building, had chanced to glance across the way to the square. The image still burned vivid in his mind, but then he wasn't really surprised. He had seen what he had been half-expecting to see for days, yet had been hoping he would not. But discretion had never been one of Victoria's strong points. He had watched them as they'd stood beneath the spreading limbs of the old tree in the square and embraced. The anger he had felt at seeing them still burned within him. Why did her betrayal seem to cut so much deeper this time? Hadn't he expected it? Waited for it? He had sensed, or somehow known, that her loss of memory was just another ploy, yet there had been a few times she had almost convinced him of its sincerity. He'd wanted to believe she'd changed, but deep down inside him he'd always known, albeit subconsciously, that nothing was different; she had always been, and was still, Victoria.

He had decided, only moments before she'd returned to the room, that he would play her game, would go along with whatever scheme she was unraveling around him and attempting to draw him into. But this time he was ready for her, this time it would be Victoria who would come out the loser.

Guy sighed deeply and gazed down at her sleeping form again. Much as he disliked what she was, what she had done, and what she hoped to do, he could not deny the fires she caused to burn within him. But it had not always been so, and that puzzled him. For almost five years now there had been no physical contact between them, and none wanted on either side. Why then, since the accident, had that changed? Why now, every time he looked at her, every time he was near her, did he want to possess her again?

Tori woke abruptly. She sat up and looked around, momentarily disoriented. This wasn't her room at Shadow Oaks. She stared at the broadcloth coat that lay across a wing chair near the window. Moonlight settled soft and golden on the black folds of cloth. A noise, like that of something small being set down drew her attention to an open doorway on the opposite side of the room. Her head swung around. Light shone from the doorway. Another sound, and then footsteps. Tori pulled the sheet up to cover her bare breasts.

"Well, I was wondering if you were just going to sleep all night." Guy appeared within the doorway, a black shape against the golden light. He chuckled lightly and finished securing the cravat at his neck. "Come on, beautiful, or the dining room will be closed by the time we get there, and frankly I'm famished."

Memory assailed her, followed by a swift sense of relief. They were at the St. Louis Hotel. She and Guy. And he had made love to her. Everything was all right. Dragging the sheet with her, and holding it to her breasts, Tori grabbed the pantalettes and stockings he had earlier slipped from her legs and carelessly tossed to the floor. Her camisole lay next to them. She scooped that up too. "I'm afraid it's going to take me awhile to get ready."

He grabbed the jacket from the chair and shrugged it over his shoulders. "Well then"—he strode across the room, closing the distance between them with only three strides of his long legs, and pulled her into his arms, holding her near-naked form tightly against his length—"how about if I go on down to the dining room and make sure they don't close up on us?"

She nodded. "I'll be there as soon as I can."

He pressed his lips to her forehead. "Good, and I'm

316

going to get out of here before I change my mind, ignore my growling stomach, and just take you back to bed."

Tori laughed as he left the room.

Once in the hallway a string of pithy oaths escaped Guy's lips. This was not going to be easy. Drawing her to him like that had been all he had dared do. One more moment of holding her naked body in his arms, of having her pressed up against him like that, and food would have been the last thing on his mind. But he had to maintain control of himself. If he was going to see this thing through, and win, he had to keep his wits about him.

The hotel's dining room wasn't as empty as he'd thought it would be at this late hour. About fifty other patrons sat at various tables, though at least several hundred guests could be accommodated. Guy ordered their meal, and a bottle of wine, and then settled back to wait for Victoria. He unfolded the pages of the *Picayune News,* handed to him by the *maître d',* and began to scan its articles. One in particular, on page three, caught his attention almost immediately.

The body of Madame Mariah Chartonneau was found today in the back of her shop, Madame's Potions, on Rue Dumaine. She had been bludgeoned to death. Money left in her cash box suggests that robbery was not the cause of Madame Chartonneau's murder. Her cousin, Doctor Yah Yah, will perform funeral rites in Congo Square tomorrow night.

Guy reread the article several times. John had once said that he had spotted Darin patronizing Madame Chartonneau's shop, but when asked about it, Darin had become enraged and claimed John was lying. Guy's gaze dropped to the bottom line of the article. Hadn't Hannah told him, not more than a few months ago, that she had heard rumors Victoria had gone to see this voodoo priest, Doctor Yah Yah?

Twenty-nine

Tori stepped into the grand dining room. Her first impression was one of splendid elegance. The place was immense, its high ceiling a masterpiece composed of murals painted around ornately carved plaster medallions from which sprung the golden chains of four elegant chandeliers. Each were three tiered and dripped with over a hundred teardrop crystal prisms that caught and reflected light in a dazzling rainbow of translucent color. The walls were covered in panels of highly polished, rich cherrywood, and on the street wall, white corinthian pilasters stood between each tall, gold brocade-draped window. Tori looked about the sea of linen-covered tables for Guy. Several men seated nearby paused in their conversations and returned her gaze. She ignored them and finally spotted Guy seated at a table near the bank of windows that overlooked Rue Royal. He was intently reading a newspaper and had not noticed her arrival. Tori weaved her way through the tables toward him, holding the skirt of the apricot silk gown she had chosen to wear so as not to bump the chairs she passed, for the huge hoop-cage beneath her crinolines swayed first to the left, then to the right. "Is this table available?" she asked, chuckling softly as Guy looked up, somewhat startled by her teasing question.

He smiled. "I'm sorry, Victoria, I didn't see you enter." He rose and pulled out a chair for her, then resettled himself on his own.

"Guy, would you please call me Tori." She shook her head and laughed. "I'm sorry, but I just can't seem to get used to being called Victoria. It sounds so formal."

His eyes studied her harshly, but his voice was congenial when he answered. "I'll try, but since I've never called you anything but Victoria, it's not easy."

"Fair enough. Now, where's a menu?"

"I've already ordered. They were awaiting your arrival before serving."

"Oh. What are we having?"

He opened his mouth to respond, but she continued before he could.

"Lord, a huge cheeseburger and a plateful of greasy, hot French fries sure would hit the spot right about now. And a coke. Or maybe a root beer."

His mouth hung agape in shock.

Tori smiled, reached over, and playfully pushed his bottom jaw up with her fingertips until his mouth was closed. "What's wrong? I was only teasing. I'm sure they don't serve cheeseburgers and fries here."

Guy cleared his throat and pinned her with a pointed glare. "What in the hell is a cheeseburger, Victoria?" he said under his breath. "And would you please explain greasy, hot French fries."

"Oh, come on Guy. A cheeseburger, you know, a hamburger?"

He stared, obviously uncomprehending.

"Beef, lettuce, tomato, pickle, and bun. Oh, and cheese." She smiled, satisfied with her explanation.

Guy glowered. He didn't know what the hell she was up to with this "cheeseburger" thing, but he wasn't going to play her game, not in public, not in the St. Louis, and not at this moment.

Their dinner arrived before he could comment again. After Tori oohed and ahhed over the gumbo, bernaise salmon, shrimp creole, and various accompanying dishes for several seconds, they began to eat.

"I read an interesting article in the paper," Guy said, breaking the silence that had developed between them at the onset of the meal. He lifted the bottle of wine the waiter had placed in a silver ice bucket at one side of the table and poured a generous serving into both their glasses.

"Oh?"

"Yes. There was a murder in the Quarter today, or possibly last night. The police aren't exactly sure of the time of death."

Tori looked at him expectantly.

"Madame Chartonneau," Guy said. He slipped the tip of his knife into the center of a small, red potato and waited for her reaction.

"Do we know this woman, Guy?" Tori asked innocently.

He looked at her sharply. "I thought you might. She was a cousin of Doctor Yah Yah."

Tori laughed, then realized he was being serious, and caught herself. "I'm sorry. Doctor Yah Yah?"

"He's a voodoo priest."

Tori felt a sudden chill, and any suspicion that he had been joking fled her. "Voodoo?" She stared at him for a long minute. "Why would I know a voodoo priest?"

He shrugged. "It's no secret you've dabbled in voodoo, Victoria—sorry, I mean Tori."

"I did?" Tori felt suddenly sick. If someone had just told her that Guy Reichourd was a murderer she would have found it as difficult to believe as the notion that she had dabbled in voodoo. Every instinct within her rejected these ideas as ridiculous.

"So I've been told."

"Then I must have been crazy," Tori muttered. She looked back up at Guy. "Do they know who murdered this woman? Or why?"

"No."

"Do . . . do you think I had something to do with it?"

"No," Guy said. "I just thought her name might stir your memory a bit." He sighed, though it was more in relief than frustration. "Obviously I was wrong."

Both turned their attentions back to the meal, but the conversation remained in their minds, stirring up questions neither had answers for.

"Ah, isn't this a pleasant surprise."

Tori nearly rammed the tines of her fork into the roof of her mouth as her head jerked up upon hearing the familiar and unwelcome voice.

Guy looked up more slowly, almost insolently, his features remaining stoic and unreadable, though definitely devoid of any warmth or welcome. "Hello, Darin. I agree, this is a surprise. Weren't you supposed to be in Baton Rouge?"

"Oh, yes, well, I just arrived back about an hour ago. Finished my business early." He reached over to pull out a chair. "May I join you?"

"I think not," Guy said easily. "Victoria and I have some private matters to discuss." He picked his wine glass up by its stem, twirled it slowly between his fingers, and smiled up at Darin, the gesture contemptuous, almost challenging. "Husband-and-wife talk. I'm sure you understand, Darin."

The expression of congeniality Darin had worn instantly disappeared, as did any pretense of familial warmth. His pale gray eyes darted toward Tori, and she nearly cringed at the loathing she saw reflected in those cold, fog-colored pools. "Husband-and-wife talk," Darin echoed. "I see." He bowed deeply, the wide sweep of his arm and the haughty cock of his head making a mocking exaggeration of the otherwise gallant gesture. "Then please excuse me, dear brother"—he nodded toward Tori—"and *sister*. I certainly would not want to intrude on such a rare conversation. Perhaps another, ah, less private time. *Bon soir*." He spun abruptly on his heel and strode from the dining room, his back ramrod straight, his shoulders stiff, an air of rage about him.

Guy turned a satisfied smile back to Tori. "I do not think my dear brother is particularly happy."

She stared after Darin. Not happy was putting it mildly. Darin was enraged, and that scared Tori beyond belief. He was, she sensed, capable of doing anything to get what he wanted, and what he wanted was everything his brother Guy possessed. She shivered, knowing that included her.

Guy watched her through half-lowered lashes. He had expected some kind of signal to pass between Darin and Victoria, some look of acknowledgement or a stolen smile. None had, and that puzzled him. He had not failed to notice the startled spark in her eyes at Darin's appearance or the expression of hesitation as the two men had conversed. Both could have been put down to surprise at Darin's change of traveling plans. But the fear he saw registered on her face now, the ghostly pallor that had come over her at Darin's brusque reaction to Guy's words, *that* he didn't understand at all. He studied her for several long minutes as she turned her attention, and her gaze, back to the food on her plate and moved it idly about with the tines of her fork. Unless, he decided at last, she thought Darin believed she'd betrayed him, that she had decided to turn away from whatever scheme it was they had concocted together.

Darin slammed his fist against the headboard and then threw himself down upon the mattress.

The woman beside him flinched, but otherwise did not move.

"She'll be sorry for this," he swore, his eyes shining with hatred. "Damned sorry." Too restless to remain still, he sat up, grabbed a bottle that sat on the table next to the bed, and tipped its neck over a shot glass. Whiskey splashed into the glass and sloshed over its rim, staining the delicate white table covering. Snatching up the drink, Darin gulped it down greedily. He felt the golden liquor slide down his throat, hot and burning, blending with the fires of his anger, then threw the delicately etched crystal glass carelessly to the floor. It bounced on the rug and rolled beneath the bed, leaving several small drops of amber liquid glistening atop the cream-colored woolen weave. "No one turns away from me like that, no one! I should have known better than to trust her."

"Perhaps it is not what you think, *chérie,*" Celestine said. "Could your brother have not, on his own, figured out what it is you are up to?" She smiled sweetly up at him, but the thread of satisfaction, the hint of loathing in her tone belied the curve of her lips.

"No," Darin snapped. "That damned, conniving shrew told him. Guy's too stupid to figure anything out. He's just like John was." A deep, throaty laugh bubbled up from his chest, a diabolic sound filled the room with darkness and sent rippling chills over Celestine's golden brown skin.

She held the sheet to her breast and prayed to God—and John—to give her the strength she needed to continue. "What do you mean, like John was?"

"Nothing, except John wasn't as smart as everyone thought. I'm the smart one. Unfortunately, I was born last."

"So, what will you do, *chérie?*" Celestine asked, her tone now comforting and sweet. She stroked his bare thigh with the tips of her fingers, letting her long, elegantly manicured nails move lightly over his hot skin.

Darin jerked his leg away from her. "Not now, bitch." He glared down at her. "You whores are all alike, you know. Colored or white, you're all the same. You can never get enough." Smashing the butt of his cheroot into a small crystal bowl on the table beside the bed, he suddenly whirled on Celestine. One strong hand grasped her jaw, his fingers tightly clasping her delicate face and squeezing cruelly, biting into her bone, his nails piercing her flesh. "And you have absolutely no loyalty, do you, Celestine?" he demanded, just before his lips slammed down atop hers.

His teeth cut into her lips and his tongue plunged deeply into her mouth, choking her. Darin rolled on top of her, his weight pinning her to the bed, crushing the air from her lungs as his hands groped at her breasts and his knees forced her legs apart. His hips rose into the air and a second later the hard, throbbing shaft of his passion rammed into her.

Hot tears seeped slowly from the outer corners of Celestine's eyes, but she lay still beneath him, her body pliant, unable to respond but submissive to his needs. The only thing that kept her from screaming, from crying out and thrashing against him, from denying him entry to her home and to her body, was the thought of John.

Darin's mouth left hers, and Celestine breathed a sigh of relief at the small reprieve. Her lips were already bruised and swollen from his earlier taking of her. She brushed a hand across them to wipe away his saliva and tasted her own blood. His lips covered one of her breasts, his tongue curled about the chocolate brown nipple, and as she knew would happen, his teeth grazed her flesh.

Still, she remained silent and staunchly ignored the rape of her body, her eyes tightly closed to block out the sight of him, her upper lip caught between her teeth to prevent her screams, as her thoughts, her memories, remained fixed on the only man she had ever loved, John Reichourd. Somehow, deep down inside her where only raw feelings dwelt and cold logic had no place, she knew that Darin was responsible for his older brother's disappearance. God help her, she knew Darin had killed John. But before she could avenge John, she had to be sure, totally sure, and so, when it had become painfully obvious that John was gone, that something dire had happened to him and he was not coming back, Celestine had done what she had to do. She had gone to Darin, seduced him, and taken him as her protector. No one had thought anything of it, even Darin. After all, she was one of the most beautiful quadroons in the city, and quadroons were meant to be *placées,* the mistresses of rich planters. That was their whole purpose in life. Being Darin's *placée* was what Celestine had chosen to be. Someday, she felt certain, because Darin loved to brag and boast of his accomplishments, he would slip and reveal to her what had happened to John, he would give her the proof she needed. She smiled into the darkness, knowing when that day came, Darin Reichourd would die.

Thirty

They walked through the quiet hotel lobby. Without the loud cries of the auctioneers and the steady hum of bidders and spectators, the huge area seemed almost deathly still.

"I don't think I've ever seen anything so magnificently beautiful," Tori said, gazing about the ornate cavern.

"You've been here a thousand times or more, Victoria."

She smiled up at him. "Tori."

He nodded. "Tori."

"I don't remember being here before, Guy. I . . ." She paused and pirouetted slowly, her gaze moving over the galleries above, the ornate pilasters, the stained glass of the huge dome overhead, the portraits of prominent citizens that hung on the walls. "I feel as if I'm seeing this all for the first time."

"Shall we retire?" he asked, placing a hand on her back.

Tori looked up at him. "Must we? I'm really not tired."

"We could sit on one of the dais for a while, and talk."

"Could we hire a carriage, Guy? Could we just take a ride around the city? It's so quiet and peaceful now."

He motioned toward the door that led out onto Conti. As the hour was late, nearing midnight, only two carriages were at the curb of the banquette beside the door. The doorman instantly waved to the driver of the nearest carriage, and the man slapped the reins over the horses' rumps.

"Are you sure you don't want to get a wrap, Vic—Tori?" Guy asked as he helped her into the carriage.

"No, I'm fine," she said. "And anyway," she continued, her voice dropping to a whisper as he settled onto the seat beside her, "if I get cold, your arms can keep me warm."

Guy slipped an arm around her shoulders and pulled her close. She was a consummate actress, he would give her that. Never before had he seen her seem so sincere and loving. A cynical smile tugged at his lips. But then never before had she had so much to lose, he reasoned. "Just drive us around the city," he said to the driver.

The old man nodded and snapped his whip over the rumps of two bay geldings. The carriage moved forward, the *clip-clop* of the horses' hooves on the cobbled street echoing through the nearly deserted Quarter.

"Oh, Guy, what's that? Can we stop?"

He turned to look where she pointed, and laughed. The two-story building blended in well with the others lining the banquette on either side of it; stuccoed walls painted ivory, an arched *porte cochère* for arriving carriages, cypress shuttered windows, and a row of second-story French doors that opened onto a wrought-iron gallery. "I don't think you really want to go in there."

"Why? It looks beautiful."

"Did you notice the sign over the door?"

Tori looked back over her shoulder. "No."

"That's The Golden Fleece, the Quarter's most popular casino."

"Casino?" Excitement lit her eyes. "Oh, let's go in, Guy.

329

I love slot machines. The nickel ones were always my downfall."

A shadow passed across his handsome features. It was at times like this that his confidence waned, his assurance that she was faking and this was all just another ploy began to waver. A furtive glance shook him further, as he saw no sign of deception on her face, no duplicity in the sparkle of her blue eyes. Anger at the possibility that he was wrong, no matter how slight, overtook him. "What the hell is a slot machine?"

Tori looked at him as if dumbfounded by the question. "You've never played a slot machine?" She laughed softly. "I don't believe it."

"I asked you what it was," Guy said, his tone hard, almost threatening. His eyes were suddenly the shimmering black of a midnight lake, silver-gray swirls of moonlight flashing intermittently within their cool depths. "Or can't you answer the question? Perhaps you've forgotten what it is?"

Tori sobered quickly at his tone, realizing instantly that his mood had changed, that something had gone very wrong between them. She hadn't the faintest idea of what had caused the change, only that it had definitely occurred at her words. "It's a machine that you put coins into, then pull a lever, and three or four cylinders with pictures on them spin." She paused, searching his face for a reaction, for a smile that would tell her he was teasing, but found only cold silence and stoney features. "If the same pictures stop together on a line painted across the glass front," she finally continued, "you win money."

"There is no such machine," Guy said simply.

"There most certainly is," Tori snapped back. She didn't know why he was so irritated, or why he was calling her a liar over something so silly, not to mention easy to prove, but she didn't like it one bit. And she was getting a little tired of his changeable moods.

Guy leaned forward and tapped the driver's shoulder. "Take us back to The Golden Fleece."

The carriage immediately made a wide sweeping turn and headed back in the direction they'd come. It stopped before the casino.

"Wait here," Guy instructed the driver. "We'll only be a minute."

"Not if I get my hands on a slot machine," Tori quipped lightly. She smiled, trying to make light of the matter, but Guy's scowl remained intact.

He placed a hand at her waist and guided her across the banquette. The quiet of the night instantly disappeared as they passed through the tall red doors of the casino.

Tori couldn't really have said what she'd expected, but what met her gaze was not it. They stood at the entry of a spacious foyer, its walls covered to waist height with dark oak paneling, and from there to the high ceiling with murals; the scenes depicted the English countryside, pheasants in flight, and a fox hunt. Through the tall arched doorway to their left, Tori could see a crowd of elegantly dressed men crowded around what appeared to be a roulette table. Several more stood before a spinning wheel of chance, and even more around a craps table. In the room to their right she saw at least a half-dozen gambling tables. She recognized a baccarat box on one, and at another the men seemed to be playing blackjack, or something similar to it. But there were no slot machines in sight.

A beautiful woman, blond hair piled high upon her crown and one lone sausage curl draped over her left shoulder, walked from a crowd of men to greet them. Her red painted lips curved into a wide smile, but Tori noticed there was definite hesitation in her almond-shaped blue eyes when they moved from Guy to her.

"Monsieur Reichourd, welcome to The Golden Fleece. You visit us much too rarely, *chérie.*"

"Thank you, Felicity, but we won't be staying. My wife," he looked down at Tori, "was just curious to see the inside of the casino, and I thought I'd indulge her whimsy."

"But of course." The woman laughed softly, and Tori found herself reminded of the tinkling ripple of wind chimes. "Welcome, Madame Reichourd."

Tori suddenly realized there were no other women in the casino. She turned to Guy. "Is this strictly a man's club?" she whispered.

"If you want your name to remain untouched by scandal, Victoria, then yes, you could say it is strictly a man's club."

She glanced back at their still-smiling hostess. By the look on the woman's face when they'd entered together, Tori had the distinct impression she had recognized her, which meant that, although she didn't remember, she had been here before—and obviously not with Guy.

Had she been here alone? She glanced around at the throng of men gambling. That seemed unlikely. With Darin, perhaps? Or Jermonde? A sudden thought struck her, and she nearly groaned aloud. Please, God, don't let there be any more men in her life. She didn't know if she could take it if another past lover crept out from the shadows. The two she supposedly had were bad enough. She couldn't help the shudder that rippled over her. How in the name of all that was saintly could she have preferred those two to her husband? But for some unfathomable reason she had.

"Do you see a slot machine?" Guy asked.

Felicity frowned, not understanding the question, but remaining silent as it was obviously directed at Tori.

"No," she said softly, feeling chastised and not liking it one bit. Just because this casino didn't have any, didn't mean another wouldn't. "Is there another casino?"

"Yes, but this is the best. If The Golden Fleece doesn't have it," Guy said coolly, "no one does."

Tori bristled. "I know what a slot machine is, Guy. I've played them dozens of times."

"When?"

She opened her mouth to answer, and nothing came out. When? She didn't know when? Tori closed her eyes for a second and tried to think. Nothing came. No answer, no images. Absolutely nothing. She opened her eyes and shook her head. "I don't remember."

"I didn't think you would," Guy said. He looked back at the blonde. "Good night, Felicity." He placed a hand beneath Tori's bent elbow and urged her to the door. When she hesitated, his grip tightened and his fingers exerted just enough pressure to let her know he was in no mood to linger or argue the point.

Once out on the banquette Tori jerked free and whirled on him. "I know I've played a slot machine, Guy. I'm not making this up, and I'm not crazy. There must be other places, other casinos, that have them."

"It's not that important, Victoria. And it's late. Let's just go back to the hotel."

She reboarded the carriage quietly. Something was wrong. She glanced quickly back at the facade of The Golden Fleece as the driver snapped his whip in the air and the horses pulled the carriage forward. Something was definitely wrong. She just didn't know what it was.

* * *

The small interior of Maspero's Exchange was crowded, in spite of the lateness of the hour. A half-dozen men, engaged in a heated discussion of politics, sat in one corner of the dimly lit old coffee house, while several more stood in the center of the room discussing the attributes and possibilities of a certain young quadroon whose protector had just gotten himself mortally wounded on the field of honor. Senator Perillout was at a table near the door, having a late-night brandy with an old friend who had just arrived that evening by schooner from England, attested to by the man's portmanteau, which sat on the floor next to his chair. Blackjack Moreaux leaned lazily on another table, diligently emptying the contents of his third bottle of whiskey. Between gulps he spewed a steady stream of curses on the gambler who had managed to take him for almost everything he had that day while both traveled downriver from Natchez.

The tall doors that made up the complete street-side wall of the Exchange had been left open, allowing the stuffiness of the room to blend with the sultriness of the night air.

Darin sat at a corner table, alone and in shadow, the weak yellow glow from the chandelier that hung from the ceiling's center not extending to the outer reaches of the room. For the past hour he had remained quiet, talking to no one, acknowledging no one, sipping on his brandy, and watching Jermonde St. Croix. He'd had no plan when he'd entered Maspero's earlier, nothing more than desperately wanting a drink to soothe the rage he'd felt after his confrontation with Guy and Victoria. Even now, the mere thought of either of them turned the blood in his veins to hot lava and left him aching to commit murder. A malevo-

334

lent smile spread across Darin's face. And that was exactly what he was going to do.

He downed the last of his brandy, pulled a pair of gloves from the inside pocket of his cutaway, and rose slowly from his chair. With an arrogance born of years of self-indulgence, Darin sauntered across the room, passing the senator, who nodded a silent greeting, Moreaux, who was too busy cursing to look up, and a dozen other men he knew, but cared little for. Finally, he paused. "Jermonde St. Croix," Darin said loudly, pronouncing the man's name as if it were filth on his tongue.

Jermonde, who had been sitting at a table near one wall conversing with one of his fencing students, looked up, displeasure at being interrupted clearly etched on his handsome face.

Before Jermonde could do little more than turn toward him, Darin raised a hand and brought it down again swiftly. The kid glove he held in his hand slashed across Jermonde's cheek.

The distinct sound of leather against flesh seemed to echo within the tiny room and a deathly hush fell over its occupants as all tongues froze and all eyes turned toward the two men.

"You have insulted my honor, sir, and that of my wife, Victoria Reichourd. I demand satisfaction."

Jermonde shot up from his seat, his chair tumbling backward to crash against another and then fall to the floor with a loud crash. Hatred and fury burned brightly in his black eyes as they narrowed above high cheekbones. A fist clenched at his thigh, but his arm remained ramrod straight. Fisticuffs were for the *hoi poi*. Gentlemen settled their differences on the field of honor, and in spite of the fact that many of the New Orleans gentry

335

refused to consider Jermonde St. Croix a gentleman and had died because of it, he thought himself one and would kill to prove it.

The room was instantly charged with tension.

Jermonde shook with rage, and as he spoke, it laced each word. "You are a fool, *monsieur,* but I shall honor your challenge and provide you your opportunity for satisfaction. I believe, however, it is my choice of time and place, as well as weapons."

Darin nodded. "My seconds will call on you in the morning."

"Non," Jermonde said, surprising everyone. "We shall meet this morning, beneath the Dueling Oaks de la Rhonde. Five o'clock. As for weapons"—he smiled slyly—"my seconds will call on you in one hour, with my choice."

Darin smiled. It couldn't have worked out better if he had written a script. "I am staying at the Hotel St. Louis." He puffed out his chest, so pleased with himself he felt about to burst. In a few hours he would be rid of Guy, then, in a few months, he would take care of Victoria, and later her two brats. Or, if the worst happened, he'd be rid of St. Croix and he'd have to kill his loving brother himself. Either way was fine. "Room two B," Darin said. "But"— he lifted a warning finger arrogantly—"please have your seconds knock quietly so as not to arouse my wife. You have caused her enough discomfort, Monsieur St. Croix, there is no need to cause her further worry."

"As you wish." Jermonde's fury was slowly ebbing, and he was beginning to feel a deep sense of satisfaction at this new turn of events. Wasn't this exactly what he had wanted? With one slice of his rapier he would rid himself of the lone obstacle between him and Victoria. He almost laughed with delight. And he hadn't been forced to make the challenge himself. The dolt had come to him.

Darin turned and quickly strode from the Exchange, intent on escaping before any of its patrons became suddenly clear headed and realized it wasn't Guy Reichourd who had just foolishly issued the challenge to New Orleans most famous and deadliest *maître d'armes*, but his younger brother, Darin. He kept his features set hard and his eyes cold, but once out on the street and away from any curious eyes Darin found he could no longer hold back the laughter that had been struggling to escape. He only wished he could be at the Dueling Oaks in the morning, and at the hotel tonight when Jermonde's seconds arrived to announce Guy's choice of weapon. Watching his brother die would be such a pleasant experience, but an impossible one. If they were seen together like that someone might realize the truth. Guy would know instantly, of course, but that didn't matter. He would accept the duel, he had no choice, because if he didn't his honor would be forever destroyed.

Thirty-one

Guy downed the last of his brandy and set the glass back on the bar. For several long minutes he stared into the huge mirror that was the centerpiece of the back wall's ornate paneling. The cold silver glass reflected the spacious interior so elegantly appointed, the hotel lobby beyond the open archway, and as far as he was concerned, the emptiness of his life. He let his head droop and stared at the polished mahogany bar top. "Give me another brandy," he said quietly.

The bartender moved to comply.

Guy had intended to fight her, to match wits with her and win. But he had forgotten how damned seductive Victoria could be. Worse though, he'd forgotten how cunning she was, to what depths of evil her thoughts could delve. He almost laughed. How could he possibly have hoped to figure out her scheme in time to thwart it? He had been a fool. She was toying with him, as a damned cat does a helpless, cornered mouse; and there seemed nothing he could do about it, short of sending her away. But that was no guarantee either. She was his wife. Even if the judge granted his request for a divorce, many would never recognize it. To them, Victoria would always be his wife. He could banish her from Shadow Oaks, send her to one of the other Reichourd plantations in northern Louisiana, even send her to France, but he could not keep her from eventually returning to New Orleans, from scandalizing not only him, but the children.

This time, though, was unlike those others when she had embarrassed or humiliated him, threatened his honor; it was worse. This time Darin was involved, and that made Victoria dangerous. Before her schemes had been merely a nuisance. Now Guy actually felt scared. Not for himself, he could protect himself. It was the children that concerned him. He couldn't allow anything to happen to Martin and Alicia, yet without knowing what Victoria and Darin were up to, how could he prevent it?

And that thought brought another. What was he going to do about Darin? More to the point, what *could* he do about Darin?

The bartender slid another tumbler of brandy before Guy and silently retreated to the other end of the bar.

Guy downed half of it immediately. The rich liquor slid down his throat like liquid fire, warming him, yet the relaxing languor that embraced him suddenly disappeared as a stab of pain ripped through his stomach. He grimaced and his fingers tightly clutched the small glass. He closed his eyes, waiting for the pain to subside, and a sharp hiss slipped through his parted lips.

"Monsieur Reichourd," a deep voice said from behind him.

Guy looked up and into the mirror. Two men stood behind and to one side of him. He recognized neither. They were young, probably no older than nineteen or twenty, one blond, one dark. Both wore expensive clothes. Obviously they were the sons of people he most likely knew but at the moment he didn't care to try and figure out their identities. "Yes?" he said finally, without turning. "What do you want?"

"We are Monsieur St. Croix's seconds," the dark-haired one said. "I am Alexandre Dubonneau. This is Robert Sinqueax. We are here to inform you that Monsieur St. Croix has chosen rapiers and will meet you beneath the de la Rhonde Oaks at five o'clock this morning, as scheduled."

Guy straightened, turned slowly, and looked at each young man. "Rapiers? Five o'clock? What in the hell are you talking about?" he snarled.

"The *duello, monsieur,*" Sinqueax answered.

"Duello? What *duello?* I know nothing about a *duello.*"

"Monsieur," Dubonneau said patiently, but with a definite distaste for Guy's response, "Monsieur St. Croix accepted your challenge like a gentleman. He will expect you to honor it as such."

"My challenge?" Guy had sobered quickly, the languorous effects of the liquor having dissipated the moment the word *duello* had been spoken. *"I* challenged St. Croix?"

A knowing glance passed between the two young men. Guy knew exactly what they were thinking; either he was too drunk to remember his challenge, or he had experienced second thoughts and was trying to find a way to get out of going through with it.

"Oui, monsieur," Dubonneau said. "Barely an hour ago at Maspero's Exchange, you issued a challenge to Monsieur St. Croix—to defend your wife's honor, you said. We were there, with Monsieur St. Croix. You did issue the challenge."

Suddenly Guy knew exactly what had transpired. So this was their game. They couldn't afford to have another

340

Reichourd brother disappear mysteriously, and obviously anything that would look remotely like murder was out of the question. Guy had thought Darin and Victoria would arrange some sort of accident, but his little brother was too smart for that. A *duello*. How perfect. With Jermonde St. Croix, one of the best *maîtres d'armes* in New Orleans, and without doubt the deadliest. Guy knew St. Croix did not believe in victory at first blood. He fought to the death. It was rumored he had killed over ten men in the last few years, one for merely brushing against him at a quadroon soirée, another the father of a *jeune fille* St. Croix had decided he wanted to marry. The father had objected, as any respectable father would have, and consequently was challenged to a duel, St. Croix claiming his own honor had been damaged by the rejection. Hours later the girl's father was dead. But St. Croix had not gotten his bride. Rather than marry him, the girl had, upon hearing of her father's death, instantly taken her own life.

"The de la Rhonde oaks." Guy pulled a gold watch from his pocket, flipped open its cover and glanced at the delicate black hands on its white face. "Five o'clock," he said, and flipped the cover closed.

"Oui, monsieur. And rapiers."

"Yes." Guy looked long and hard at the two young men. "I would expect nothing else from St. Croix." He tilted his head in acceptance. "Rapiers."

The young men bowed and hurried from the bar, as if not wanting to be seen in Guy's company any longer than necessary. There were only three other patrons in the place, and each left almost immediately after Guy's acceptance of the terms. Guy turned back to the counter. "Pour me another brandy."

The bartender looked at him curiously, but did as he was told.

Guy didn't bother returning to the room. Five o'clock was only a few hours away. No doubt Victoria knew exactly what was happening, but if she were confronted she would, he felt certain, feign complete innocence. Anyway, he didn't feel like seeing her now. Hell, at the moment he wished he never had to see her again. He pushed away from the bar. Damned if he would use one of St. Croix's rapiers. He wouldn't put it past the scoundrel to slice its blade part way through at the base to weaken it. One soundly placed thrust or riposte and Guy would be left without a weapon. No, he had to get to Pepe's house. His old teacher would loan him a rapier, and perhaps give him a few tips on how to avoid finding St. Croix's foil embedded in his chest.

Victoria tossed and turned continually, her sleep fitful and fraught with threatening dreams and images that made no sense. She heard the crashing of metal against metal and felt the chill of early morning air on her skin, the dampness of icy dew on her feet. But everywhere she looked, seeking the origin of the sounds, she saw only blackness, empty, infinite blackness. She snuggled deeper into her wrap, pulling its folds around her, but the cold and darkness were inescapable, the deadly clinking almost deafening.

Then the images changed completely. She pushed off the bed's coverlet as her flesh became suddenly hot. Sounds of the bayou echoed all around her from the impenetrable gloom of night. She tried to cry out to Guy, needing him, desperate to know he was safe, but her voice was frozen somewhere deep inside of her throat. A step forward brought her foot into contact with something soft and wet. She looked down, and a scream filled her chest as her gaze fell once again on the body of a man floating atop the murky water of the swamp. His lifeless eyes stared back into her own, his mouth was open wide, as if to speak, but no sound emanated from the still, blue lips. His body moved slowly with the swirling waters, half-covered with the debris and refuse of the swamp, and his outstretched fingers bumped softly against the toe of her shoe.

Tori moaned and rolled over, burying herself once more within the coverlet and the mountains of pillows. Instantly the picture of the murky water with its ghastly offering faded from her mind and another image took its place. Guy and Darin stood on a small strip of raised land within a clearing surrounded by the eerie foliage of the swamp, the bulbous stumps of long-dead cypress and the moss-covered trunks of trees still struggling to survive within the primeval forest. Darin was holding a gun toward Guy's chest, and laughing crazily. She heard the heinous sound, felt it surround her, and tried to block it out, to deny its existence; but it seemed to penetrate her flesh, her heart, her very soul.

Suddenly a figure emerged from the depths of the stagnant black waters, his arms outstretched, his lifeless gray eyes seeking, his parted blue lips screaming. The debris of the swamp covered the rotting threads of what had been elegant clothing; moss dripped, like shredded cloth, from his raised arms; and his hair, which had once been a rich black, was now colorless and tangled, streaked with the swamp's mire. He moved toward the two men. . . .

Tori screamed and bolted up from the pillows. Her heart raced within her breast, its maddeningly accelerated beat

echoing in her ears. Her pulse raced, her blood rushe
through her veins and she gasped for the breath that th
scream had stolen from her lungs. Her body shook vio
lently. "My God," she whispered, once her teeth ha
stopped chattering. She squeezed her eyelids tightly shu
What in God's name did these nightmares mean?

She looked at Guy's side of the bed. Empty. Had he eve
returned to the room. She glanced at the settee. Only he
gown and crinolines lay across its back. Her gaze droppe
to the floor where Guy's valise sat. It was still closed, an
did not appear as if it had been moved or opened. A sens
of alarm stole over her, but she fought it down.

Throwing back the coverlet, Tori slipped from the be
and walked quietly to the big window that looked out o
the square. It was not yet dawn, and the city was still snug
gled securely in bed. Here and there a lighted windo
could be spotted, perhaps a tavern that was still open,
wife leaving a light on for her husband, or a business pre
paring for an early morning opening. But those lights wer
scarce. For the most part the city remained in slumbe
shrouded in darkness, except for the lanterns that hun
about the Quarter at the main intersections. These o
lamps were suspended from the center of ropes whose end
were attached to buildings on opposite sides of the stree
They cast a soft yellow glow over the center of the inte
section above which they dangled, but left the banquette
and storefronts in inky darkness.

Tori turned away from the window and began to pac
the unlit hotel room. She tried to tell herself she was bein
silly, that she had merely experienced another nightmar
and it had left her shaken, maybe even a bit scared. Bu
no matter how logical her reasoning seemed, the feelin
of dread, of imminent danger, wouldn't leave her.

Finally, when she could stand the silence no longer, when her shaking hands refused to stop their trembling and her mind would give her no peace, she decided to try to find Guy and assure herself, and her runaway imagination, that he was all right.

Hurriedly fastening her shoes, Tori grabbed a gray mantle from a hook at the back of the door where she'd hung it earlier, slipped the heavy folds around her shoulders, and secured its front over her nightgown. She pocketed the key to their room and walked swiftly down the hall toward the stairs. Most likely Guy was still in the hotel bar. Or perhaps, after several drinks, he had sat down on one of the winged-back chairs that dotted the lobby and fallen asleep. There was nothing to worry about. Absolutely nothing.

Tori kept trying to tell herself that. She repeated it with each step she took down the wide staircase, with each glance around the empty lobby; but her panic continued to mount, and the sense of danger grew more intense with each second that passed. She hurried toward the desk.

"Have you seen my husband?" she demanded of the clerk. "Guy Reichourd. Have you seen him?"

The man looked up from a pile of papers he seemed to be sorting. *"Oui,* Madame Reichourd, I have, but not for at least an hour."

"Where was he then? Where did he go?"

"He was in the bar, *madame.* I saw him there when I came on duty."

Tori spun around and raced toward the bar. She knew she wasn't supposed to go in there. Guy had told her so earlier when she'd suggested they have a drink together, but at this moment she didn't care. Propriety was the least of her worries. She had to find Guy.

345

Two gentlemen were just coming out of the bar as Tori ran for its doorway. She dashed past them without a glance, heard their clucks of disapproval and ignored them. "Where's Guy Reichourd?" she called out to the bartender who was busy stacking bottles at one end of the bar. "Where is he? The desk clerk said he was in here."

"Yes, *madame,* he was, but Monsieur Reichourd left, maybe forty minutes ago."

"Where did he go?" She practically screamed the words at him, the unreasonable, unexplainable sense of panic overtaking her now. "Where?"

"The oaks, *madame.*"

"The oaks?" Tori repeated. Was that another bar? "Where's that?"

"The Dueling Oaks, *madame,*" the bartender said, as if that explained everything.

"The Dueling Oaks? He's gone to fight a duel?"

The man nodded. "He made a challenge, and was called upon to honor it."

"A challenge? Guy challenged someone to a duel? Why? Who?" Her heart was racing so fast Tori felt almost faint. Her dream was coming true. She looked wildly about the room. But he couldn't be fighting a duel. Why would he?

"I heard the man's seconds say they were here for Monsieur St. Croix."

"Jermonde," she echoed, and clung to the bar's edge. Her entire body had begun to tremble. "Where are these oaks?" she asked, nearly breathless with fear.

"The de la Rhonde oaks, *madame.*"

"I heard you say that before," Tori snapped, her patience gone now in the face of terror. "Where are they?"

The bartender quickly gave her directions, which Tori realized too late, after wasting time listening, she didn't need. She ran through the lobby and barged past the entry doors. The doorman, sitting on a small chair nearby, jumped to his feet in surprise.

"A carriage," Tori said, "I need a carriage."

The man frowned. "It's not a good hour for a lady to be out and about alone, *madame*," he said slowly.

"I need a carriage now!" Tori demanded, gracing the man with a scathing glare that, she hoped, left him with no more urges to be protective of her virtue.

He waved a hand and a carriage seemed to emerge from the tenebrous shadows that hovered over the street. Tori climbed into it before the liveried doorman could even offer a hand to assist her. "Take me to the Dueling Oaks," she ordered.

The carriage driver turned in his seat and stared down at her, hesitation in his eyes. "You wants to go to the Dueling Oaks, *madame?*"

"The de la Rhonde oaks, yes," she said. "Take me there, and be quick about it, please. Extremely quick."

He needed no further explanation. It was obvious what was happening. He took up the reins in one gnarled old hand, and grasped his whip in the other. A quick snap of the whip and the horses lunged forward.

Tori had no idea where they were going, or how long it would take to get there. She clung to a small leather strap that hung above one window and swore softly to herself as the huge wheels of the carriage seemed to find every hole and rut in the road. The clattering hooves of the galloping horses echoed within the vacant streets of the Quarter, the sound bouncing off of one stuccoed wall only to bounce off another, and then another.

Within minutes they had left the city behind and were racing across open countryside. The carriage swerved again. Tori looked about while still holding frantically to the strap. They were passing beneath a long arch of oak trees, the gnarled limbs spreading widely, meeting overhead, entwining, and creating a canopy of foliage that allowed only an occasional glimpse of the sky. Long strands of Spanish moss hung from them like wispy curtains of gray lace, lending further eeriness to the macabre passageway.

Tori clutched the side of the carriage, stuck her head out the window and tried to peer around the driver. What met her eyes sent a cold chill through her. The driver pulled up hardily on the reins and the two big geldings came to a stop.

Tori thrust the carriage door open and rose from her seat. She was about to alight when the carriage driver swung around and reached out a warning hand to stop her. "No, madame," he said quickly, "it is too late."

Some yards away two men stood facing each other, little more than five feet of space between them. They had stripped to their trousers and shirts, their coats and cravats having been handed to their seconds to hold. In the pale glow of moonlight that filtered down through a sparse opening in the canopy of tree limbs, the threads of their white shirts seemed to shimmer iridescently, and the thin blades of the rapiers, held taut and upright before them, reflected a dazzle of silver sparks.

"En garde!" Jermonde suddenly said. Both men jumped to readiness, their swords clinking against one another.

Tori's heart jumped into her throat and lodged there.

Thirty-two

Tori watched, horrified, her heart pounding frantically as each man lunged at the other, their movements graceful yet deadly. The thin silver blades of the rapiers slashed out, metal hitting metal, one blade sliding down the length of the other and then both abruptly drawing back, circling, swiping, the blades' soft swishing as they cut the air the only sounds in the beautiful grove.

Jermonde lunged. Guy parried, deflecting his opponent's thrust, but just barely. The tip of the *maître d'armes'* blade stabbed the voluminous fold of Guy's shirt sleeve and ripped the delicate silk threads apart . . . but no blood was drawn.

Tori slapped her hands over her mouth as a scream threatened to burst from her throat.

"After our last time together," Jermonde said, "you should have known better, Reichourd, than to challenge me." A smile of supreme confidence curved his lips.

"Perhaps I did," Guy shot back, regaining his composure instantly. Years ago, when both men had barely been able to claim that designation, they had faced each other on the field of honor, and as now, that confrontation had

349

also been over the affections of a woman. Guy's eyes strayed to the scar on Jermonde's face. He had never meant to slash the man so visibly.

"Hah!" Jermonde laughed and lunged forward.

Guy instantly brought his wayward thoughts under rein and deflected the striking blade.

Another thrust, a lunge, a hold, a parting, and another lunge. And on and on for what seemed endless minutes in which Tori hardly dared to take a breath.

Blade clinked against blade, each gesture made with such swiftness it was difficult to follow their movements. Tori studied Guy's face. His features were taut, the line of his jaw a slash of granite, his brow furrowed with intense concentration as his eyes remained fixed on his opponent's blade. Suddenly Jermonde's rapier pulled away from Guy's, sliced downward and across the folds of white silk that hung loose just above the waistband of his trousers.

A soft gasp emanated from the small crowd of onlookers and Tori's heart nearly stopped. Please, God, please, she prayed, keep him safe.

A thin veil of perspiration glistened on Guy's forehead and his fingers moved to reaffirm their grip on the rapier's handle. He was not doing well. It had been a long time since he'd held a rapier in his hand, even longer since he had faced an opponent who was anything more than a fencing partner. Pepe's quick hour of brush-up instruction had helped, but Guy wasn't sure it had helped enough to get him out of this mess Darin had gotten him into.

And then he thought of his children. If he lost this *duello,* if Jermonde killed him, as he so obviously intended to do, what would become of Alicia and Martin? The thought of leaving them in the precarious care of Victoria, and under the constant threat of Darin, gave Guy the impetus he needed to succeed.

Jermonde parried, his blade bearing down swiftly toward Guy's chest. A quick step to the left combined with an excellently maneuvered riposte carried both Guy's and Jermonde's blades, harmlessly, in a wide arc to the right. Jermonde responded instantly, his foil looping back toward Guy, but he was not quick enough. Guy's blade crashed against Jermonde's, slipped away, and struck again, time after time.

Then Jermonde, seemingly in an almost desperate move, lunged at Guy. His foot slipped on the dew-covered grass, and the tip of his rapier, aimed at Guy's chest, dropped to pierce the trouser leg at Guy's thigh. At almost the same moment, Guy's blade embedded itself within the muscle of Jermonde's shoulder.

Jermonde, started, jerked away from Guy's blade and stared down in disbelief at the front of his shirt, which was beginning to turn crimson as blood flowed from the wound.

Tori scrambled from the carriage as the two men stood glaring at one another, neither moving. She ran toward Guy, his name a breathless cry of relief on her lips.

"Not yet, Victoria," Benjamin Lecoix said, and stepped in front of her to block her path to the two men. Grasping her arm firmly with his old fingers, the doctor steered her to the side of the clearing. "It's not over."

"But"—Tori looked from Guy to Jermonde—"they're both hurt."

The old doctor nodded, but said no more.

"Blood has been drawn, St. Croix," Guy said. "And honor has been avenged."

"Non," Jermonde said, his eyes dark with hatred. "First

blood means nothing." He straightened and, ignoring the freely flowing blood that had stained the tan kerseymere of his trouser leg, held up his blade in readiness. *"En garde!"* he announced.

Guy remained motionless. "You're not fit to continue."

"En garde!" Jermonde said loudly, his voice a demanding command that echoed across the still, gray clearing. He assumed the starting pose. " 'Til death," he declared, and lunged at Guy.

Having no choice, Guy executed an instant parry, followed immediately by a blindingly quick riposte. Once again his blade found its mark, slashing across Jermonde's wrist. The cuff of St. Croix's sleeve was ripped apart, and a spray of blood rained upon the grass only seconds after his rapier fell to the ground.

Jermonde staggered backward, the fingers of his left hand clutched tightly around the bleeding wrist of his right, his eyes never leaving Guy. Benjamin rushed forward to tend to Jermonde's wounds and, grasping Jermonde's arm, forced him to turn away, but not before Tori saw and recognized the seething hatred that burned within the dark eyes still directed at Guy.

Tori ran toward Guy. Caring not a wit for propriety, or anything else except that he was safe, she flung her arms around his neck. "Oh, Guy," she cried, tears welling up in her eyes. "I was so afraid. Why did you do it?"

He stood ramrod straight, stiff and cold in her arms. "It seems I was not given a choice in the matter, Victoria, as you well know."

Suddenly aware of the glacial look of him, and of his hard words, Tori slipped her arms from around his neck and stepped back. Illumination came to her like a flash of lightning across a dark sky. She felt certain Guy had not offered the challenge that had resulted in this duel. Somehow, and she swore to find out how, either Darin or Jermonde had goaded Guy into duelling, and whatever it was they'd done, they had implicated her. She didn't know how she had realized this or why she felt so sure that was what had happened . . . she just did. "What do you mean, as I well know?"

His dark brows rose skyward and a haughty sneer of disbelief twisted his handsome features. He grasped her arm roughly, his fingers curling about her tender flesh like the claws of a bird of prey, exerting just enough pressure to make her wince and follow him. They moved hastily away from the others. "I will admit, Victoria," he said, his words low and harsh, "that of late you have been a consummate actress. Better than I could ever have imagined. There were even times I found myself believing you."

He heard his own words and saw the look of surprise that came over her face at them, but instead of the satisfaction he had expected to feel—the triumph—he felt empty. Cold, hard, and empty. Dammit. Why did she always win? Why now, when he should want nothing more than to rejoice at beating her at her own game, or at least this portion of it, did he feel such a sense of loss? Such a gnawing, aching, sense of loss?

In an unconscious movement, his fingers tightened around the handle of the rapier he still held, clenching the cold metal until his knuckles were white from the pressure. He still wanted her, damn the saints. In spite of everything she'd done, in spite of the hell she had put him through, in spite of the fact that he knew she wanted him dead, he wanted her with a hunger that threatened to destroy him.

"Guy, please," Tori said, "if you'd only listen to me."

"I did that once, Victoria, long ago. If I hadn't, perhaps

you and I would have gone on to lead much happier lives without each other. But there is no point in recounting what might have been." He began to turn away, then paused and looked back at her. "I must admit, though, coming here like that"—his eyes raked over her mantle and the ruffled hem of the nightgown which peeked out from beneath the thick cape—"does lend an air of authenticity to your concern, for those who do not know you as well as I do that is." He laughed softly, a derisive sound that told Tori, more than the granite stare of his eyes, more than the icy tone of his voice, that nothing she could say at this moment would change his mind.

She turned and began to walk back to the carriage, her head held high against the stares of the other men still loitering about on the duelling field.

"Victoria," Jermonde called out.

Tori stopped and turned back to look at the man who had spoken her name, the man who had helped to perpetuate the rift between she and Guy. A gasp left her throat at the ghostly pallor of his flesh, and her anger at him was momentarily suspended. "Oh, my God." She had forgotten Jermonde had been wounded. Overcome by compassion, Tori lifted her skirts and hurried toward where he sat hunched over on the seat of a nearby buggy. She might have no pleasant feelings for him, no love in her heart, but she had never wished him dead or injured. "Jermonde," she said, "you must get to a hospital."

"Non." He waved a dismissing hand at her words. "The doctor is here and has seen to my wounds."

"What happened Jermonde? Why did you duel with Guy?"

"Because it had to be, *mon cœur.* But"—a hateful gleam sparked his black eyes—"it should have been Reichourd

354

lying here, and not merely wounded. I underestimated your husband, *chérie,* but"—he shook his head—"I will not make that mistake the next time."

"Next time?" Tori's eyes widened in alarm, and her pulse began to race again. "Listen to me, Jermonde, there isn't going to be a next time. There is nothing to fight about. Do you hear me? Nothing."

"We belong together, *chérie,* you and I, and I will see to it that we are together. Fortunately for me, your cuckold of a husband believes honor is avenged with the drawing of first blood. I do not."

"Ohhh!" Tori whirled around and abruptly stopped in mid stride. Everyone was watching her. Everyone had been listening to the exchange with Jermonde. Everyone, including Guy. "Well, good," she mumbled angrily. "I hope they got an earful." She stalked toward her hired carriage, hoisted her skirts in a very unladylike fashion, which drew several gasps from the gentlemen, and climbed not too daintily into her seat. "Take me back to the hotel," she ordered.

The carriage lurched into motion immediately.

Tears filled Tori's eyes and blurred her vision. She angrily wiped them away. Ever since she'd come to New Orleans nothing had gone right, and now Guy was fighting duels over her, and at the same time telling her he wanted nothing more than for her to remove herself from his life. A small sob broke from her throat, then suddenly she bolted upright and her eyes widened. *Ever since she'd come to New Orleans?* What the hell did that mean? Why had she thought that? She'd been born and raised here. Guy had said so, and he had no reason to lie about that. Did he?

She shivered against the cool morning air and drew her

355

cloak more tightly around her, then settled back into the deep seat of the carriage. Her thoughts were a jumble of confusion. "And I'm beginning to think things that don't make any sense whatsoever. If I'm not careful they'll be sticking me in a looney-bin." She would have to talk to Guy again, reason with him, make him listen to her. A long sigh left her lips. She didn't know how he had been drawn into that duel, or how she had been implicated as its cause, but she had to get Guy to talk with her. Darin was behind this mess, she knew he was, even if she didn't know how. But one thing was certain, she'd be damned if she'd let Darin kill Guy. Though she wasn't exactly sure what she could do to stop him. Especially since Guy wouldn't listen to her. She shoved a fold of the cloak under her neck, cutting off the draft of cold air that blew in through the window and nearly chilled her to the bone. "Well, I'm just going to have to find a way to make him listen," she muttered angrily.

The light of dawn had crept over the area almost unnoticed, but then every eye had been intent on watching the two men duel. Only an occasional glance was spared the woman who had come, uninvited and unwelcome, to the Dueling Oaks. Everyone in attendance knew who she was, and that she was the cause of the deadly encounter, but no one voiced this opinion or made any other acknowledgement of her presence, except for the old doctor.

Darin stepped quietly from his vantage point behind one of the thick oaks a good thirty yards away from the clearing. Fury burned in his eyes. Jermonde had proven a fool, obviously resting on his laurels for the past few years rather than maintaining his expertise with the rapier. And

Guy had proven himself much more adept than Darin would have believed. Most likely, while Victoria had been enjoying her dalliances over the years, he had been preparing for the inevitable task of defending his honor. Darin swore softly. He wanted Guy dead, but remembering the embrace of Jermonde and Victoria in the square, he would have been just as pleased if Guy's blade had buried itself within Jermonde's heart. Unfortunately, both men had walked away from the *duello* with no mortal wounds.

Darin sniffed. Well, if he couldn't count on Jermonde to do the job with Guy, he would just have to do it himself. But he would have to be extremely careful. He dropped his cheroot into the blanket of green grass at his feet and ground out its simmering tip with the heel of one boot. He lifted a hand to his breast pocket and felt the small bottle nestled snugly within the fabric of his blue camlet coat. Madame Chartonneau had proven to be an old fool. Darin smiled to himself. The witch had thought she could play both sides of the road—sell poison to Darin, then, for another fee, warn Guy. But Darin had arrived at her shop half an hour early. She'd been in the back room preparing the potion and mumbling to herself of her plans and hadn't heard him come in. Lucky for him no one else had been about to see him enter. A sigh of frustration left his lips. He'd silenced that damned old witch and gotten the poison, but now he couldn't use it because he couldn't be sure Victoria hadn't told Guy about his plan. That meant he'd have to find another way to get rid of his dear brother. It would have to look like an accident, a very deadly accident. And possibly one that included Guy's dearly beloved wife. He smiled. The children could be taken care of later.

Of course, if he couldn't figure out a plausible accident, he would have to find some way to make Guy's death look like self-defense, or some such rot. Darin nearly laughed aloud, but caught himself just in time. He didn't need to draw attention to the fact that he was there.

Guy returned to the hotel room only minutes after Tori had entered in a whirl of anger and frustration. She met him at the door, intent on talking and clearing up whatever was going on.

"We must talk," Tori said.

He brushed past her and made for the dressing room. "I have an appointment with my *homme d'affaires* this morning, Victoria," he said, "and I need to wash and change clothes."

"Guy, please, we have to talk about what happened."

"There's nothing to say. Your scheme didn't work, that's all. And it's not going to."

Tori's temper was rising. How in heaven's name was she going to get through to this man? To make him listen to reason when he was so willing to believe the worst of her? "Guy, you've got to listen to me," she began.

"Victoria, I've been up all night and was just forced to fight a duel with a man who's obviously besotted with you and would like nothing more than to see me dead. I'm tired, I'm angry, and I do not want to talk."

"Guy, please," Tori pleaded.

He was fighting to hold on to his temper, though he wasn't exactly sure why. "My appointment most likely will only take a couple of hours. When I'm finished I plan on departing for Shadow Oaks. If you want to return with me in order to get your things together, then be here and be ready when I return. I'm sure you can find something with which to entertain yourself while I'm gone. Or perhaps I should say someone," he added calmly, as if it didn't matter. He slipped a gold stickpin within the silken folds of the blue cravat at his neck. God, how he wished it didn't matter, but he would rot in hell before he'd let anyone, especially Victoria, know that it did. He had allowed himself to hope, almost to believe, that her memory loss was real, that the change in her was genuine. And making love to her, that had been nothing but brash stupidity. It had brought out feelings within him he had thought long dead; know he didn't know if he could ever truly be rid of them again. What a fool he'd been. What a total, senseless fool.

Tori's temper reached the flaming point. She had promised herself to remain calm, but his arrogant, self-righteous manner was leaving her anything but calm. "We need to talk," she said through clenched teeth.

"There's nothing more to say, Victoria. I believe your memory has returned sufficiently, if in fact it was ever gone, so that you can move to Rive des Fleurs, my plantation near Mississippi. You can begin to pack when we return to Shadow Oaks."

Tori's heart began to race. "Guy, damn it, we have to discuss what's happening."

"No." He picked up his cutaway coat from the chair beside the bed.

"Fine, then if you won't talk, I will." She moved to block his path to the door. "You can just listen," Tori snapped. "I don't know why you challenged Jermonde to a duel, but it was ridiculous. I don't care one twit's damn about Jermonde. And for that matter, I don't care about Darin either. But I do care about you, and Darin is going to—"

"Darin is going to leave Shadow Oaks," Guy said, "as you are. Whether you leave together or not is up to you."

He slipped into his jacket and walked around her. "And irrelevant to me."

"Guy, please, Darin's going to try to—"

He paused at the door and looked back at her, his gray eyes so icy she almost shivered under their glare. "Darin is going to do nothing, Victoria. He's not going to get Shadow Oaks, and he's not going to get me. He may, however, if you still wish, get you." With that, he stepped into the hallway and closed the door behind him.

Shocked, Tori stood, mouth agape, and stared at the paneled door.

Guy strode down the hallway, his back stiff, eyes straight ahead. If everything he'd said to her had been the truth he would have felt fine. As it was, he was making a concerted effort to keep his emotions under control. His mind might want her to leave—logic told him it was the only way—but the rest of his body just wasn't listening. A steady stream of curses rumbled softly from his lips. He had never believed in the old custom of plaçage, never considered taking a *placée,* but perhaps now was the time. He definitely had no intention of ever taking another wife.

Tori stamped a foot on the carpeted floor. "Damn the man," she cursed. "Damn him, damn him, damn him!" Whirling around, she nearly ripped the wrapper from her shoulders and then pulled the nightgown over her head, tossing both carelessly atop the still open valise she had been packing.

Well, if Guy wouldn't listen to her, maybe Darin or Jermonde would. She jerked on her pantalettes and camisole, poked a hole through her stockings with a fingernail while trying, to secure them in place, and nearly lost her balance while fighting to get the folds of her skirt settled over the mass of crinolines that draped her hoop-cage.

"Archaic, ridiculous, idiotic way to expect a woman to dress," Tori mumbled. She looked in the dressing table's tall mirror and adjusted the puffed sleeves of the gown she'd chosen to wear, then paused. Why had she said that? Wasn't this the way she'd always dressed?

No. The answer came to her almost immediately, but without explanation. She remembered the incident with Guy's trousers. It had seemed natural wearing them, as well as riding astride, though Suda and Robert had both assured her she had never done either before.

She glanced back at her image in the mirror. Her gown was a lightweight cambric, its plaid design a combination of varying shades of lilac, pale green, and white. The neckline was scooped, her lower arms bare, and her waist was girdled by a wide sash of lilac muslin. The gown had a matching Basque-style cape that reached barely to her waist. It was made of lilac muslin, then trimmed with a ruffle of plaid cambric. Tori slipped it over her shoulders, picked up the black-beaded reticule she'd left on the dressing table earlier, and turned toward the door. Why she had the feeling that her clothes were beautiful but archaic and unnatural, when they were obviously the height of fashion, she didn't know, but it wasn't something she had time to worry about at the moment. There were other, more important matters to attend to . . . like convincing Darin and Jermonde that if either of them tried to harm Guy again, she'd personally bash their brains in.

Determination squared her shoulders as she stepped out into the hallway.

But by noon she still hadn't located Darin. She had inquired in all the Vieux Carré's hotels, checked the square, and had even ordered her carriage driver to slowly tour the Quarter's streets in the hope she would spot him walking along one of the banquettes. With a sigh of frustration Tori decided to turn her efforts toward Jermonde. She leaned forward on her carriage seat. "Driver, doesn't Mr. Jermonde St. Croix have some kind of fencing school in the Quarter?"

The man, whose hair, brows, mustache, and face all seemed the same shade of gray as the top hat he wore, turned and looked down at her as if she'd just asked if birds could fly. *"Oui, madame,"* he drawled finally.

"Take me there, please."

He sent her a frown of disapproval. "It is not proper, *madame,* for a lady to enter one of the *académies.*"

Tori stared back at him. She was beginning to get a little tired of hearing those words. "I don't care if it's proper or not. Now please, if you want the fare, take me there."

The man turned in his seat and snapped his reins over the horses. The carriage turned onto Royal. Minutes later, they swerved left onto Rue de Bienville and before going more than half a block, stopped. "Monsieur St. Croix's *académie* is there." The driver pointed down a narrow alleyway. "Second entry on the left."

"Wait for me, please," Tori said, and descended. She walked quickly to the door the carriage driver had indicated and knocked.

There was no answer, yet she could hear voices from within, quite a few voices, and more than a little commotion. She pulled on the metal latch and the door opened easily. A little black bell hanging overhead tinkled merrily as the top of the door struck its scalloped rim. Tori hesitated at the musical sound, then, gathering up the front of her skirts, she stepped across the threshold and into Jermonde's *académie*.

The eyes of at least ten young men turned toward her instantly, as did those of the two men who had been fencing in the center of the room. One of the duelists raised his face guard, tucked his rapier beneath his arm and approached her. Tori recognized him immediately. He was one of the young men who had been at the Dueling Oaks. He bowed gallantly, but his eyes never left hers. "May I help you, madame?"

"I am here to see Mr. St. Croix," Tori said.

"Ah, but Monsieur St. Croix is not here, Madame Reichourd," the man said.

"You know who I am?" Tori said, somewhat surprised.

He smiled. "Everyone knows of the beautiful Madame Reichourd."

Tori wasn't sure if the comment was meant as a compliment or not, so she decided to ignore it. "Do you know where I can find Mr. St. Croix? It's important I speak with him."

The young man shrugged. "Perhaps, but"—he shrugged—"it is not for me to say."

Tori's patience was waning. "I must talk with him. It's urgent. Please."

The man remained impassive to her plea. She looked about the room, her gaze falling at last on the other duelist, who stood several yards away, his features still hidden by the mesh mask he had not removed.

"Please," she said again, "I must talk with Mr. St. Croix."

The room remained silent.

Infuriated, Tori lifted her skirts and turned back toward

the door. "Thank you, gentlemen, for your courtesy," she said, flinging the words curtly over her shoulder.

From behind the protective mesh of wire Darin watched Tori leave the academy. He had come there that morning to work out his frustrations with a little exercise, and the rapier was his favorite way of doing so. There were more than a dozen other academies he could have gone to, but somehow, coming here to St. Croix's gave him a perverse sense of satisfaction, even though St. Croix himself wasn't present. He turned his attention away from the now empty doorway and the chittering gossip of the spectators. Why did Victoria want to talk to St. Croix? Did she suspect what he had done in challenging the disreputable Creole in Guy's name? Or was she merely running to him to assure herself that her lover was all right? Fury burned in Darin's breast. She had betrayed him with Guy, and she had betrayed him with St. Croix. Soon—he smiled—she would never betray anyone again.

Tori stepped back out onto the street and nearly screamed as a huge, scarred black hand snaked out of the shadows of the overhanging portico and touched her arm.

"Mizzy wants ta know where she can find St. Croix?"

Trembling violently and making a concerted effort to compose herself, Tori paused. Squinting against the sun, she looked up at the tall figure who stepped into the light. He was huge, his skin darker than the shadows from which he had just emerged, his eyes like two pools of liquid onyx. "You're the man . . . from the auction," Tori said. He was no longer dressed in ragged trousers, but a fine suit of what seemed exceptional quality.

"Yes, miz," he said. "You wants ta know where you can find St. Croix?" he repeated.

"Yes. Do you know?"

"He's at eight-hundred and twelve Rue de Toulouse." The moment the words slipped from his lips the man disappeared back into the shadows as quietly, and quickly, as he had appeared.

The carriage stopped at the corner of Toulouse and Rue de Vendôme.

Tori looked about in confusion. "Driver, why are we stopped here?" she said, "I need to go to eight-hundred and twelve Toulouse."

"That's it back there," he said, pointing at a two-storied townhouse they'd passed in the center of the block. "But you'll need to get out here so's you can cross the slab onto the banquette."

Sudden understanding came to her, and she descended the carriage, at the same time realizing they were only three or four blocks from the St. Louis Hotel. She paid the driver. "Thank you. I can see myself back to the St. Louis when I'm through," she said, and descended. She walked to the corner and held her skirts up as she trod carefully across a concrete slab which spanned the open sewer trench that separated the banquette from the unpaved street.

A carriage sat beneath the arched roof of the deeply shadowed *porte cochère* that gave entrance to 812 Toulouse. Tori hesitated to enter. Jermonde was evidently not home alone. "Oh, so what?" she snapped at herself. She needed to talk to him, and that's what she was going to do. Anyway, the carriage was most likely his. She walked past it, through an open courtyard whose center fountain was surrounded by a lush array of potted plants, all in colorful bloom, and then ascended the three shallow steps that led to the entry door. She knocked quickly, before she could lose her nerve.

The door opened seconds later, swinging back on quiet hinges, and Tori started in surprise.

"Bon jour, Madame Reichourd," Celestine Dubois said.

Thirty-three

"Miss Dubois," Tori said, finally finding her voice. "I . . . I thought this was the residence of Jermonde St. Croix."

Celestine smiled, stepped back from the door, and motioned for Tori to enter. "It is," she said simply, continuing at Tori's look of puzzlement. "I have been caring for him since the"—she glanced quickly at Tori—"since he was injured this morning."

"Oh, I didn't realize you two . . . I mean, I was unaware there was a relationship between . . ." Tori's voice trailed off and she looked at Celestine, uncertain how to finish her sentence.

Celestine smiled knowingly. "Jermonde is my half brother," she said, giving Tori another shock. "And I believe there are some issues we three need to discuss. Please"—she swept her arm wide and indicated an open doorway at the opposite end of the foyer—"come in."

Tori followed Celestine into the room. It was spacious, though nowhere near the size of the rooms at Shadow Oaks. An intricate chandelier of brass and crystal hung from the center of the ceiling, but the room's light came from a tall oil lamp that sat on a lemonwood table near a black-faced fireplace, and the two tall windows that flanked it. A huge gilt-framed mirror hung above the fireplace, reflecting the room's richly appointed draperies and cushion coverings of burgundy damask, its highly polished and intricately carved woods, and its crystal bric-a-brac situated randomly on the shelves of a corner whatnot.

Tori's gaze slipped over the furnishings and settled on Jermonde. He lay stretched out on a long settee, a coverlet pulled over him to the waist. His shirt was open, and a bandage covered half of his chest.

"Jermonde, we have a guest," Celestine said, though there was really no reason for her announcement. Jermonde's gaze had locked on Tori the moment she'd appeared in the doorway, and just as quickly he looked away.

Tori had forced a smile to her lips upon entering the room. She'd known this was going to be difficult. Jermonde hadn't impressed her as the type of man who would take a woman's rejection of his attentions too kindly, but it had to be done. She didn't want him going after Guy again when there was absolutely no reason. But the air of haughty arrogance she had expected to encounter from Jermonde did not seem to be there. Rather, he appeared almost embarrassed to see her.

"Please, Madame Reichourd, be seated," Celestine said. "We will have coffee." She indicated one of two ladies' chairs that sat opposite the settee on which Jermonde reclined.

After both women had seated themselves, Celestine turned to her. "It is obvious my brother is not going to explain himself or the situation to you." She threw Jermonde a scathing glance, then continued. "So I will."

"Please, Miss Dubois," Tori said. "I only came here to

368

inform Jermonde that, regardless of what feelings there were between us in the past—"

"There were none," Celestine said, interrupting.

Tori gawked at the woman. "Pardon me."

"Feelings," Celestine said. "There were no feelings between you and my brother. Before your carriage accident you didn't even know one another."

"But I thought . . . I mean, Jermonde said . . ."

Jermonde kept his gaze directed to his view of the courtyard beyond the window, while Celestine threw him another disapproving glare. "Jermonde only proved himself the despicable rogue everyone says he is." She handed Tori a cup of coffee. "Let me explain it all from the beginning, Madame Reichourd. Maybe then you will understand and not think too unkindly of my brother, even though he deserves it."

Tori nodded, too confused and shocked to do anything else.

"First, as I said, Jermonde is my half brother, a fact only a few people in New Orleans are aware of. We share the same father, but have different mothers. Jermonde's was a young Frenchwoman of, shall we say, less than desirable reputation, who came to New Orleans looking for a better life and made her way working as a seamstress. Our father met her quite by accident. Jermonde was born a year later. His mother returned to France and married a *maître d'armes* who treated Jermonde as his own son." She sipped her coffee. "My mother was black, one of my father's slaves."

"But Guy said you were a quadroon, only a quarter black."

"I am an octoroon," Celestine said, "but it is of no matter here in Louisiana. Mulatto, quadroon, octoroon, or manneloque, it makes no difference. Black blood is black blood." She waved a hand as if in dismissal. "But that is *n'importe.* So that you will understand Jermonde, I must explain myself. I was John Reichourd's *placée,* and I loved him, more than anything in the world. Then one day last year, he disappeared"—she snapped her fingers—"like that. He is dead. I know that in my heart. His body was never found, but someday I will prove that he was murdered, and the man responsible shall pay with his own life."

Tori stared at her, a thousand questions buzzing through her mind.

"After John had been gone awhile, and my tears came less often, I knew what I had to do. I took Darin Reichourd as my protector, I became his *placée."*

"But why?" Tori gasped, feeling a churning wave of revulsion deep within her at the mere thought of this beautiful woman with Darin.

"Because he is the one who killed my John. I know it, but I cannot prove it, and that I must do. As his *placée* I am close to Darin. Someday maybe he will let something slip. When he feels sure of me, when he trusts me completely, maybe he will brag a little, then I will know."

"But what has all that got to do with Jermonde and me? And this foolish duel?"

"Jermonde was supposedly"—she put a sneering emphasis on the last word—"helping me. He was to befriend Darin, give him free dueling lessons and such, to gain his confidence and friendship. Instead, he befriended you."

Tori glanced at Jermonde, but he kept his eyes averted.

"I was unaware until just recently, when he nearly got himself killed, of Jermonde's diversion from our plan. When he heard of your memory loss Jermonde decided to act on his own. You see, my brother has a small problem with money. He has gone through the inheritance his step-father left him, as well as the monies our real father provided him when he turned of age. And lack of money has made him reckless, if not unscrupulous. Unbeknownst to me, Jermonde made up a tale of a great *affaire d'amour* between you two, and why not? He figured, you had no memory so you couldn't deny it. If he could manage to convince you that you were in love with him, then all he needed to do was get your husband out of the way and the Reichourd fortune was his for the taking. A simple and devious plan."

Both women turned blazing eyes on Jermonde. He met their gazes, head held high, but within seconds he looked away.

Tori didn't know what to say. She felt like laughing she was so relieved, yet she also felt like throttling Jermonde. Then she remembered the duel, and anger overtook her. "You could have killed Guy," she said softly, "and all for nothing."

"Jermonde got exactly what he deserved," Celestine said. "He has been paying more attention to his dalliances of late than to his business, and Monsieur Reichourd's skill with the rapier reminded him of that. He is lucky his little folly did not cause him to lose more than his pride and my respect."

Tori stood. "Is there anything I can do to help you, Miss Dubois?"

Celestine looked at her curiously. "I do not understand, madame. What could you do to help me? And why would you want to?"

Remembering the nightmare that had haunted her ever

since the accident, Tori resumed her seat. "Do you have any idea where John was killed?"

Celestine wiped a tear from her eye and shook her head. "It is as if he disappeared into thin air. He was to be at my house that evening. When he did not come, I knew something was terribly wrong. John always came when he said he would. The next morning I received a note from your husband stating that John had disappeared."

"But how do we know, then, that he's dead?" Tori asked.

Celestine inhaled deeply and released the breath with a long sigh. "His horse returned to the plantation without him."

"Oh."

"But why do you ask where his . . . where it might have happened?"

Tori closed her eyes for a brief second before answering. She didn't like to think about the nightmare, but maybe it would help. Perhaps she knew something that she wasn't aware of. "As of late I have been having a nightmare. Almost every night, it is the same. I am walking in a swamp, and I see a man's body. He is floating face up . . ."

"Ohhh," Celestine slapped a hand over her mouth.

"I thought my nightmare meant something was going to happen to Guy in the swamp, but now"—Tori shrugged—"I'm not sure."

Celestine looked at her brother; then they both turned their gazes to Tori.

"Do I have permission to search the bayous of Shadow Oaks, Madame Reichourd?" Celestine finally said softly.

"Of course, and if you need help, please get word to me."

Tori left the Toulouse Street house feeling extremely buoyed. At least she didn't have to worry about Jermonde

372

any longer. But there was still Darin. At that thought her spirits instantly plummeted.

The sun was high in the sky, and the afternoon air was heavy with humidity. She crossed the street to walk in what little shade it afforded her and picked at her sleeves, trying to pull the fabric away from her hot flesh. "I feel like a beach bunny in ski clothes," she mumbled to herself, then stopped. What did that mean? Beach bunny? And what were ski clothes? Damn, why couldn't she remember things that made sense?

She began to walk again, but before going more than two steps her attention was drawn to a black man leaning against the arched entry to a house a few feet in front of her. His lanky arms were crossed at his waist, and he stood watching her, his posture one that combined casualness and intense study. His shirtfront was open, and a series of swirling white spots dotted his chest. There were more on his upper arms, and in the center of his left cheek. As Tori neared, she realized each spot was a small mound of scar tissue that formed a design in the man's flesh. She met his gaze then and found his eyes, glistening like spheres of ebony beneath a bush of wirey black hair, seemed to look not at her but into her, as if searching. She shivered at the thought and determined to walk past him without another glance.

"Who are you?" he demanded suddenly as she came alongside him.

Tori started. "Victoria Reichourd," she said automatically.

He shook his head. "No. Doctor Yah Yah knows Victoria Reichourd."

"You're Doctor Yah Yah?" Tori asked. His name brought

back the memory of Hannah accusing her of studying under the voodoo priest.

The old man nodded, said nothing, but continued to rake his gaze over her, assessing.

"I was told that I studied under you."

The man shook his head. "Not you," he said simply.

Tori frowned. "But I was told—"

"No. Victoria Reichourd, I teach her the voodoo, but not you."

"But I am Victoria Reichourd."

"No," Doctor Yah Yah said. "You look like her, but you are not her." He turned then, abruptly ending the conversation, and went into his house.

Tori stared after him. "Now what did that mean?" she murmured.

Suddenly a team of horses pulling a long dray screamed around the corner. The animals' hooves pounded the hard-packed earth and sent up a thunderous rumble. White foam flew from their lips as the driver of the dray snapped his whip over the horses' flanks, urging them to more speed, and they strained to comply. People crossing the street scattered to get out of the way, and a small dog jumped into the sewer trench to keep from being caught beneath the flaying hooves.

Tori watched the speeding dray in fascination, but in her mind she saw a completely different vehicle: a long, brilliantly red truck, its black wheels spinning furiously, white ladders glistening beneath the sun, siren and bells clanging in warning of its approach. She shook her head to rid it of the unfamiliar image as the dray sped out of sight. What was happening to her? Could Doctor Yah Yah be right? Was it possible that she wasn't Victoria Reichourd? That she was someone else? That she was from some other place and not New Orleans, and these things she was seeing in her mind, these words that kept popping out of her mouth, were from some other country or civilization?

She frowned. It would explain why everything felt so alien to her, so unfamiliar, and sometimes even archaic. But, if she wasn't really Victoria Reichourd, then how did she get here? And where was the real Victoria?

She shuddered as a chill swept over her. If she wasn't the real Victoria Reichourd, then who was she?

Thirty-four

"I met Celestine Dubois today," Tori said. She fingered the ribbed hem of her traveling suit's brown jacket and stared out at the scenery as they passed.

Guy's gaze remained riveted straight ahead, his attention seemingly on the two horses trotting before the carriage. He held the reins loosely, draped through his fingers.

"She seems like a very nice woman. But she's convinced that John was murdered, and that Darin did it."

Guy looked at her sharply. "She's a smart lady."

"She loved John very much."

"I know," he said quietly.

"Can we help her, Guy? Find out what happened to John, I mean?"

"Are you trying to tell me that you don't know?" His tone was caustic, and as cold and biting as an arctic wind.

Tori fought back the tears that threatened to fill her eyes. Guy hadn't returned to the hotel until mid afternoon. For two hours before his appearance she had paced, stared out the window, and turned over everything, every word, every thought that had occurred to her since the accident, which, among other things, she still didn't remember. By the time

Guy had arrived, she had just about convinced herself that, as unbelievable as it seemed, Doctor Yah Yah had struck a cord of truth when he'd said she wasn't Victoria Reichourd. Physically she was, but mentally, emotionally, she had become another person, and if there was any chance of a relationship between her and Guy, which was what she desperately wanted, she had to find some way to convince him of that. And she had to find a way to make him listen to her when she said his life was in danger.

"Guy, I know you believe I'm playing some kind of game with you, that all of this . . . this amnesia is fake, but it's not. I love you, Guy," she laid a hand on his arm, "and I'm scared for you, for us."

He looked incredulous at her words. Love? He had never once heard that word slip from Victoria's lips, even in the midst of one of her ploys. And now that he had heard it, he was in no mood to believe it. He jerked his arm from her. "Victoria, the game's over."

Her temper instantly flashed hot, anger replacing the cajoling softness of only a moment before. "Damn it, Guy, I'm not playing a game, and I'm not Victoria. I'm Tori. The woman you knew as Victoria is dead, can't you see that?"

He pulled up on the reins. The carriage stopped, and he swung around in his seat to face her. Desire battled fury within him. He wanted desperately to believe her, to trust her again, but he knew he couldn't. It was the last thing he could do. "What I see, Victoria, is that you are sitting next to me, very much alive and, I believe, well."

She wanted to slap him, to beat her fists against his chest until he listened to her, until he believed her. At the same time she wanted to throw herself into his arms, to feel his lips on hers again, washing away all the fear, all the unknown, all the past she didn't remember and he remembered too well. Instead, she held her hands together tightly in her lap and forced her voice to remain calm as she spoke. "Guy, I can't explain what happened. I don't even remember the accident, but ever since it happened I've felt strange. Words I've never heard of pop out of my mouth, images I can't explain come into my mind, as do ideas I don't understand."

His eyes narrowed cynically.

"I know it sounds ridiculous, and from what you and others have said I was like before, I don't blame you for believing this is some kind of trick, but . . ." The tears threatened again. She stiffened, determined not to cry. "But it's not." Her voice dropped to a soft whisper. "I do love you, Guy, very much, and I don't want to lose you."

"Victoria, I—"

"Please, call me Tori. Victoria just . . . just doesn't feel right."

He closed his eyes for several long seconds and remained still, then opened them and looked directly at her. He saw the tears glistening at the corners of her eyes, heard the note of fear in her voice, and felt the tremors that shook the arm that touched his. His body was hard with need and want of her, his blood boiled within his veins, but he clung to his self-control and to his doubts about her. "Tori," he said with a sigh, "if there ever was any genuine feeling between us, it's gone, and has been for a long time. I've made arrangements for you to live at Rive des Fleurs."

"No," Tori said, the word little more than a rush of air from her lips.

"But, if you and Darin decide you'd rather stay elsewhere, that is fine—as long as it is far from Shadow Oaks." With that, he turned to pick up the reins.

Tori's feeble hold on her temper snapped. Before she even realized what she was about to do, she clenched a fist and smashed it into his arm. "Haven't you heard a word I've said? What's the matter with you?" Tears poured from her eyes and ran down her cheeks as she hit him over and over. "Listen to me," she cried. "Listen to me, for God's sake. Listen, listen, listen."

He grabbed her flailing arm by the wrist, holding it tight within the circle of his hand. "Stop it, Victoria."

But she couldn't. Something had snapped within her, and she was desperate to make him believe her. "Listen to me, listen to me," she wailed. "Please, before it's too late. Please, Guy, please."

"Tori, stop it." His voice cut through her wailing like the rumble of thunder.

She looked up at him through eyes blurred with tears.

He stared down at her, and for one brief flash of a second Tori thought he was going to pull her into his arms, drawing her into the safety, the security, of his embrace. Instead, he turned back toward the horses, picked up the reins, and whipped them over the animals' rumps. The carriage lurched forward and Tori slumped back in her seat.

They rode in silence, Tori's mind working desperately to find some way to reach Guy, some way to convince him she was telling the truth, Guy staunchly trying to deny and ignore the passion she had once again stirred within him.

Suddenly the sound of a gunshot shattered the afternoon quiet, cracking the air. A dozen birds burst from a nearby grove of trees and took flight toward the heavens at the same time a bullet smashed into the buggy's wooden support rigging. The wagon rigging smashed against one of the horses and the reins were nearly jerked from Guy's hands as the animal reared, screamed, and plunged back to earth in a forward lunge of blind panic.

"Hold on," he yelled to Tori, but she needed no urging. One hand tightly gripped the railing behind the seat, while the other grasped the fabric of Guy's jacket. Her gaze remained fixed straight ahead yet unseeing, as another time and place enveloped her, and the image of another harrowing ride unfolded within her mind's eye. It was night, and she was on this same road, only it was no longer dirt, but hard, solid blackness. She was seated in something that resembled a metal box, and she was steering it with a wheel. A storm was brewing overhead. Lightning snapped. Thunder rumbled. And suddenly, a jagged bolt of lightning hit the ground directly before her. She screamed and jerked on the wheel. The metal box swerved from the road and plunged over an embankment.

Another shot pierced the air. Guy's left hand snapped back as the bullet smashed into his forearm.

"Guy," Tori screamed as the sound yanked her from her reverie and she felt Guy smash against her.

The reins slipped from his grasp, and he grappled to retrieve them with his other hand as blood spurted from his wound and streaked the gray sleeve of his jacket.

"Damned son of a bitch," he cursed beneath his breath. A bead of perspiration trickled down his right temple, and a lock of black hair fell onto his forehead.

The carriage careened wildly down the road, its axles and rigging rattling furiously, its huge, spoked wheels finding every rut, bump, and hole that existed in the narrow road. Tori stared down at the two galloping horses and prayed. Their long legs stretched across the earth, and their hooves pounded down violently, only to be lifted immediately. Their backs, shoulders, and flanks rippled with flexing muscles, their necks strained forward, their dark manes and tails ripped about furiously, and a white lather began to speckle their glistening, sweating bodies.

Guy struggled with the reins. He wound the thick leather strips around his good hand and pulled back, bracing one heel against the footboard, the other on the buggy's brake lever. A grimace twisted his face as he threw all of his strength into the task of pulling on the reins. "Whoa, damn you," he yelled at the horses. The animals tossed their heads, fighting the pressure of the bits in their mouths and the command to stop. Panic had them in its grip. "Whoa, damn it," Guy yelled again. He threw his weight against the reins and pushed down on the brake lever.

Blood poured from his arm, but he ignored it.

Tori grabbed the reins, just below Guy's grip, and began to pull back in an effort to help him. The horses jerked wildly. Guy pushed the brake lever harder, and their combined efforts and the resistance of the carriage as it braked forced the horses to slow. They rolled to a stop beside the road. Guy stood and grabbed Tori's arm roughly. Before she knew what was happening, she was sprawled on the ground in a heap of skirts and dust.

Guy pulled her into the shallow gulley that edged the side of the road. "Stay down," he ordered, when she attempted to right herself.

"I am down," she snapped back. Then she saw his arm. "Let me do something with your arm," she whispered, horrified at the amount of blood still pouring from the wound.

"Forget it," Guy snarled. "I've got to get to my valise."

"Why?" Tori looked at him, confused.

"Because like a fool, I packed my damn gun in it."

"You think whoever shot at us is still out there?"

381

Another bullet hit the ground a few feet from where they crouched. Dirt and rock sprayed the air.

Tori ducked but a shower of earth fell over her hair and back.

The horses, still skittish, bolted.

Guy and Tori watched helplessly as the carriage careened down the road away from them.

"Great," Guy muttered, "just great. No damned carriage and no gun."

Darin cursed to himself. He never had been that good with a rifle. Moving stealthily away from the bushes that fronted a grove of trees to one side of the road, he refastened the weapon to his saddle and mounted. He had hoped, if not to kill them with his shots, to at least frighten the horses enough so they'd bolt out of control. A carriage accident would have been perfect. Now, unfortunately, he would have to come up with another plan.

Two hours later Guy and Tori walked up the winding drive of Shadow Oaks. She had ripped a ruffle from one of her petticoats and tied it around his arm. The bleeding had stopped, but the grimace on his face told her that the pain had not subsided, and the pallor of his skin attested to the loss of blood.

A sigh of relief stole from her lips as the house finally came into view. He had barely spoken to her during their long trek, but Tori was too enmeshed in her own thoughts to worry about that. The image she'd seen while the carriage had careened down the road haunted her. It meant something, she knew. Something important, she just didn't know what.

"Oh, my Lord, what happened?" Hannah cried, when they walked into the foyer. She saw Guy's arm, the blood that had soaked both his jacket sleeve and the white cuff of his shirt, and let out a wail. "Moses, get to town and fetch the doctor."

The old man scurried out the back door and headed directly toward the stable.

Suda appeared at the top of the stairs and hurried down, wide-eyed at hearing Hannah's cries.

"I'm going to see to Guy's arm," Tori said to her. "Will you please arrange baths for both of us?"

The girl nodded and hurried toward the kitchen.

Hannah glared at Tori. "You can go and take yourself upstairs, missy," she said. "I'll tend to Michie."

For a moment Tori stared up at Hannah, uncertain just who the hell Michie was; then she understood. "No," she answered, her voice firm, "I will take care of Guy's wound."

The two women stared at one another for a long moment, but it was Hannah who finally relented. Her dark gaze dropped away, and she turned toward the warming kitchen. "I'll get some hot water."

Tori followed Guy into the warming kitchen and began to help him off with his jacket.

"You don't have to do this," he said. "Hannah knows how."

"I know better," Tori said, then wondered at her own words. What did she know about doctoring someone? She grabbed one of the rags Hannah had placed on the table, dipped it into the hot water, and began to cleanse Guy's wound.

383

He sucked in a sharp breath.

"Sorry," Tori murmured, "but it has to be clean or it will get infected." She looked over her shoulder at Hannah. "Do we have any antiseptic?"

The old woman's face remained blank.

"Antiseptic—disinfectant."

Hannah shook her head.

"Bactine? Mercurochrome? Anything?"

Hannah shook her head again. "Got liniment."

Tori wrapped a clean bandage around Guy's arm. "Well, we'll just have to wait for the doctor then, but it looks like the bullet is still in there. Probably lodged against your bone."

"I could have told you that," Guy said through clenched teeth.

Tori moved to sit on the bench beside him, but jumped away as Guy suddenly hissed, clutched at his stomach and bent over.

"What is it?" She grasped his shoulder. "Guy, what's wrong?"

"He having another attack," Hannah said.

"Attack?" Tori echoed. She remembered the last time this had happened, just after he'd kissed her. Darin had appeared and she'd thought he had already tried to poison Guy. She whirled on the housekeeper. "What's happening, Hannah? What's wrong with him?"

Hannah shrugged. "Doc don't know. Gives him laudanum to take, but Michie don't want it."

Guy straightened and took a deep breath.

Tori turned concerned eyes to him. "The pain, it's in your stomach?"

He nodded, his concentration on ignoring the last gnawing aches rippling from that part of him.

"Do they come often?"

"Every few days," he said, his voice ragged.

Tori's mind spun. Cancer? Ulcer? She'd rather think it the latter. "Hannah, get him a glass of milk. A big one."

The housekeeper stared.

"Hannah, get him a glass of milk, damn it, now!"

Hannah ran into the pantry. A few minutes later she emerged with a glass of milk and handed it to Guy.

"What's this for?" he questioned.

"I think you have an ulcer. Milk will make it feel better. And I want you to stop drinking, and don't eat any fried foods for a while." She draped his shirt over his shoulders. "I'd say relax and try not to be under any stress for a few days too, but under the circumstances I guess that's impossible."

"What's an ulcer?" Guy looked at her, suspicion clear in his eyes.

"It's like an abrasion of the stomach. A burn or hole."

"How do you know all of this?"

"I . . ." Tori's mind searched for an answer to give him and found none. "I don't know. I just do, that's all."

He looked down at the milk, and suddenly she knew what he was thinking; was it safe to drink? Should he trust her? She grabbed the glass from his hand and took a long swallow of the white liquid. "There's nothing wrong with it." She handed it back to him. "Now drink it."

He emptied the glass and then looked back at her. "Go upstairs," he said.

"I'll wait with you for the doctor."

"Go upstairs and take your bath," he repeated. "I'll be fine. Anyway, I want to be alone for a few minutes."

Feeling as if she had just been rejected, again, Tori rose and left the room. As long as they were in the house, and

Darin wasn't here, she could relax . . . somewhat. She would find some way to get through the stubborn maze of brain he had beneath that granite skull, but first she had to do as he'd said and take a bath. Her dress was covered with dirt, grime, and sweat, as was she; her skirt and petticoats had been snagged and torn, and her feet were throbbing, to say nothing of her head.

Tori spent a relaxing half-hour luxuriating in the violet-scented bathwater, letting her limbs relax and her muscles turn to mush. Finally, when she felt so wonderfully languid she was on the verge of falling asleep, she forced herself to rise from the midst of white bubbles that covered the water's surface. But she was too relaxed now, and the sight of her bed, turned down, was too much to resist. With nothing more than a towel draped around her still-damp body, Tori slid onto the bed, just for a few minutes she told herself, and promptly fell asleep.

Guy stood in the open doorway. She hadn't returned downstairs. Nor had she rung for Suda to request a dinner tray be brought to her room. All he'd wanted to do, he'd told himself, as he had approached her door on the way to his own room, was make certain she was all right. Though even admitting he needed to do that stirred his anger.

His gaze traveled over her naked form curled on the bed, her skin turned golden beneath the touch of moonlight that shone into the room from the window. Her dark hair was spread across the pillow like strands of black silk atop a blanket of snow, and one arm was raised, her hand lying palm up beside her head. A dark bruise encircled her upper

386

arm where he had grabbed her earlier and forced her from the carriage.

He felt the inseam of his trousers begin to tighten as his gaze moved to her breasts, perfect mountains of flesh, each topped with a rosey peak. Her waist was narrow, her hips subtle and well curved. His eyes moved to the small patch of dark hair at the apex of her thighs and desire threatened to overwhelm him as memory of those silken curls against his flesh, of the taste of her on his lips, assailed him.

Then, through the haze of passion that had begun to cloud his mind and heat his blood, Guy noticed something else, something he had seen before, had speculated on, but in the midst of everything else that had happened, had dismissed. Now he snapped to instant and cold attention. Her breasts, and the flesh surrounding that tantalizing triangle of hair, as well as a line of flesh over both hips, was a creamy white, while the rest of her body was golden, obviously touched by the sun, and not once or twice, but many times.

He frowned. The Victoria he had known for the past five years would never have willingly gone into the sun . . . for any reason.

Thirty-five

The morning sun was blazing through her windows when Tori woke, but she knew instantly it hadn't been the brilliant yellow-pink light that had awakened her. She sat up, senses alert, listening. Voices drifted through her open window from the garden below. Angry voices. Tori slipped into the wrapper that lay across the foot of the bed and walked to the window. She unlatched the jib door and stepped onto the gallery, then moved to stand behind one of the thick white pillars that supported the gallery. Remaining in its shadow, she peered over the railing.

"I want you off Shadow Oaks today, Darin," Guy said. "You have your own properties to run. Pick one of them and make your residence there—you're no longer welcome here."

"Ohhh, aren't you afraid of what people will say, dear brother?" Darin sneered. "Kicking your beloved kin out of the family's ancestral home. Remember Guy, you wouldn't want a lot of scandal to touch darling Alicia and your son, Martin."

"Scandal be damned," Guy said. "You're lucky I don't kill you. I want you off my land, Darin. Today."

Darin's sneering attitude suddenly changed to one of antagonistic outrage. "This is just as much my home as it is yours, Guy," he growled. "I was born here, too."

"Shadow Oaks was left to John, Darin. When he . . ." Guy hesitated at using the words, because much as he didn't want to admit they were true, in his heart he knew they were, "His will left his estate to me."

"At least half of Shadow Oaks should be mine."

"You inherited quite a bit in your own right from our father, Darin. It's high time you saw to your own business and got out of mine."

"Oh, like Victoria business?" Darin snickered. "Maybe we should ask the lady what *she* wants. Or have you bribed her with some promise of new jewels? Or a trip to Paris? Or maybe a townhouse in the Quarter?"

"Victoria is also leaving Shadow Oaks. Whether it's with you or not is up to her."

Darin spun on his heel and began to stalk toward the stable. "Who says *I* want her?" He laughed nastily. When he had met her in Europe, before Guy had known her, he'd wanted her, and had had her, but in marriage she'd chosen someone else. Later, when she had been Guy's fiancée, and Guy had been in love with her Darin had wanted her, and had had her. When she became Guy's wife, and Guy had cared about her, Darin had wanted her, and had her. But now she had betrayed him, and if Guy was sending her away, he obviously didn't care about her anymore. . . . Neither did Darin.

"Today, Darin," Guy called after him. "I want you to leave Shadow Oaks today."

Tori turned and walked back into her room. Leaving, was she? Well, maybe she'd have a thing or two to say about that. She tore off the wrapper and began to pull on the undergarments Suda had laid out on the settee earlier. Guy Reichourd was going to listen to what she had to say if she had to hogtie him to a chair to get him to do it. But first, she glanced over her shoulder into the cheval mirror standing in the corner, she was going to take special care getting ready today. After all, she needed every advantage she could get.

She looked in the tall armoire. A white gown of Caledonian silk caught her eye. A sea of sky blue threads woven beneath a layer of pristine white ones gave the fabric an almost iridescent quality. The skirts voluminous folds shimmered against the sunlight as she pulled it from the armoire, and the deep blue velvet sash at its waist shone richly. "Perfect," Tori proclaimed. She pulled the gown over her head and struggled to get the massive folds spread over her hoop-cage. This was not an appropriate morning dress. It was an evening gown. She knew that, and she didn't care. She wanted to look especially pretty for Guy— for her attack against his bullheadedness. After the accident, Suda had been forced to explain to her the differences between morning dresses, day dresses, evening dresses, and ball gowns, since Tori's memory loss had obviously resulted in a lack of knowledge as to even how to properly clothe herself.

She ran a brush vigorously through her hair but left it flowing loose over her shoulders. A touch of rose petals to her cheeks and lips left them both a soft pink. Giving one last look in the mirror, Tori left the room. Feeling suddenly nervous, she wondered if Guy would refuse to listen to her? Well, she'd just have to make him, she decided. She was halfway across the foyer toward the entry door when she spotted Martin sitting in the parlor. He was hunched over a book that was propped open in his lap and was writing in it. "Good morning, Martin," she said, smiling widely.

The boy looked up, frowned, and snapped the book closed.

"What are you writing?" Tori asked.

"My journal." He stood, turned his back on her, and walked from the room through a door set in the opposite wall from which Tori stood.

"Journal," she repeated, her words so soft as to produce little more sound than that of a butterfly's wings on the still morning air. "Martin Camerei Reichourd's journal," she said again. Suddenly the world spun out of control. Tori clutched at the doorjamb for support as her knees turned weak. The room around her began to darken and blur, its rich hues melding into a kaleidoscope of colors that whirled crazily around her. Nausea welled up within her, and fear sent a ripple of shivers dancing over her cold skin.

Abruptly the spinning colors disappeared and suddenly she was no longer standing in the parlor of Shadow Oaks, but sitting in what seemed to be an old attic filled with trunks, boxes, and cartons. She was on the floor, with an old, leather-bound book propped in her lap. Her great-great-grandfather's journal. She looked down at the words scrawled in what appeared to be a young hand on the open page before her.

A scream of denial rose in her throat and she began to tremble violently, but no sound left her lips. The world righted itself on its axis, the room stopped spinning, and the image disappeared. Tori, maintaining her death grip on the doorjamb, looked around, momentarily confused. "He's going to kill him." Suddenly lost memories came flooding back into her mind, sweeping over her consciousness and leaving her astounded at the reality of what had happened. Now she knew, finally, why everything about her life had seemed so strange, so archaic and old-fashioned, even why the man who was supposed to be her husband seemed like a stranger. She had never been to Shadow Oaks before, never known these people or their customs. Somehow she had traveled through time, had been thrown a hundred and thirty-four years into the past. But there was no time to dwell on that now, or even to wonder about it, because the man she loved, the only man she would ever love, was about to be killed. She whirled around and ran toward the door. "Guy!" she screamed. "Guy!"

At the edge of the gallery Tori paused, her eyes frantically scanning the gardens, the entry drive, the path to the stables. There was no one about. "Guy!" she screamed again. Her only answer was the soft chirping of a cardinal, the bird's brilliant red plumage like a tiny sunburst amid the green leaves and white blossoms of a nearby magnolia.

She forced herself to stand still, to close her eyes and try to remember what the journal had said. The swamp. Martin's journal had said Darin had somehow gotten Guy to go into the swamp. Grabbing up the folds of her gown, Tori practically flew down the fanning entry steps and around the house. On the path that led to the stables she nearly ran over Martin. She grabbed him by the shoulders. "Martin, help me, please," she pleaded.

The boy tried to pull away from her, his face screwed into an angry scowl, but Tori's grip only tightened.

"Darin's going to kill Guy," Tori cried. Tears of panic and fear filled her eyes. "You've got to believe me, Martin, please. You've got to help me stop him."

He jerked away from her, and without a word, ran toward

392

the house. "Martin," she screamed, stunned at his reaction. She turned and hurried in the direction of the bayou. Terror filled her, chilled the blood in her veins, and nearly stilled her heart. Martin didn't believe her. Wouldn't help her. Darin was going to kill Guy, and somehow she had to stop him.

She rounded a corner of the stable. The skirt of her gown snagged on the split rail of the corral and jerked her to a stop. Startled, Tori fell face down in the dirt, the breath knocked from her lungs. For a split second the world went black and spots of bright light flashed before her eyes. She fought the sensation and tried to struggle back to her feet. A sob of frustration broke from her throat. She had to get to Guy.

"Mama, Mama," Martin yelled. He ran up beside her, grasped her by the forearm and helped her rise. "I've got Guy's gun." He raised the weapon proudly toward her face.

Tori shook her head to clear it and gasped in air. She nodded and took the gun. "Come on," she finally managed, and grabbed Martin's hand, "we've got to hurry."

Celestine had been in the bayou since the first rays of dawn had crept over the horizon and snaked their way in amongst the thick stand of cypress. But where the brilliant pinkish yellow rays were a radiant spread of light everywhere else, in the primeval growth of the swamp, filtered by leaves, curtains of moss, and dank, peeling branches the beams were forced to circumvent or pierce, the illumination was weak and eerie. For the first few hours of her search she had carried a torch, the dancing fire held high above her head creating even more shadows and haunting images within the primitive landscape than already existed.

The skirt of her riding habit had been pulled up and tucked within her waistband, but the effort to keep it unsoiled had been futile. Too many times she had slipped on the moss-covered ground and fallen to her knees, or accidentally stepped from the trail of raised earth altogether and into the black waters of the swamp. Her riding shoes were caked with mud, her stockings were torn, and twice she had caught her skirt on the protruding stump of a dead cypress, tearing the fabric and leaving it ragged. The neat chignon into which she had arranged her thick black hair that morning had slowly worked its way loose, and long black strands now cascaded over her shoulders and down her back. The hair at her temple was muddied from where she had brushed it aside with her hand after falling into the swamp, and she had long ago discarded her gloves.

A long sigh of defeat left her lips. Hope had swelled once again in her heart when Victoria Reichourd had mentioned her dream, but it was, admittedly, a thin thread to hold onto, and obviously a false one. She was exhausted, and she had accomplished nothing. It was time to go back to town. She turned to retrace her steps and stopped abruptly. To her left, only a few yards away, and nearly obscured by the tall growth of ferns and wild grasses that lined the bank before it, was the small cabin she had sought all morning. Celestine almost cried with joy.

John had told her long ago of a small cabin in the swamps of Shadow Oaks that he and his brothers had built, and played in, when they'd been boys. He had continued to visit the tiny island the cabin was built on, he'd explained to her, whenever he needed to be alone to think. Somehow, she had felt certain, if there was an answer to John's disappearance, to his murder, it would be at or near the childhood playhouse of the Reichourd boys.

In her excitement to get to the dilapidated structure, Celestine splashed through the water, stepped in the oozing quagmire of the soft bank, and snagged both skirt and blouse on a cypress. Panting softly, she stood in front of the playhouse and looked around. There was no sign of a body, no indication of a newly turned and hastily dug grave. She walked around the playhouse and peered into it through its windows, its sagging doorway, and a space in the rear where two slats of the wooden wall had fallen away. With nervous fingers she pushed aside the ferns and grasses that surrounded the small structure, and forced herself to stare into the water that stood stagnant in the winding swamp lanes on each side of it, anxious to see what was beneath its murky surface, yet terrified of what she might find.

Finally, sighing in defeat, she sank to the ground and began to weep. She missed him so much. He had been not just her protector, the rich Creole planter who paid her expenses and occasionally shared her bed, he had been her entire world, her everything. John Reichourd had been the only man she would ever love, and now he was gone. But there was no grave for friends and relatives to grieve at and pay their respects, no date to acknowledge as that of his passing, no explanation of what had happened to him to offer the little girl who lay in a bassinet at the home of Celestine's mother. That little girl, born six months after John's disappearance, had the same dark gray eyes her father had possessed.

Overhead the sun moved and a new beam of light pierced the bayou waters. A spark of gold beneath the nebulous surface drew Celestine's gaze. On hands and knees she scrambled toward the bank, curious and once again hopeful. She plunged a hand beneath the black water, unheeding of the deadly creatures that called the turbid depths home. Her fingers closed about the smooth, round object, and she drew it up. As her hand raised from the water and the object came into clearer view a gasp of surprise and happiness burst from her lips, yet at the same time her heart was filled with the sudden and definite knowledge of loss. She spread her fingers wide and stared down at the gold watch that lay in the palm of her hand.

He would never have voluntarily parted with it. She flipped open its lid and her eyes fell on the familiar inscription: To John, my beloved, my world, Celestine. Tears once again filled her eyes. She looked out at the vast meanderings of Shadow Oaks bayou, her tears glistening as they ran, like silver rivers, over her cheeks. "I love you, John," she said softly. "I will always love you."

Clutching the watch tightly in her hand, its gold chain dangling free, Celestine rose and turned to walk from the swamp. The watch proved, at least to her, that John was dead, but finding it this way didn't prove that Darin had killed him. She sighed. Perhaps tonight she could use a bit of belladonna to make Darin confess his crime. She pressed the watch to her heart. Yes, she would do that. And tonight was the perfect time. Jeannette could remain at her grandmother's, and Zakar, the slave Celestine had purchased at the St. Louis Hotel auction, was scheduled to leave New Orleans on a schooner at five. She had given him his papers, and enough monies to live on while he tried to establish a life up north. Celestine smiled to herself. Yes, tonight was a good night for the belladonna. It would render Darin paralyzed, physically helpless, but he would remain lucid and totally aware of what was happening . . . and he would tell her the truth.

A voice pierced her thoughts, and Celestine stopped, thinking for a moment that it was in her imagination. Then she heard it again. A shiver of apprehension coursed through her, while at the same time the burning heat of hatred filled her breast. She looked around quickly, searching for a place to hide, and her gaze fell on the small, half-broken playhouse. Gathering up her skirts quickly, Celestine ran toward it.

Thirty-six

Tori ran, gasping for breath, her dark hair flying out wildly behind her. She gripped the gun tightly in the fingers of one hand, with which she also held her skirts bunched up at her waist so as not to trip. Her other hand held Martin's as the two plunged from the bright sunlight of the fields into the dank, humid depths of the bayou.

Silence surrounded them instantly. The only sounds that broke the eerie quiet were the pounding of their feet on the soft, damp earth and the panting gulps of air each took as they ran. Tori's grip on her skirts slipped and they tumbled down before her, the huge hoop-cage springing back into place. She stumbled, nearly fell, and stopped, hurriedly gathering the skirts back into her grasp.

"Which way, Mama?" Martin said, looking at the never-ending landscape of cypress, fern, and stagnant water that enveloped them. "Which way do we go?"

Tori looked up, her eyes wide. Which way? her mind repeated. Which way? She looked around wildly, frantically. Everything seemed the same. In every direction the landscape was identical. She closed her eyes and tried to remember what the journal had said. Then the thick ruche of earth-brown lashes parted again, she looked down at Martin. "A cabin," she said. "Like a playhouse, I think." Her eyes darted about, searching. "Is there something like that in here, Martin? Some kind of little cabin?"

He nodded quickly. "Guy showed it to me once. They built it when they were kids, my father and John and Darin. It was their secret place. John still used to go there. He said he liked the quiet."

"Can you find it?" she asked anxiously. He was their only hope. The journal hadn't described how to locate the little cabin, only what it looked like, and that it was in the swamp.

Martin nodded again. "I think so, come on." He jerked her hand as he darted forward and Tori ran after him.

Oh, God, let him find it, she prayed. Let us be in time. Please, God, let us be in time. Her mind whirred with the memory of what she'd read in Martin's journal. Darin had killed Guy and made it appear as if he, too, like John, had disappeared. Then a year later, while in a violent argument over money, Darin had killed Victoria. Alicia had met with a riding accident, though a suspicious one. Martin, fearing for his own life then, had run away and never returned to Shadow Oaks.

But now everything was different, everything had changed . . . because she was there and she loved Guy. How it had happened that she'd been tossed back in time to 1859, she didn't know, nor why. And she didn't care. All she cared about was saving Guy. She could think about all the questions later. Then another thought struck her as she ran, panting and gasping for air, her feet sinking into the soft morass of the swamp, splashing through the murky waters, stumbling over broken tree limbs and protruding stumps; what if there was no later? What if her reason for being thrown here was only to save Guy? What if, accomplishing that, she suddenly found herself back in her own time, in 1993, and without Guy? She would never see him again.

Her heart screamed a denial and tears filled her eyes, but she forced herself to keep running.

Martin stopped abruptly and yanked on her arm. Tori nearly stumbled over him and then fell to the ground as he pulled her downward. "Sssshhh," he hissed, and pointed past the thick, drooping fronds of the fern they hid behind. "Look."

Celestine crouched low to the ground and peered around the corner of the small, singular window that had been built into the Reichourd brothers childhood playhouse. A wash of relief filled her as she saw Guy Reichourd break through the surrounding foliage and walk toward where she hid. She moved to rise and greet him.

"Remember this place, dear brother?" Darin said, his tone scathing.

Celestine froze and her heart nearly stopped beating. She clutched John's watch tightly in her left hand, and willed herself not to give in to the rage that had begun to build within her at the sound of that voice. Acting according to the sense of self-preservation that had been bred into her long before she had met John Reichourd, Celestine slid her other hand beneath the folds of her gown to a strap attached to her slender thigh. Her fingers wrapped around the curved walnut handle of the tiny derringer she always carried sheathed there and slipped it free of its binding.

"Our playhouse," Guy said. He turned to face Darin, but ignored the gun his brother held pointed at his heart. "So, is this where you killed John?"

400

The breath stilled in Celestine's lungs.

Darin's brows soared into two curving black arches, and his eyes widened in surprise. His lips curled in a nasty grin. "I'm surprised you hadn't thought of this place before. Do you remember when we used to come here, Guy? Every day after we finished our studies with Mr. James." He shook his head slightly. "I always hated that horrid little man father hired to tutor us."

"You've always hated everything, Darin," Guy said calmly.

Darin frowned, as if considering Guy's words. Then he smiled again, and shrugged. "Yes, now that I think about it, I guess you're right. Although I have to admit I did delight in Victoria . . . for a while."

"But only for a while," Guy said. He edged slowly toward an old, rotting stack of wood that was piled near the playhouse.

"Well, I never would have chosen her for a wife." Darin laughed. "I mean, she was used, Guy, soiled by another man's touch. And who needs the baggage of someone else's child?"

"Used," Guy repeated thoughtfully. "And yet you took her to your bed."

Darin's smile widened. "Of course, but"—his tone was caustic—"you didn't really think I cared about her?" He shook his head. "I might have cared about her once," he said, remembering the liaison in England before she'd met Guy, "but, honestly, I seduced our dear Victoria mainly because she belonged to you."

"And Celestine," Guy said, "what of her?"

"Oh, she meets my needs . . . for the moment," Darin answered, his manner offhanded. A wicked gleam sparked in his eyes. "And I find I receive a rather perverse pleasure in bedding our dearly departed brother John's *placée.*"

"And when you tire of her?" Guy persisted. "Or she no longer meets your needs?"

Darin shrugged. "I'll sell her."

"She's a free woman," Guy said.

"She's a woman of color," Darin sneered. "And I'm a Reichourd. In another city, who would question my right to sell her?"

Celestine's finger tightened on the delicately curved trigger of the small gun she now held securely in her hand. Rage filled her, burned within her like a gnawing ache, but she held still, knowing that when she made her move it had to be precise.

Guy looked around. "So, I assume you brought me here to kill me too."

Darin tipped his head in acknowledgement. "You assumed right, dear brother. Once I'm rid of you, everything will be mine."

"Is this where you killed John?" he asked again.

Celestine stiffened, every muscle tense, her senses alert, as she waited for Darin's confirmation of what he had earlier intimated, of what she already knew in her heart to be true.

Darin looked momentarily surprised; then a satisfied smile spread across his narrow lips and he laughed. "As I said before, I'm surprised you didn't think of it before. You've searched everywhere else." A malicious laugh escaped him. "Of course this is where I killed him. It was so simple. Like leading a lamb to slaughter."

"He trusted you," Guy said. "You were his brother."

Darin shrugged. "His mistake."

Guy inched closer to the woodpile as Darin gloried in

his triumph. "I really didn't intend to kill him, you know. Not at first. But, well, it just happened." He sighed. "We were riding the fields together that morning, and he mentioned that Celestine was expecting a child and he wanted to move her to Shadow Oaks, to set her up as his wife." Darin's voice had risen with his words. "Can you believe that? Set that black wench up as his wife. Of course, John knew he couldn't marry Celestine, not unless he wanted to go to jail, but that wasn't going to stop our dear brother from bringing her to the plantation and flaunting her in everyone's face."

"And that's why you killed him?" Guy asked in astonishment.

"Oh, for heaven's sake, Guy, think of the scandal. Between John parading that whore as his wife, and your lovely Victoria running all over town bedding anything and everything in trousers, our name would have been ruined."

"You killed him so he wouldn't bring Celestine here?" Guy couldn't believe what he was hearing.

"Well, not really. I mean, I didn't set out to kill him. Just talk some sense into him. I knew he was going into town that night and caught up with him on the drive. I rode awhile with him, trying to talk to him, but he just wouldn't listen, said he was going to bring Celestine out here, to Shadow Oaks, and if I didn't like it, I could leave." Darin smirked. "Imagine, he chose a black whore over his own brother." He shrugged. "I became angry. I warned him I wouldn't stand for it, but he just laughed and told me I had no choice. So"—he shrugged again—"I shot him."

"Damn, Darin, how could you?" Guy whispered in horror.

"It was easy really. He was going to bring scandal down on us, the kind we'd never dig out from under. I couldn't let him do that, so I saved him from himself." His smile returned. "And then, after I brought his body here and tossed it into the water I started thinking; I could have it all . . . if it weren't for you. So you see, Guy, I have to kill you."

The blood in Tori's veins turned to ice, and she knew at any moment her heart would cease its constant, though thunderous, beat. This couldn't be happening. The journal had said that Victoria had lured Guy to the swamp where Darin waited, hidden. But the real Victoria wasn't here. Tori's mind whirled. This was all wrong; yet Darin was pointing a gun at Guy. As Martin had written in his journal, he'd pull the trigger and Guy would die.

"Martin," she whispered, clutching his forearm, "I'm a good shot, but not this good. We need a diversion, something to draw Darin's attention away from Guy. Can you work your way around to the side of them without being seen?"

He nodded.

"Good. Then be quick, but for heaven's sake be careful. When you get there find a rock or a piece of tree limb, or something, and throw it at the playhouse."

He nodded again and, crouched low, loped away from her and disappeared within the swamp's tall reeds.

Tori looked down at the gun Martin had given her. "God, it looks like something out of a museum," she muttered beneath her breath. But it wasn't. It wasn't even old. In fact, it looked fairly new. She buried it within the folds of her skirt and pulled the hammer back until she felt it cock. The fabric of her gown had muffled the sound. Holding the gun tightly with both hands, she prepared to stand.

Tori saw the rock Martin threw from his hiding place behind a fern soar through the air. It crashed against one wall of the playhouse with a loud thud, which was followed instantly by a shrill scream.

Guy spun around in surprise and stared at the small cabin.

Darin, clearly startled, took a step to the side and held his gun out, swinging it slightly back and forth so as to cover both Guy, and whoever had screamed from within the crumbling shack.

"Come out of there," he ordered loudly.

Tori had jumped up from her hiding place, her arms raised stiffly in front of her, hands clutching the gun and pointing it toward Darin; but her mouth had clamped closed upon hearing the scream. Now she stood silent.

Celestine rose to her feet and stepped into the open doorway.

"Well, well," Darin clucked, "what do we have here?"

"I found John's watch," she said, her dark eyes fixing on Darin. She held it out toward him.

"Well then, I hope your little treasure was worth dying for, Celestine. I had thought to get a little profit from you, but I guess I'll just have to forgo that now, since you'll be staying here with my dear brothers."

Celestine's fingers tightened around the handle of the gun she held hidden within the folds of her habit. Her eyes flicked away from Darin for a brief second and lit on Tori standing, still unnoticed by Darin, behind him in the shadows and foliage. She looked back at Darin. "You took my life, Darin, when you killed John." She smiled. "So you see, there really isn't anything further you can do to hurt me." She took a step toward him.

"Stay there, Celestine, or I'll shoot." He smiled. "And

I'm certain a bullet piercing your beautiful breast would hurt."

"Stay back, Celestine," Guy said softly, warning in his tone.

She took another step forward. "You murdered your own brother, Darin," she said softly. "Your own brother. And he loved you."

Tori glanced toward the spot where she knew Martin crouched. Why doesn't he throw another rock?

Suddenly Martin stood. "Hello, Darin," he said jovially. "What's going on?"

Darin swung around and pointed the gun at the boy.

There was no choice left for Tori. "Darin, drop the gun," she screamed, suddenly filled with more fear than she'd ever felt before.

He whirled around, the gun searching for her at the same time his eyes found her. "Damn you, Victoria," he growled. His finger drew down on the trigger.

Celestine's arm snapped up. The glistening silver barrel of the tiny derringer she held cradled in her palm caught the sunlight and reflected it back in a brilliant spark of light.

Tori blinked at the near-blinding reflection and instinctively pulled on the trigger of her own gun. Her shoulder jerked back at the repercussion and she stumbled erratically in an effort to keep from falling.

Celestine fired with a calm and deadly aim.

The quiet swamp exploded into a deafening roar as all three guns erupted. Guy yelled Tori's name and ran toward her, his heartbeat thundering as cold fear filled him.

She felt Darin's bullet pass close to her head, and then heard a thud behind her as the lethal projectile slammed harmlessly into a tree.

A bullet crashed into Darin's shoulder and he screamed in both pain and rage, the sound reverberating endlessly through the dense swamp. His arm jerked to the side, and the gun flew from his fingers. It plunged into the black water and disappeared instantly. The impact of the bullet had knocked Darin off balance and thrown him backward. For one brief yet seemingly timeless moment, he flailed wildly trying to recapture his stance, one foot teetering on the moss-covered bank, the other circling aimlessly in the air, searching for a foothold. Fear of what was happening, and panic that he could not control or change it, contorted his features, and in his pale eyes was the horror-stricken knowledge of what was yet to come. Blood gushed from torn flesh only inches above his heart, rivulets of red that saturated the front of his once pristinely white silk shirt, and when the delicate threads could hold no more of Darin's life fluid, the ruby droplets fell into the water.

"Guy!" Martin screamed.

Everyone turned toward Martin, who was pointing at the opposite bank from that on which he stood, but the same one Darin was toppling from. The thick foliage rustled softly and the grasses swayed.

Screaming with fear and outrage, Darin fell backward into the water.

"Sweet Jesus," Guy muttered. He grabbed the gun that had dropped from Tori's hand to the ground.

"What is it?" she cried, but at that same second the question ripped from her lips, the alligator moved into the light, and she needed no answer. "Oh, God."

Guy cocked the hammer, aimed, and pulled the trigger. The hammer slammed down with a click, but no explosion of gunpowder followed, no bullet burst from the barrel.

The alligator's leathery hide, nearly black with age and

the remnants of clinging swamp debris, glimmered as he crawled from the shadows of his hiding place among the lush ferns and tall reeds and into the sunlight. He paused for only one brief second, alert to his surroundings, his lance-shaped body lying flat to the ground, stubby short legs bowed, claws dug into the earth and ready to push him forward. His long, tooth-lined jaws parted ever so slightly, and he moved with the deadly intent and primeval grace of his prehistoric ancestors to slip quietly beneath the water.

"Son of a . . ." Guy swore. He glanced down at the gun. It was wet. He cocked the hammer again and his gaze searched the pond for the reptile, but only a soft ripple moved across the top of the water now as Darin, his wound turning the water red, bobbed to the surface and gulped for air.

Suddenly his eyes bulged and his mouth opened to scream, but before any sound could tear from his throat, he was yanked beneath the water's surface.

Tori, unable to help herself, cried out for him.

As if in answer to her, Darin shot up from the blackness. His death scream filled the still air, and his hands and legs thrashed frantically. The dark water, so still only a moment before was now a foaming, spraying deluge.

Guy aimed at the churning waters beside Darin and pulled the trigger, once, twice, three times. Again and again the gun clicked but no explosion sounded. In resignation he lowered the gun. "God help you, Darin," he said softly, knowing there was no way that he could save his brother.

Celestine, her arms hanging limp at her side, the derringer still cradled within one hand, stood motionless and watched.

The huge alligator's steel-like jaws clamped tighter around one of Darin's thighs, razor-sharp teeth embedded deeply within the soft flesh. Darin's blood, pouring now from both his chest and thigh, covered the gator's jaws and was fast turning the small black lagoon into a crimson pond. The reptile's long, spear-shaped tail slapped at the water as it fought to subdue its prey. Darin's screams echoed endlessly through the primitive glade for several long seconds, and then, abruptly, as man and beast finally disappeared beneath the murky surface, all was quiet.

Tori, sickened by the sight in spite of her loathing of Darin, turned and pressed her face to Guy's chest. His arms wrapped around her, and he held her securely against him.

"It's over," Celestine said, coming to stand beside them.

Tori turned and looked at the bayou. Except for the red tint of the water there was no evidence of the horror that had just occurred. But she, better than anyone, knew that it wasn't over.

Thirty-seven

With his arm still securely wrapped around Tori, Guy looked at Celestine.

She held John's gold watch to her breast for a long moment, then sighed and slipped it back into the pocket of her skirt.

"Why did you come here?" Guy asked quietly.

Celestine shrugged. "I knew in my heart that Darin had killed John. I have been searching for months now around the Quarter and docks, and even on the road leading to Shadow Oaks for something, anything, to tell me what happened." She closed her eyes to fight the tears that still threatened to come, inhaled deeply, and then reopened them. "Yesterday Victoria came to Jermonde's. I was there."

Guy looked quickly down at Tori.

"There was nothing between them," Celestine said, seeing the shadow that had come over Guy's face at the mention of her half brother. "Jermonde made it all up. He is a greedy man and will use any means or ploy he can to get what he wants. In this case, under the guise of assisting me in trying to prove Darin killed John, and hearing of

Victoria's memory loss, he saw a chance to get the Reichourd fortunes. I am sorry."

"There is nothing for you to be sorry for," Tori said. She reached past Guy and took Celestine's hand. "Nothing."

Celestine nodded and turned her attention back to Guy. "When Victoria came that day she said that she, too, believed Darin had killed John, and began to talk of her fear for you. I remembered something then that John had once said to me. When I'd told him I thought I was with child and he had begun to talk of bringing me to Shadow Oaks, he had mentioned the playhouse in the swamp that you three had built and played in as children. He'd wanted to fix it up so that our children, too, could play there." She looked wistfully at the small cabin.

Guy nodded. "We had some good times here."

"Yes," Celestine said, choking back a sob, "he remembered."

Martin thrashed his way through the thick ferns and came to stand beside the trio. "Is everything okay now, Papa?" he asked anxiously with a glance toward the still red-tinted water.

"Yes, Martin," Guy said softly. "Everything's fine." He wrapped his free arm around Martin's shoulder and then looked down at Tori, "but we have a lot of talking to do when we get home." He turned back to Celestine. "Will you join us?"

She shook her head. *"Non,* thank you. I must get home to Mamière and Jeannette. Now that I know what happened to John, and that his killer has paid, my daughter and I will be leaving New Orleans."

"Where will you go?" Guy asked.

Celestine shrugged. "France, perhaps. Or maybe just up North. But to some place where John's daughter can

411

have the chance to be something other than a rich man's *placée*."

"You don't have to leave," Tori said quickly. "It's going to change."

The small trio looked at her sharply, puzzled by her words.

She hurried to explain. "There's going to be a war, Celestine, between North and South. It will start next year, in eighteen-sixty, I think. Or sixty-one." Damn, why hadn't she paid more attention to her Civil War history? She hurried on with what she could remember. "By eighteen sixty-five the slaves will all be free, and the old customs and traditions of the South will no longer exist."

"How do you know this?" Celestine asked quietly.

Guy just stared.

Martin gawked, his mouth hanging open.

Tori looked at those gaping at her, her own gaze moving from one to the other, recognizing their shock, disbelief, skepticism; and she knew she had a lot of explaining to do . . . now that she remembered it all. "This is going to be a long story, and I think"—she looked around at their surroundings and an involuntary shiver shook her—"that we would be more comfortable back at the house."

Tori stepped across the threshold of the parlor and saw that Guy, Celestine, and Martin were already there, waiting for her. When they'd walked in the door of Shadow Oaks, an hour earlier, Hannah had taken one look at them and insisted that they clean up before settling down to talk. No one was going to "set" on *her* chairs caked with swamp mud, the housekeeper had declared. Baths had been prepared immediately, Celestine shown to a guest room, and coffee and *beignets* prepared.

The sweet aroma of the fat, deep-fried donuts, which were covered in powdered sugar, filled the room. Their scent proved a delicious accompaniment to the tangy aroma of chicory coffee that emanated from the silver pot set on the table before the settee.

"Sorry to keep you waiting," Tori said, and entered the room. She chanced a glance at Guy and felt suddenly shy and awkward. For the past hour she had been trying to decide how to explain to him who she was, where she'd come from, and what, as best she knew, had happened. She looked at Martin. And how would he take the news that she wasn't really his mother, but his great-great-granddaughter?

Guy stood by the fireplace, an arm resting casually on the mantel, one foot propped upon the brass fender skirt that encircled the hearth. He held a freshly lit cheroot, its white smoke wafting up into the air in a wispy stream and giving off the scent of apricots and tobacco. He watched her enter, watched her walk across the room, pass him, and take a seat on the settee; but he didn't move or speak.

Tori poured a cup of coffee for Guy, Celestine, and herself.

"You were going to explain how you know about this war you claim is coming," Celestine said.

Tori took a deep breath and, like a diver flipping off of a highboard, plunged into the truth. "I know about the war," she said, "because I'm not Victoria Reichourd."

"Victoria," Guy said, his voice holding a definite warning note.

She held up a hand. "No, Guy, please let me finish. What I'm telling you is the truth. I am not your wife. My

413

name *is* Victoria Reichourd, but it's Victoria *Elizabeth* Reichourd, and no one has ever called me Victoria, except my mother, and only when she gets mad at me. I've always been called Tori." She took a deep breath and, when no one interrupted, continued. "I was born in Walnut Creek, California in nineteen sixty-six."

Guy snapped straight and flung the cheroot onto the cold grate. "All right, Victoria, you've come up with some pretty ridiculous schemes, but this—"

"It's not a scheme, Guy," Tori said calmly. "And I told you, no one calls me Victoria but my mother—I think it's safe to say you're not my mother."

Martin giggled and Tori smiled at him, relieved to see her words hadn't angered him, too.

Celestine remained quiet, studying Tori.

"Now, if I may continue?"

Guy resumed his casual position against the fireplace, but it was obvious his limbs were stiff with tension and his gray eyes had grown as dark as a midnight fog. "My grandmother died a few months ago, or rather, in March of nineteen ninety-three. I went, along with my mother, up to my grandmother's house in Grass Valley, which is in the Sierra Nevada mountains, to help her pack a few things and clean the place." Tori paused and looked at Martin. "The house was left to my grandmother by her grandfather, Martin Camerei Reichourd."

Martin's eyes widened, but he remained silent.

"Anyway," Tori continued, "while I was going through some of my grandmother's old things that had been stored in the attic I came across a journal. I was curious so I began to read it, and soon I was mesmerized. You see, we didn't know anything about my great-great-grandfather having come from Louisiana."

"This is ridiculous," Guy muttered.

Tori ignored him and went on. "The journal's author wrote about some murders, in particular that of his uncle, John, and his stepfather, Guy, both committed by his other uncle, Darin, and Martin's own mother, Victoria. Later he wrote that during a heated argument Darin also killed Victoria, then arranged a riding accident in which Alicia died."

Guy glared at her. "Do you honestly expect us to believe this wild tale?"

She ignored his outburst. "To avoid being killed himself, my great-great-grandfather, Martin, ran away from home and traveled alone to California, where he eventually settled." She looked at Martin. "Reading the journal, learning of what happened to the Reichourds, was like reading a murder mystery, and I was fascinated. I made a few quick phone calls. . . ." She hesitated. "A telephone is like a telegraph, only faster." Martin nodded. "Anyway, I made a few quick telephone calls and found out that Shadow Oaks still existed, in nineteen ninety-three, and that there were still Reichourds living on it. I was between jobs and had the time so I decided to travel to New Orleans and meet our long-lost relatives."

"And that brought you to eighteen fifty-nine," Guy sneered. God, how he wanted to believe her. He had been hoping, when he saw her aim the gun at Darin, when she had attempted to save his life, that she had truly changed, that all his suspicions were wrong and that somehow, by some miracle, she had become the woman he had always dreamt of, the woman he'd thought he had married. But now. . . . He shook his head in self-disgust.

"No. My plane landed safely in New Orleans, and I rented a car."

"Your what landed safely and you rented a what?" Guy growled, his patience wearing thin.

Tori sighed. This was going to be more difficult than she'd imagined. If she wasn't careful she was going to have to explain every other word that popped out of her mouth. "My plane landed safely. In nineteen ninety-three we can fly."

Guy's eyes rolled heavenward, and Martin gasped in delight.

Celestine remained quietly sober.

"And I rented a car—I guess you'd call it a horseless carriage."

"A carriage that moves with no horses to draw it, is that what you're trying to tell us?" Guy said.

"Yes."

He stalked to a table and drew another cheroot from the pink crystal decanter that sat there. With his pocket clip he snapped off one end and rammed the cheroot into the corner of his mouth. "I think we've heard enough." He scraped a lucifer across the marble tabletop and, as its tip burst into flame, held it to the cheroot.

Tori's patience was almost at its limit, but she held on, knowing that she had to convince him, not enrage him. "Guy, please, will you just listen?"

He glared down at her. "All right, so how did you get here?"

"I was on the way to Shadow Oaks when I suddenly found myself in the midst of a lightning storm. Lightning has always terrified me, so I was nervous. A bolt struck the ground in front of the car, I swerved the steering wheel and the car left the road. It plunged over an embankment and hit a tree. That's all I remember of the accident"—she

416

looked at Guy—"until you pulled me out of the wreckage and brought me to Shadow Oaks."

"I pulled you out of a wrecked carriage."

"Yes, you did," Tori agreed softly. She rose and moved to stand before him. "And I can't prove any of what I've been saying, Guy, but I swear it's the truth. Somehow, when my car hit that tree, I was thrown here, to eighteen fifty-nine, and I can only assume that your real wife, Victoria, is in nineteen ninety-three, with everyone trying to convince her that she is me."

He stared down at her, wanting to be convinced, wanting desperately to believe her. It would make sense then, his loving her so desperately, his wanting her as he never had before, his needing her with an ache that threatened to consume him. But it was such a preposterous tale.

She turned away from him and went to stand before Martin. Tori took the boy's hands in hers. "In your journal you wrote that Darin and Victoria were lovers, and that you had overheard them talking about having killed John, but you were too scared to say anything, even to Guy, for fear they'd kill him, and you, too. Then they did kill Guy, and a year later Darin killed your mother and Alicia. You feared for yourself, knowing it was only a matter of time, so you ran away to California."

"To the gold fields?" he asked excitedly.

"Yes, to the gold fields. You married, settled down and had a family, but you never came back to Shadow Oaks, and you never told anyone what had happened here."

He nodded. "But none of that happened, except for John. And we didn't let Darin kill Guy."

Tori smiled. "No, we didn't." She turned to Celestine. "Martin never knew about Jeannette or you, so there was

417

nothing in his journal about either of you, but if Guy agrees I'd like you both to come and live here at Shadow Oaks."

Celestine smiled through the tears of surprise that came to her eyes. "John would have liked that," she whispered.

"Yes, I think he would have." Tori looked at Guy. He nodded his approval, and she turned back to Celestine. "Will you come?"

Celestine shook her head. "No, but I thank you from the bottom of my heart, both of you. I still think it best that Jeannette and I leave New Orleans."

"Then leave with the Reichourd name," Guy said, "and wear it proudly. It belongs to you, as does John's estate. I will see that all of his finances are put in your name immediately."

Crystalline tears slipped down her cheeks. "You are a good man, Guy Reichourd, as was your brother John." She moved across the room and stood on tiptoe to press her lips to his cheek. Celestine turned to Tori and clasped her hands. "You have been a good friend to me, Tori Reichourd, and I shall never forget you. Perhaps, after this war that is to come is over, I will bring my daughter home to New Orleans and introduce her to her father's family."

"We'll look forward to it," Guy said.

At the door Celestine turned back one last time. "Thank you," she whispered, and then she was gone.

Tori sighed and looked at Guy and Martin.

"You're not my mother?" Martin said. "Really?"

"No, Martin, I'm not."

He nodded, his head hanging, and walked from the room.

Tori watched him leave and felt a small part of her heart break away.

"So, now what?" Guy growled, his tone hard and commanding.

Tori jerked out of her reverie and stared at him. "I don't know, Guy." She walked toward him. "I know what I've said is hard to believe, but it's all I have to offer, except"—she paused before him, their bodies mere inches apart, her midnight blue eyes peering deeply into steel gray ones—"except that I love you with all my heart."

Thirty-eight

"No, no, don't make me get into that thing," Victoria screamed. She stared at the black and white metal box. "Please, no."

Officer Pellichout gripped Victoria's upper arm tightly and placed his other hand on the top of her head to keep her from bumping it on the doorframe of the police car. "Come on, ma'am," he said in his best soothing voice, "we've got to get you back to the hospital."

She tried to twist away from him, but they'd secured her hands behind her back with some kind of metal fastenings that cut into the flesh at her wrists. "No," she screamed. "Get away from me. Don't you know who I am? I'm Victoria Reichourd."

"Yes, ma'am," Officer Pellichout said. His partner walked around the rear of the car to assist him.

"I'll see you rot in a cell for this. I'm Victoria Reichourd, I tell you." She slammed a lavender-slippered foot against the car fender and pushed against the officer. "You can't make me get into this thing. I won't let you."

420

Just then an ambulance arrived.

"Thank God," Pellichout's partner said.

Two paramedics ran up. One stopped and stared. "Hey, this is the woman we pulled out of that wreck a few days ago," he yelled to his partner. The partner looked up from where he'd knelt to open his medical case. He glanced at Victoria. "Yeah, she was looney then, too," he said caustically, showing no regard for Victoria's feelings. He readied a syringe and while the officers and his partner held Victoria still, the paramedic plunged a needle into her arm. "That'll quiet her," he said.

"Where's my carriage?" Victoria yelled. "And my husband? Where's Guy? And Darin? I . . . have . . . talk . . . Dar . . ." Her eyes rolled out of sight and her head suddenly drooped.

"Thanks, guys," Pellichout said.

"Yeah, we'll take her from here," the paramedic who'd given her the shot said. "Don't know why they didn't put her in a security room in the mental ward in the first place."

Thirty-nine

New Orleans, Louisiana
Shadow Oaks Plantation
June, 1865

"Miss Tori, Miss Tori," Suda called. Excitement had caused her voice to rise several octaves so that its high-pitched squeal echoed through the large old house, down to the stables, and across the fields.

Startled, Tori dropped the hoe she'd been using to break the ground beside the old kitchen building where she and Alicia were planting a garden. She looked toward the house, then quickly reached for the rifle she'd placed against the building's rock chimney. It had been over six months since she'd received a letter from Guy, four since she'd heard from Martin. Every day she kept a smile on her face for Alicia and the twins as well as for Suda, Hannah, and Moses, but every night when she stood on the wide gallery and looked out at the horizon, her arms empty of the man she loved and her heart breaking just a little bit more with worry for him, the tears came, as well as the curses. And with each storm, each strike of lightning, she prayed not to be ripped from the life and family she loved so much.

She could tell the future outcome of the War Between the States, she could predict the changes in the country, the inventions, the hard times and trials, even who was going to be President, but she couldn't predict whether or not her husband was going to come home from the war. With her appearance in 1859, almost everything she'd read in Martin's journal in 1993 had changed, so that, at least as far as the Reichourd family was concerned, their future was as uncertain to her as was her own, except for Martin. He, she knew, would survive.

"Miss Tori," she heard Suda call again.

"Go into the house, Alicia, quickly," Tori whispered to the young girl she now loved. "And take Jimmy and Crista with you."

"Is it Yankees again, Mama?" Alicia asked in a hushed tone.

"I don't know, honey. Just go, and hurry." Tori watched Alicia urge the twins toward the back door before she dared move away. She had to be sure they were safe. Alicia was eleven now and already a young lady. Tori sighed. She only wished the child hadn't been forced to endure the hardships the war had placed on her homeland, but then, Shadow Oaks and the Reichourds were not as bad off as many who had been caught unexpectantly. At least Tori had been able to warn Guy of things like cotton prices dropping to near nothing and of Confederate banknotes being worthless. But she hadn't been able to remember many of the battles or their outcomes. Who had won Antietam? Petersburg? Yellow Tavern? Fredericksburg? She didn't know and it didn't really matter because regardless of who won, men died. And she was so deathly afraid that

Guy would be one of those brave men in gray who fought valiantly and fell, never to know the joy of another sunset, of his children's smiles, or his wife's love.

Five years old, Crista and Jimmy both turned back to her before being pushed into the warming kitchen by their older sister. "You give them ol' Yankees what for, Mama," Jimmy yelled.

"Jimmy, shhhh," Tori admonished. But she couldn't help but smile through her anxiety. Looking at Jimmy she felt she was seeing how Guy had looked as a child; a little blustery soldier with a mop of wavey black hair and beautiful, deep gray eyes.

"Be careful, Mama," Alicia said solemnly.

"Be careful, Mama," Crista echoed, mimicking Alicia's warning.

Tori's gaze shifted to her youngest daughter. Crista, too, had Guy's lustrous black hair, as well as thick, delicately curved lashes, but they surrounded eyes as blue as the deepest sea. Tori nodded and motioned for them to close the door. "Go on in now, hurry," she ordered in a whisper. They disappeared into the warming kitchen, and the door shut quietly but soundly behind them.

"Miss Tori, Miss Tori," Suda cried out again. "Come quick. Hurry!"

The urgency now in Suda's voice sent a shiver of fear through Tori. She snapped up the old rifle and settled it against her right shoulder, her left hand held the barrel outward, and the index finger of her right curved expertly around the trigger. Staying close to the house, under cover of what shrubs were left, she moved quickly and stealthily around toward the front. The news that Lee had surrendered to Grant at Appomattox Courthouse, Virginia, and that the war was over had swept over the land several weeks before like a great tidal wave. But in dire contrast to the North, where cheers of joy that it was finally over had been heard everywhere, in the South there were only tears of grief that the Confederacy had failed in its attempt to gain freedom from the Union. But even though the fighting was over, that didn't mean that the foraging had ceased, or that the guerrillas had stopped their raiding.

Tori moved cautiously toward the front of the house, prepared to fire her rifle if necessary, to kill if that was what she had to do to protect her own.

Just last week a group of raiders had crossed Shadow Oaks. Luckily all they'd been intent on was grabbing a few chickens, which the plantation could easily spare. The children, Moses, and the women had locked themselves in the house and not been bothered. Darin's son, Robert, who was now sixteen, had gripped one of Guy's pistols and insisted on standing beside Tori. The raiders had left quietly, satisfied with the chickens. But this time, Tori knew, they might not be so lucky.

She pulled back the hammer on the rifle and tightened her finger on the trigger, lifted the barrel to a firing position, and stepped around the corner of the house. Her gaze quickly scanned the front lawns, the shadows beneath the trees, and the long winding drive. She saw nothing. Were they already in the house? Cold fear gripped her. She stepped forward hastily and swung around to look at the front door. It stood open, wide, a black hole gaping in the center of white walls that needed a fresh coat of paint. A shudder wracked Tori. "Oh, my God," she gasped, "the children." She began to run toward the steps, but caught a movement on the drive out of the corner of her eye. She spun around, rifle raised, ready to face whatever threat had come to Shadow Oaks.

Three figures walked toward her on the winding drive; two black women and a white man. Tori's heart began to pound furiously, and tears instantly blurred her eyes. She hurriedly uncocked the rifle and set it against the house, then wiped the moisture from her eyes and, almost afraid to look, turned back to the drive again.

He was limping, favoring his left foot as he walked between the two women. His once immaculate gray uniform was tattered and mended almost beyond recognition, so frayed as to be near threadbare, and the gold braids that had curled across his sleeves in such radiance four years ago were now soiled to near obscurity. His glistening, rich black hair had become streaked with gray and hung, dull, almost to his shoulders. His handsomely chiseled face was covered by several days' growth of whiskers. Even so, the short beard could not hide the deep hollows in his cheeks any more than the clothes could hide the fact that the sinewy body she knew so well was now much leaner than she remembered.

"Guy," Tori whispered, so filled with happiness and relief that for a brief moment she could not move. Tears of joy streamed down her cheeks. Then, as if every nerve cell and fiber within her suddenly exploded, she cried out his name, loudly, happily, joyously, and ran toward him.

He swept her up into his arms, lifting her from the ground, crushing her against him, melding the lithe shape of her to the lean hardness of his own body. They both laughed and held tight to one another, as if afraid to let go and find it all a dream.

"I was so afraid you wouldn't come back," Tori said softly, her lips moving against his ear.

His arms loosened about her waist, just a little, and she slid downward until her feet touched the earth once more.

She looked up at him, into the dark gray eyes she knew so well.

"And I was so afraid you wouldn't be here when I did," Guy admitted. He had prayed every day that whatever unknown force had brought her to him would not see fit to take her away. And he would continue to offer up that prayer for the rest of his life.

"Papa, Papa!" Jimmy cried, bursting past the front door like a runaway colt. He bounced down the entry steps and sped across the drive toward them, his little legs moving as fast as they could.

Crista and Alicia, hearing Jimmy's cry, ran onto the gallery and, both spotting Guy, laughed happily and followed in Jimmy's footsteps.

Laughing, Tori stepped back and, as Guy knelt, Jimmy propelled himself into his father's arms. Within seconds Crista barreled into them and the three hugged and laughed. Finally, Guy stood and Alicia stepped up before him. She stood on tiptoe and kissed his cheek.

Guy smiled. "So, my little princess has grown up too much for me to hug?"

Alicia threw herself against him then, her arms wrapping around his waist, her head burrowing into his chest. "Oh, Papa, I was so afraid you wouldn't come home."

He held her tight and rocked back and forth. "But I did, Licia," he said softly, and kissed the top of her head. "We're all together now, and we always will be."

With Jimmy and Crista holding to his pantlegs, Guy looked over Alicia's head to Tori and held out a hand to her. She moved into the circle of his arm, and luxuriated in the feel of its strength wrapping around her shoulders.

"And we always will be," Guy said again.

Epilogue

New Orleans
June, 1999

"Come on, Mama, there's nothing more we can do for her here," George said, taking his wife's hand and leading her away from Victoria's room.

"I know, George, I just hate to see her trussed up like that, tied down to her bed and all. Even if she isn't really our Tori, she looks so much like her it makes me feel bad, committing her to an asylum, you know?"

He nodded. "Yes, Carrie, I know." He held up Martin's journal. "It's still kind of hard to believe, and I suppose if we told anyone what happened they'd think we made up the whole thing, even doctored this old diary."

Carrie looked momentarily stricken. "What if we'd never read it, George? What if we hadn't paid any attention to that woman's rantings that everything in your grandfather's journal was a lie. We might never have read it, George, and we would have continued to believe that this woman was our daughter. We would never have seen Tori's note to us in the back of that journal, or known what really happened to her."

"But we did read it, Carrie, and we do know. Somehow, through some freak of nature, our little girl got whisked back in time, and this woman, this Victoria, who was evidently her great-great-great-grandma, got thrown up here." He looked at the old journal again. "And according to what both Tori and Martin wrote, this Victoria is not exactly a wonderful human being, so I guess she's getting what she deserves." George wrapped an arm around his wife's shoulders. "But Tori's happy, Carrie, back there with him, with Guy Reichourd. She loves him, and she's happy, and that's all that matters." He glanced down at his wife. "Isn't it?"

She smiled up at him, her midnight blue eyes as radiant and bright as her daughter's. "Yes, dear, it is."

Author's Note

Cheryln Jac is the pseudonym of Zebra author, Cheryl Biggs who, under her own name has written Zebra historical romances *Mississippi Flame, Across a Rebel Sea,* and will debut 94 with the first two books of the four book Braggette Series, *Hearts Deceived,* in May, and *Hearts Denied* in November.

Shadows In Time is her first time travel for Pinnacle. Her second, *Timeswept,* will be released in 1995. Also in 1994 her first paranormal romance for Pinnacle, *Night's Immortal Kiss,* will be an August release.

Cheryl loves hearing from romance readers and would be happy to answer their letters, questions, etc., as well as send them any bookmarks or promotional materials she has on her books. Write to her at P.O.B. 6557, Concord, CA 94520 and enclose an SASE.